A New England Escape

Jilly Bourne

First published in 2024 by Oakham Press

This book is a work of fiction. Names, characters, and incidents are either a product of the author's imagination or are used fictionally.

The town of Oakham is real – the name changed.
Any resemblance to actual people, living or dead, is purely coincidental.

Paperback ISBN: 978-1-0686214-0-6

Editor: Sian-Elin Flint-Freel
Formatting: Michelle Catanach
Illustrator/Book cover: Beki Hawley
Photograph: Sharon Isted
Publisher: Oakham Press

Website: www.mytop5ofeverything.com
Instagram: mytop5ofeverything
Facebook: Jilly Bourne

PROLOGUE

Jon, eyes closed, had already disappeared and was unresponsive, despite the beeping. I was suddenly grateful for the time we had been able to spend together that afternoon. We talked about something and nothing between bouts of sleep. The words are etched in my memory, precious and few. I tucked his ice-cold hands under the blanket, knowing it was to no avail, they would never be warm again. A last act of kindness, it made me feel better. Slightly. We sat at his bedside – his parents, his sister Katie, and his best friend Ben – all assembled after a frantic phone call informing us of Jon's sharp decline.

Months of appointments, treatment, chemotherapy, caring and watching him die inch by painful inch, completely unable to help. It had come to this, a long night listening to Jon's laboured breath, waiting, waiting for the final one. At around seven in the morning the sky turned a glorious fresh peachy pink, and we all turned our attention to the garden outside the claustrophobic, airless room. The colours were achingly beautiful. Within the hour he breathed his last and

I was a widow.

What struck me first was the silence, the chasm of silence. All the beeping stopped, our breathing hushed, no words. I expected tears. Tears of sadness or relief that the suffering was over – for him, for me. But nothing. Numbness. I wanted my heart to stop too, stop the pounding in my chest, to stop beating and ease the pain that seeped through every fibre of my being. For months we had dealt with anguish, fleeting moments of complete joy, plenty of sadness... now this. He'd gone.

How could I carry on without him?

What was I supposed to do now?

1

Standing at the garden gate, in the middle of the white picket fence, I look right and left: to the left it is obvious by the increasing number of buildings, shops and vehicles that the road leads into town; to the right the road leads to who knows where? I glance back at the Oakham Inn at 1516 Main Street. It has wood-framed windows, weather-beaten grey clapboarding, a front porch with the obligatory wooden swing seat. Facing the street and dithering for a moment – decisions, decisions, never a forté of mine – but given that I must go somewhere and can't stand here like an idiot all day, I decide to turn right and start to walk, glad I brought a coat with me because the wind is chilly.

It is a bright mid-April New England morning and when I get to the corner at the top of Main Street, another decision, another direction – left or right. Over the rooftops, I spot a lighthouse and, without considering what might be in the other direction, I stride purposefully, impatient to catch my first glimpse of the sea.

Within ten minutes I reach my destination. In England, it would be 'the sea', but here in Oakham, Cape Cod, Massachusetts, it's an ocean, a vast blue expanse. The biting onshore breeze takes my breath away momentarily. I sigh. The ocean has that effect; it is huge and untamed and offers the possibilities of travel and adventure. And today, here, a new adventure begins.

Sitting on the low wall, I swing my legs over, face the ocean and let my eyes wander back and forth from the pale grey beachside homes with huge windows and balconies, across the wide expanse of the bay to the sand dunes and back again. My shoulders drop an inch or two as all the worries and stresses of the past two years are gently, momentarily soothed by not only the sight, but also by the briny, seaweed, sand and sagebrush-covered dune smell of the ocean and the sound of the crashing waves whipped up by the wind. Again, I sigh.

Suddenly, the familiar pain above my eye signals tears, which seep silently, warm and wet, blurring my vision. Two years or more this has been happening. The accumulation of worry, caring and then the grief have sapped the essence out of my life, leaving me bereft and deflated. In my head, I hear the familiar words: *I wish he was here – Jon would have loved this.* I push the thoughts aside, put them back in the box marked 'Jon'.

Standing abruptly, I brush away any hesitation along with the tears. I resolutely tell myself, *Not today! I will not think about him today!* But who am I kidding? He will always be there, the love of my life, the one who has left a massive hole in my being, the one whose absence causes an ache so deep I find it difficult to breathe. But I must. I must breathe. I must go on.

At the end of the low wall that separates the dunes from the pavement and parking area are steps down to the beach. The surface is uneven. Holding tight to the bleached wooden handrail, I eventually reach the soft sand and, for a brief second, contemplate taking off my shoes, but down here the wind is decidedly brisk and biting. Not today – another day. After all, I am here for six months.

What made me decide that six months was the right length of time? Not too long that I would settle in and miss being away from home, family and friends (although I know I will). Not too short that it would feel like a holiday. I chose the pretty seaside town of Oakham in the most disorganised, random kind of way – I stuck a pin in a map. Yep! Me! Me who struggles to make decisions. Me who does things instinctively and then reflects and worries, especially now that I am on my own, without Jon. Tears threaten once more so I shake my head and focus on the ocean ahead.

As I walk toward the roaring white-capped water,

my ever-active mind turns frenetically from here to there and back again. Worry about my parents; Dad suffered an angina attack just before I left and the wrench of leaving him and the rest of my family sets my heart racing. My mind turns back to yesterday when I had closed the door to our home – well, it is my home now and I still cannot get used to the idea – and placed my hand on the wooden doorframe to steady myself. "Goodbye," I had whispered. "Wish me luck." And here I am strolling on a beach thousands of miles away, in my mid-thirties; I have left my home, my life as I have always known it, and leapt out of my comfort zone into the unknown.

Yesterday. My thoughts return to the drive to the airport. It proved to be tough – on all four of us. There had been acres of quiet space as no-one had known quite what to say. Then someone would quietly utter a word or two and we all nervously rushed to join in the conversation that inevitably turned out to be stilted before we faltered back into silence. The atmosphere had been heavy, my stomach had churned as it is wont to do in moments of distress, and I had been acutely aware that my father's knuckles were white as he gripped the steering wheel of the Land Rover and negotiated the traffic on the A556 towards Manchester. Sitting next to him in the car, my mother's face had a pinched, tired look. I knew she hadn't slept the night before, neither had I, nor I suspect, had Dad. I had heard her padding around downstairs at four in the morning and assumed they'd asked me to stay at their house in a uniting bond of sleeplessness. Katie (Jon's sister and my best friend) had been sitting beside me in the car, staring out of the window, her left hand endlessly playing with the tassel on her Radley handbag.

After check-in I had wanted to leave, to be able to breathe normally again. But I also wanted to stay and hold them and tell them it would be alright, that I needed to do this, and yet all explanations had already been given, accepted or not, so I had taken the initiative, to hug, kiss and walk away. I had turned just in time to see Mum put her head on Dad's shoulder as Katie waved and mouthed "Bye."

The mental images evoke feelings of guilt. Why did I put them through this? I'd hurt them all by leaving, even if only for six months. But today is not a day for regrets, it's a day for doing, so I plod on, face to the wind. At the end of the beach I stop, breathe, and tell myself I CAN DO THIS! The wind, now behind me, is blowing me along as I head back to the steps.

"Good mornin'!" A man greets me with a cheery smile that lights up his round, tanned face. He has a full head of pure white hair and stands tall with a military bearing, not stooped. His keen blue eyes are only slightly dimmed with age.

"Morning," I utter, trying to catch my breath after the strangely invigorating walk. I lean on the handrail at the top of the steps.

"We noticed you walkin' on the beach, all by yourself. D'ya come here often?" he asks.

The old lady holding onto his arm, whom I assume is his wife, nudges him. "You say that to all the pretty girls!" He grins and squeezes her hand. Her kindly face may be wrinkled and her bright eyes framed by crow's feet, but they hold a sense of mischief and she is beautiful. "We've been walking here the whole of our lives, haven't we, dear?"

"We have." His whole attention is given to her in that moment as they smile at each other. "Eighty years Oakham born and bred!"

My heart skips a beat at the beauty of their obvious love for each other. Fragments of a memory of Jon smiling at me in the same way appear, but I push them away, determined to be present in the moment.

"So, this is your first time?" he asks me.

I confirm with a nod. His eyes now focus intently on me, as though he wants to know, and I am the only person in the world he is concerned about at this precise moment.

"What d'ya think?"

I turn back to look at the ocean. "It's beautiful!"

"It truly is awesome, right? That view's what made

me wanna go to sea. So, where you from, young lady?"

"I'm from England."

"What brings you here?"

My smile tightens. I pause at the unwelcome question. "Many things. Many reasons."

"Dear, don't pry!" The lady taps his arm gently.

A huge warm smile, his eyes almost close with the joy of the moment. "Maybe one day you'll tell me."

The muscles in my face relax as I find myself smiling back at him and thinking, *Yes, maybe I will.*

"We'll be off then. Goodbye."

I watch them go, pushing down memories of my Popa and Grandie, shaking my head and attempting more mental channel changing. Starting back in the opposite direction towards the inn, I try taking in my surroundings: the trees which are about to burst into life, the spring flowers heralding a new season and the promise of warmer, longer, sunnier days. The houses, so pretty with their painted clapboard of pale grey, light blue and yellow, their gardens surrounded by the ever-present white picket fences, are all neatly kept. Oakham is picturesque in a quaint and charming way. Typical New England.

Back at the inn, I wave and smile at the receptionist, who is distracted, her expression professional, distant and cool. Any fleeting attention to my presence evaporates as she returns to her previous conversation with a forthright lady who keeps jabbing the papers on the reception desk in front of her. This lady strikes an imposing figure, dressed in brightly coloured linen layers that make her appear elegant, yet at the same time slightly bohemian. She has a mass of dark hair, tied up with a linen band, the colour of which matches her outfit. She enforces her opinion with a further stab and I feel sorry for the desk. Moving her reading glasses from the end of her nose onto her forehead, she looks directly at the receptionist. Her accent is New York (5th Avenue, not the Bronx). I slow my step slightly and as the conversation halts I feel their eyes on me. A prickle of apprehension makes my fingers tingle. As I quickly make my way up the stairs, away from them, the hum of conversation returns.

The traditional brass key unlocks the door to Room 12. Taking off my coat, I hang it on the back of the door and take a peek at my reflection in the mirror: pale blue eyes staring back at me, the freckles on my nose and cheeks are accentuated by my pink windswept skin. I wince at the damage to my hair, which has taken on a life of its own. A mixture of blonde and brown, it is naturally curly but prone to frizz. Resigned to its wildness, I head towards the welcoming fire in the grate and curl up in the armchair. The light and airy room is agreeable decorated, a cross between beach and vintage with its comfortable looking bed piled high with an assortment of cushions, lace blinds and striped curtains adorning the large window. There is a vase of fragrant spring flowers on the bedside table – daffodils and tulips. They remind me of home.

When I am thawed out and my hands are warm, I move to the little desk by the window and glance at the huge beech tree in the garden; its branches are currently bare, but they will provide cool shelter when the heat of summer arrives. In the desk drawer I find letter-headed paper and a pen. I will write to Mum and tell her that I have arrived safely and fill her in on what I've seen, who I've met – I know she'll laugh as she reads my description of the two harpies at the reception desk! I begin to feel myself relax as I write about the old couple I met by the shore. Then the guilt seeps in: leaving my sister to support Mum and Dad while also having to tend to her own family needs while I, in her words, "swan off across the Atlantic". My fingers falter as I quickly finish the letter, place it in the envelope and leave it, abandoned on the desk.

The next morning, after a light but delicious breakfast, I am out onto Main Street again, turning left out of the gate. My first thought on waking is always Jon. Every morning is the same. Every morning there is the pain of no longer having him in my life. Taking a deep (yet slightly shuddering) breath, I march resolutely into town, grateful for the weak spring sunshine and blue sky to lift my mood.

Despite what may appear to be a random choice for my sabbatical, I did do something sensible and checked Google before I booked my flight. I also looked at maps, pictures and reviews. Oakham, a small town, is quaint and immediately arouses my curiosity to discover more. I get the sense it will be a bustling place in the summer, though presently, the gift shops are closed, the shelves bare and covered in cobwebs, the clothes shops have empty racks, all waiting for the season to start. There is a perception of a town about to emerge from hibernation after a long, cold winter of inactivity. The bar is one of the few places open, though it too is quiet, and as I stroll along, I note a couple of cafés. Towards the end of Main Street, I am drawn to the Blue Brolly Bookshop, which is open, so I venture inside.

I love bookshops: the sight of the books neatly lined up on the shelves; the sum of unread words; the endless possibilities of unexplored places and unmet people; and the smell of books and paper. Don't get me started! As a child, one of my greatest joys (apart from peanut butter) was to visit a bookshop, coins in my sticky little hand, and taking hours to choose a new book. Old memories. Before.

The shop is empty, and the quiet purr of Bach fills

the air. The owner is perched on a chair behind the counter, glasses on the end of his nose, eyes down, concentrating. Momentarily he glances up at me and greets me warmly with a cheery word and a smile, which I return before wandering to the back of the shop, taking the odd book that catches my eye off the shelf to read some more and then returning it carefully to its place. Nothing particularly grabs my attention until I reach the front of the shop. By the window is a low table covered in books written by local writers. I glance at the variety of hard and paperbacks before picking up *A Year by the Sea: Thoughts of an Unfinished Woman* by Joan Anderson. Turning it over and reading the back page, it pulls me in, and I read the first page, the second and then the third. It calls to me and I cannot wait to read page four. This is the book for me.

Bought and paid for, I hurry to leave, impatient to read more. As I reach for the handle, the front door of the shop opens abruptly. I jump back and let out a quiet yelp of surprise, quickly withdrawing my hand. Looking up, the most amazing green eyes are smiling at me. Concerned, he apologises.

"Yes. Yes. I'm fine." I turn away, conscious that I might, just might be staring. His face is handsome in an unconventional way: a few laughter lines around his eyes, his goatee and moustache flecked with a little grey, as is his hair, cut short.

"You sure?"

"Yes! Really, I'm alright." Flustered now. *Leave me alone.* "You surprised me, that's all!" I glance up again, feeling the heat rising up my neck.

"Great choice," he tells me, indicating to the book in my hand.

I glance down at the cover, unable to think of anything to add to the conversation and slightly embarrassed by my reaction to his presence.

"She lives on the Cape… the author," he offers.

I look at him again, only to quickly avert my eyes when he smiles. My heart does an involuntary somersault. "Does she?" I mutter.

He nods. "Great writer, you'll enjoy reading it."

"I'm sure I will," I reply, feeling a little pathetic before mumbling something inane and leaving the bookshop.

Out on the pavement (or sidewalk, as the locals would say), where it somehow feels much cooler, I take a deep breath and then another. Turning abruptly for the inn, I almost collide with its receptionist, who is staring through the bookstore window at the green-eyed man inside. Jolted from her reverie, her eyes shoot daggers at me. Shocked, I take a step back and wonder why. What have I done to upset her? Frowning, I step to one side to pass her and head to the safety of my room, disturbed by the whole experience.

2

Rummaging in the desk drawer, I gather my art equipment — pencils, crayons, paper — and fill my backpack, leaving Room 12 with one purpose in mind: a woman on a mission. These art materials came with me to help me find myself, to rediscover who I am. I was creative in my former life and I am determined to be creative again.

Before my foot has hit the last step, I am slightly terrified by a terse "Morning" from behind the reception desk. The dour-faced receptionist glances at her wristwatch as if to say, 'What time do you call this?' Admittedly, I did sleep late and miss breakfast, but I am on holiday! I mumble a reply, reluctant to start a conversation after our previous encounter outside the bookshop and hurry out through the front door and onto the street, away from the unfriendliness.

Back outside the Blue Brolly Bookshop, I see a bench on the pavement opposite. It is bathed in early spring sunshine, the perfect place to sit down with a perfect view to paint. I settle myself down, clutching my bag tightly and recalling the last time I was here as a flash of green eyes and a handsome face runs through my mind. Ready to create, yet reluctant to start just in case I can't remember how to paint, my mind races and my heart thumps. A mum strolls past with her young son who waves and says hi, bringing me sharply back to the present. I smile and take a deep breath.

Opening the bag, taking out the contents, I lay all the crayons and pencils on the bench beside me, only to discover that the curve of the seat makes them all roll away. They clatter on the ground, rolling towards the couple on the next bench who stop their enthusiastic chattering and scowl at me as I scramble around their feet, apologising profusely whilst collecting them, hoping the uncomfortable blush spreading across my face is not obvious. But doubt it. I am trying to be inconspicuous and it's not happening. Panic rises. Fear, like a shadow that creeps across the ground on a sunny day. NO! I grip the pencils and crayons tightly, my knuckles white. Closing my eyes, I breathe in and out slowly. Again, I wonder what I have done. Why am I here? How is being somewhere different going to transform how I feel inside?

I have not drawn anything for myself, for my own pleasure, for almost two years. Not since… But one of the reasons for coming to the US was to start creating again, to draw, to paint and to be absorbed in the process with no time to consider anything else. Focused. Concentrated. Effort. Jon had been so encouraging, motivating me to return to my art, especially in those months of sitting by his side as he slowly faded away from me. This morning, revisiting the paper and pens feels intrinsically linked with the loss and accompanying pain in my heart. I shake my head, push the disquieting thoughts away and unclench my fingers. The crayons are now placed where they will not roll away and I blow on my hands to release the tension, to get the blood flowing.

The first attempt is well… frankly, it is rubbish. Dissatisfied, I tear out the page, screw it up and put it in my bag, slightly concerned that I may have lost the ability. A sense of frustration bubbles up and battles with the 'can do' attitude and the sense of letting Jon down. What am I thinking? That a change in place will alter the sense of hopelessness I have carried with me over the last few years? A rash decision brought me here. What if I can't settle? How could I possibly face everyone if I went home early?

Another deep breath. My hand quivers slightly. I stare at it, willing it to be still. It takes some time but thankfully, my second attempt at drawing the bookshop is an improvement and shows a measure of potential, if not talent – at least the lines are straight! I allow the page to stay in my beautiful new sketch book with its luxurious watercolour paper and tactile felt cover that I bought before I left England in the vague hope that it might inspire me. As a child, if I ever received unexpected money as a gift, if I couldn't find a book that I wanted, then I would buy pens, paper, brushes or crayons. Art has always been a part of my life and my heritage – my father, paternal grandmother and several aunts are all artistic and the joy of paper has never left me, for painting, for reading. I love paper! Sad maybe, but true.

The third attempt actually resembles a bookshop. (Ignoring people – I don't draw people. It's a whole different skill set and not to be attempted on the first day.) The pencil lines in place, I pick up a watercolour crayon: blue – appropriate! And when I am satisfied with the result, I wash the colour with a wet brush, let it dry and outline the image with a fine fibre-tip marker. Focused. Concentrated. Effort. I hold the sketchbook out at arm's length.

"Hey! That's real pretty. Good job!"

So absorbed in the task, I have failed to notice the man standing beside me – the old man from the beach. He smiles and I am strangely comforted by his presence.

"Hi!" he speaks softly. "You come here often?" There is a twinkle in his eyes as he echoes our previous encounter.

"No, it's my first time." I smile back.

"Stan!" He thrusts out his hand and I shake it.

"Jane! Nice to meet you."

"Again!" he reminds me, asking if he might look at my work as he sits down. "It's good."

"Thank you – it is the third attempt," I admit.

"Mind if I take a closer look?" He turns back a page but only finds the second attempt.

I reach into my bag and pull out the ball of paper to pre-empt his next question. "This is the first attempt and no, you may not."

He laughs, throwing his head back. He seems so full of joy. "How long've you been in town?"

"Just over a week."

"How long you here for? Where you staying?" He surveys me with the same intensity I saw at our first meeting. He senses a mood change from my facial expression. "There I go again. Like Shirley says, 'Stop pryin', dear!' Askin' too many questions."

There is a quiet moment between us before he resumes talking in a voice low and gentle, calming my heart.

"We get many visitors here, you know, and it's one of the first things we ask… but… you're here early in the season. Unusual that. And you've come along way too – from England, right?"

I nod.

His words are measured and considered. "We get folks here around Easter time, folks who own a holiday home and the like, but they've gone back to the city now and they don't normally return 'til probably Memorial Day. That's the end of May, by the way," he adds when he sees my frown of incomprehension. "Then when school's out for the summer, we get folks comin' for weekends and vacations, and day trippers." He halts, watches me, waits a moment before asking, "I guess you're stayin' for longer than a week?"

"I am," I admit. "I'm staying all summer."

The words are out before I know it. Once spoken, they cannot be withdrawn. All summer, eh? Maybe I will settle, maybe I can do this.

Totally unaware of the internal battle in my head, the elderly gentleman continues. "Nice! It gets pretty busy around here once the weather has warmed up some." He glances up at the sky. "Breezy and cool today. No rain though."

I look up too. The clouds high, white cotton wool balls.

"But later in the week it's gonna rain for sure."

"You sound like an Englishman – we talk a lot about the weather."

We sit in companionable silence for a while.

Then he asks, "You painted down by the ocean yet?"

"Not yet. It's my first day today and besides, I find

the sea a challenging subject."

"Me too. It simply won't sit still!"

Another shared smile and I feel the warmth of the sun radiate through my body.

"You paint?"

"After a fashion. My dear wife, Shirley, you met her, she likes my paintings but I ain't gonna win no prizes for 'em, that's for sure."

"What do you like to paint?" I ask, taking a shine to this lovely old man. Maybe there are nice, friendly people in this town after all.

"Flowers." He holds his hands up. "Yep, I know."

He grins and I cannot help but smile back at him.

"But I grows 'em and I paints 'em and Shirley loves 'em!" He groans slightly as he pushes himself up from the bench to stand. "Well… I best be goin'. I'll see ya' round town, I guess?"

"You will," I admit happily.

"Nice talkin' with you!"

I gaze after him as he slowly shuffles off down the pavement. Turning my face to the sun's rays, I smile to myself as I realise I am going to be here a while and hope I will see him again.

Later in the week, having attempted a few subjects – an umbrella, a flower, the bandstand in the park and even a man sitting on a bench – my confidence is returning enough to attempt to paint the sea (sorry, ocean). So, collecting my materials, sketch book, and the easel and canvas I bought the day before from the art supply store next to the tourist information stand on Main Street (thinking big now), I set off to sit on the low wall at Lighthouse Beach on Shore Road. Nervous and excited at the same time, this is my first big painting adventure. I can do this.

I set up my easel then position the canvas, fixing it tightly in place. Looking up at the sky, I consider the old man's forecast. Immediately, my 'artistic' brain switches on and I establish that the clouds will require several colours: Payne's grey (which means there is the possibility of rain), a small amount of yellow ochre with a touch of alizarin crimson where the weak sun turns the clouds pink, and perhaps some cobalt blue for the bits of visible sky beyond the clouds. Soon I am lost in the process. I concentrate on what I see – the light, the shadows – absorbed in trying to find a likeness and an image that perfectly reflects the day, oblivious to the cool breeze blowing off the ocean.

Part way through I decide to leave the canvas for a moment, let it settle and I sketch: the lighthouse behind me, the houses over to the left that face the water, the steps, the wooden rail, the sand dunes, anything – even the figures walking on the beach. Thrilled that I can paint, I can draw, I can do this, feelings of long-forgotten joy and a contentment sweep through me, easing the tension in my shoulders, lifting my heart from the darkness of the grief and stress I've experienced. These sensations are not accompanied by any sense of guilt, which is a relief. I retrieve my camera from my bag and take photographs for reference purposes, should I want to revisit the paintings and sketches later. Camera back in the bag, I squint at the canvas, tilting my head left and right, stepping back to view it from afar. Satisfied, I go back to work until it is time to stop. The art of painting includes knowing when to stop. It's time to stop. Besides, the clouds are now dark grey and ominous, and I want to get everything back safe and sound to Room 12. The old man was right, it is going to rain today.

My pace quickens as the breeze picks up and feels fresh on my face. All of a sudden, the heavens open and it starts to rain so I run – ungainly, given I have a huge bag on my back, a canvas under my left arm and an easel under my right! Not attractive. I'm not going to make it back to the inn and I am thankful for a nearby café. I lean on the door only to realise it opens out. Now I'm soaking wet (and annoyed) and struggling to pull the door open with my little finger – the only digit not holding something. I stumble inside, dripping all over the wooden floor. Frustrated, I launch my bag off my back, dropping it on the floor with a resounding thud, and put the canvas up on the side to dry – it too is dripping! I sigh deeply – such a good morning and now it's ruined.

A young waitress comes to my table to enquire if I am alright, and I gratefully order a hot drink. When the coffee arrives it is deliciously milky, warming and comforting and it helps me regain some perspective as I assess the rain damage. Maybe the painting isn't ruined after all.

The café is humid, the aroma of damp woollen coats mixes with the smell of coffee, the windows steamed over with condensation. Several other soaking wet people arrive, including a brash sounding southern couple who fill the quiet café with noise and movement.

"Oh, my Lord, what a day!" erupts the wife, a woman with bleached blonde hair piled on the top of her head.

She is trying to engage me in conversation, but I deliberately avoid eye contact and concentrate on my coffee.

"Dear," she almost whines to her husband, "could you get me an iced tea?" She sits down at the table next to me with a large, exaggerated sigh and her eyes take in the dripping canvas. "Oh my, what a beautiful painting! It sure does capture the mood of the day!"

"Thank you."

"You painted this, dear?" she asks as she points at my canvas, her gold bracelets clinking on her wrist.

Her voice carries across the room, a voice that could shatter glass at forty paces. A tingling sense of doom inches through me as heads turn, eyes stare.

"It is soooo beautiful!"

She goes to touch it, but I intervene and put my hand up to stop her.

"It's still wet," I warn her, stating the obvious.

Her husband returns with a tray, and she enthuses to him about how beautiful it is.

"I have to have it, dear. It reminds me of our vacation and the awesome day we've had," she implores.

I get the impression that anything she wants, she gets. That lingering sense of doom is making me uncomfortable. He looks at me with eyes that say, 'please help me here'.

I muster up the courage to tell him that it is not for sale.

"I am sorry, but it has been ruined by the rain."

"Oh dear" – she touches my arm with gnarled fingers which have bright pink, pointed nails and I decide I do not want my painting in this woman's hands – "but that's why we love it."

It's 'we' now?

"It will always remind us of today. Dear, I have to have it!"

Out of the corner of my eye I notice a lady standing behind the counter on the other side of the room frantically trying to attract my attention. It is the tall, dark-haired lady who was in reception at the inn on my first day in town and I assume that she is the owner of this café. Today she is dressed in a voluminous pale green linen smock and matching headband. She moves her glasses from the end of her nose to her forehead as she beckons me over.

"Would you excuse me?" I say to the couple in my best English accent used on formal occasions and go over to the counter. I gulp down the lump in my throat and ask, "Yes?"

Her hand shoots out and I shake it. Her grip is vice-like.

"Martha," she hisses in a stage whisper. I assume that is her name. Before I can reply, speak, say anything, she ploughs on, "I think you should sell the painting – it's really good."

"But I don't particularly want to – it's been ruined by the rain," I reply, aware that I have lowered my voice to match her conspiratorial tone.

"That doesn't matter! What matters is that they love it. And they want to buy it! You should sell it. Look" – she lets go of my hand and I gently rub it as the bones relax – "We'll go fifty: fifty."

"What?"

"OK – sixty: forty then?"

"No, hold on a minute. This is my painting we're talking about here. Why should I give you anything?"

I am irritated by the weather, the door that opens outwards, the fact that I am soaking wet, and all I want to do is scream! *What is happening here?* I came in to shelter from the rain, I've got an old battle-axe of a woman demanding my painting (which I think is ruined) and another woman insisting I sell it to the battle-axe and her long-suffering husband!

"Well, I'm not an art expert, but it is really good, and if you are going to sell it in my café, drinking my coffee—"

"Which I paid for!" My voice raises above a whisper and heads turn. I want to tell her it's none of her business. It's my painting. Did I mention it's ruined? And besides, I don't trust her as she's friends with the distinctly unfriendly receptionist in my hotel!

"True!" she confirms.

We regard each other, sizing each other up. My heart thumps in my chest.

"But selling the painting is my idea and I believe that deserves a cut!"

Refusing to allow her indomitable spirit and slightly scary directness to win me over, I take a deep breath and pause to think. I suppose I could walk away and take the painting with me, but maybe, just maybe, I should convince myself that I can sell my work for no other reason than it is admired and appreciated. But no! Suddenly the realisation slaps me about the face. No! I don't want to sell it. Indignation fizzes in my head. How dare she! I stand tall and grow an inch.

"Sorry, it is NOT for sale!"

"But…" she splutters as her eyebrows shoot up.

I hold my hand up to prevent her from speaking, turn on my heel and blunder across the room, knocking a chair. I grab all my belongings, my bag, the painting, and turn to storm out of the café. Then I realise I need to pay, so I put everything back down and rummage in my bag before slamming a five-dollar bill on the table and heading for the exit, pushing the door so violently it bangs back on its hinges with a loud thwack. I can hear a collective intake of breath from behind me and out of the corner of my eye, see the friendly waitress, coffee pot in hand, mouth open wide. Making friends in this small town is now going to be harder than ever.

In my haste to leave, I don't see the man in front of me, so bash into him (What is it with me and my propensity for bowling over the local population?). Apologising profusely (all I seem to be doing nowadays!), I glance up to see his green eyes aren't smiling. The need to cry, the need to run and hide, is overwhelming and drenches me as the rain soaks me a second time on my walk back to the inn.

3

"Ah!" The receptionist, dressed in black, descends upon me like a crow in full flight. I cannot avoid this encounter, much as want to sweep her aside and hide in my room. "I'm glad you're back." Her words do not seem to agree with the expression on her face, pinched with a hint of a sneer.

She steps back a pace or two when she sees the rainwater dripping from every item of clothing. It pools at my feet, but frankly, I am beyond caring.

"Oh dear..." The sneer turns to a self-satisfied smile as she passes me an envelope, making every effort not to sully herself on my soaked attire. "Your bill," she states, retreating to behind her desk.

Embarrassed that she appears to be gloating over my appearance, a frisson of anger courses through me, and I shuffle past, making sure I leave wet impressions on each tread of the stairs. Still seething, I deliberately drop my bag on the carpet outside my bedroom door until it leaves a stain, while inwardly berating myself for being mean. Today is not turning out as I had expected and having potentially alienated every person in this small town where no doubt everyone knows everyone's business, I head for the shower, warm and soothing.

When I have recovered my equilibrium, I settle by the fire, my legs tucked up under me, covered with the soft blanket from the bed. I read my book for several minutes before my eyes drift to the painting, propped up against the wall. Ruined. Turning my head to one side, I peer closely. Or is it? The people I encountered earlier thought it was a good painting, worth selling. Why was I so reluctant? Is it a lack of confidence, or something else?

As I get up to look more closely, the envelope given to me by the receptionist falls from within the pages of my book. Retrieving it, I find the bill for the first week. Ouch! Expensive. I cannot rebuke myself for the indulgence of such a pretty room as I knew how much it was going to cost. I had at least planned the expenses before I left England but knowing the expense and seeing it in black and white fills me once more with doubt. Also, the daily living costs of eating out, books and painting equipment is a bit more than my usual. Oh dear! I worry what Jon would think of me spending the last of our money on such an extravagant and self-indulgent trip. Always careful with money, we spent the savings we had on lifesaving (not saving his life) treatment and now, I am splurging what remained on this. Maybe I should have sold the painting. I close my eyes and squeeze out a sad, lonely tear.

The following morning after breakfast, avoiding the receptionist, I make my way up Main Street towards the café. I have to apologise for my behaviour yesterday. Humble pie is not my dessert of choice, but my conscience kept me awake for most of the night and I know I will not be able to settle to anything – reading, walking, painting, anything – until I have apologised.

As I pull open the door and enter, all eyes turn to me. Thankfully, the aromatic waves of rich coffee draw me towards the friendly waitress who greets me with a smile and happily takes my order, inviting me to take a seat. I avoid the area that was involved in yesterday's embarrassing saga and sit by the window, watching the people walk up and down the pavement outside, willing my heart to stop thudding in my chest.

I glance up as the mug of steaming coffee is placed on the table in front of me by the owner, not the waitress.

"So…" Martha says, sitting down opposite me, uninvited. "Have you recovered from yesterday's hissy fit?" There is not a hint of a smile on her guarded face.

I nod.

"Good! You want to tell me what happened?"

I shake my head.

Her eyes narrow slightly. "And your name is?" she asks.

"Jane." I manage to find my voice.

"She speaks!"

I have the decency to turn a shade pinker. I mutter an apology then finding a measure of poise, I sit up straight and speak more clearly. "I am sorry about yesterday. I behaved badly."

In the silence that follows, I take a sip of my coffee and notice her shoes are the most extraordinary creation of lilac and white embroidery, a perfect match to her outfit of the day. She has a certain style; I'll give her that.

"And..." she says eventually, her head on one side, her eyes piercing.

Now does not seem the right time to tell her about the internal wranglings of my mind, my history, my grief, my reasons for being here, and I struggle as to what exactly I should tell her about what happened, other than the fact that I was upset.

"I just felt..." I pause a moment. "I just felt that the painting was ruined, and I didn't feel it was worthy of them paying for it." There, that was a good answer. I allow my shoulders to return to their natural position, no longer wearing them as earrings.

"But we all felt it was a good painting..." Her voice

fades as her face softens slightly.

"I know, I know."

"And having apologised, in a manner of speaking, how do you feel about selling the painting today?"

The waitress, who had obviously been listening to our conversation, tells us that the couple are staying at Oakham Wayside Inn, along the coast. I knew small town knowledge would come in useful.

Martha looks at me and her eyes widen a tad in anticipation. "Well?"

Later that morning, I watch Martha as she advances towards the couple who are waiting for us in the bar of their hotel. She walks with style and purpose, like a duchess at a finishing school with a book balanced beautifully on her head. She thrusts out her hand towards the husband. He shakes it and winces. I hide a grin.

"Hi," she says. "I can only apologise for the incident in my café yesterday."

The man nods slowly, tentatively. He glances briefly at me as though he's apprehensive about what I might do next, like I'm a rabid dog, or more accurately, a mad English woman. He's agreed to this meeting but appears reluctant at the same time. His wife smirks.

Martha continues, "On reflection, Jane and I have discussed things and the painting is for sale—"

"Oh! Thank you!" The wife claps her gnarled hands together like an over-excited child, her bracelets join in with their own clanking.

Martha ignores her, focusing on the husband. "And it sells for one hundred dollars."

Wow, I think, *she's good!* We hadn't discussed prices before we arrived, and to be perfectly honest, I am just grateful that Martha is taking control as it will stop me from backing out and embarrassing myself a second time.

"That's fine." He sounds relieved and glances at me again before extracting a roll of money from his pocket. He proceeds to peel off ten-dollar notes and hand them over.

"Dear," the whiner starts, "do you think Doris and Ed would like a painting too?"

I look from her to the poor long-suffering husband. His eyes glaze over.

"I'm not sure…" he hesitates as he flops down into his chair.

"I'm sure they would. D'y'all have any more paintings?" she asks Martha, then focuses her sharp eyes on me, knowing she is making me uncomfortable.

Before I can speak, Martha says, "As you can see, this painting is kinda unique. It clearly reflects what happened yesterday and the weather as well as the fine talent of the artist." She pauses for a moment and seeing my dazed expression, her eyes dart back to the couple. "What would Doris and Ed like?"

I cannot believe what I'm hearing.

"I think maybe a painting of the café so we can tell them the whole story of our wonderful day. And I know Joan would like a painting of the ocean too, dear – you know how she loves the ocean."

The man visibly shrinks in his seat, his eyes firmly fixed on his hands. I panic.

Martha merely smiles and adds, "You're staying until when?"

"We leave Monday afternoon."

I get the impression that the time of departure cannot come soon enough for this henpecked husband.

Martha turns to me. "Monday afternoon, eh?"

I am stunned into silence yet choke down the mounting rage and panic within. She's doing it again! But can I afford for her not to? I press the emotions down as I watch Martha turn back to the man and inform him that the paintings will be ready. She adds, "The price for each one will be negotiated at the time, based on their size, *et cetera!*"

He nods and the gnarled-handed woman smiles smugly.

Back at the café, Martha bustles over to where she told me to sit, bringing with her some coffee and cake.

"So, could you have the two paintings ready for Monday morning?"

"I don't appear to have much choice, do I?"

I know I sound like a petulant child but again things have moved outside my control. One painting was fine, but several? I trusted Martha enough to allow her to sell my painting, but now, now I'm wondering if this was such a good idea after all.

"Well, we did agree to have them ready by then." She starts to eat her cake with the small fork, delicate and precise.

"We? Again, I don't recall being given much choice."

"True," Martha admits and gives a hearty laugh, "but I'm sure you are more than capable. That painting was excellent, by the way."

I confess that it was my first attempt and the only one I have painted since my arrival in Oakham. I regret the words once they are spoken as Martha looks slightly horrified and her lips, perfectly made-up lips, form a letter 'o' but no sound is emitted.

"In which case, you'd better get started!" she says eventually before returning to her cake.

We quietly eat our cake, and once it's cooled, I cradle the coffee mug in my hands, savouring its aroma. I notice Martha is giving me a concentrated stare, like her handshake, firm and direct.

"Are you here on vacation?"

"Not quite..." I pause, unwilling to open up. Not yet. My trust only goes so far, but I realise she is only being kind, so add, "Well, not really."

"How long're you here for?"

"Some time."

Martha frowns and tilts her head slightly at my vague response, but before she can ask any further questions, the café door opens. She smiles and waves her hand in greeting. My back is to the door, and I assume it is one of her regular customers. I finish my coffee and, remembering my manners, thank her for her generosity.

"You are welcome – it has been a good day all round." She smiles, perfect teeth. "I hope to get to know you better while you are here for... some time."

I know she is mocking but I smile anyway.

A man comes into view and plants a kiss on Martha's cheek.

"Gotta run," he tells her, turning to me and flashing a huge grin which reaches his green eyes.

My heart does what it does whenever he is in the room.

4

Sleep is a refuge from the pain and emptiness, a place where somehow everything is the same as it was before. Each morning, when the balm of sleep rubs off and I am wrenched into a new day, the knowledge that Jon is no longer around hits me with such force that it often takes my breath away. But this morning, after my encounter with Martha my first thought is not about Jon. My first thought is *I must paint,* and I feel panic, not pain. Anxiety not emptiness. The pressure to produce makes me shudder as uncertainty and nagging doubt returns. Then I think about Jon, and oddly, I feel slightly guilty for putting him in second place.

Yesterday was quite the day: the stress of having to apologise, summoning the courage to face Martha, the sale of the painting, the sensation of being in and then out of control with a woman I barely know, followed by the heart palpitations as I revert to being a teenager whenever I see that damn man with the green eyes – it's ridiculous! I have enough on my plate without having some crush on a random stranger – and that is exactly what it is as there can never be another after Jon. Exhausting!

I force myself out of bed and head into town to find breakfast —not at Martha's. I do not need external pressure to add to the internal turmoil. Instead, I go to a small diner at the crossroads near the bookshop. It's also a bit cheaper! There, in spite of an agitated stomach, I am able to consume a delicious plate of pancakes served with maple syrup and strong black coffee to fortify me for the task ahead. Then I go back to the sea and simply draw what is in front of me, waiting for the churning inside to subside. After all, I agreed to this, and I do have three full days to complete the work. I can do this.

When Monday rolls around I am seated in the café before ten in the morning, apprehensive about how the couple will react. Will they have changed their minds? What if they've decided they don't like my art after all? I have drunk two large coffees and need to visit the bathroom but dare not leave my seat. I wriggle uncomfortably.

I have produced the two commissions, which have been framed by the kind gentleman in the art supplies store who was apologetic at having to charge me so much for the rush job. I was simply appreciative. And I have to say, I am happy with them. My style is returning. They are not the best I have ever produced, but I am happy. I wipe my sweaty palms on my jeans and take a deep breath in a vain attempt to tame the inner storm. After all, I have fulfilled my responsibilities and I'm pleasantly surprised. A small smile. Now I have to wait.

Much to my relief, Gnarled Hands and her husband love the paintings and pay the (what many may consider to be an over-inflated) price that Martha negotiated without any fuss. They are happy. I am grateful and Martha seems pleased as she hands over the cash.

"Sixty: forty – right?" That hearty laugh proves she is joking as I count the dollars. She shakes her head and instructs me to sit. "And I'll make us a celebratory" – she checks her watch – "and early lunch!"

Food appears to be intrinsic in her life as she eats with gusto and talks between bites of ham and cheese, tomatoes and salad with crusty bread and olives. My body feels heavy after all that has happened and I struggle to eat, taking small, measured mouthfuls as I listen intently. This woman is taking me on a journey full of unexpected twists and turns and I'm not quite keeping up with the pace.

5

The following morning, I am strangely drawn back to the café. The morning buzz and the smell of baked goods and coffee is calming, and for the first time in days, I feel the tension evaporate. No sweaty palms, no tight shoulders. Alone but not lonely, I listen to conversations and people watch for a pleasant hour.

Then as I see Martha advancing towards me, that heart skip and a jump returns. What now?

"I've been thinking," she states as she joins me.

This sounds ominous.

Glancing around the small café, she adds, "You know, this place could do with brightening up some."

I have to agree with her – the café is cosy but bland, and the wooden tables and chairs are tired and dated, the walls and window blinds plain and ordinary.

"Now that you've finished with the commissions, how would you like to exhibit your paintings from here?"

We make eye contact. I try not to flinch. I don't have

any more paintings; I think but keep quiet. I am being swept along by events outside my control once more, swimming against the tide, so to speak. I take a further moment to look around the room. It's a long time since I had an exhibition, probably a decade. It might be fun – not quite what I had in mind, but fun, nonetheless.

When I cannot find the words due to the dryness of my throat, she carries on, reiterating her previous sentiments in simple words that even a child would understand.

"How about you bring your paintings, hang them here and we'll see what happens?"

She tilts her head and smiles at the idiot in front of her. Me! I see once again that she has perfect teeth. She may be an eccentric dresser, but she is beautiful, striking even. The rest of her make-up, like her lipstick, is expertly applied.

"Could you do some sketches too?"

I nod.

"Watercolours?"

Nod.

"Greetings cards?"

Nod.

"OK. Good, bring them all."

She pauses. I fight down the fluttering inside. All? I have nothing! Do I tell her?

"And we'll split the proceeds sixty: forty!"

I cannot help myself and snort with laughter as I hold out my hand. Unbelievable. Let's go for it. Forget the doubts, the lack of resources, just do it. "That sounds like a great idea."

We shake hands to seal the deal. This time I know what is coming and grip her hand in return. There is a moment of silence as we appraise each other, and I need to know so I ask, "Why?"

"Business, dear, business!"

There is a momentary pause as she locks eyes with me. Then the corners of her mouth twitch.

"And I'm the patron saint of lost causes," she chuckles.

I wonder what she sees in me.

"And you, my dear, look lost."

Do I? Am I? Her eyes tell me she understands, and she trusts me. I am hesitant and loath to let my guard down and reciprocate.

"But…" she pauses for dramatic effect, "…do not take this as a sign of weakness on my part as it does not, I repeat NOT extend to dogs or children!" She wags her finger at me emphatically and smiles once more.

Several days later, days filled with painting and sketching and bargaining with the kind man in the art supply store, I'm back in the café and received warmly. Sally, the friendly waitress, already knows my order and prepares it the moment I enter. It is beginning to feel welcoming and comfortable.

Martha tells me, "You go ahead and hang these," as she examines the pile of frames and prints.

When I'm convinced, finally, that they are worthy of being here, that they look good, I take a couple of photographs and WhatsApp them over to Katie, Mum, and my sister Jo with the comment, 'I got an exhibition!'

The receptionist from my hotel flutters in to chat with Martha. As she leaves, she comments in a voice bordering on a sneer, "Nice work…if you like that sort of thing!"

I turn to say 'thank you' just in time to see her leave and close the door behind her. Unperturbed by her rudeness, I stand back to admire the results as Martha emerges from the kitchen with two large plates of food. She set them down at one of the tables and goes back for more: bread, two glasses and a bottle of champagne.

"You came through!" she announces, "and I have to say, I'm impressed." She surveys the room. "They look really good. Unusual arrangement, but if you're happy…" Her voice drifts off while she pops the cork, pouring the bubbling liquid into two glasses. "Cheers!"

Later in the day, I email Katie to bring her up to date on events but play down my apprehension about being here and my concerns about finances. I also keep my reservations about the receptionist to myself, unsure why she behaves as she does and wondering if I have mis-understood something. I want to tell Katie I'm settled, to share my excitement about the exhibition. Subdued excitement, it's true, but excitement, nonetheless. I type and retype so that the email sounds upbeat and positive, knowing she will share it with Mum and wanting to give her a good impression despite my niggling doubts. Her reply lands within minutes.

From: Katie [mailto: Katie@Katiesplace.web.com]

Sent: 30 April 16.20

To: janenjon28@web.com

Subject: Afternoon!

Hi BFF! Sorry for the later reply - just finished work.

Glad to hear you are safe and well. I called round to see your mum yesterday - she got her letter. She looks fine so please DO NOT worry about her. I will call her and chat with her again tomorrow and get back to you. She will survive without you! I haven't seen your Dad yet, but I promise I'll go over and visit them at the weekend. Promise.

And congrats on the exhibition and sale! Love the photos and I always knew you had talent. My brother would be so proud of you!

Speak soon.
Love you x

I read the reply, looking for hidden words, signs, nuances. Nothing. She seems genuinely pleased and I feel a stab of guilt at not being entirely honest. But she's right – Jon would be proud.

6

After an early morning walk through the back streets of town and the park to clear my head – sauntering, discovering and exploring new places and sights – I pick up a local newspaper to search in the rental section. I have paid the bill for the first week but deep down I know I cannot afford the luxury of Room 12 for more than a couple of weeks – max – even with my new income stream, particularly as that might not continue. My head is still full of those doubts: Will I have to go home early? Will everyone at home then think I'm a failure after I convinced them I could last out for six months?

Despite the turmoil of thoughts in my head, the walk has done me good. I settle in my chair in the spacious, elegant reception at the Oakham Inn, with polished wood floors, wicker chairs with plump white cushions, light décor and large sash windows which allow the wonderful light to flood in. The local newspaper, *The Cape Cod Chronicle*, is spread out before me on the coffee table and, with pen in hand, I am circling anything that appears to be a possibility.

However, I realise that my relaxed mood has made me vulnerable, and I should have done my research in my room, away from the prying eyes of the all-seeing, all-knowing receptionist whose name I have discovered is Jessica. She brings over my coffee and cinnamon bun on a bright red tray, setting it down firmly while craning her swanlike neck to see what I am up to.

"What ya doin'?" she inquires in what appears to be a friendly way, which is unnerving. Her darting eyes take in the newspaper and they narrow slightly.

I don't trust this change in manner. From the few conversations we've had to date, I am wary. If I was standing, I would take a step back at this point. I am on my guard.

"Checking out the local property market," I tell her unthinkingly. I grit my teeth. Stupid!

On the defensive, she draws her thin frame to her full height and retorts, "You're not happy here? I thought you were booked in for at least another week. Yes?"

"Oh yes, yes I am!" OK – pause and think, handle this carefully. "I love it here and I love my room and these cinnamon buns are delicious!"

She preens, her ruffled feathers are soothed.

"But I'm afraid I can't afford to stay here long term,

so I'm looking for a place to rent."

"Oh? How long are you gonna be in town? For the summer? Yes? You're a bit early for a summer rental, normally that's around the end of May. I know you'll find most summer rentals are expensive." She emphasises the word 'expensive.' "Much more than staying here…" She is on a roll and the words flood forth. "You know the prices are much more affordable" —her face tells me 'for people like you' — "further down the coast."

I shove my unruly hair behind my ear and rearrange the top I'm wearing that has seen better days. I may not be the smartest of people, I may not have taken the best care of myself while I've been caring for Jon, but my money is as good as anyone else's. I bristle.

The front door opens and in walks the man with the green eyes. This is all I need right now as my body reacts in the now familiar manner: racing heart, dry throat, wet palms, all of which is made more disconcerting by the huge grin that lights up his face when he catches sight of me. Jessica is up out of her seat in a second and advances towards him in a manner she must think is sultry but actually makes her look like a flat-footed duck. I'm surprised by this sudden change of demeanour and supress a smile.

"Daniel!" she purrs.

His eyes move from me to her. His smile becomes

frozen and cool.

"Jessica."

"Thank you so much for coming over." She takes hold of his elbow and guides him out of the room.

The moment over, my body returns to normal.

Sometime later she returns, ostensibly to collect my plate and empty cup, and greets me with her faux politeness and a cat-like smile.

"You found anything?" she asks.

Again, my guard is up.

"There are some possibilities… but like you said, this is an expensive area. I think an apartment might be out of the question. I'm probably looking at renting a room."

Having finished, I realise I may have said too much, revealed my hand. Why do I do that?! There is something about her that makes me not want to confide in her too much, something untrustworthy, and yet I speak without thinking and at the same time I have the feeling that anything I share with her will be the knowledge of the whole town within hours. And yet what have I just done? Again! And given the poor first impression I have given so far, I don't really want people coming to their own conclusions before they get to know me. There's also my pride to think of. I hardly want to be considered destitute!

She sees this revelation as an opening and settles

down in the chair next to me, turning the paper to see what has been marked. She scans the circles and passes comment, poking the paper each time. I observe her sharp-featured face as she reads intently. She is probably in her early 40s, with great skin, a beak of a nose and those wonderful straight white teeth that all Americans seem to have. I wonder why she is behaving as she is towards me – inquisitive, almost to the point of an unhealthy interest.

"Not there – weird neighbours." Pause. "That won't work." Pause. "You wouldn't wanna stay with her – husband's creepy. Yes?"

She looks like she has just sucked on a lemon. I try to stifle a laugh, but it erupts as a snort which I try and disguise as a cough, causing her to look up.

"I am serious. Serious!"

I stop smiling. She resumes her analysis of my choices until she reaches the final page and sits back satisfied.

"There are a few possibilities. You should find something." She sounds dismissive, as though she has exhausted her attention span on this topic of conversation. But then she thinks and adds, "Unfortunately, after the end of the booking we have for you, your room is booked and the inn is full. So, you'll have to be quick."

I listen in silence, shocked and stunned by her

contempt.

"Or go home!" she adds.

We stare at each other and I blink first.

"Oh! And by the way, Daniel..."

She lets his name sit between us for a moment as I rack my brains as to who 'Daniel' is, then remember it was the name she purred to the green-eyed man. I blush as I wonder if my reaction to his mere presence was plain for all to see.

"I'm telling you to save you from heartache; don't trust him."

Back in Room 12, stung by her words, I am reverting to type and overthinking the morning's events, my mind flitting from one thought to the next. How can she say the man is not to be trusted when she seems to be close to him, on friendly terms and clearly changes her behaviour when he appears? She can't possibly be jealous of the way he smiled at me. Oh boy, that's all I need! As if I would be looking for a relationship! Life, death, and grief have knocked the corners off my confidence, and I'm experiencing such a maelstrom of negative emotions that starting a relationship is the last thing on my mind. I feel despondent and miserable because I probably can't afford to rent in Oakham. My 'well thought-out plan' – which clearly it wasn't remember the pin in the map approach? – is not going as expected. Things aren't helped by feeling swamped with a sense of loneliness and isolation from my dear friend Katie, and Mum and Dad. Although I keep in regular contact with them, as well as getting frequent updates about my grandparents and regular Facetimes with my sister and adorable niece, it's not the same as being able to pop round for a cup of tea. Thinking of my father, I hear him telling me, "You can come home if things didn't work out, my dearest girl." But I cannot give up at the first hurdle – there must be a solution.

I lie on my big, warm, soft bed and the pain over my right eye returns, the one that signals tears. The room is quiet. I miss my husband. There is no sobbing now, no sound. Done that and got the T-shirt. Tears seep out silently. What have I done? Why did I come here? The feeling of exhaustion flows over me as the pain subsides and sleep proves to be a faithful friend. However, my sleep is not without interruptions, and echoes of the cause of my anguish play out in my dreams.

The woman sitting opposite was crying. I stared at her; she seemed crumpled, small. I briefly wondered if I looked like that when I cried. Crying makes you look – how does it make you look? Sad, yes. Vulnerable, maybe. I felt sympathy for her. Instinctively I wanted to hug her and tell her it'd be OK

– I felt empathy too. This tumble of thoughts, watching the woman sitting opposite in the bright clinical waiting room, is interrupted as a man dressed in brown faded cords and a knitted tank top calls my name.

"Jane?" I looked up and smiled at Peter, my grief counsellor. "You ready?"

I nodded and rose from my plastic chair, glanced one more time at the woman who was still crying, and followed him down the corridor into the consulting room. There the atmosphere was more cosy, less stark. The chairs were covered in a pale blue fabric, comfortable and conducive to chatting.

"How have you been?" he asked softy.

"Better, I think."

I told him about my week at school, the kids I had taught and the art.

"But how have you been?" He repeated his question, both of us fully aware that I hadn't actually answered honestly. "You've told me what you've been doing, but..." His voice faded.

I sighed as his words hung in the air.

"I know."

There was a stillness in the room.

"That woman out there – she's crying. Just sitting there crying."

I paused. He waited.

"Do I look like that when I am crying? She looks" – I paused again, trying to find the right words to sound mildly

intelligent – "she looks all folded in." I had failed. I scrunched up my body as an alternative to words. "Like she wants to disappear."

After a moment, when he had carefully chosen his response, Peter asked softly, "Is that how you feel? Like you want to disappear?"

"Sometimes. My favourite place to cry," I said, smiling as if this was normal, "is lying on the floor in a ball next to my bed. If I were smaller, I'd crawl under the bed like I did when I was a child."

"As a child?" he prompted when I stopped.

"Yes, whenever I was afraid, I'd hide under my bed. I didn't do it often, but it was my safe place." I didn't want to go down that road so changed the subject quickly. "I am fed up with crying, Peter. It's exhausting."

We sat in silence for a time. I crossed and uncrossed my legs, leaned back, and stared at the ceiling.

"I have had enough." I looked back at him to gauge his response.

"Of what?"

"Life." Then I realised what I had said and hastily explained. "No! I don't mean that, not life, per se, as in I want to die. It's more in the sense of my life – my home, my job, my misery. I want to run away and go and live somewhere else and do something different – almost reinvent myself. I want to live. I feel like I'm becoming a victim of this situation, like the woman crying. I want it to stop. I want to run away and start again."

"And that will help how?"

I wake with the question ringing in my head: "And that will help how?" I lie there, staring at the ceiling, before checking what time it is and rousing myself. I've slept for an hour and it is now late afternoon. A big sigh escapes, like air leaking from a flat tyre, as my thoughts battle back and forth. I've come halfway around the world and seem to have created new problems and challenges and yet at the same time a measure of confidence seems to be re-emerging. The fresh sea air is doing me good, giving my cheeks a glow that's been missing, though it has yet to revive my still sunken eyes. And what's been happening at home? How is Dad? I make a mental note to call him. That'll put my mind at ease. I snuggle deeper into the duvet and then my stomach feels like a huge weight as I remember my predicament – I must find somewhere to stay.

I'm getting nowhere with this mental fight so I jump out of bed to make myself a refreshing cup of coffee which brings me back to life. An unexpected thought pops into my head and I dive under the bed to retrieve my suitcase. Brushing the dust off it, I take a brown paper-wrapped package from inside and place it on a chair, close the case and slide it back under the bed. It takes a moment or two before I can untie the string because I know what's inside. I haven't run for over two years, not since… Back then I had taken the trainers, the shorts and the iPod and wrapped them in brown paper and tied them up with string. I don't know why I didn't throw them out. I don't know why I kept them wrapped up in the wardrobe at home and I don't know what possessed me to pack them and bring them to America, and yet here they are.

The paper reveals its contents and I sigh once again at the sight of them. Do I want to run again or not? I sit on the bed next to them and contemplate. Running. Running always helped me when times were tough. Running helped me to forget. Running kept me from going mad.

It seems like today is a day when I know I am overthinking, and I tell myself to simply get on with it. It's been a tough day with some harsh realities, and yes, I am tired, but I am no longer sleepy. There is no inclination, but deep down I know I need to run.

Running helps me to cope.

At the garden gate in the middle of the white picket fence, I stop. The huge tree in front of the inn has green flecks on it as the leaves begin to unfurl. The daffodils along the fence are in full flower. Spring is in bloom. I tell myself, *Don't think, just go!* I turn right and start to jog. Within seconds my body is screaming, "WHAT THE HELL DO YOU THINK YOU ARE DOING?" I slow to a walk and endeavour to get my breathing under control. In two, three, four. Out two, three, four. In two, three, four. Out two, three, four. The counting rhythm helps and, with my breathing sorted, I step up the pace and this time my body does not respond so violently, it accepts and remembers how it feels to run.

As I get closer to the sea, I pick up the pace a little more and my legs carry me past the low wall, the steps and the lighthouse, and down Morris Island Road to the headland. The views are amazing. It is early May and the sky is bright blue, fading to indigo as the sun slowly sets. It is the best time to run, and to run in a beautiful setting makes it special. Now I remember why I enjoy running. My body settles into the rhythm and the endorphins flow.

When I reach the furthest point of my run at the headland, the wind picks up and the waves crash against the shore. I feel visceral. I feel alive. Grief, guilt, frustration and exhilaration whirl around me with the wind. I take a deep breath and scream towards the setting sun.

7

Sally greets me with a cheery smile, welcoming me to a place that is a warm cocoon amidst the turmoil of my mind.

"Morning! You OK?"

I nod and smile.

"I'll be back in a minute. Coffee?"

My morning ritual, my visit to the café and chatting with this young girl, calms me. She is open and honest, and I can see that she would like to know more about me, for no other reason than she wants to be friends. There is no agenda. My inner scepticism does not, as yet allow me to feel secure enough to be honest with her. This adds to the burden of guilt, the one I carry: guilt at leaving my parents in time of Dad's need, the guilt I feel when a moment of joy fills my world.

I am preparing to leave when Martha bustles in through the front door, dressed in peacock colours: blue, green and turquoise linen layers. She looks amazing. Even the reading glasses perched precariously on her head perfectly match her outfit.

"Morning!"

Her cheery presence lightens my mood and I smile broadly.

"Good morning!"

"You look bright," she comments.

Little does she know. But I carry on with my false optimism. "I feel it today – thank you."

"Is there a reason?"

I hesitate. "I am trying desperately hard to be positive," I divulge, then hesitate again, but decide I can trust her with more information, "because I have to find somewhere to stay."

"You're not happy at the inn?" She pulls out the chair opposite and joins me.

"Yes, I am, but it's, well, I simply can't afford it long term." I reach for the folded newspaper and hand it over, not telling her about Jessica's threat.

She brings her glasses to the end of her nose and sees the circles, reads without commenting, then mutters, "Mmnnnn!" She folds the page, puts it on the table and looks me straight in the eye. "How long you looking to rent?"

"I bought a six-month ticket – so 'til about the middle of October."

"All summer, eh?"

I shrug.

"What can you afford?"

"Not a lot." I point at the paper.

"Wrong zip code, sweetie!"

"I am beginning to realise that. I've thought about trying further afield away from the coast, but I would like to stay in town where it feels comfortable and safe. It is lovely here."

"It is… I'll keep my ear to the ground for you." She pauses when she sees my smile. "I'm not promising anything, mind you!"

I nod. I know.

Martha sits back in her chair, folds her arms, and gazes intently at me over the top of her glasses. "Whereabouts in England are you from?" she asks quietly.

"Just outside Manchester, it's in the north of England."

She nods. "Yes, I know where it is."

"You've been?"

"A long time ago. I was in England for work – as I say, a long time ago." She shifts in her chair, looking slightly uncomfortable, and then her face takes on a softness, a memory perhaps? "So, why are you here? Why'd you come to our small town?"

I blush under her scrutiny. "This is going to sound silly, but it was totally random. I stuck a pin in a map."

Her eyes tell me that she understands but still she

asks, "Why?"

Now – how much do I tell her? I pause to consider my response and settle on telling her it was a "crossroads moment".

"Sorry to interrupt," Sally interjects. She looks at Martha and nervously informs her that Patty didn't turn up for work again this morning.

Martha explodes out of the chair, surprising us both. Sally wisely moves out of the way as Martha advances across the room.

"That's the chef," Sally whispers to me as she moves closer.

"The chef?" eyes on Martha, I whisper back.

"Yes, Patty hasn't shown up now for two days." Martha can be heard banging about in the kitchen, her voice raised in outrage, so Sally moves closer. "And she's not paid her rent on the apartment either. I checked!"

Those customers who are present drink up quickly and within seconds the place is empty.

"So, no breakfast this morning. Sorry."

My stomach rumbles in protest. Recently, I've been eating breakfast like a king, lunch like a prince and eating a snack or a sandwich in my room in the evening to eke out my dwindling funds. And as a happy consequence, I have lost a few pounds and feel better for it, my body feels lighter and heathier. But disappointment swamps me as the bacon, eggs and toast are removed from my daily schedule. My stomach reacts violently and noisily, and Sally apologises again.

"Can I do anything to help?" I ask Sally.

Martha's sharp retort from the kitchen, "I doubt it," echoes across the room.

I exchange silent glances with Sally as a sliver of my fragile trust with Martha splinters and my hand shakes. I hide it from view as it is disconcerting. I know Martha has bigger issues to deal with now, but I was hoping to revisit our earlier conversation and find out if she knows anywhere I can rent. I return to my coffee as Sally nervously approaches her boss.

Quiet returns. The front door opens and in walks my favourite old man, Stan. He beams as he sees me then takes in the empty room, the banging pots in the kitchen and Sally's slumped shoulders as she approaches the kitchen, then shakes his head.

"Not a good morning?" He instinctively knows to whisper too.

Is this behaviour a pattern they're all aware of or are they all afraid of Martha? I shake my head. No words are uttered as Martha flounces out of the kitchen to the counter and another tirade about chefs and letting people down and running a business with half-wits erupts from her. A look of horror on Sally's face brings Martha up sharp as she realises she has gone too far and mutters, "present company accepted."

Stan smiles, Martha stops, we all hold our breath.

"May I have a coffee please?" His words quiet and calm as he approaches the counter.

Sally, grateful for something to do, makes his drink, and places it with a fresh cup for me on my table. Stan nods his thanks.

"Martha, Martha, there must be a solution." He takes hold of her hand and brings her towards me. I sit up straight.

She slumps in the chair. "I never really trusted Patty—"

"But she could cook," Stan reminds her.

Martha nods. Calm seems to be restored, but I worry it might only be temporary.

"True." Martha drinks from my cup but I bite my tongue. "But where am I going to find someone to replace her?"

"I can cook!" I announce and all eyes turn to stare at me and my instinctive outburst! "Well, I can!" I tell them. I might not be a trained chef but how hard can it be to cook a few breakfasts, make some sandwiches and bake a cake or two?

Sally and Martha exchange glances. Sally smiles and realisation rises from my canvas shoes up through my body – I've just volunteered for something I might not be able to fulfil. Suddenly the shaking of my hand intensifies as worry about letting them down sinks in.

8

Thursday morning, I wake with the sudden realisation that today is my first day at the café and anxiety kicks in – first day at big school, first day at uni, first day at work. So many firsts and this one an entirely new experience. Glancing at the clock – 6.30 a.m. – there is time for a short run and a shower before work starts at eight., so that everything can be baked and ready for when we open at ten. I briefly snuggle down in my bed amid the deliciously cool white French linen. There is a moment when I know I have to get running but my body isn't going to comply. I hate the idea of running but know, at the same time, that it is beneficial and I will feel better afterwards. I must make a choice – to run or not to run.

I decide to run without music, to listen to the town as it wakes up. The month of May has shrugged its shoulders and the clouds have fallen away to reveal a gin-clear sky. It is my favourite time of the year when everything is new, full of potential and the world is bright. I have no clue where my life is heading but I cannot wait to find out. I make a mental note to send a card to Mum and tell her how life is for me and tell her about my new job – at least for now.

Feeling the sea breeze on my face, I run down Main Street to the crossroads and left down Stage Harbour Road, down Bridge Street and along the shore, past the lighthouse and the cobalt blue ocean and back onto Main and home – a short, sharp burst of a run and into the shower.

My mood is much calmer and I'm ready for my first day at work. I quickly dress in my 'uniform' of black crop jeans, T-shirt and comfortable black trainers, and head over to the café, which is quiet and peaceful, empty of customers. Sally, dressed in the same 'uniform' – which somehow looks better on her than it does on me – starts my initiation into the workplace by instructing me on how to make a good coffee using the temperamental machine that spits steam and hisses. She is a confident and enthusiastic teacher. I am a fearful but obedient student, willing to learn, which Sally thinks is admirable. I am grateful for her encouragement.

Martha bustles in dressed in navy and white.

"Nice outfit," I compliment her.

"Thank you." She preens visibly.

Though not expecting a compliment back, her lack

of comment about what I am wearing pops a worry bubble in my mind – do I look smart enough? Martha asks If Sally is helping me to settle in.

"She is, yes, thank you, though I'm not sure I'll get the hang of this thing." The coffee machine hisses at me and I step back quickly.

"You're an intelligent woman, you'll get the hang of it."

She pats my hand and Sally snorts with laughter.

"What?!" Martha exclaims, eyes wide with mock astonishment.

"From a woman who never makes coffee!" Sally retorts.

I glance from Sally to Martha and back again, expecting a repeat of the outburst I experienced earlier in the week. I hold my breath.

"I don't need to make coffee. I have you guys!" She waves her hand at us and retreats outside.

I look at Sally for confirmation and breathe.

"It's true, she has no idea how this machine works!" she whispers, shaking her head, her ponytail swinging from side to side as she makes her way into the kitchen to introduce me to the fridge, the cooker and the menu for breakfast.

Thankfully, there appears to be sufficient cake to last several hours so I only have to focus on making breakfast and not multi-tasking, which is a huge relief.

These instructions continue until we open at ten. Sally smiles at everyone who enters, locals and tourists alike. She introduces me to those she knows by name: Tim, the guy from the harbour on his way to work, who takes his coffee triple shot Americano with no chit-chat; Stella, the tiny delicate lady who runs the dress shop next door, who takes her expresso extra hot with soya milk. I worry about all the convoluted alternatives. Surely coffee is coffee. Apparently not!

There is an array of folks passing through, ordering coffee to go, or perhaps sitting a while to catch up on town news. I notice that the smile and greeting the tourists get is slightly different, more professional, less personal. However, everybody is welcome and made to feel at home. I also notice how the customers interact with Martha, friendly and respectful. She too makes them all welcome, like she has with me. This adds a further brick to my little wall of trust for a woman who has taken a leap of faith in me after all and let me loose in her café. I am determined to try to reciprocate.

The breakfast menu has a thankfully small list of dishes and nothing proves to be beyond my culinary skills. Thankfully, none of the customers complain about the food I produce, and I am both relieved and proud of my first service.

The mid-morning rush subsides, I serve customers, make my first coffee and then rather than stand around not doing much, I return to the relative peace of the kitchen to bake a cake or two.

A couple of hours later, excessively and probably overly pleased with the results, I bring my bakes out and place them on the counter. Then I see Jessica, the receptionist, coming in through the front door at the same time I hear Sally whisper, "Oh no!"

Before Jessica reaches us, she stops and holds what looks like confidential talks with Martha, constantly looking over her shoulder at me. My paranoid instinct kicks in – are they talking about me? Maybe Martha isn't as trustworthy as I thought. I quickly rattle the thought from my mind – she's offered me a job; she cares about me – don't be stupid. I tell myself to play it cool, to be professional.

"Oh hello!" Jessica says to me, her voice highly strung, her hands gripping the countertop. She smiles with her mouth but not her beady eyes and I remain wary. "Fancy seeing you here." She lets the words resound around the café.

"What can I get you?"

"You are working here now? Yes?" Her eyebrows shoot up in mock surprise.

She seems to already know the answer to the question, and I guess Martha told her. Maybe it's that cake I am holding, or the apron emblazoned with the name of the café that's the giveaway, but my mind tells me they were talking about me. Oh dear, what have I got myself into? I simply nod and wait, not wanting to be drawn into that topic of conversation.

"I'll have a latté, please, and a piece of that cake you're carrying."

"Take a seat and I'll bring that over to you."

She seems reluctant to leave but makes her way to the seat by the window. Her head flicks back and forth, watching me and glancing outside as though she is expecting someone to show up.

Sally whispers in my ear, "Well handled."

I'm not sure what to make of the whole thing but begin to prepare her order. Suddenly, she jumps up and shrieks at me that she'll take her coffee to go! She snatches it from my hand before it hits the counter and runs outside towards a man who turns at the sound of her voice. So, she was waiting for someone! It's Daniel! A man she says I shouldn't trust.

"What's that all about?" I ask, confused on both levels.

Sally tells me, "Oh boy! She's at it again. Will she never learn?"

"Learn what?"

"Never mind. Just warning you. Be careful!"

I watch Jessica and Daniel disappear from view and wonder why I need to heed this advice and who do I need to be careful of – Jessica, Daniel, or both of them?!

9

Routine, the calm passing of days, painting and selling my paintings through the exhibition, working and making friends, all of this helps. I feel a sense of peace, quiet and small but peace, nonetheless. And I like it. This is what I came for. This is what I needed. This means I am beginning to find myself, to discover what I want from life. The sense of guilt at this new sensation is still there but it's tempered somehow, and I am living with it.

Each morning that I am working, as the routine takes over, my mind begins to rest, and I hum a little tune to myself as Sally and I settle into the working day. The smell of freshly brewed coffee and cooking bacon fills the air as the early morning customers arrive. I can cook. I can prepare breakfasts for the customers and make coffee using the hissing machine, over which I have finally found mastery.

This morning, I am lost in my activities when I realise someone the other side of the counter, watching, waiting. The handsome man with the green eyes stands in front of me. Daniel. He greets me with a smile that once again reaches his eyes and asks for a coffee.

"You're working here now?" he asks.

I nod as my heart does its fluttery dance. "Yes." My throat so dry, it sounds like a croak not a word.

"Yes, Jessica did tell me. You're from England, right?" he asks.

I nod again, slightly awkward under his scrutiny, his mention of Jessica throwing me slightly.

"Well, welcome to Oakham, it's good to have you around."

I blush, desperately trying not to, but unable to stop the warmth from spreading up my neck and into my cheeks. "Thanks," I manage to say, berating myself at being unable to speak like an intelligent human being whenever he is near. I swallow the lump in my throat and ask him again what he'd like to order. He takes his coffee strong and black. I even manage to inform him that I will bring his coffee to him if he'd like to take a seat – a whole sentence containing words of more than one syllable. A proud moment. But before I can practice my language skills any further, Martha bustles in and he forgets me, turns his attention to her and they embrace warmly.

"Daniel! How wonderful to see you! How long have you been in town?" Martha asks, guiding him over towards what I consider to be my table, my favourite place to sit. She's friends with him too. She seems to trust him.

"I drove down yesterday; the city's getting too hot," he tells her.

"So, you here for the summer?"

I listen more carefully, noticing the lovely sweater he is wearing and berate myself for wanting to know his answer. And for noticing.

"I don't think so, not yet. I've got a big contract to finish up with some clients, but maybe in a couple a week's I'll move down. I need to get some down time and go fishing."

"Stan was asking after you last week."

"How's he doin'?"

"He's OK…"

I move out of earshot to collect a tray, wipe down a table, then go into the kitchen. I don't need to hear any more. Frankly, I'm vaguely disappointed in myself. Standing at the sink, arms straight and tight, I stare out of the kitchen window and tell myself, *Pull yourself together, you stupid girl!* Yes, this man is attractive, but I have seen attractive men before, it's not like he's the first! I also know I do not want to find him attractive and I have no interest in complicating my life further, especially as I'm being warned off. The last thing I need is to get between him and Jessica. So, I tell myself once more to stop it!

10

"So…" Jessica sneers as I stand in reception paying the bill. "Where are you going tomorrow?"

My mouth is dry, my palms are damp, and I have to steady my hand as I punch in my PIN number. I cannot be honest with her and give her any satisfaction. I feel stupid, like a stupid teenager.

"I have options," I decide to say, forcing a smile to hide my anxiety.

Being homeless is not on my to-do list and in my defence, I have been searching for alternative accommodation. I've called nearly every hotel in town and only yesterday Stan told me he would ask a neighbour if their basement was free. Sally had let me know that if I was desperate I could sleep on her sofa. I'm sure that Stan would do the same if he realised the urgency of my situation. I am getting desperate but not desperate enough. Not yet. Martha hasn't mentioned the subject again and I didn't want to ask as she is now my boss.

"Because you won't be able to work at the café if you're leaving. It's a shame that." She pauses a moment, then narrows her dark beady eyes. "Leaving Martha in the lurch like that. Yes?"

I have no intention of leaving Martha in the lurch. I tell her so. Politely but firmly so she knows.

Upstairs, packing my case, the tears flow. What do I do now? Who do I tell? And how much do I say? It seems that neither Martha, Stan nor Sally have discussed my situation with Jessica, for which I am grateful, but can I really trust them with the reality?

I decide to be perfectly honest with the one person who knows me so well and send an emotional email to Katie. I get an instant response.

From: Katie [mailto: Katie@Katiesplace.web.com]

Sent: 15th May 16.20

To: janenjon28@web.com

Subject: Afternoon!

Hi BFF!

Come home, Jane! We will be so happy to see you and you've proved so much to yourself, really you have. Now it's time to come home and stop causing yourself all this stress. It's not worth it, Jane.

Come home x

I guess this is the response I expected, though it's not actually the response I want. I want her to tell me I can overcome this challenge and deal with this, that I am strong enough to cope and that I can see this through. But I got the response I expected and burst into tears again.

Filled with a sense of hopelessness, I wipe my hands across my face then pick up my phone and tap in my parents' number. My thumb hovers over the green 'call' symbol. I hesitate, knowing I will cry at the sound of their voices, and they too will tell me it's not worth it, to come home. Closing the phone, I throw it on the bed. In the ensuing silence I am alone with the tumultuous thoughts of an overactive mind and the silence. Lonely.

I close the door of the lockup at the bus terminal, turn the key, locking my worldly goods inside. The terminal is silent. It is five in the morning; I cannot risk anyone in the community seeing me hiding my things; I cannot risk Jessica seeing me leave the inn. No-one must know.

Heart thumping, and three thousand miles from home and without somewhere to sleep tonight, I am afraid. I go for a walk, down the wooden steps, taking care on the uneven surface, holding the bleached rail tightly, my body tense in the knowledge of what's going to happen later today. I wish Stan was here, knowing he'd make me feel better. At the end of the beach, the waves are gently lapping on the sand; I stop, breathe and watch the sun rise. Totally in the moment, surrounded by the beauty of creation, I tell myself I can do this. There has to be a solution. I will deal with the things I can control and try not to worry about what I cannot.

At work, I find myself retreating into my mind, constantly sorting the information, filing, and dismissing thoughts as they emerge and disappear. It is hard to be engaged with the others as I am constantly thinking about what I am going to do next. Sally asks if I am alright, and I tell her I'm OK. She doesn't believe me.

After breakfast, I take a break and sit on the steps by the back kitchen. I'd picked up a timetable from the bus terminal earlier in anticipation and take it out of my pocket. The names of the towns and places mean nothing to me – where do I go?

"Hi!" A quiet voice breaks the silence.

It's Daniel. He smiles and my heart leaps.

"Saw you sitting here all on your lonesome. You OK?"

I nod, unable to speak as tears are too close.

"May I?" He sits next to me. Far too close but the step doesn't leave room for manoeuvre. "Where you planning on going?" He points at the timetable.

"I'm not..." I cannot complete the lie that is coming from my lips as I look into his kind eyes. "This is just in case..."

He frowns.

"Just in case I can't find somewhere to stay."

"I thought you were at the inn?"

"I was..." My voice fades as I know I've said too much, hoping he won't ask any more questions.

His frown returns as he tilts his head to one side in a most appealing way. I try to give some clarification.

"Look, I'm sorry. You must think me either very rude or an idiot, or both. It's a tough day..." As if that explains everything.

"Can I help?" His smile reaches his eyes, as it always does.

"Not unless you have an empty basement or a spare room." I blush as the words gush out. Here I go again. "Or you know of a room to rent?" I mumble, hoping it will get me out of the hole I've just dug.

Shaking his head he tells me, "I'm afraid I don't. I've had a leak in my house and so I've got some people in to sort it out and redecorate. The only rooms that are habitable are the kitchen, bathroom and my bedroom..." His voice fades as a deep crimson blush creeps up to his face. "...but I can keep my ear to the ground if you like?"

"Thanks, I'd appreciate that," I say quickly, trying

to ignore my mind taking me on a virtual tour of his bedroom. "There's no rush anyway." I long to tell him to hurry up and find a place NOW but he knows enough, and I am reluctant to tell him the truth of the situation and it's probably too late.

"So how come you're moving out of the inn?"

"My room is taken with a new booking."

He looks confused. "Who told you that?"

At the mention of her name his confusion turned into pursed lips and he tuts. Circumstances aside, it makes me laugh and I tell him he looks like he sucked on a lemon.

He chuckles softly, a nice sound. "She has that effect on me..."

It's my turn to frown as my impression was that they were friends, but before I can speak, Sally pops her head around the kitchen door and tells me there's an order come in. A split second later she sees Daniel, grins then laughs.

"Back to work," he tells me, holding my hand a moment longer than is necessary as he pulls me up off the step.

I close the kitchen door and lock it, placing Martha's keys safely in my apron pocket. My heart is in my mouth as I move stealthily into the alleyway between the café and the dress shop. Eyes alert to anyone around.

It is only a fifteen-minute walk to the bus terminal to collect my case, but I am wary, wondering who's watching. Oakham is – without too many tourists – a small town. It does seem like everyone know everyone's business. My bags collected, I hurry the short blocks back to the café, dive down the alley and quickly unlock the door, enter, and relock it behind me, attempting to breathe properly now I am safe, relatively speaking.

That afternoon, Martha, despite having watched me all day, seeing me make silly stupid mistakes, watching me wipe away tears, had asked me if I could lock up the café and open up in the morning. Eventually she had handed me the key, having held on to it a little longer than necessary, as if unsure whether to give me the responsibility. She had been desperate as she had an urgent appointment to keep and Sally had to leave mid-afternoon as she had the early signs of a migraine. If I believed in God, I would have thought that a miracle had taken place. I wanted to hug her and tell her how much I appreciated her trust and how she had given me a refuge and a chance to think, if only for the night, but she would never know because I would never tell.

I decide against turning on the lights once it starts to get dark. The blinds are pulled down, and no-one can see inside but I want to stay hidden. For want of something to do, I remove the cushions off the bench seats and make a makeshift bed away from the windows and doors, tucked in a corner. I set an alarm for the morning, giving me time to hide the evidence of a night spent on the floor. Alone, in the dark, the café smells different. There is a faint hint of coffee and stale food, the life has gone out of the place now the people are missing. The silence, the dark envelops me, and I feel a strange sense of calm knowing I have dealt with today, but this peace is swiftly replaced be fear; I am afraid of what will happen tomorrow. Suddenly the coffee machine hisses and I jump at the sound, my heart racing. I want to cry but tears do not come. I'm beyond it. Helplessness leads to exhaustion and a dreamless night.

I miss the alarm and am woken in the morning with, "What the hell?" Martha. Standing, hands on hips, her face is stern. "I trusted you with the keys. What the hell do you mean by sleeping on my floor when you have a perfectly good hotel room?"

Woken suddenly from a deep sleep and in shock, I promptly burst into tears.

"How dare you!" Her voice is raised. "Do you know how much trouble I could get into if the authorities found out you were sleeping on my floor? They could close my business!"

The tears flow and my sobs get louder as the distress of the previous days flows out of me. Martha's face is stone-like, not showing any emotion.

Sally arrives and joins in the fun. Thankfully, she proves to be sympathetic, getting down on the floor next to me, holding my hand as I ramble and mumble my way through the events of the last days: Jessica's behaviour and all that has happened and how sorry I am to have caused Martha so much trouble.

"The inn is fully booked —"

"It can't be," Martha exclaims, her face finally showing some expression, a look of confusion. "I booked my friends in there just last night. Into Room 12!"

"My room!" I splutter.

Martha's face takes on a horrified look and Sally gasps.

"I don't believe it!" Martha stamps her blue-shoed foot. "How could she?"

"Because she's a witch!" Sally exclaims, then immediately throws her hand to her mouth, disbelieving that she has spoken so bluntly about her boss's friend.

I want to agree but keep quiet. Martha tuts loudly and storms out of the room, through the kitchen, slamming the back door behind her. Sally and I sit in silence, reflecting on what just happened. I wipe the tears away with the back of my hand and sniff loudly as my heart thumps with worry about what Martha will say or do when she speaks to Jessica, as that is where

I'm convinced she's gone.

"Come on!" Sally stands and pulls me up.

We hug and I hold on to her a moment longer, not wanting to let go, realising how much I need that human contact, that quiet reassurance.

"Let's get you all packed up."

I am grateful for our friendship and her care.

"You should have told me," she quietly remonstrates with me. "I told you that you could sleep on my sofa if you were desperate."

"I didn't think I was desperate."

Sally shakes her head in disbelief.

Less than an hour later, while I am making an order of omelettes for breakfast for our first customers, Martha bustles back in without a word. We work quietly together, walking warily around each other, getting on with the day as if nothing has happened and yet it clearly has, and my predicament still hangs in the air. Homeless. I might have slept on the floor of the café last night, but where will I sleep tonight?

When I get the chance of a break, I go outside and sit on the step. For a brief second I recall my companion from yesterday and hope he doesn't reappear today. Not what I need right now. I take out my phone and the local rental pages, now tattered around the edges and scribbled on. My options are decreasing on a daily basis and with the prospect of using my ticket to fly home looming, I tap in the next number on the list. The answers are the same: no vacancies, too expensive, we have next Wednesday night free but nothing until then. Sorry. Sorry not sorry. I sigh and decide that I will have to look further afield, along the bus route, for somewhere to stay. Unable to face it at this moment, I put the paper and my phone back in my pocket. Later.

I rest my head back on the warm bricks and sigh again.

"Why is that woman so nasty? Jane's such a sweet person?"

My ears prick up at the sound of Sally's voice coming from the kitchen.

"You know how she can be."

"I do, but this is beyond what we've seen before. You know she outright lied to her about the room! Left her homeless, for goodness' sake! And only yesterday I was in the store and Jessica was telling Bonny about Jane being from the wrong side of town and how she couldn't be trusted. Bonny was kinda lapping it all up and Jessica was saying that she could tell whoever she wanted, but why?"

I held my breath waiting for Martha's response.

"Look! Gossip is like releasing feathers to the wind and her dishonesty requires a speaker and a listener, so don't listen—"

"Jessica didn't know I was there," Sally defended herself.

"Good. She doesn't need any encouragement and she's unlikely to come in here again for a long time."

"You gave it to her?"

"Both barrels."

I can only imagine what Martha had to say.

"She's envious is what it is —"

"Why?" I need to be a part of this conversation.

After their initial surprise at my sudden appearance by the back door, Martha continues, "because you're the new girl in town."

Sally sighs. "And you have to understand, she was born and raised here in Oakham. She's a small-town woman with a small mind mentality."

"Sally!" Martha warns.

"Well, it's true, and over the years she's managed to annoy or insult almost every person in town, including my mom."

"She strikes me as a bit of a busybody; she wants to know everything about everyone." I add.

"Nosy!" Sally adds, again ignoring Martha's warning expression.

There is a moment or two of silence before Martha adds, "But when someone's like that there's usually a reason; maybe something happened to her in the past."

"Maybe," Sally concedes. "I heard that her father

died when she was about fifteen years old, and her mom never really recovered. I think they were dirt-poor but kinda proud at the same time if that makes sense. Like 'stand tall, girl, be proud', like we're not from the wrong side of town' kinda attitude. Life was probably hard for her growing up. I dunno."

"Makes sense."

We pause to reflect.

"That makes me feel a bit sorry for her," I admit.

"No! Don't go down that road, please." Sally becomes agitated, shifting her weight from one foot to the other while she relates more of the insults her mother endured. "Besides, I know she's jealous because Daniel likes you!"

"Daniel?" I stutter. "What's he got to do with all this?"

Sally is on a roll. "Jessica thinks that she has a chance with Daniel."

Martha gives her a stern look that only momentarily stops the words before Sally carries on, ignoring the warning, "When Daniel's wife left him" — *His wife left him. When? I didn't even know he was married!* — "Jessica thought that she'd be in with a chance, and she hounds the poor man. He's far too polite to tell her where to go and she is so delusional, thinking he's ever going to look at her, and then along you come, new in town, pretty as a picture, and bam!" She slams her hand down on the counter, making us all jump. "She has to get you out of town someway."

"But...?" I hesitate then I decide to tell them.... "But she told me not to trust Daniel?"

Both take the same stance, hands on hips, mouth tight, frowning.

"Ridiculous!" Martha states.

Sally adds, "He's one of the nicest guys I know."

They exchange glances.

"I think she told you that to keep you away from him."

They both nod.

"She's the one not to be trusted."

I agree wholeheartedly.

11

Thankfully it's a busy morning with only one incident: Jessica walks along the sidewalk, past the window. There is a collective intake of breath as she looks as though she will come in then changes her mind. Martha shakes her head and the moment passes. Thankfully.

With the lunch rush over, Martha takes a moment and calls me into the kitchen. My insides churn at the thought that she might dismiss me for what happened earlier, so I'd be homeless and without a job or money. I would have to go home. I nervously watch and wait as she returns her glasses to their original place on top of her head and in a matter-of-fact manner states, "Come with me!"

Following her through the kitchen door, we go down the side of the building and up a set of iron steps. At the top, she opens a small gate onto a balcony, then taking a key from her purse, opens the door to an apartment. The place looks dilapidated and unloved. Frankly trashed.

Martha takes a deep breath and apologises, "I guess I should have thought about this before but didn't think your situation was so dire." The apartment has a big square open plan living room, a kitchen area off to the left... but the light, oh the light is wonderful as it floods in through the skylights and big casement windows. "This place was where Patty lived before she abandoned me... AND without paying her rent for the month." She sighs. "It's just about habitable."

Down the short hallway, I find a bathroom and two bedrooms, each one empty, dusty and in need of some TLC. I close each door and go back to where she is standing.

"If you can fix this place up, it's yours while you're here."

Her eyes are lit with a sharp intelligence that make plain, without words, that she will not suffer fools. I have only known her a short time but already I sense there is a connection between us that I am happy with and do not wish to break. But now I must be totally honest with her.

"I can't afford to rent a whole apartment."

Hands clenched; I am trying desperately to hold tight to my emotions. I would love to live here, but it is not possible. I cannot afford this. I know it will be expensive from what I have already seen in the paper. A whole apartment with two bedrooms – it'll be hundreds of dollars a week. I try to suppress the tension that threatens to swamp me. Do not get your hopes up! Nope, it is not going to happen.

"I can't. I'm sorry," I admit sadly.

"You haven't heard how much the rent is yet."

"If it's anything like the rentals I've been looking at, I know I can't afford it."

"That's true, but how about we do you a deal."

She moves towards the window and gazes at the park beyond. I hold my breath and wait. She turns back to face me.

"You have come through on the painting thing, sales of your artwork are good, and the season hasn't really gotten going yet. And you can cook!"

We both smile.

"OK…"

She pauses. I wait.

"How about this? You do up this place." She sweeps her arms wide. "Right now, it's unloved, as you can see, but I guess you can do something with it. You obviously have an artistic eye, and you are pretty handy in the café making sure things look good. So… do it up and you can live here at a rent you can afford."

I make a move to tell her what I can afford and it's definitely not this.

Martha raises her hand to stop me.

"You are getting some income now from working

downstairs and you have your tips. Also, like I said, your paintings are selling well. You must have budgeted for accommodation?" I nod, unable to speak because of the lump in my throat. How can I go from the depths of despair in the darkness, homeless, to this, the possibility of renting a whole apartment? "Like I said, I have a tendency to be the patron saint of lost causes and frankly, my dear, when I first met you, you looked like you'd lost your reason to live. I don't know why and I'm not asking why, but your crossroads moment just got some direction. Besides, I like you. You've come through on everything I've asked of you to date so I know you are reliable, even though I've only known you a couple of weeks. I'm usually a good judge of character." Her face darkens and I'm not sure if she's thinking of Patty or Jessica. "And I believe I can trust you."

There is an expectant pause while she peers at me encouragingly, eyebrows raised. This woman with her indomitable spirit, mixed with warmth and a sense of humour, she believes in me, is being honest with me. She wants me to succeed. She seems to understand me. I have to let go, allow the connection because I get the feeling we are going to become good friends and I can trust her.

I hold her gaze and wonder at her generosity, straining to withhold the smile which threatens to flash across my face. I feel like I've passed some sort of exam I didn't even know I had taken and now see the room with a different attitude and vision; there isn't much furniture, there's dust and dead insects in each and every corner. Where to start? The realisation slaps me roundly; Oakham could feel like home and having a place to stay, people to spend time with, could actually give my life a sense of purpose once more – something that's been sadly missing these last few years. Yes, I am relying on the kindness of strangers and yet inside my emotions bubble as I talk myself in and out of the agreement.

"We gotta deal?" Martha asks quietly and patiently, almost as though she can hear the conversation I have been having with myself.

She tells me the rent she expects. My eyes open wide. I can afford it! I glance around. I can live here. A home. A place of refuge. I smile.

"We have."

"You continue to work for me and if things gets really busy during the summer and you have to work more then we re-negotiate."

"Thank you!" I add, grinning from ear to ear.

"You are doing me a favour; the place is a mess. You can take that suitcase out of my kitchen and bring it up here now."

"Yes ma'am!"

She smiles too and hands me the key. "Get started! You can have the afternoon off; I think we can manage without you!"

"Yes ma'am!"

I have no clue where my life is heading but it's a better direction than yesterday and does not include a bus timetable.

12

A moment of silence envelopes me as I close the door to the apartment. The noise from the kitchen downstairs, the sound of chatter from the café and traffic from the street, all of it turned down to a mere whisper in the distance. My heart rate slows, the pounding in my ears fades as a sense of calm I have not felt for several years flows through my veins. I am safe. The weight lifted from my shoulders lightens my mood and a smile threatens to emerge. A deep breath or two, and I glance around the trashed apartment.

Without taking a step, I assess what is mine: a comfy looking blue sofa, a lamp on a painted side table. There is small table and two chairs that l instantly decide should be moved over beside the window so that I can see the park. My smile broadens. Some shelves and an awful painting of a house that I know is going in the bin downstairs. The kitchen has a broken drawer front and a cupboard door is missing. That can be fixed, or a small curtain can be made, French style.

Placing my keys on the counter, I explore further by opening cupboards and finding sufficient cutlery, plates, cups and bowls for my needs. There is a kettle, some pots and pans. Yes. Enough. Down the hall I am frankly appalled by the state of the bathroom, but a quick resume shows it's complete, just needs a HazMat suit to tackle the grime. My smile broadens as I imagine what my mum would be saying: "Roll up your sleeves, girl, and get on with it!" I wish she was here. I miss her. She'd be good company for what lies ahead.

The smaller of the two bedrooms is empty except for a solitary chair, cobwebs, and an assortment of dead flies. The main bedroom has built-in closets and a small set of drawers, both of which are thankfully empty. The double bed makes me shudder. Whoever crawled out of it… well let's just say a laundry will not be necessary – all the bedding will be finding its way to the bin. Clean, fresh bedding for me. There suddenly seems so much to do.

"OK, let's get started." Taking a deep breath, I repeat the mantra "I can do this!" over and over. I tell myself, *At least finish cleaning the whole place first before you start to panic!*

Once the floor in the main room is swept – too vigorously, with clouds of dust and much choking – I consider sanding the planks and painting them before dismissing this grandiose idea and just sweep, this time less vigorously. I wipe walls, the whole of the kitchen and then the huge windows. The view over the park is incredible, with swathes of grass and large trees turning green with fresh leaves (when I paint the scene I will use terre verte, I think). There are children playing, squealing, and enjoying the spring sunshine. I move the table and chair, now spotlessly clean, and position them just so. This is where I will start every new morning.

A knock on the door allows me a moment to stand up, straighten out my taut limbs and stretch. Martha enters and smiles.

"Great job!" she tells me. "Stan is downstairs. He'd like to see you."

I stare at my hands, my knees, the dirt that must cover me from head to toe.

"No worries, he's seen worse. Come on!" she insists.

Stan laughs at the sight of me. "You've been busy, I see."

Sally joins in the laughter, and once I've collected myself, I too laugh. A strange sound, not much heard around these parts. But there it is.

"You gotta minute? I've got some stuff to show you," Stan says, his eyes sparkling.

Stan takes me to his place, and in the car on the way over asks me, "Seems like the last couple 'a days have been tough on you. How ya bearing up?"

Tears overwhelm me. I have only met this man a couple of times, but he makes me feel safe. And here in the comfort of his car, I finally give way and weep silently.

He continues chatting calmly. "Martha tells me that you've been hard done by. Just remember, not everyone in town feels the same about you. We're glad you are around."

I gulp and stare out of the window through the veil of water that flows down my face. I wipe away the drips but with little impact as Stan thoughtfully gives me some space and concentrates on his driving.

"And Martha gave her the keys to the apartment upstairs," he informs Shirley when we get to their house.

She has enveloped me in her arms and is comforting me, her small, fragile body feels like my grandmother's and my heart is wrenched with missing her.

"So, I was kinda thinking that some of the stuff we have stashed in our garage might be of use to this young lady. What do ya think, dear?"

Shirley agrees and once we have had a cup of coffee and I have finally cried my last, we go and see what is stashed away. There is an array of household items. I choose a chair which matches the sofa in colour if not in style, some pretty plates, cups and saucers, and linen napkins which look ancient and precious.

"I can't thank you enough," I tell them. Not just for the items but also for their love and attention.

"Do you have any bedding?" Shirley asks, "Or towels?"

I shake my head and she rises from her chair, asking me to follow her. In the hallway stands a beautiful oak antique dresser with glass doors and inside is the most wonderful array of linen. "These were my mother's, and her mother's before her," she informs me, gently touching the folded sheets and blankets.

"I couldn't possibly..." I couldn't. Really, I couldn't.

"But my dear, I only use one set at a time, and all this is sitting here, just kinda looking pretty. I'd love you to have them, to use them for the purpose they were made."

"On one condition!" I demand. "That you have them back when I leave. I will only be the temporary custodian."

She smiles and her eyes light up. "But of course, my dear. What a splendid idea!"

Shirley takes down an old lilac eiderdown quilt which I know will look beautiful on my bed. She explains that she made it many decades before and I tell her I will treasure it and bring it back to her. She then creates a pile of two pillows, sheets, and a blanket, together with a spare set. Overwhelmed by her kindness, I hug her, and a tear falls at her generosity.

After a cup of tea and a homemade biscuit, Stan drives us back to the apartment. Sally has come over to help. Such generosity of spirit soothes me.

"We have such happy memories of this place," Shirley says as she glances around the apartment.

"You do?" I enquire but don't get an answer, as Stan arrives with the box of china.

"That's the last of it." He sits down at the table, grunting with the effort.

I worry that I have over-tired this lovely old man.

"I like this over here; you can see the park."

"Oh yes, you can," Shirley agrees.

I tell her it's where I'm going to eat breakfast each morning and she thinks this is a "splendid idea!" Sally emerges from the bedroom, having deposited the bedlinen, and thinks it's a great idea too, as does Martha as she appears at the door. I glance around at the folks gathered before me. My heart feels full. I have people I care about, who care about me; they are kind and friendly. Finally, for the first time, I feel welcome in town.

Later, once everyone has left, I potter and the place looks habitable, clean, and tidy and all the furniture is where it should be. Everything I want to dispose of (after asking permission from Martha) is now in the bin. My bed has been made and I am looking forward to sleeping in my own bed in my own place. Smiling and filled with a deep sense of satisfaction, my watch tells me it is past eight o'clock. No wonder I'm hungry.

Entering the Squire opposite the café in Main Street, I sit at the bar and order something to eat. A handsome young barman with sepia brown eyes, a strong jaw and cheeky grin flashes a smile and asks, "How you doin'?"

"I'm very well today, thank you – yourself?" I cannot quite believe the words. It's been a long and arduous day and yet yes, I'm doing OK. I made it through. I can do this.

"You from England? I just love your accent!" He beams again and asks what I'd like to drink.

Over the course of the evening, I eat a salad, drink some beer from the bottle, and we flirt – it is sweet and gentle, kind and unthreatening. By the time I leave, I am exuberant and in high spirits.

Later, in my big comfy double bed, under clean crisp white linen and my gorgeous antique eiderdown, I text Katie as she has been pleading for information.

I've had the best day! 23.30

How come? 23.31

Remember me telling you about Martha who owns the café and sells my paintings? Well, turns out she owns the apartment over the café and it's empty. Well, it's empty apart from the dead flies and spiders but she said I could live there at a reduced rent! 23.31

I didn't want her to know about the fear, the loneliness nor the scene in the morning, I only want her to know the good bits. I want her to be happy for me.

Kidding??? 23.34

I'm not! I spent the whole afternoon cleaning and I think it's going to be OK. I'll send pictures tomorrow. 23.36

Does that mean you're staying and not coming home? 23.38

I can sense the disappointment in her text. Having spoken to my Dad, I know he is OK, so I'm definitely not needed at home. No, this is about Katie, and I wonder if she isn't as enthusiastic as I'd hoped because she's not ready for me to move forward with my life without Jon, her brother. I shake the thought away. Maybe she's simply missing me – as I miss her.

Yes, I guess so. I really want to make a go of this. I think I'm ready. 23.40

It seems an age before she replies and my worries increase with each passing second. I think I'm ready to move forward. I feel I have overcome so much these last few weeks. And I want to prove to her and to the rest of them back in England that I can do this.

Ok....... 23.45

I want to reach out to her but cannot find the words. I want her to understand but a text isn't the way to do it. I'll call her tomorrow. And I won't mention the Rob Lowe lookalike and the flirting. A step too far.

13

The fragrant evening air is unseasonably warm, offering a hint of the summer heat to come. Sally, her boyfriend Ricky and I stroll along the sidewalk to the Squire. When we enter the bar the place is quiet, so with plenty of seats to choose from, we find a booth. The handsome young barman from the night before comes over to our table. I can't help but notice how tight his white T-shirt is over his broad shoulders.

"Hi!" he says, smiling at me as he hands out the menus. "Nice to see you again. Two days in a row, eh?"

I try not to blush.

"So tonight, the specials are listed on this sheet." He places it on the table next to me as Sally muffles her giggles. "I'll give you guys some time to choose what you wanna eat. Can I get you a drink?"

"Beer," Ricky states. Sally agrees.

"Three beers please." I flash him a smile. I can do this!

"OK. Be right back."

When he leaves, Sally leans forward and whispers, "I think you pulled."

"No. He's being polite."

"He said you were here yesterday?"

I'd failed to mention this when she had invited me to join her and Ricky for dinner tonight. We'd had a much happier day at work and she had insisted.

"No," Ricky agreed. "You pulled!"

I glance at the young man, his dark hair pulled back in a bun, his face clear and open. "Give over, I'm old enough to be his mother!"

They both laugh at me, thus setting the tone for the evening.

Devouring a bowl of clam chowder followed by a chicken Caesar salad, Sally and Ricky share the most enormous plate of BBQ ribs and we drink more beer. Well, technically it's lager, but it goes down easily and lubricates the proceedings and the laughter.

When Ricky goes to the bar for a third time, I take the opportunity to ask Sally, "Where did you two meet?"

"In High School," she says. "Junior year. I thought he was kinda nerdy to start with, but you know what I like about him is he's deep."

"He gives the impression of being very quiet." He'd only said half a dozen words the whole evening so far, which made me worry that I was playing gooseberry on their date night.

"He is, but you know, he's never solemn or moody and I like that. Maybe he's quiet with you because he's shy 'cause he doesn't know you too well yet. Once you get him talking you can't shut him up!"

I cannot imagine this scenario and smile at the thought.

After dinner, Sally and Ricky dance close together and I experience a sharp pang of sadness. There he is again – Jon – never far from my mind, always close. He would be loving this adventure I am having. I wish he was here to be a part of it too.

"Would you care to dance?"

The young barman smiles at me as he stands by the booth. I have no idea how long he has been there as I was deep in thought.

Suddenly flustered as this flirting seems to have taken an alternative route, I mutter, "Err no – no thank you, I don't dance." I wave a hand to reinforce my refusal.

"You don't? You surprise me. Come on, give it a shot?" He smiles again.

The barman is annoyingly handsome and sensing it will do no harm, I accept gracefully and take his hand. I guess I am mildly flattered by his invitation given his youthfulness. Out of the corner of my eye I see Daniel enter the bar with two friends. He gives me a non-committal nod and a smile that does not reach his eyes.

My heart having somersaulted at the sight of Daniel starts to pound as I take to the floor. This is the first time I have stood close to a man in a long time and he smells 'male'. Jon hated dancing, claiming he had two left feet and no sense of rhythm. Even on our wedding day he protested about the first dance and reluctantly caved in under considerable pressure. These powerful links with the past, vivid pictures and memories are simultaneously joyful and painful. And tonight, my body is rigid, all my senses acutely alert.

We make polite conversation but as soon as the song ends, I smile and tell him, "You're very sweet, but…" My voice trails away. I mutter an apology and return to my seat.

My overloaded emotions: fear and loneliness, finding a safe space, generosity and kindness, and my body's reaction to all that has been happening in last few days overwhelm me and exhaustion hits. I want to escape. It's time to go back, out of here. I make my excuses and leave.

The air outside is fresh and I breathe it in deeply.

Despite a disturbed night's sleep with acres of awake time when I miss my husband so much and want him to reassure me that I can keep going, I finally awaken from a short dream in which I'm walking towards Jon. I know it is him but when he turns to face me I see

Daniel, who offers me a curt nod. I look for Jon and he is nowhere to be seen. Dreams are disconcerting and have a way of influencing my mood and this morning my heart aches with a gaping hole of grief. It is a struggle to face the day. I want to hide in my lovely warm bed.

I have always enjoyed my own company, and even when Jon was around there were times when I needed to be by myself, to think and meditate on life and things. I have never equated being alone with being lonely and in this space, in my new home, I am alone and yet, as I lie here and think about it, I'm not lonely. Just tired.

After breakfast, looking out onto the park, I decide to stretch my legs and get some fresh air. The jaunt up and down Main Street in the early morning sunshine reinvigorates me and involves visiting the newly opened souvenir shops and purchasing some things for my place. I smile as I think about it. My place. I consider the small expense worthwhile to make 'my place' feel more like home: a couple of ornaments for my shelves from the gift shop that opened last week for the summer season, a picture frame or two from the art supply store and a box of second-hand cookery books from the Blue Brolly bookstore. "We'll bring them over for you later," they promise, as the box is too heavy for me to carry. As I leave and my hand reaches for the handle on the front door, I recall Daniel. Quickly, I shake my head as though trying to dislodge the memory.

Turning into the alleyway, a wide, paved area between the café and the dress shop that links Main Street to a side entrance of the park, I see a man dressed in dusty overalls sitting on my steps.

He rises to his feet as I approach and asks, "Hi, you Jane?"

"Yes."

"Hi! I'm Joe."

We shake hands.

"Martha sent me with this." He indicates towards the white van parked next to the café. "It's some stuff for your apartment."

"Stuff?"

"Yeah, stuff. Come see!"

He opens the back doors to reveal a treasure trove of boxes, small and large.

Martha appears at my shoulder.

"Morning!" she says to Joe as he takes the first box up the steps.

He mumbles a breathless reply and I feel a small pang of guilt for not helping him.

"Hi!" My eyebrows rise in Martha's direction and she understands my unspoken question: Why?

"I've had these things in storage, you might as well use them," she tells me in her matter-of-fact way.

"That's very kind of you but you didn't need to do that, I'm fine." Oh, independent me.

"I wanted to."

We look at each other. I see a minute shift in our relationship.

"Thank you." I smile. "I appreciate it, and all that you've done for me." Then I hug her.

Almost instantly and instinctively I move away from her. I am coming to realise, by her reaction, that her mask of coolness may hide something that she keeps locked deep inside. Or maybe, as my landlady and employer, she wants to keep a professional distance; maybe I misread the signs. This might be a fine line to walk.

"When you have finished unloading everything, ask Joe nicely and he might take you to the store to get anything else you need." She hands me an envelope. "This is your share of the proceeds from the sale of your artwork last week."

Inside is four hundred dollars. I look up at her, my surprise obvious by the slackening of my jaw and gaping mouth.

"Fifty: fifty right?" A cheeky smile brightens her face.

I realise she is not offended by my hug and laugh with relief.

"And then when you're done with shopping you better get painting again as my walls are decidedly bare!"

She turns her back, physically, and emotionally, her East Coast upbringing coming to the fore; her emotions are returned to their proper place and I smile as she walks away.

"Thank you!" I shout and she raises a hand in acknowledgment.

I want to say thank you properly, but 'the hug' puts me off – she did give the distinct impression of not being amused even if she wasn't offended. I mull over some ideas while I open the boxes and take out the kitchen utensils, place items in the cupboards, and arrange my few pieces of furniture. Finally, I decide to write her a little handmade card of thanks rather than approach her face to face, and maybe make her a cake – I know she has a soft spot for sponge cake. Getting personal with Martha is going to be difficult. I am intrigued by her cool reserve that occasionally slips with the resulting smile that lights up her face. I am puzzled by her generosity and kindness despite her cool facade: the reduced rent on the apartment – well I suppose that's off-set by working for not very much – but the furniture, the exhibition? All very interesting.

I take pictures and WhatsApp them to Dad and Katie with a promise to email soon. My father texts back: "Cosy!" Is he pleased that I am settled or disturbed by what he sees? I tell him I miss him. He sends me back a big red heart. I wonder how Katie feels, given the conversation we had the day before. There is no response and I feel torn between the enjoyment I am experiencing in my new home and the worry of how my best friend is reacting to my new life.

14

I collect my crayons, paints and paper, pack them into my bag and head to the low wall by the beach. It has become my favourite spot to paint and meditate on life, and the perfect place to go on my day off. I had spent the morning assembling a pinboard which I put up in the kitchen. It is now adorned with brightly coloured pins holding a shopping list (currently blank), a wooden heart on a wire that Katie has sent that says, 'Friends like you are precious and true', and several photographs to remind me of home: me as a young child aged about six sitting on my dad's knee with Mum next to him, holding my baby sister Jo in her arms. We were on holiday in Wales. Another of a group of friends holding wine glasses and grinning drunkenly at the camera. And finally, one of Jon and me on our wedding day. A black and white casual shot, unaware of the photographer, lost in our own world. Reminders of England and home. What was home.

The weather is warming up and summer is on the

horizon; the air is heavy with the scent of late-spring flowers and there isn't a breath of wind. For the first time, I venture out without a jumper – or as Martha would say, a sweater. A sense of freedom drives me to the beach, which is quiet. The sky is cloudless and the ocean is flat calm ultramarine, and equally uninspiring artistically, so I sit on the wall at the far right and look over to the houses in the distance. Today I will paint the houses and put all thoughts of Jessica and the past few weeks at the back of my mind. And breathe!

Stan comes past, stops and asks, "May I join you?"

I shuffle over and make room for him. His mere presence brings a warm glow to my senses. I like him.

"Thought I might find you here – I bought my sketch pad and pencils today." He shows me. "Let's see what happens!"

People pass; visitors are starting to arrive in town. Some stop to watch us, some chat a while and some take no notice. Stan and I share the space and the quietness that exists comfortably between us. I hold up my pencil, close one eye to measure and try to get the perspective correct; my houses give the impression that they will fall over given a strong wind and I am frustrated at my lack of progress. At the same time, I'm aware of the need to supply Martha with new paintings to hang on the walls.

Stan can sense my growing frustration and he starts

to chat.

"I remember the first time we met," he states. "It was right here." He puts his pencil down, folds one hand over the other and stares out to sea. "Feels like a long time ago."

I remind him it was April.

"Ah yes." I can see him recalling the windy day. "Shirley was with me." He seems to withdraw into himself.

I wait a moment then fill the silence. "Is she OK?" I sense she may not be.

"She had a fall about a week back. She was shook up a bit, but she's OK, I guess. She needs time to recover. I left her restin' up, but I am hopin' that she'll be OK to go out of the house tomorrow."

He is quiet again as we both gaze out toward the ocean.

"You told me you'd come to Oakham for many reasons…" His voice fades as an invitation to explain myself.

"That's true."

The pain over my right eye is sharp. Why does the truth reduce me to a pitiful teary state and make me wish that the one man I want in the world to be here, right now, cannot be here? No-one knows why I am in Oakham. Is it time to tell? Reluctantly, I continue.

"There are many reasons, it's true, but I think the

main reason I came…" I pause. "I came to find out who I am." Again, a pause, unsure if I want to tell him.

The familiar old emotions flow back. I have started to get a sense of place here, a growing sense of contentment and a measure of happiness without the accompanying guilt, but the probability of this conversation reliving old memories is painful. I swallow the lump of grief.

"My husband, his name was Jon, he died over two years ago now. Cancer."

Stan doesn't interrupt. I sense he is listening, and I plough on despite finding it difficult to talk about it all, even now.

"I kind of got lost along the way."

I exhale softly and suppress the tears. The pain above my eye vibrates. It was once familiar and ever-present, now it is strange and upsetting. I muster up some resolve. I will not cry. I sit upright, shoulders back.

"I miss the life we had, the life we had before he got sick – I miss it." I try to smile as I remember. "When he was going through chemo and was really ill, I would go out painting, like now. We'd take along a comfy chair for him to sit in. He would read a book and usually he'd fall asleep, and I'd paint with the sound of him snoring."

The memory is a sorrow deeply embedded, a sword in my heart. I breathe deeply and swallow back the lump that has reappeared in my throat.

"When he was gone, there was this overwhelming sense of helplessness and isolation. I was a lost soul…"

Finally, my voice trails away as I lower my eyes, remembering. It's all I have to say. No more. Not yet.

Stan sits quietly, non-judgemental and without comment. I am glad. This old man makes me feel safe; he has a measure of peace about him that I covet – a quality I want to find in myself. He pats my hand lightly to show that he understands and we resume drawing in companionable silence.

The next time I am in work, I amble down the iron steps with my healthy green breakfast smoothie in my hand. I have noticed that my work jeans are a little snug around the waist – must be all those hearty carb-filled breakfasts – and so this morning I pledged to start eating healthily again. As I make my way to the front door of the café, I reach for the handle then pull up sharply. The door opens outwards and I see the same green eyes I met in the bookstore all those weeks ago.

"Daniel!"

He smiles. "We're gonna have to stop meeting like this!"

I hear him chuckle softly before he steps aside to let me pass, holding the door wide.

"Thank you," I mutter, feeling a blush rise on my cheeks.

"You're welcome."

And he is gone.

Startled by the encounter, my heart beats faster. It's unsettling. Despite what Sally and Martha have said about him, I'm still unsure and I berate myself for feeling this way every time I see him, as well as for the accompanying sense of guilt at even considering him after losing Jon. I hope that the routine of work will soothe me.

Thankfully, it does. And so does baking – today, choux buns. The morning passes quickly. Tim, the harbourmaster, greets me by name now as he collects his morning brew on the way to work. Only the tourists are surprised at my accent and comment, "Are you from England?" or "You're a long way from home!" I smile and politely agree, serve them, clear up after them and wish them well.

Later in the afternoon, Stan arrives with Shirley, who is wearing a floral shirt dress belted around her enviably small waist. He holds the door open for her, gently helps her to her seat and listens to her every word. You can see the deep love they have formed over the years. He is courteous and kind, and it warms my heart. I am genuinely pleased to see them and hurry over to welcome them.

"Hello Stan. How nice to see you!"

He puts his arm around my shoulder, and for an old

man, has a firm grip.

"Hello, my dear." Shirley leans forward and takes my hand in hers. Her skin is paper thin, but her fingers are strong. "It is lovely to see you again." Her smile is genuine. "Have you settled in upstairs?"

"I have, yes, and thank you for all the lovely things you LOANED me. They make my apartment feel so much more like home."

"I'm glad. Stan's been telling me about your painting sessions together. He really enjoys them." Her face lights up when she smiles at her Stan, her small eyes almost disappear amid the lined skin. Yet there is a certain youthfulness about her, despite her white hair.

"Stan tells me you had a fall recently. How are you feeling?" I ask.

"I'm much better, thank you. Today is the first time I've had the chance to walk some. Stanley has been so caring and protective, but I did need to get out and about. And the weather is lovely today, don't you think?"

"It is and I'm glad you're here. What can I get you?"

They gaze at each other and Stan says, "A couple of coffees?"

"I made a special treat this morning, and I'm really pleased with them. Do you like choux buns? They're delicious. Can I bring some over for you?"

They nod and smile. My heart swells.

The week before, I found some beautiful plates, cups, and saucers in a flea market – English fine bone china, a long way from home. Now is the time to bring them to the attention of the customers, and in particular Stan and Shirley. I quickly make my excuses and run upstairs to get the delicate china cups and saucers and arrange everything on the tray. I want to make everything special for them, so I place the choux buns in a pile on one of the plates with two napkins neatly folded. Satisfied with the presentation, I take it over to them and proudly bask in their pleasure and praise.

Back behind the counter, I glance across the café to where Stan and Shirley are sitting, their chairs close to each other, their conversation lively and filled with love. They remind me of my grandparents – I must write to them. I sense Martha is behind me, watching the same scene.

"I hope you don't mind that I brought my china down for them. I wanted to make it extra special as it's Shirley's first outing in a while."

"Sure. Good job."

"He's such a nice man," I comment quietly. "You know he comes and sits with me sometimes when I am painting. He sits all quiet and calm. I enjoy his company."

"They've been married over sixty years," she tells me.

"Family? Kids?"

"Nope, just the two of them."

We stand and watch them some more.

"Look at how they are with each other, they're like a couple of newly-weds. He is so caring…" I let the words hang in the air and think of Jon. "Have you known them long?"

I glance at her and see distance in her eyes, memories.

"Yes, a long time. Good friends when I needed them most. When I first arrived in town."

"You needed friends?"

My words sound unintentionally harsh. I immediately apologise.

"Of course!" She tries to sound affronted but fails. "We all do."

"Why, what happened?"

"Never you mind!"

Later that evening, I pick up my phone to give Katie an update. I want her to know that I am coping and dealing with life. I want her to be happy for me.

> Hi Best Friend! How you doing? Miss you.
> 22.09

Hi BFF! You ok? 22.11

Kind of… work's going OK, finally got the hang of the hissing, spitting coffee machine. Very proud of this minor achievement, I can tell you! The weather's warming up too. It's a Bank Holiday here so it's been busy in the café today - they call it Memorial Day - not sure what it's about but it seems to spark the start of summer, so they tell me. 22.12

I am happy, I guess but I have been thinking about Jon a lot last couple of days. Miss him. Miss you. 22.14

That's bound to happen. You can move away physically, even a continent away, but you take your feelings with you. You take Jon with you and unfortunately, there's nothing you can do about that. Why not reflect on some of the advice Peter gave you

after Jon died - that might help? Don't worry about it - and I know you will - but try not to - AND BREATHE 2, 3, 4. I miss you too.
22.24

The following morning is my day off – no work, no painting, no running – so my shorts and flip-flops are given their first outing of the year. The bright sun and the warmth of the June day draw me outside. I settle in my rocking chair, head back, resting on a pillow, eyes closed, skin slightly tingling with the heat – breathe in and out slowly. Peter taught me breathing techniques and the benefits of being truly present in the moment and mindful.

Mindful of what I can hear: The children playing in the park, squealing with joy at being chased by an older sibling or parent, their laughter when they are caught. My mind flies to my sister Jo and her adorable daughter. I can hear the sound of birds in the trees, the gentle buzz of a bee, and the quiet hum of cars slowly making their way up and down Main Street. Lots of sounds but little noise.

Mindful of what I can smell: The jasmine plant by my side gives off the most delicious aroma that is mixed with the baking cake smell from downstairs; Sally must have the back door to the kitchen open. My mouth waters.

Mindful of my body: In the rocking chair, left foot resting on the ground, pushing gently then letting go, push and let go, rocking back and forth. My body is relaxed and comfortable as the sun warms my skin.

Feelings of contentment are welcome, yet still they

take me by surprise, and I consider the fact that it has been a long time since I have sat and enjoyed the pleasure of the sun on my skin with a sense of inner peace and security of mind. I count the weeks since arriving in Oakham – eight weeks – and despite the fact that Jon has been in my thoughts since my conversation with Stan, I feel renewed. It is a strange mix of emotions, which I decide includes happiness and – I think – it is allowed. Part of me feels untethered and thankfully the feeling of guilt that once accompanied any happy moment is fading.

I was ready for a change, ready to embark on an adventure, ready to face a new future by myself and here I am with a place to live, a small group of friends and a job in a café. Who knew?

15

My life has inadvertently developed a rhythm and routine. It's not without its blips; I dread the fact that I might bump into Jessica, and I seem unable to control my body's reaction to Daniel, but all in all, I'm doing OK. Just. However, there is one big grey cloud that follows me around, one blot on the landscape – the conversation with Stan. It has left its mark and circles in my head. I cannot stop thinking about Jon, the good times and the not so good.

Finally, at the end of another working day, once the café is clean, the ovens are switched off and the door closed, I hobble home on aching feet. I wish the sun was shining so that I could sit on my rocking chair and relax, but the skies are grey and the air is cool. For want of something better to do (despite my feet), I decide to go for a run – to 'blow the stink off', as my mum would say. Frankly, there's not a lot of motivation for this activity, but deep inside I know it's for the best and will do me more good than harm, so I change into my running gear, do my stretches, fix my playlist, and set out down Main Street. The unrepentant overcast sky is darkening by the minute. I mentally replan my route away from the back streets, sticking to the roads that are lit – it may be a small seaside town, but you can never be too careful.

As I round the headland, the ocean – stormy, dark Paynes grey and brooding – comes into view, but it is instantly forgotten as the iPod plays a tune that sends shockwaves through me. It's a playlist I haven't listened to in a long, long time and I suddenly realise that it's the list I made days before Jon died. The shot of adrenalin that sears through me makes me stumble and I slow to a walk. Before I know it, tears are streaming down my face and the sobs rise in my chest. Deep in my memories, I feel overwhelmed. The weather is closing in as dusk turns the sky indigo blue. The wind is whistling and there is no-one around. I throw back my arms and lift my face to the sky. A primeval scream is released into the world from deep within.

Exhausted, I stop and rest my hands on my knees, leaning over, gasping for air. Sobbing, gasping, and crying all at the same time. The tune ends. Slowly recovering from the shock, wiping away the tears with the back of my hand, I rip the earbuds out to stop any further sounds from wreaking havoc on my emotions. I stand upright and take a huge gulp of air.

This may be my new life and yes, it brings a measure of contentment (if only in brief flashes and moments), but the past is never far behind. The music and the grief of losing Jon, these links are still having a powerful effect.

Walking home past the dunes, the huge grey clouds appear almost menacing. The hairs on my arm bristle at the passing breeze and there is the sound of the reeds rustling. I hesitate. And listen. Unsettled, I suddenly need to be at home. I need my sanctuary. I quicken my pace slightly, but my body isn't ready for a heart-thumping run. It's not recovered. The muscles in my calves burn, so I mentally map my route home. How far have I got to go? Not too far. Keep going, slightly faster. Come on. Back down Main Street and I can see the café, the alleyway – home. I turn off the street and sprint the few yards to my steps, taking them two at a time. Inside, I lean on the door, now locked. Home.

I get a drink of water and try to clear my head. After a quick shower I go straight to bed and hide under the covers. My sleep is fitful.

It's closing time and I get the sense that I don't want to be alone after work. I'm tired and though I am no longer responsible for cooking breakfasts (Martha has found a short-order chef named Jake to do it for her), the effects of the last few days – Stan, the music, Jessica,

Daniel with the green eyes – have all disturbed my equilibrium and the emotional effect is draining. I want company so I seek out Martha.

"I don't know if you have plans for later, but would you like to join me for dinner? I'd like to say thank you for all you've done for me."

She agrees.

"Seven then?"

She nods, and I smile then realise I have to figure out what to cook – something simple, as I visualise the meagre contents of the fridge and freezer.

At seven o'clock precisely, Martha knocks on the door and lets herself into the apartment.

"Hi! Thanks for coming. Come in, please. Sit down."

I have taken a lot of time to make the place clean and a lot of care and effort (with a nod to Nigella – the domestic goddess) to make the table look pretty and welcoming with a small tub of fresh flowers, candles and matching crockery and cutlery, and of course, the obligatory fairy lights – I found a set in the gift store that has opened for the summer, selling seaside memorabilia.

Dinner is a quiet affair and to start with talk is stilted. I think it is because this is the first time we have spent time together in a relaxed setting. We are in unknown territory and neither of us is sure how to react. We are landlady/tenant. We are boss/worker. Yet here we are having dinner together and politeness and manners are uppermost in both our minds.

After we've finished eating – a simple salad and some homemade bread accompanied by a glass or two of chilled white wine – Martha rises from her chair and moves over to the bookcase, noticing my growing number of cookbooks, some bought from the store, some old ones I found at a flea market, and the couple my mum sent me last week.

She picks one off the shelf and whilst flicking through the pages asks, "This is quite a collection of books – you like cooking?"

"I do, yes. My mum's a… was a cookery teacher."

"Home Ec.?"

"That's right, and she's been teaching me how to cook and bake since I was old enough to stand up and handle a wooden spoon."

"How did she feel about you coming here? Does she miss you?" She replaces the book and takes her seat once more at the table.

"When I told her about my plans, she said, 'Why don't you go to Wales instead? You love going to Tenby, why not go there?' To be honest, I do love Tenby – it's such a pretty seaside town and I have many happy memories of the place; as a family, we had some great holidays there. Happy times when Dad used to take me sailing, we would all eat ice cream and fish and chips after we'd been on the beach all day. We went on fishing trips to catch mackerel. It's one of my favourite places, but I knew I needed to go someplace new. Someplace I've never visited before, and I wanted to make new memories."

I recall watching my mum the morning we had that conversation, noticing for the first time how grey her hair was becoming, the skin on her face still smooth even without makeup, her eyes sharp and intelligent, taking in everything. I knew by the expression on her face that she was both horrified and frightened at the same time, for herself and for me. Martha is watching me closely and I am suddenly aware of the silence so continue.

"I remember telling her, 'I need to go, Mum.' She said, 'I understand you need to make a change, Jane, especially after all you have been through in the last few years… but America?!' Her voice rose with indignation as she said that last bit." I smile to myself at the memory of that afternoon.

"She's special to you – your mum?" Martha asks.

"Very. Mums are special, don't you think?"

I notice an unusual expression flash across Martha's face – hurt, pain, what? So, I quickly change the subject.

"But dads are different. I'm not as close to my dad as my sister is. I love him, don't get me wrong, but it's Mum I go to – always."

There is more pain in her eyes this time. I cannot understand what is happening. She is quiet, staring at her wine glass, twirling it slowly between her finger and thumb. So, I search for another topic of conversation and tell her about the first time I tried to paint the Blue Brolly Bookshop and meeting Stan.

"Now he's a lovely man," I say with a smile. "What's his story? He told me he was at sea?"

"That's right, he served in the Navy for years. He saw action in Vietnam too. He doesn't say much about it, but I think he was genuinely affected by the things that happened out there. When he returned home, Shirley told me he had changed; he was quieter, more withdrawn. But over the years, he's mellowed some."

"He always been kind to me, gentle too. He has this unhurried aura, don't you think?"

Martha agrees as she returns my smile. "He does."

"And Shirley is such a sweet woman; she clearly adores him."

"She does. She may be sweet, but she can be feisty sometimes too. You should see how she deals with Stan!"

She relates a tale or two about them and then starts to tell me a little of her own life prior to owning a café on Cape Cod: her life in New York; her job as a buyer for a major department store. It sounds like a résumé, but I listen and do not interrupt until it's appropriate.

"So how come you came here from New York to open a café?"

She takes a minute and I can tell she is considering what to say next.

"It's a long story. Crossroads moment, I guess."

I know that's all she will say for the time being.

"I understand how that feels." I smile. "And long stories tend to require quantities of gin."

"Yours too, huh?" She smiles back.

Encouraged by her opening up (not much, but slightly), I show her some more of the fine bone china I have been acquiring and explain about the history of where it comes from and why it's so popular in England.

She murmurs her approval. "I saw that tray you made for Stan and Shirley; it looked real pretty." And then another sudden change of conversational topic. "So why did you come here? Apart from sticking a pin in the map?"

"You remembered!"

She laughs. I pause – it's time to tell her. I have spoken the words out loud to Stan. I can do this.

"It was about two years ago, my husband Jon died after fighting cancer for, oh, twelve to fourteen months. When the second anniversary of his death came around in March this year, I suddenly felt trapped… No, that's not the right word – lost? Maybe? I don't know." I'm playing with my napkin, smoothing and folding then unfolding it, thankful I can speak the words without tears. "But, you know, it struck me that I needed to get away. To be in a place where no-one knows my name or who I am and what's happened to me. I wanted to get away from my house, my job, my life, everything, and do something new, something different. I also wanted to try somehow to get over it, or move past it, the grief? Oh, I don't know."

I feel like I'm blurting it all out, but Martha smiles, and I suspect she understands though she doesn't seem to want to share the reason behind this empathy.

"Do you enjoy working downstairs?" she asks.

Another total change in the direction of the conversation. It's like a game of chess.

"I do, yes! It's very different from being an art teacher. But you know what I like best? I like early mornings before the customers come in, when it's all quiet and I'm baking and getting everywhere ready. Not that I don't like having the customers there," I add quickly when I see the expression on her face! "It's just that I like the peace." I think about my time at the café. "But sometimes I like to have the radio on and sing and dance my way around the room!" I find myself grinning. "Yes, I love it."

"Do you feel the café could do with a new lease of life?" she asks suddenly.

I am struggling to keep up with this – another change and frankly I'm surprised that she would seek my advice, given her air of self-assurance. I take a moment to gather my thoughts and decide against a full-blown inventory of what I would do to breathe new life into the place as I do not want to disrupt our new-found and fragile friendship, therefore I hesitate momentarily and then ask her, "Why?"

"I've been thinking about it recently, and you know, I've come to the conclusion that it is getting to be a little dated. It needs more than a coat of paint; maybe it needs modernising. After all, it has been like it is now for some time…" Her voice trails off and I top up her wine glass as a diversion and encouragement. "Of course, we'll have to include Daniel in any changes. He's an architect, you know?"

I didn't. My stomach leaps and I worry.

16

It's a bright summer morning and thankfully, the bad weather has blown itself out when I return to the café a couple of days later. As I come down the steps towards the back kitchen door I can hear voices coming from inside. It's Jessica talking with Martha. *Oh no, not again!* This woman is beginning to get under my skin. Tentatively, I move slightly closer to listen. All senses alert.

"Who is she, Martha?" Jessica snaps.

Martha sounds taken aback. "I'm sorry?"

"Jane? Who is she?"

"Why are you so interested?"

I can almost hear her draw herself upright and reply, "I'm not interested! It's just, well, she's new in town – I'm concerned, is all. I know how you are about taking on lost causes. Yes?"

"Concerned? For me?"

"Yes. For you! What do you know about her? Why is she here? Can you trust her? She's only been in

Oakham, what, a couple of months? She's selling her paintings in your café—"

Martha interrupts her, "Because I asked her to!"

"She lives upstairs."

"The place was empty and besides, I invited her to live upstairs."

"And now she works in the café, yes? And you mentioned yesterday that she was giving you some ideas on how to improve your business!"

She sounds annoyed. I bristle.

"All of which is true, but her ideas are good. They make business sense, and again, I asked her for advice and help. What is with you, Jessica? I'm a big girl – I can take care of myself and decide who I want to live upstairs and who works for me!"

I should not be listening to this conversation.

"I'm worried, that's all. She's definitely trying to ingratiate herself into your life. Now why would she want to do that, I wonder? Does she know you have a soft spot for waifs and strays?"

There is a moment of silence and I consider moving away but my feet are still firmly rooted to the spot.

"We have known each other a long time. We look out for each other, yes? You're my friend, that's what friends do, right? What do you know about her, her past, apart from the fact that she comes from England?" The words tumble out fast and furious. Charmless.

My arrival in town and into the lives of these people is having an impact. Yet as I hear Martha sigh, it's like she's heard it all before. I wonder how Jessica has the gall to come back to the café after what she did.

"She told me she was at a crossroads in her life. It seems that life had been good back in England, then" — she pauses, and I wonder what she will say next and think *please don't tell her, please don't tell her* — "then she had a tragedy in her life that made her rethink her priorities. She came here to find herself, and Jessica, we both know what that feels like."

There is another pause. I hold my breath. I wonder what Martha's tragedy is. She came here from New York; she's had a crossroads moment. What was it? And what's Jessica so worried about? What's her story?

"Look, I know from the time we've spent together that Jane's honest and hardworking, she's reliable, and you know what, I like her, and I've come to trust her. She bakes great cakes, can cook up a storm. She cooked dinner for us both a couple of nights ago and it was delicious."

Thanks, Martha!

"And the customers, they love her, and so does Stan." She laughs, a short burst of laughter. "Stop thinking the whole world has an agenda! You'll come to like her too. I know you will."

"I doubt it!" Jessica states as she emerges through

the doorway. She sees me, her eyes open wide in shock, and she almost growls before literally pushing me aside. "Get out of my way!" she snarls menacingly.

I watch her retreat down the alleyway, Martha at my shoulder.

We spend the next half hour getting the café ready for the day ahead. There is a slightly awkward atmosphere as neither of us purposely talk about what has just happened.

When Sally arrives, we are both relieved at the break in tension that is palpable in the room. Thankfully we have our inaugural staff meeting to distract us and give the morning some focus – an innovation Martha considers to be important 'for the team!' Sally tries not to snigger. I elbow her. Martha's face takes on a stern expression, making us both feel like naughty schoolgirls in front of the headmistress. As we are not sure what to expect from this new turn of events and there is no agenda, we bumble along for about fifteen minutes before a frustrated Martha orders us to get to work.

"Maybe we could have the next meeting after the working day?" I suggest.

I can see Martha is making an effort and she responds encouragingly with "that's a great idea."

Sally chips in, "Maybe we could have a designated snack next time, test a couple of new recipes?"

Martha smiles briefly at us both and nods, heading to the front of the café to unlock the door. There it is again – why is she making such an effort to make us a team, to include us in the decision-making process? Especially me, when I have only been here five minutes and am still an outsider with a ticking clock and a return flight home. Why does she seem so nervous when she does so? Where is that self-assurance? She wants to include us and yet why does she seem to be finding it so hard? It's a brief thought – let the working day begin.

I am writing price labels and arranging the cakes and pastries in an aesthetically pleasing way on the counter when the bell signals that the front door has opened. I look up. It's him. *Oh no!* is my first thought. There is an unwanted movement inside my chest as my heart does an involuntary somersault and I can feel my pulse quicken. What now?

"Hi!"

He smiles and I notice that the skin around his green eyes crinkles. I feel like I'm fighting my body all the time as it's telling me 'Go for it!'

"Good morning! What can I get you?" I decide on the professional approach.

"I'll have a large black coffee" — he gazes at the breakfast bakery I have arranged — "and a croissant, please."

"Sure, take a seat and I'll bring them over."

He walks toward my favourite table. *It's my table,* I think territorially. He is gazing out of the window but turns and smiles at me as I approach with a tray. Setting down the plate, I notice he moves it slightly and that he's left-handed. Once I put the mug of coffee down on the table, he moves that too so that it is exactly next to the plate. Weird!

"Thank you! It seems quiet this morning?"

"It is early, I guess."

"You like working here?"

This takes me by surprise. "Yes, it's fun. It's different from what I used to do."

"And what was that?"

"I taught art in school."

He persists by asking another question. "Whereabouts in England are you from?"

"Manchester."

"How long've you been here in Oakham?"

What is this? Why is this unnerving man giving me the third degree with a barrage of questions?

"I'm sorry, but you only get three questions per cup of coffee." I smile and walk away. Trying to focus on the job in hand and ignoring the butterflies in my stomach.

Sally comes back from running an errand at about eleven and I decide to find out more about this unnerving man.

"Cute or what?" she replies, not telling me anything as she slips into the kitchen to drop off the parcel she collected on her errands, then returns to find me waiting patiently. She grins at me. "Bit old, but hey, like I said, cute!"

I glance across the café through a sea of faces. *Old? I don't think so.* I blush.

"Martha told me he's an architect."

"Yeah. He's got a business he runs in Boston, lives there most of the time but he has a house in town, up the road a way. He's a good friend of Martha's."

"Oh right."

"No, they're not friends in that way."

My facial expression is easy to read. She grins again, flashing her perfect teeth and my blush deepens. This is all very disconcerting. I notice that he's wearing faded Levi's and expensive brogues, a white collarless shirt and a brown waistcoat – kind of cute. He smiles when he realises I am staring. Am I staring? My face flashes heat and turns a beetroot colour. He gets up and comes toward the counter and I want the ground to open and swallow me. I will not panic. I. Can. Do. This.

He pushes his coffee cup towards me. "Three more questions please."

You have got to give it to him. I fill the cup and push it back across the counter to him.

"Go ahead." I lay down the challenge.

"How long have you been in Oakham?"

I hold up my hand and touch my index finger. He chuckles softly to himself.

"Since the middle of April," I reply.

"And?"

"Is that a question?"

He holds up his hands in mock surrender and laughs, "No, no, it's not, it's just that you weren't very forthcoming—"

"Nor would you be," I point out.

"OK. I'm sorry!"

"Choose your questions carefully," I caution him.

Sally puts down a tray of dirty crockery on the counter between us. It clatters noisily and she grins at me, teasing. I want to slap her, but keep my expression neutral, take the tray and empty the contents into the sink, cup by cup, then wipe the counter down, grateful for something to do. The task complete, I look at him – he's still standing there. I decide to turn the tables and ask him a question.

"Why do you want to know?"

"Well… Martha told me you started work here," he admits, "and that you have moved in upstairs. I was merely curious. New kid in town and all that stuff." He looks around, pauses, and then asks, "Are these your paintings?"

I hold up my hand and point to the second finger and he chuckles again; it is a pleasant sound.

"Yes, they are. Martha sells them for me."

He moves effortlessly across the room and studies the paintings thoroughly and carefully, one by one, not briefly, he really examines them. "They're good."

"Thank you."

"Are they all for sale? And no, that's not one of my questions."

"Yes, they are."

"I like this one." He points to a small watercolour of the dunes, the grass, and the sea under a stormy sky, which I completed soon after I arrived. "It looks amazing – I know exactly where to hang it at home. Is it for sale?"

I hold up my hand and point to the third finger. He smiles and despite myself, I smile back. I sense Sally watching us intently as I take the painting off the wall. Bringing it back to the counter, I wrap it and hand it over.

"You have captured the light. I know where you were standing when you painted this – it's perfect, thank you!"

He smiles and holds my gaze. I am lost for words. He pays and leaves.

Sally coughs next to me then laughs out loud. "Like I said before, cute or what!"

Martha turns the delicate saucer over and reads the label underneath 'Made in England'. She makes a familiar humming sound as though she is considering something.

"I love them." She puts the saucer down and picks up the cup, holding it gently, running her finger around the gold-painted rim.

"These are slightly different to the ones you've seen before," I tell her. "The others were Doulton. I found that one and that cup in a flea market; they're made by Wedgwood."

It's an extravagance I can only afford because the paintings are selling, but I love the lightness and yet the strength within the fine bone china. And it reminds me of home and my grandma's china collection.

"Very delicate," she comments, carefully setting the cup onto the saucer. "Are these what you would use for afternoon tea, like we talked about last week?"

I nod, then and fetch some other pieces I have been collecting, including a rather impressive cake stand. It is made of three tiers of plates, the largest plate on the bottom then a slightly smaller one in the middle and the smallest plate at the top, all held together with metal struts and a tiny handle to carry the stand. Each plate is decorated with an intricate pattern of birds and flowers.

"Wow! What's that for?"

"That's what you serve the sandwiches and cake on. Nice, isn't it?"

"It's beautiful!" She turns it around gently. "You told me that afternoon tea is a historic thing, right? From about 1840? That long ago…" Her voice fades as she picks up the cake stand. "Kinda heavy, but fragile at the same time. And you Brits do it all the time? Take afternoon tea?" She attempts an English accent.

I try not to laugh but cannot hide a smirk. "No, not all the time, it is still a special occasion thing, like taking tea at the Ritz—"

"I had lunch at the Ritz in London once," she interrupts suddenly. I can see in her eyes that she is filled with the memory. "A long time ago. Previous life." She almost shakes herself free from the past. "It was delicious, refined."

"I can imagine."

"You've never been there?"

"No, I haven't."

Martha seems surprised. "Oh! But you have had afternoon tea?"

I nod.

"So, what would be served?"

"Well, generally speaking it consists of a cup of tea, well, a pot of tea, maybe some tiny sandwiches and lots of lovely small delicate cakes, maybe biscuits, but not normally."

She looks up at me as she sets the cake stand down on the counter, obviously wanting to know more.

"Would you like me to make one for you and explain what all the elements are then?"

"That would be interesting. Yes, that sounds a great idea!"

"Tomorrow?"

"Sure. We're normally quiet 'til about eleven, so before then?"

That evening, grateful for something to occupy my mind and block out the thoughts of the man with the green eyes, I get out my paper and paints and make a beautiful menu to accompany the food.

The next morning, up early baking bread and cakes and getting everything ready, I am excited but a little nervous. I want Martha to enjoy the experience and I would like her approval. A lifetime thing: firstly parents, then teachers and friends. The need for approval. Also, I would like her to take it on board and maybe introduce it onto the menu in the café. It would be like having a little bit of home in this corner of the world.

The table nearest the kitchen is set with a white tablecloth and the china, including the cups, saucers and plates. The colours are all mismatched, mainly because I am struggling to find complete sets of crockery, but it's a pleasant mix. I put the menu onto her plate and stand back, satisfied.

In the kitchen, I cut the freshly baked and cooled bread into slices about quarter of an inch thick and spread butter thinly. Some I fill with traditional cucumber, some with egg and cress. Crusts removed, I cut them into dainty two-bite-size mouthfuls and arrange them on the bottom tier of the cake stand. I cut a sponge cake filled with jam and cream into inch squares, then wonder how we are going to sell what is left of the mangled cake, so cut it all into chunks and quickly place it on the counter, hastily writing a price label to match the portion size. I slice the fruit scones in half, spread each half with strawberry jam and ladle on a huge dollop of thick, heavy whipped cream and place them and the cake on the top two tiers of the stand. Again, I stand back to admire my handy work before setting it in the right place on the table as Martha comes in through the front door.

"It's not ready yet; give me five minutes," I state.

She sits down at the table anyway and takes the delicately folded napkin, placing it elegantly across her lilac linen lap.

Back in the kitchen, I warm the teapot, spoon in the loose-leaf tea and top it up with hot water. Then I collect the small jug of milk and go back into the café.

"Now…" I take a deep breath. "Let's start with the tea. So… black tea used to be the most common type of tea consumed in the UK and it comes from India, an historic colonial thing. But you can get good tea from China too. Mostly we drink blended teas, which are a mixture of two or more tea varieties. Earl Grey is mild-tasting and fragrant, scented with bergamot oil which gives it a citrus note, but I couldn't find any at such short notice. You could also have had Lapsang Souchong – I am not a fan, it's too pungent for me. So, I'm serving English Breakfast Tea."

"As part of afternoon tea?"

"You've got a point, but it is blended to be drunk with milk and is a good accompaniment to sweet foods such as we have here."

Martha doesn't look convinced, but I plough on regardless.

"Making a pot of tea is important. It's not a case of putting a teabag in a mug, you know. Really good tea deserves attention and thought. I have used loose-leaf tea. Firstly, I warmed the pot, adding some freshly boiled water from the kettle, swishing it around and then emptying it. Then I added the tea, one teaspoonful per person and one for the pot."

She looks confused. "One for the pot?

"Yes, well, sorry." I stop and breathe. "I'm a little nervous," I admit.

"What on earth for?"

I rub my sweaty palms on my apron and swallow

down the words 'I want your approval'.

"I want you to enjoy what I've prepared."

She smiles at my honesty, sits back in her chair and encourages me to continue. "One for the pot?" she reminds me.

"Ah yes. That extra teaspoon of tea 'for the pot' makes the tea that slightly bit stronger. Freshly boiled water is added to the tea, and it should be left to stand for three to five minutes to brew."

Martha checks her watch and I take the tea strainer to collect the tea leaves and pour the brewed tea into the cup.

"Now one other thing: milk! Some people say the milk should go in first and then you pour the tea, and some say it should be the other way around, tea first then milk. I don't think it matters, to be fair, but there are two distinct camps on this matter." I pour the milk, knowing full well I am babbling but cannot seem to stop. "And on the stand, you will see the sandwiches, the cake and scones." I'm aware that I look slightly stupid pointing at the food and internally berate myself for being so eager to please. I almost curtsey! I want to explain about the order of the jam and cream and the differences that arise with the order in Cornwall (jam then cream) and Devon (cream then jam), but I know it will only bemuse her and I know I have talked for too long.

"Leave me to get on with it and I'll give you my opinion when I am done." She waves her hand to dismiss me.

Back in the kitchen, out of sight, the nerve-shredding wait is agonising. I polish every surface and clean out the fridge. Eventually, Martha calls me back and I pull up a chair to hear her verdict.

"The tea is OK, though I'm not sure about all the fuss that goes with it. We can't be giving the customers a full lecture before they get to drink it. And as for the milk first or second, well, you Brits!" She shakes her head as though not quite believing we could make such a fuss over something so insignificant. "The cake is a hit, but then we've had that one before, haven't we?"

I nod.

"Victoria Sponge, right?"

I nod again.

"These are delicious; they're scones?"

I momentarily consider explaining the different ways to pronounce the word 'scone' but decide against it. It will only add to the confusion. The English language has its own nuances.

"But the sandwiches, I am really not sold on these – they're far too small!"

"Afternoon tea size."

"Where are the crusts?" she asks.

"Ah, yes! The rules are there are no crusts, you cut

them off."

"And where's the filling?"

I can feel myself beginning to panic. "That is the filling, it's cucumber."

"Gherkin?"

"No, cucumber."

"And where's the rest of the filling?"

"That is the filling. A cucumber sandwich. OK, you have to understand the English traditions here." I pause and consider where to begin. "In the past — we're talking Victorian, Edwardian times at the end of the nineteenth, early twentieth century, before the First World War, I guess, maybe a bit earlier, but definitely by then — well-to-do folks had lunch at, say, twelve to twelve thirty. Then dinner would not be until maybe eight in the evening. It was often a formal affair that people dressed up for or maybe went out to eat."

An expression of enlightenment crosses her face. "Like Downton Abbey on TV!" she states.

"Yes!" Relieved she knows what I am talking about. "So, you see, there's this gap in the middle of the two meals. And so, one goes out for afternoon tea with one's friends at four in the afternoon." I put on my best posh English accent and Martha laughs. "Sometimes this would be at home but sometimes in a hotel, and the Ritz Hotel in London does by far the best afternoon tea."

"Proper like!"

"Proper like!" I agree.

Martha looks at the remains of her meal and I can see her contemplating her next move.

"So, do you think this might be a hit with the customers round here? It might be an added attraction alongside the normal menu?"

"I think so, yes."

"Maybe we could modify it a bit to make it more suitable – to start with we could make these" — she holds up a sandwich — "a whole lot bigger!"

I agree.

Martha studies the table. "It might work. What do you think?" She gazes around the room and speaks almost to herself, "Is it time to make some changes round here?"

17

I am packing my bag and preparing for a delightful painting day with Stan when I catch the sunrise from the corner of my eye, a pink sunrise that links so tightly to the past and the morning Jon died. The colours were achingly beautiful on that sad day. Today the sky is achingly beautiful, but there are no tears, simply a warm and pleasant glow. A friend told me once that 'when you can tell your story without tears, you're healed.' *Am I healing?* I wonder. I survey the room – my room, my home…for now.

My favourite place to sit in my apartment is at the table by the large windows overlooking the park. Over the recent months I have seen the new lime green leaves appear, the white blossom has fallen from the cherry trees and the leaves darken to my favourite colour in the paint box, Hooker's green, so that they almost glow in the late afternoon sun. But first thing in the morning, like now, just after sunrise, is the best time.

My bags checked a final time – I have all my

equipment and a packed lunch for us both – I head downstairs to wait for Stan, checking my watch. A huge American pickup truck comes into view, dark grey in colour – a Ford F150. It pulls up to the pavement and stops. The window lowers slowly and Daniel beams.

"Hi!"

"Hello."

"Hop in."

"No, no! I'm waiting for Stan." Flustered, I shake my head.

"Yeah, I know. Hop in and we'll go pick him up."

I have no choice. I do hope he's not going to be with us all day as I am looking forward to being with Stan (and maybe asking him some questions about both Daniel and Martha!) Damn!

Stan and Shirley's house is commonly described as a 'ranch style' property (I would call it a bungalow myself). It's in a street dotted with similar style houses and is set back from the road by a broad front lawn and surrounded by tall oak trees. The grass is neat and tidy, the borders full of echinacea and hostas. The house has dark grey clapboard and a wide window at the front, next to the front door which is painted bright red. There is a standard issue porch and a rocking chair surrounded by pots and pots of pretty plants and grasses. Such a welcoming sight as Daniel pulls into the driveway after an excruciatingly quiet ride.

"I am so looking forward to today, thank you for letting me borrow your husband!" I thank Shirley as I skip down the porch steps ten minutes later.

"Hey, no problem!" she calls out and links her arm through Daniel's. "I get to go out with this handsome guy!"

He looks down at her with a tender expression and they smile at each other. She pats his arm and winks.

"My toy boy!"

He throws his head back and laughs loudly. There is an easy warmth between them.

"Come on, Mrs. B, you're far too old for that kinda nonsense," Stan tells her as he loads his things into the car.

"Speak for yourself! Be off with you!"

At the lake, we unload, and once we've settled, Daniel leaves us to return to Shirley – thankfully. Now I can relax. While I set up our easels and canvases and get everything ready, Stan flops down in his chair with a sigh. He surveys the view in front of him.

"I love it here."

I agree; the shoreline of the small inlet is dotted with boats of all sizes and colours, some are moored on the water and some stranded on the shale beach in front of us. Reeds, dogwood, and flowers such as lead plant and daisy add to the picturesque scene. The early morning sun shimmers and reflects off the hardly moving water.

"What you going to paint first?" Stan asks, keeping a close eye on me.

"Hmm," I mutter, "not sure." There are so many possibilities. "You?"

"My first thought was those flowers but, you know, I'm gonna try my hand at that boat."

"Good idea. I like that small one there, on its side."

Having settled on my subject, quiet descends, broken only by the sounds of nature all around us: the water lapping gently on the shore, the birds, the buzz of the occasional bee and the scratching of my pencil on the canvas as I tentatively start to draw. Gentle faint strokes. Just enough to put everything in its place, establish the correct perspective and make it pleasing to the eye. The sun is warming up. On with the floppy hat. I swish my brush in the jar of water, my big brush to add pale blue to the sky, and then a slightly darker shade of the same colour, slowly bringing the foreground into view. I love watercolours as there is an immediacy to the work, drips and happy accidents which bring a painting to life. I pause to allow the washes of colour to dry in the sun. Then picking a smaller, finer brush and a red paint, I start to outline the little boat. Concentrated effort, a deep sense of pleasure as I can see the struggle to recapture my artistic abilities is finally paying off to the soundtrack of nature – this is why I love painting outdoors.

Several hours later and with the sun high in the sky, we move into the shade of a tree to avoid the fierce heat of the day. I retrieve the food and water from my bag and offer Stan some refreshment.

"Thank you." He sits back, examining his painting. His verdict: "Not a bad start. Don't think it'll float mind!" He laughs. A happy sound.

We tuck into the egg sandwiches, and I ask him, "How did you meet Shirley?"

His face lights up at the mere mention of her name. "I first laid eyes on her in High School. She was a freshman, and I was a junior. She'd moved in from a different school. Her hair hung long and straight down her back. It was a most wonderful colour – like mahogany. She smiled at me, and I was in love – just like that. I have never looked at another woman from that date on." He smiles at the decades-old memory. "Did you know she graduated top of her class? She could've gone to college but even then, she totally wanted to be a homemaker and be with me. I knew I'd have no trouble from her when I went into the Navy, no trouble."

"She's a good woman."

"The best."

"But then she's married to a good man."

He winks at me. "I think you might be a tad biased."

"Just a tad." And he is right, I am beginning to love

this man. "How long have you been coming here?"

"Oh, since I was a kid. My dad brought me and my brother here, taught us to fish and to sail in a boat like that one. First ignited my love of the ocean." His eyes seem to focus on the distant memories rather than the view. "It was a long time ago." He glances back at me and smiles.

I find such pleasure in sitting and listening to him reminisce about his childhood, before the invention of cell phones, tablets and technology that somehow rob children, everyone, of the simple pleasures and activities in life and the freedom to explore the world around them.

"I sailed with my dad too," I tell him.

"You did?"

"Yes, when I was younger. I remember he would make us do a capsize drill every time we went on holiday, just to make sure we could get back on board and get the dinghy upright again. I hated it, but I guess it was a good idea."

"Very good. Safety is key on the ocean. You have to respect it, or it will bite you in the butt!"

Lunch over, we start again, and without his gaze on me, I decide to quiz him for information.

"How long have you known Martha?"

"Martha? Oh, maybe ten years, I guess."

Silence. I hold my breath. 'And?' I want to ask, but

I know from experience that he will tell me more in his own time. Sure enough, he tells me the story.

"She came from New York, and we met her when she first came into town, funnily enough in the café about a week after she had arrived." He smiles. "I remember her trying to work with that coffee machine and deciding it was below her pay grade!"

He laughs and I'm about to interrupt when he continues, his voice a tone quieter.

"Looked kinda lost back then, though you wouldn't think it now. And we became firm friends."

Silence.

So many questions. Why did she leave New York? Why did she look lost?

"She's been very kind to me." I tell him.

"Has she?"

I nod. "And generous."

He looks at me. "And maybe you deserve it."

"Who knows?" I shrug and know that's all he will say for the time being, so I change tack and try to sound casual in my enquiry. "And Daniel?"

I concentrate on my painting, but I can feel Stan's eyes on me. There is another moment of silence. I hold my breath, knowing I asked without thinking and now I'm embarrassed.

"Young Daniel, eh?"

He waits. I look at him. He smiles. I blush.

"My fishing buddy and my wife's toy boy! I guess I've known him a lot longer. He's been coming to Oakham close on twenty years."

I can see him considering what to say next. Be patient.

"I am very fond of young Daniel, he's like a son to me." He pauses, chewing the end of his paintbrush contemplatively. "He's a good man. Been through a lot over the years, almost broke him, but in the last five years he's been the happiest I've ever seen him." He dips his brush in the paint and applies it to the canvas, a flash of colour. "I care a lot about him and don't want him hurt."

His words hit home as a warning.

'And?' I want to ask.

Moments later he asks me, "Why do you ask about Daniel?"

That puts me on the spot.

"He keeps turning up in my life, smiling and teasing me and asking questions. Always questions. I find it all so unnerving, Stan. I find him unnerving. I… I… I've no idea," I admit, shaking my head. "I'm confused about him as he seems so kind, he's always been nice to me and you obviously think the world of him, but I've heard various things–"

Stan cuts me off sharply. "From whom?"

I look shamefaced. "Jessica," I whisper.

"Ah, Jessica!" He sighs and puts his brush down, folding his hands together in contemplation. "That woman has some serious issues, I'm afraid. And jealousy is one of them."

This confirms what Sally said.

"Unfortunately, it's not an emotion she keeps to herself, and it can impact on others." He looks directly at me. "Do not get sucked in. Daniel is a kind and gentle man, honest and trustworthy, and if he's nice to you, take it for what it is. And be nice back to him. He deserves it."

Now I know the truth.

"I can see that."

There is more silence between us then he pats the back of my hand and quietly asks, "Why did you come here?"

He has asked me this question before and he knows about Jon, so I figure he is asking again for another reason. I take a moment to answer. Honesty is the best policy and my confidence in him is solid.

"To find out who I am, I guess, and to… I don't know, to start again. Life seemed empty after… and I suppose I'm trying to find out what I want now that I'm by myself." I gaze off into the distance. "I really enjoy being able to paint again. It brings me peace, helps me forget and stops me from overthinking. I'm good at that – overthinking." I smile at him. "And running away. I've always wanted to travel; Jon and I would go on holiday, but he was very much a home bird. Then when he got sick, I felt hemmed in, knowing I couldn't go anywhere and feeling guilty. After all, he had cancer and was dying. Then initially I couldn't face leaving home. I was afraid… until now…" *Because, now here with you, I don't feel afraid,* I want to tell him.

"What did you expect when you arrived?"

"Not sure, to be honest. I didn't really come with any expectations. I was perfectly happy to be someplace new and to experience whatever came along."

"So why do you doubt?" I look at him with a frown, so he continues, "You doubt yourself. Doubt Martha's kindness and generosity, and you even doubt your ability to paint."

How insightful. My first attempt from the morning is pretty good and I think, *it's rather lovely – so why do I doubt everything? Maybe it's more a lack of confidence?*

"Like I said, I overthink. And Jon's death knocked all the stuffing out of me, all the confidence." Yes, maybe that's it. "But you know, I am having the best time with you guys. You've both proved to be such good friends to me, you, and Martha. Thank you."

"Pleasure."

"And my friend Katie keeps telling me to enjoy this new life, and to be happy."

"She's right! You should. Life is too short, my

dear. Just take your time and be patient with yourself. Sometimes answers don't come from the places we expect."

We look at each other again and he smiles.

"You'll work it out, my dear. You will."

18

Despite the regular and much-improved staff meetings, I can sense that today's meeting – scheduled for four o'clock when we close the café – is going to be different. To start with, when Martha announced it this morning, it was with a tone that implied no questions. Then she handed out an agenda – small and beautifully formed with only three items, but an agenda nonetheless:

```
1. The present café
2. Afternoon tea
3. The future
```

Sally and I look at each other. *This is new!* Sally shrugs her pretty shoulders.

At a quiet moment in the morning, I peek at the agenda again and wonder why a meeting today? Later, I ask Sally, "What's this is all about?" She says she has no idea and I push the thoughts to the back of my mind and tell myself to stop overthinking. Again.

Four o'clock comes around and once Martha closes the front door, we collect the remnants of cake and fresh mugs of steaming coffee and settle at the table by the counter. She pauses. We wait. She coughs slightly, nervously, and points to the agenda. This is not the Martha I have come to know: she's a professional woman running her own business, normally cool, calm and collected.

"I have been considering your suggestions about afternoon tea."

I hold my breath — I seem to be doing it a lot these days.

"Agenda item one," she says somewhat formally. "This café has always been successful" — her eyes do a circuit of the room — "but, as I mentioned before, I believe it might be time for a change; a time to see this business with fresh eyes. With your eyes."

She points at me, and I jump and pull a face of mild panic. Normally this would make Sally snigger, but not today.

"The café's been like this since I took over " — she looks around again — "but… I must admit it is dated. It will be a big change" — she repeats herself, her face guarded — "and I have to make sure that any changes are for the right reasons and make business sense too. The customers I've asked seem to like the idea of updating the place."

Martha has been asking the customers' opinions. Interesting. She formally announces agenda item two.

"The cakes you make, Jane, are popular. We always sell out. Well, nearly always." She takes a bite of the remnant of Madeira cake and sips her coffee, taking a moment before focusing once more. "I really enjoyed the afternoon tea you made, it was delicious, though we will definitely need bigger sandwiches and I am not sure about all the milk first/second stuff."

I nod my head in agreement. I want to defend my actions and argue her comments but don't want to interrupt her thinking process. This looks almost painful for her.

"So… the menu. Breakfast, that'll stay the same, I guess." She picks up the breakfast menu to briefly check and agrees with herself. "But from lunch onwards" — she takes a longer look at the lunch menu, then moves her glasses from the end of her nose to her forehead — "this needs to change. The sandwiches and pastries can stay – we need to keep cakes on sale by the slice in case people want just one. But let's add in the afternoon tea on one of those three-tier plate things?"

She glances up at me and I nod in agreement.

"I think that might be the first step and then I… Well, if I go ahead and do this, it is going to be a big change."

She pauses. No-one moves. I hardly breathe.

"And the cakes you make have always sold out—" She repeats herself. Again.

My heart beats faster. I have never seen Martha so… so uncertain. Indecisive, despite the formal agenda.

"And delicious," Sally interrupts, only to be given a sharp look by Martha.

"Thank you, Sally. And delicious. So, I have decided to call this meeting then we can all discuss a plan going forward to possibly…" She puts her hands up. "I am not saying I will, but like I said, I am open to the possibility of change and to transform this place into an English tearoom." She picks up the sheet of paper. "Agenda item three!"

Silence.

"Well, say something!"

"It's a great idea!" said Sally.

They both look at me. I start to cry. With relief. With a sense of excitement and slight embarrassment. She likes my idea!

"You mean it?" I whisper.

Ignoring my emotional outburst, she gathers herself to voice something she has been thinking about but not fully considered. "I do. Possibly. Like I said, a change of menu initially to test the water and see how the customers react, but I am interested to hear your ideas about changing this place first." She sweeps her arms wide to encompass the whole café.

I take a deep breath. Tumbling thoughts. *This is a six-month trip that I am nearly three months into already and yet here I am making plans, long-term plans with these people. Am I ready to invest time and energy in this project? Have I started something I might not be here to finish? But if I stay?* The thought worries me – *I have elderly grandparents back in England and if I stay what happens to them? I did have a life back then – not much – but I did. And I have good friends, yet this place feels like home now. I'm happier than I have been for – oh ages – I have new friends. But I never intended to stay longer than six months – can I stay longer? I sigh. Oh well, maybe I should resign myself to helping Martha get the place going – but then I'll have to tell Martha that I am leaving. I suppose the least I can do is tell them what I think: thoughts about the food we could serve, the plates, cup, and saucers we could use. The need for teapots.*

Suddenly becoming aware that my inner dialogue has left a long silence, I notice Sally and Martha's expectant faces, so I get up off my chair and move around the room, the animated arm movements return as I explain, "An English tearoom can sometimes be quaint, with small tables and white tablecloths, but I don't think that would work here. So, maybe a jumble of different table sizes – square, round, oblong – all painted, kind of lime-washed in pastel colours with an assortment of chairs, also lime-washed colours, but all pale – like the houses by the sea, you know? And unusual lights, something unique." The words tumble out as my long-held thoughts and ideas flow freely. I indicate where we could put everything to maximise the space. "Over here, then maybe here?"

Sally adds, "That would look awesome! There's no place in town like that. At. All!"

"And maybe repaint the walls, I don't know, perhaps white or pale blue? And get some new blinds and maybe some bunting?"

"You could paint a mural? You could do that, right?" Sally moves over to the wall by the front door. "Over here?"

I love her youthful openness to all these new ideas we are throwing around and silently thank her.

"You could paint a row of houses, like the houses by the sea?"

Our enthusiasm is infectious and even Martha joins in, beginning to add her thoughts to the discussion. Together, as a team, we decide that a mural would be wonderful. A lively conversation follows as we throw ideas about between us, then suddenly there is a knock on the door.

Martha gets up and unlocks the front door. In walks Daniel. I stop. I do not want him involved. *This is my idea, our idea, for us to discuss. Why are you here?* I remember that he's an architect so maybe Martha has asked him here for that reason. Uncertainty makes my knees wobble.

"Go ahead." Martha waves her hand at me as she sits back down.

Daniel pulls up a chair and sits next to her. In the quiet moment that follows, he takes in our facial expressions, looking from one to another.

Astutely, he says, "I've interrupted something, sorry."

"Daniel, no, it's fine." Martha pats his arm reassuringly. "We're having a staff meeting and Jane here is giving us her ideas on how to change the café into an English tearoom."

Daniel looks from Martha to me and back again. "Why change it?" he enquires.

"I have given it a lot of thought and I consider it'll be good for business," she replies. "And you have to admit, this place could do with a bit of an upgrade. It is beginning to show its age."

The first assertive, positive statement we've heard all meeting, and it took the attendance of Daniel to bring it out. I am standing in the middle of the floor, feeling awkward (and slightly annoyed), not sure if I should continue or sit down.

"Jane and I discussed the idea a couple of weeks back. Then she made me an afternoon tea and I was rather impressed. Almost as good as the Ritz."

Martha smiles at me and I am reassured.

"I have been talking with some of the regulars about things as they are now, but the kind of things we might serve on a new, improved menu, and they seem to be open to something different around here, and frankly, I like the idea. Jane was just telling us about how we could maximise the space in here." Martha's confidence seems to have returned.

"Well," I sigh. "I was almost done with that."

Daniel gets up and walks round the room territorially, allowing me the opportunity to sit down before my legs give way. I breathe deeply and tell myself he is clearly checking things out and simply asking questions. It is obvious that Martha invited him (though failed to tell him what would be happening and why he had been invited), so I pause and tell myself to be willing to hear what he has to say.

"So, where you going to put the counter?" he asks, running his hands along the wooden surface.

"Leave it where it is as it's next to the kitchen," I state, trying not to see this question as a sign of disapproval but as a desire to help. It isn't easy.

"Is it the right size?"

He turns and puts all his attention on me. A shiver runs down my spine.

"I think so," Sally adds, sensing a change in the atmosphere in the room.

"We don't need it to be this long, maybe we could shorten it a bit," I add as Daniel turns away and paces it out.

"Taking off a couple of feet will give you more space." He inspects the room with a technical eye then asks, "Are you keeping all the tables and chairs?"

"Not necessarily. We might keep some of them," Sally tells him, "And paint them different colours."

"Or maybe we'll get a few new ones," Martha suggests, "different shapes and sizes. We haven't decided yet."

"Painted pastel colours – walls, chairs, you know," Sally adds.

I get the feeling I have sold the idea to them and as a united front we are somehow selling the idea to him. Daniel keeps asking questions.

"I know I invited you here but what's with all the questions?" Martha demands to know as she laughs. "Why don't you come up with a plan?" she teases.

"No! No!" Hands in the air, surrender. "I like Jane's plan," he states.

We are all digesting this snippet of information when there is another knock on the door and Stan is admitted. *Why is everyone here?* I stare at Martha with the sudden realisation that she has orchestrated this: she wants their opinion; she needs their encouragement and reassurance that she is doing the right thing. She invited these two men, but she didn't tell them why. The indecisiveness, the hesitation, the need for reassurance – this is a big deal for her. And it is obvious that she's not used to relying on people and yet here they are!

The inner critic throws a thought into the ring. She needs a second opinion. She doesn't have full confidence in me. I dismiss these thoughts immediately as now is not the time for self-doubt. Martha needs me and she needs them.

"Join the staff meeting!"

Martha invites Stan to sit down, patting the chair next to her, and we go through the details again for his sake. He is supportive and quietly enthusiastic and, as always, says little but what he does say is important. I sense his support and watching Martha, I can see she does too.

"You'll have to close the café for a time to get all the work done." Daniel states the obvious.

"Obviously!" Sally retorts. *See! Obvious.*

"Hey, wait a minute. I haven't decided yet. You guys might think it's a great idea, but I need to see plans, lists, costings, timelines, prices, and a schedule of works – there is a lot of work for you guys to do." She points at me and Daniel. The old business-like Martha gets up out of her chair. "Meeting closed. You must all have homes to go to!"

I am stunned. I cannot believe what just happened!

We started out with an uncertain Martha, the three of us discussing plans, and end up with five of us coming to a few conclusions. Now Daniel and I have been asked to work together to carry the project forward. What happened?

19

The meeting at the café has filled me with a strange anxiety that I am struggling to comprehend. Martha's initial behavior was out of character and seeing her so insecure and needing reassurance from both Daniel and Stan plays on my mind. I need to be alone and rebuild a connection with myself, slow down and unwind. I need to process the day, the events, and what people said and did, and file them away. What seemed like a simple idea to start with – an afternoon tea – has brought up lots of other ideas and also some interesting relationship dynamics. They obviously have years of history together, the three of them, and the bond of friendship is clear to see, but do I want to get this deeply involved and invest in what is, after all, their future? Besides, it was never my intention to stay longer than six months, never my intention to… to what? Didn't I think I would meet and get to know people? Didn't I think/hope it would be a great six months?

The inner struggle continues, so I go for a run, but

my body fights every step and even motivational music doesn't help. The muscles in my legs ache and my head is pounding. At home (there I go again – home!), I take a quick shower and change into my favourite shorts and T-shirt, pack my bag with paper and pencils, and walk to the low wall – actually, it is more like a stomp than a walk, totally disgruntled by everything and feeling trapped in the middle of something I don't quite understand. This wall has become my official place of refuge, my thinking step. The sight of the water, smooth and calm and jeweled with flickering light, the sound of the ocean and the smells of iodine, dune grass and sea salt, all combine to soothe me. I manage to take a deep breath for the first time in what seems like hours.

I go to my favourite coping strategy and make a list in my head to try to organise my thoughts:

Martha – despite her initial hesitation, by the end of the meeting she appears to have become an ally. Of course, she has shown me so much support already (encouraging people to buy my paintings and giving me a home), and yet her show of vulnerability is surprising, although understandable given this is a big change for her. She has always struck me as a confident woman in control (tight control) of her emotions (and with a very firm handshake), so once she has made her mind up, I'm sure she would be fully behind it. She is difficult to read and yet deep down I believe she is my friend and I support, trust and respect her.

Sally – my workmate, my enthusiastic supporter who seemed totally on board with everything today, like a little sister. I am not sure what her issue is with Jessica. It has obviously affected her and her family deeply, but I trust Sally and will take her advice to be wary.

Stan – his quiet, reassuring presence is a comfort, and he makes me feel safe, like my grandfather. I feel I can open up and be honest when I am with him as he has no agenda. He fills the gap of not having Mum, Dad, and my grandparents around. Always a wise word and a listening ear.

Daniel – the man with the green eyes who has an unsettling effect on me whenever he enters the room. Too attractive for his own good, it troubles me that he might distract me from my reason for this trip – to find myself.

Despite how happy they make me feel (well, three of them at least), I ask myself again – do I want to help with this change that Martha seems so insecure about? Do I need to get involved in their lives? And yet, clearly I am involved, given the meeting that has just taken place. This is only temporary, isn't it? My real life is back in England. Isn't it? But then I focus on my 'why' and tell myself I came to find me – what I need, what I want.

Breathing deliberately and deeply, I attempt to quell my emotional overthinking. Slowly, I become more settled and find I am able to take pleasure in the late June sunshine as the heat of the day subsides barely a fraction of a degree. It is almost seven o'clock and I still can't get used to the idea that it is going to stay warm after it goes dark. In England, this is rare, but here it is normal, and I haven't worn a cardigan or sweater for a couple of weeks. Folks tell me that the humidity will start to kick in soon and I will need to get an air con unit for my bedroom. I make a mental note to find out where to obtain such a sleep aid.

On the beach, families pack up blankets and windbreaks, buckets and spades, shouting to their children to say it is time to go, and heading to the steps, back to cars, vans, homes. They pass me, their skin pink and shining, smelling of suntan cream and salt, laughing and smiling, happy people.

I reach into my bag for a sketchbook and pencil and start to draw a family sitting together on the beach. My figure drawing is improving, and realising that practice is the key, a certainty of pen stroke is returning to the pages. The first sketchbook charts the time when I first arrived in Oakham and there is noticeable improvement both in skill and technique. This second sketchbook, bought from my new favourite art supply store, is beginning to hold real promise of an era of artistic achievement and a return of confidence. I am totally absorbed in the process.

The sketch complete, I turn my attention to a young couple and see him lean in and kiss her tanned shoulder. She brushes her hand casually through his mop of brown hair. There is something about their intimacy and mutual affection that is natural, and I find myself coveting it. Sighing deeply, I wonder when my life might find the balance I am looking for. Coming here, I thought I'd find it. The past is a little less painful and I know I have moved on from the darkest days, but I haven't exactly found 'it' yet.

In one of those serendipitous moments, as I move my gaze from the loving couple, wondering when and from where the answers will come, Daniel steps into my line of vision as he gets out of the cab of his Ford pick-up truck. My heart beats faster as my brow furrows in a deep frown. How dare he come here! This is my place. This afternoon I had been so concerned with the meeting and the plans that I had not been aware of what he was wearing: a white T-shirt, faded Levi's and moccasins without socks. His ankles are tanned, and I berate myself for noticing. His baseball cap is pulled down low and Wayfarer sunglasses hide his eyes – damn, he's attractive – and I am annoyed at myself as tension rises inside.

He sits next to me on the wall. Quiet. I ignore him

for a short time, inwardly telling myself to calm down. Then my upbringing surfaces and my manners kick in.

"Hello."

"Hi," he replies.

An awkward silence lingers between us. So I draw, pencil scratching on the paper.

"That's good," he tells me.

"Thanks."

Silence. *Why are you here?* I turn to him and take the initiative, ask the question.

"Daniel, what do you want?"

His face shows surprise. He takes off his sunglasses and the green eyes sparkle. He holds his hands up. "I'm sorry"— he moves back slightly — "I came here to see if we could talk. I'm sorry if I'm disturbing you." He makes a move to leave.

I realise I have been both impolite and too harsh with my words. He may unnerve me with his presence but there is no need to be rude. Reaching out, I catch his arm.

"OK, go ahead – talk." Immediately, I realise that my words have come out a little more abruptly than I intended, so I try to soften them with a smile.

He sits back down. "I came here to apologise for the way I behaved."

Silence.

"Look, I know I came across, to you particularly,

maybe a bit interfering? It's Martha's café and if she wants to turn it into an English tearoom with your help, that's fine with me, and after all, it is none of my business."

I remain quiet but inwardly acknowledge his apology. The tension level drops a notch or two.

"You can add to this conversation at any time."

"I accept your apology." I know my words still sound harsh, but I cannot help myself. The inner struggle does not need to be shared.

"You have any spare paper or a pencil?" he asks.

I hand him both and he starts to draw. This silence becomes more neutral – not comfortable but less awkward. We sit and draw. The level drops another notch and I start to relax – a little.

At the top of the steps from the beach, a small child, probably about five years old, dressed in a sand-covered swimsuit and a floppy hat, walks barefoot holding an ice cream. I can see it is balanced precariously on the cone and before I can think that it might fall, it does. The scene is frozen as the child realises what has happened. His mouth opens in a silent scream and then the piercing noise hits us all, including the father, who turns around to see the child is distraught. Daniel chuckles softly then his warm smile is swiftly replaced with a pained expression. I wonder why but don't feel I can ask him as the moment passes.

His drawing is excellent and when I tell him, he explains, "I took a minor in art in college as a sideline to help me deal with architect studies"—he looks directly at me— "so when I tell you that your work is good, it's good!"

"Don't sound so pompous!"

"Pompous!" he squawks, and we laugh easily, then go back to drawing. Safer ground.

A moment later I ask, "Why architecture?"

He starts to tell me about his choice of subject, his tutors, his classmates, his alma mater.

"It's a university, by the way, not a college," I interrupt his train of thought. "You Americans have

taken the English language and ruined it."

"You're kidding." He holds my gaze. "You're not kidding, are you?"

"No! I mean it. For example, the way you all drop the letter 'r' out of so many words—"

"Bostonians."

"So, when you say, 'park a car' it sounds more like 'paahk a caah'!"

"Like I said, Bostonians."

"And that there – what's the thing at the front?" I point at the vehicle closest to us.

"A fender."

"No, it's not! It is a bumper and that's the bonnet."

"The hood."

"And at the back is the boot."

"The trunk," he retorts.

"See – ruined! And don't get me started on crisps!"

"Crisps?"

"Well, you call them potato chips, but we call them crisps, because chips are hot and eaten with a burger."

"You mean fries!" He is watching me intently.

"See!"

He chuckles softly – I can't help it; I am beginning to like the sound – and averts his eyes. The ensuing silence has taken a further step towards comfortable as we resume drawing, though neither of us is producing anything noteworthy.

Sometime later he enquires, "So are you happy living upstairs above the café – sorry, English tearoom!"

"Yes, I am, and I can't tell you how grateful I am to Martha. She's made my stay here a pleasant one." I pause, deciding how much to tell him. "After she offered me the apartment, she told me she was the Patron Saint of Lost Causes and felt the need to help me."

"A lost cause?"

"Maybe."

We talk a bit, then we stop – stilted conversation. I put down my pencil and sigh, looking out towards the ocean.

"Do you live locally?" I ask politely. I know he lives

in the city, but the silence needs to be filled.

"No, I live in Boston."

"Oh yes, I remember you saying—"

Daniel's puzzled expression causes me to blush as I only know this because I was earwigging!

"Yes, I live in Boston. I have an apartment there, near the office where I work, but then I come to Oakham whenever I can. I've got a place along the shore"—he points to the right— "It overlooks the ocean. I try to be here most weekends, holidays, Christmas, you know, and then I kinda move here for the summer – June through August. I can work remotely from my house and if there's a problem in the office, well I can always drive back to the city. Besides, I love it here."

That's clear to see.

"Me too," I whisper and then wish I hadn't.

He looks straight at me, and we observe each other for a moment longer than is necessary. He tips his head far too attractively to the left and asks, "You wanna come see my house?"

"Sure."

I say this without thinking, and once in the cab of his grey pick-up, I realise I am way out of my comfort zone and become quiet and withdrawn. Daniel senses the change and he chats away to fill the space with sound. He points out places of interest as he drives along the road, relates memories of past events, the people he knows, and when we pass the harbour, he tells me he went fishing yesterday with Stan and his friend.

Ten minutes later he pulls off the road and onto a gravel drive which slopes slightly downhill. The house in the middle of the plot of land is modest and pleasing to the eye.

"Shall we go inside?" he asks quietly as he opens the front door.

I walk ahead of him and am immediately hit by the light in the house, the simple elegant style, the clean lines. He moves past me into the lounge.

"This way," he indicates.

"Wow!" The word escapes involuntarily because the view is amazing. The whole of the back of the house is a wall of glass and the view is the ocean. "Wow!"

"Impressive, huh?"

I drag my eyes away from the view and look around the room – open plan with a kitchen area (expensive kitchen), breakfast bar, and soft, plump sofas in pale greys and washed tones that match and reflect the seascape. Impressive.

"Like it?" he asks, watching me closely.

"It's amazing! And I can see why you like being here. It's beautiful!"

He unlocks the glass door and slides it back. On the elegantly proportioned deck there are several pale wooden chairs, a table, and two loungers placed strategically to admire the surroundings.

"I knew as soon as I saw this house that the view was the most important thing. I drew up plans to transform the inside of the house and make it more open, taking down walls, you know. I wanted to make the most of the view. I was really happy when the plans got passed and then I started work… so that this"—he sweeps his arm out towards the sea— "would be the focal point. I love the ocean."

I wander around and find myself stroking things, taking pleasure from the quality.

"How long have you lived here?"

"I guess I've owned the house about twenty years. It wasn't like this at all when"—he pauses— "I bought it."

I get the feeling he was going to say 'we' but cannot be sure.

"It's beautiful!" I repeat.

"Thanks. So, tell me more about your plans for the café?"

He stands right beside me. I want to move away but it would appear rude. I reiterate what was said at the staff meeting before he arrived and put more detail into the design ideas that have been enthusiastically running through my head since Martha first asked me about it all.

"I can help you draw up the plans"—he catches

my eye— "if you want, that is? I wouldn't want to interfere… but if you want?"

"Thanks, that'd be nice." I accede to his wish to help me.

"Your creative abilities and my technical style might just make a great team."

"How long has the café been like it is now?" I ignore his comment.

"Since way back, before Martha took over."

"It could do with a change then?"

"On reflection, it probably could. You're happy to help Martha even though you are only here for… how long?"

I take a breath. I am not telling him how long. I don't know myself and questions like this bring my insecurities to the fore and I worry that he might talk to Jessica about me. Is he concerned that I'm taking advantage of Martha? Is his invitation a fact-finding mission? I decide to be cautious in my response.

"If Martha is happy with making these changes, then I'm happy. She has been so good to me since I got here and anything I can do to help her in return is OK with me." It almost sounds like a challenge.

"Then it's OK with me too."

Silence.

"I bet there is no light pollution here," I say, wondering why I say it as soon as it is out of my mouth.

"None."

"The stars must be awesome." *I can't help myself, can I?*

"You must come over one night and see for yourself."

"Yes, I'd like that."

Realising that I've backed myself into a corner, I blush profusely. He is smiling so I look away. I lean on the deck rail and try to compose myself. Suddenly it all feels too much – the tension has returned, and it is exhausting, and I need to get away from here, from him.

"Could you take me home now please?"

"You want some coffee?"

"No, I… I would prefer to go home now, please."

His frown tells me he is confused. And I don't blame him.

"Sure," he agrees reluctantly.

On the drive home, I cannot help but notice the fair hair on his tanned arms. He smells of sandalwood and sunshine, and the confines of the space become overwhelming. A feeling of panic starts to build, a huge balloon of emotion expanding and pushing against my rib cage. I become desperate to keep a tight rein on my emotions, concentrating on my breathing as I stare out of the window to search for a measure of calm. But nothing helps as I barely control the need to cry.

When we are back on Main Street and he parks up, I get out quickly, say "Thanks for the ride" and almost run home, to my safe place, my refuge. I close the door and lean back against it, my eyes closed. Slowly, with measured, even breathing my heart rate starts to slow to normal. Thankfully within minutes the panic attack is over. The first one I have suffered for a very long time, taking me totally by surprise.

With a sigh I open my eyes at the sound of my phone pinging.

Hi - You OK? 22.02

It's Katie. How does she know?

It's been a bit of a weird day. 22.02

Weird how? You OK? 22.05

I settle on the sofa and wonder how I'm going to explain what's going on inside. I tell her about the staff meeting and then try to explain how I feel. Katie is my rock, my anchor to my true home. She knows me. She understands me. But would she understand the way I am feeling now? I almost feel as though my thoughts make me disloyal to this good friend.

> I've been all over the place emotionally and yes, I've been overthinking. I'm starting to feel torn between life here and life at home. I miss Mum and Dad obviously (and you, of course) and I know Nan and Popa are not getting any younger, but I'm not sure about coming back. I like life here. It's starting to feel like home. 22.06

There is no reply to this text, and I fear I have gone too far. Been too honest. Having a place to live, making plans for a 'future', being part of a community. It's all starting to change the way I feel. It's starting to feel permanent.

The phone remains silent. I seem to be frustrating and confusing everyone!

20

It's American Independence Day – July 4th. There is no time for anything except a quick shower and a banana on the run as we open two hours ahead of normal time (at eight o'clock instead of the usual ten) to serve breakfast. So, getting up at stupid o'clock is the first order of the day. Thank goodness it is light.

Within minutes of turning the sign and opening the front door the café is full, and I am grateful that Martha allowed me to ask for extra help; we have Sally's sister and her young friend taking orders, serving customers, and cleaning the tables. Martha has chosen (on the busiest week of the year) to delegate several responsibilities to me from now on – the ordering, choosing suppliers and the whole invoicing procedure. I am worried whether I can manage all the extra responsibilities at the same time as serving customers and baking cakes at all hours of the day (and night), and yet I find myself eager to impress and keen to prove her right. I can do this!

The breakfast rush goes without a hitch with all of

us working flat out (including Martha). Well, when I say without a hitch, there was one fly in the proverbial ointment – Jessica. I'm not sure where she got the courage from, but she brazenly opened the door and came into the café all smiles and saying hello, as if nothing had happened! She ordered coffee to go from Sally and as she passed me on the way out, she said, "Martha tells me she's thinking about giving this place a facelift. That'll be your idea then? Yes?" Before I had had chance to answer, she leaned in closer, her eyes beady and sharp, and ploughed on, "I didn't know you were qualified in interior design. Or will you be relying on the skills of Daniel?" My jaw slackened as she swanned out of the café, happily greeting people as she went. What the…?

Thank goodness I don't have time to process her accusations because at around eleven o'clock Daniel appears. I am relieved that he came through with his promise to help out and that I am not at all frazzled by his presence (for once), but at the same time I'm still a little embarrassed about how we left things the last time we spoke. Daniel doesn't seem to feel the same (or at least shows no evidence of being uncomfortable) and quickly assesses the situation. All pleasantries aside, he follows Martha's advice and gets stuck in washing up plates, cups and bowls and anything else that needs cleaning. Apron tied around his waist and sleeves rolled up, he takes charge in the kitchen. We are all so busy that there is little time to chat and little time to focus on anything other than the job in hand as the morning passes in a blur and all my concerns evaporate.

After lunch there is a slight lull in proceedings. I study each one of the 'team' as they go about their duties and, with Martha's permission, quickly assemble everyone in the kitchen. I thank them for their hard work and ask them to continue with the high standards of service as the afternoon rolls along and, no doubt, as we all get tired.

Daniel apologises to us all, that unfortunately he has to leave but he promises to return around five to help us clear up at the end of the day.

"Nice pep talk," he whispers in my ear as he leaves, and I find myself covered in goosebumps despite the heat of the day.

The afternoon is slightly quieter in the sense that we don't actually have customers waiting for a table or queuing in a line out the door. We manage to sit every last one, feed them and get them out again without appearing to rush them. We work as a well-oiled machine: efficient, slick and all done with a smile on our faces. We missed the procession down Main Street, which is a shame, but by the time it had passed us by it was too late to get out there! I am reliably informed that the parade (not a procession) was "lively", the marching band "sounded great" and the floats were "pretty". About twenty thousand people came to watch – and it feels like most of them came to the café!

The day flies by, and before we know it, it is time to close up. Daniel is back in the kitchen. Martha locks the front door, turns the sign to 'Sorry We're Closed' and heaves a huge sigh of relief. We both survey the scene: every table is laden with cups, plates and rubbish and the detritus of half-eaten meals and cakes.

"Where is everyone?" I ask Martha and a flicker of a frown crosses my face as I hear laughter coming from the kitchen and see the girls enjoying a joke with Daniel.

"Quick!" He stands upright and salutes Martha and I as we enter the kitchen. "The boss is back!"

They all laugh some more. I am tired and suffer a momentary sense of humour failure until I take a second or two to look around. We are all tired. I stop myself from getting defensive and smile. Martha beams. Everyone is relieved.

"I don't know about you, but I haven't worked that hard in years," Martha tells us. "Let's get this place cleaned up then we can all go home and rest. One more push, please."

The café is locked up, everyone waves goodbye, and

I make my way back to my little balcony. I don't even bother to unlock the front door; I plonk myself down in my rocking chair and heave a sigh of relief. We did it. My body aches and my feet throb, but the gentle to and fro, to and fro of the chair relaxes my mind and I hope my body will follow.

But with a relaxed mind comes Jessica's comments from earlier. *What did she mean? Have I taken on too much? And why on earth did she mention Daniel? Is she still on that obsession and talking and laughing at me behind my back?*

Deliberately, I push the thoughts away as they produce a tightening of the muscles in my chest. No! It's been a great day; I am not going to let the petty-minded woman spoil it. I shake my head as though shaking out all the negativity, rub my sternum gently and consider getting myself a large G&T but cannot be bothered to stand up. No! I'll speak to Katie instead. I still haven't had a reply to my last text, and I worry that we may no longer be singing from the same hymn sheet. I am ready to move on, I know that now, but is Katie ready to let me go?

I send her a brief WhatsApp to tell her what's going on and then put my phone on the floor, face down so it won't disturb me. Head back. Eyes closed. And BREATHE! Within what seems like minutes (but is probably closer to an hour – I may well have fallen asleep in the sunshine), I hear footsteps on the iron steps and a voice shout, "Hello, anyone home?" It's Daniel.

"Hello," I reply.

He sees this as an invitation to open the gate and join me.

Suddenly my little balcony with my rocking chair and a few plant pots overflowing with fragrant summer blooms seems overcrowded. My heart does the fluttery thing. I can't help it.

"Hi!" He grins. "Caught you napping, eh?"

"You might be right!" I admit.

"I come bearing gifts."

He produces a small case of beers. Not exactly what I ordered but welcome all the same.

"I approve! Thank you!"

He drags a chair out onto the small balcony. I shuffle my rocking chair back into the corner to accommodate him and put space between us. We quietly quaff the first cold beer. It hardly touches the sides. It's delicious and turns out to be exactly what I need. I emit an exaggerated sigh and a gentle unashamed belch.

"That was good!"

"Another one, boss?" he teases, handing me a bottle. "You did a good job today."

"You think so?" As always, I doubt myself. "Martha really put her trust in me today. I want her to be proud of me. You know her well; will she be pleased with what we did?"

"Yep. She will be."

I'm glad, but honestly, I'm too tired to welcome the news. I rest my head back and momentarily close my eyes as we drink in peace, then I ask, "How long have you known her?"

"About ten years, I guess, since she first came to town." He says no more but confirms what Stan has already told me.

"I like her," I tell him.

He nods and we go back to drinking beer and watching the folks in the park. Surprisingly comfortable companions. Maybe I could get used to this.

"How are your plans for the café coming along?" he asks a minute or two later.

Since our agenda-led meeting I have been industrious, collecting magazine pages that reflect the style I am after, together with paint and fabric swatches. I have started a spreadsheet of costs and have even considered a schedule of works. It's been absorbing and thoroughly enjoyable.

A tad reluctantly, I fetch the preliminary drawings I have made, the mood board, fabrics, and paint colours. I value his opinion even though I am still a little reticent about his involvement, not sure I can fully trust him. He sits and quietly appraises my designs.

My fragile confidence leads me to ask, "Do you like the plans?" The conversation with Jessica from this morning pops into my mind once more and my brain goes into overthinking mode. "Should I get formal plans drawn up? I mean, I'm not exactly qualified in interior design."

Daniel glances up from the plans and frowns. "That's a strange thing to say?"

Without thinking, I admit to him what happened earlier.

"Ah! Jessica!" His mouth tightens, his shoulders tense. "That woman has some personal issues, I'm telling you. She can be strange but please take what she says with a large pinch of salt. You can do this – these plans, they're good. You have a talent."

He hands the plans back and I hold them to my chest protectively. I have put a lot of effort into them. I think they are what the café needs but Jessica's words, her spitefulness, have sucked out the small amount of confidence I had to begin with.

"You could get formal plans made up; it might look a bit more professional. But really, they're fine. Would you like me to draw them up for you?" He looks directly at me, and I realise he is being kind and there is no ulterior motive behind his offer. "Once you have decided what it is you want?" He qualifies his offer and I get the sense that he knows this decision is part of something bigger for me.

We discuss the layout of the floor space, the length

of the counter, positioning of tables and chairs and the need (or not as the case may be) for sofas and a more casual, relaxed seating area. I show him my pictures of the light fixtures I particularly like and he compliments me on my choice. When he questions the paint colours, I am inclined to agree with him and we talk about alternatives, maybe using materials such as wood or brick.

All talked out and my confidence partially restored, he asks, "You hungry?"

Am I?' "Yes, I am."

"I'll go get some pizza. Any toppings in particular?"

"Whatever goes."

He leaves with a parting smile.

That night I lie in bed and mull over the events of the day. It's been a good day is my overall conclusion, and for the first time I have felt comfortable in Daniel's company, neither threatened nor unnerved. Yes. Comfortable.

The heat of the day and the prevailing humidity of the night (I definitely need to get an air-con unit) makes it difficult to sleep and my fitful night is filled with dreams of Jon/Daniel intermingled. Disturbing.

The following day is another super busy day, but thankfully with shorter opening hours. The girls do another great job and at closing time I split the tips from the last two days between them so that they can see the financial rewards for all their hard work.

"Thank you so much for everything," I tell them again and again, grateful for their efforts and company as they hug me and leave.

And speaking of company – no sight of Daniel and no word either. A brief moment passes when I miss him.

When everyone has finally gone home and there's only me and Martha left, she emerges from the kitchen with a bottle of chilled white wine and two glasses and pours us both a large (and well-deserved) measure.

"Cheers!" Our glasses clink lightly.

"What a day!" I agree.

"But well worth it. I bet we've taken more this last two days than we've ever done before. I'll check the till receipts later, but it's been a great success. And that's mainly down to you!"

"Me?"

"Yes. You rallied the troops; you kept them all going. They turned to you for guidance. You make a good boss— "

"No, you're the boss," I blurt out.

"No, I'm the owner and they view me differently. They like you. They're afraid of me!"

I can't help but laugh.

"I'm not kidding." There is a moment of quiet

reflection, then she adds, "You did a good job. Thank you."

Before going to sleep I send off a text message to Katie, giving her the daily update: who, what when. After a longer than usual silence following my last message to her, Katie had eventually replied, encouraging me to give myself time to think things through. That was all she said. However, when I had told her about the plans for July fourth, she had replied in her usual supportive way when my doubts had crept in, telling me to enjoy myself and to remember this was a holiday. But then I do it without thinking AGAIN and read it back – oh no! I wait with trepidation at the barrage of questions that I am sure Katie will send, especially at the mention of… him.

This time there is no reply.

21

I have taken my time drawing up the plans for the transformation of the café. The mood board has been improved following my discussion with Daniel. The mural has been sketched out and I've found fabric and paint shades that, after a rethink, will complement the beautiful light fittings. He has drawn up some architectural plans which are amazing. When all the details are ready and we have come up with the costing, I present them to Martha after work.

Sitting at one of the tables in the café, I spread out the plans and mood board in front of her. Both of us are tired after a busy day, so we are glad of a sit down, drinking a well-deserved coffee and eating the last pieces of lemon drizzle cake.

"That's a good cake," she sighs as she puts down her plate and takes up the plans, diligently examining every last detail.

I watch her expression for any signs, indications of what she is thinking. As always, I want to tell her my thinking but decide to err on the side of caution and let her take it all in first. I know from past experience that she will ask when she is ready. She does, and I get the chance to explain.

"Mmnnnn," she says, her voice soft and quiet. "I like."

She takes her glasses from their perch on the end of her nose and puts them on her forehead. Her outfit is one of my favourites – the peacock one of lime green and turquoise.

"You seem happy about making these changes," I comment warily, unsure if this is actually the case. The indecision she showed in the team meeting seems to have evaporated, but I am still not sure it's been replaced with confidence in me, in herself and this major alteration she is planning. "You OK with this?"

Martha holds my gaze. "I am."

There is a silence, and I can detect an important moment is about to happen.

"I know why you're asking." She pauses. "You're an astute woman. I think it's time you got to know some things about me." She puts down the papers and plans. "We need wine."

She hurries off to get glasses and a bottle of chilled white wine that she keeps in the kitchen fridge for such occasions as this, pours me a small glass and a larger one for herself. She takes a large slurp before speaking.

"When I was about nineteen years old, my life fell off the rails, so to speak. Straight in at the deep end, eh?" She flaps her hands around (a dangerous activity given she is holding the glass of wine) and tells me I don't need to know the gory details. "My mother was bitterly disappointed in me and made it obvious that I was no longer welcome at home as I had disgraced her and the family. Daddy wasn't so sure but, as always, he bowed to pressure. Always did." She pauses and gazes off into the distance into a different time and place.

I hold my breath as she takes another huge slurp of wine. I top up her glass as she continues.

"But Daddy was so sweet, so dissimilar to her… he gave me a second chance. He found me a great apartment on 5th Avenue near Washington Square Park, nice area, and helped me get a position in a department store as a head buyer. He knew that I'd made a mistake, albeit a big mistake, but he was willing to forgive me, and I will always be grateful to him for that. I took the opportunity, that second chance, in both hands and made a damn fine job of my life."

Her confession helps me see where the spirit and resilience come from, and also the need for that cool, slightly remote exterior.

"Then my crossroads moment. We all have one in life, right?"

She looks at me again. I nod in agreement.

"Daddy died a week before my fiftieth birthday and Mother, who bear in mind had not spoken to me in three decades, refused to let me attend the funeral."

Her face becomes taut at the memory. *What had she done to offend her mother so much?*

"I was distraught, as you can imagine..." More gazing into the past, the memories. More wine. "I mourned him by myself."

I pour the remnants of the bottle into her glass, and she thanks me.

"Then a cheque arrived in the post – no letter, no nothing. A cheque for a big sum of money. It was from Daddy, and it was dated just before he died. Like he knew what would happen, like he knew how she would react, and he needed to protect me..." Her voice fades slightly. "A second chance, a second time around." She sighs. "I decided I didn't want to live in New York anymore when he wasn't there. I missed him so much and every street corner, every sunrise brought painful memories." She sees me nodding in agreement and continues, "So I decided to leave. I handed in my resignation, sold the apartment, and came out here to the Cape. I stayed in a hotel for a week or two then found this place. Sound familiar?" she asks.

"It does." My instinct is to cry, to hug her, but I hold my emotions in check – now is neither the time nor the place. But this is very insightful.

"This place was for sale: the café and the apartment, the whole building. So, I bought it off Stan and Shirley."

My eyes widen. The connection.

"Yes, they lived here before me. Before you. They retired and I took over and moved in upstairs until I could find a home of my own."

Now I know this snippet of information I can see why she has kept it the same all these years and that any change must involve Stan – he must approve too. I let this information sink in.

"I found myself here." She is watching me carefully. "Sound familiar?" she asks again.

A tear seeps down my cheek as I look at her. I have to clear my throat, which is constricted with building emotions.

"It does."

"I want to make these changes, Jane, not just to the café but to my life. I am ready for change. Are you ready? Are you willing to help me? Can you see this as your second chance?" She waves her arm wide to encompass the whole room.

This is disconcerting. We seem to have gone from an interior design project to something much bigger. This is the moment. My sensation of being torn in two grows. *Life here or life back home in England? What do I want? What exactly is she offering me?*

"I don't know what to say. Give me some time?

Please?" I plead.

She sees my inner turmoil written plainly on my face. "You got it."

22

The conversation with Martha keeps going round and round in my head. Her story, the connection with Stan and Shirley, second chances, the way life has a way of making you take a turn in the road, make a decision that will change you and the way you view life and live life forever. What had she done that was so bad? Why had her mother not spoken to her for thirty years? I guess I don't need to know – all I need to know is that she took those second chances, and she made the most of what life threw at her.

So, what was she now throwing at me? Was it the chance to make my mark on her business? Or the chance to run the business? For now? And all the time my mind keeps bringing me back to the reality:

a. that I am here to find myself – or maybe this is it? Maybe this is the new me? My new life?
b. BUT I'm only here until October – so what happens then?

Painting normally brings me comfort, but not today.

Overthinking makes me grumpy and is reflected in the work I am producing. I want to get out my big brush and make big marks on a big canvas, but I only brought my sketch book with me today. Nothing seems to help clear my mind or improve my mood. Added to this is the conversation I finally had with Katie – after a week of silence this time. She told me I had to do what was right for me (though I'm not sure she meant it), but that she misses me dreadfully. I'm the only one she can talk to, who understands her. Something is not right. I can sense it. Unease about our friendship and the strain that the distance geographically is putting on it makes the frustration build.

Then I see Stan strolling towards me and my heart is gently lifted. It's as though he knows when I need him and when I need his wisdom. He sits down next to me on my wall, groaning slightly with the effort.

"My knees," he states as a means of explanation. "Thought I might find you here. How you doin'?"

"Not good," I sigh and show him what I have been attempting to draw.

"Not up to your usual standard. You look like you're dealing with stuff?"

I stare at him, and he meets my gaze. How does he know that? Lowering my eyes, I agree with him and decide to tell him about the conversation with Martha (but not my stream of consciousness with Katie – he doesn't need to know EVERY thought in my head!).

"So, do you know what happened back then?" I ask him.

"Well, like I told you, when Martha first arrived in Oakham, she was kinda like a lost soul. You could tell she was distraught after the death of her father and in need of a purpose in life. Shirley and I, well we were getting ready to retire. We'd found our forever home and wanted to sell the building and the business. Martha was the right buyer at the right time." He laughs at the memory. "Frankly, I couldn't see her running a café with all her New York elegance and glamour and wealth, but hey, she managed it. She's done a fine job all these years."

I actually want to know about what happened when she was nineteen but either he doesn't know or he isn't telling, so I don't ask again.

"What do you think she means by offering me a second chance?"

He shrugs. "I know that she is thinkin' of retiring. She hit the big six zero last year. She says she gotta book inside her that's ready to come out – maybe she wants to step back from the café and write. Maybe she's thinkin' of offering the business to you?"

Martha retiring?

"I can't afford to buy that building! It must be worth half a million! At least! Probably more!" This is ridiculous!

"She must have her reasons."

"And I don't have a green card or residency or anything and I am leaving in October!"

I realise I am beginning to sound frantic. Here we go again. I stop and breathe, contemplating his bright blue wise old eyes as if I can absorb some of his essence. It dawns on me that my first response was about the costs, not whether I'm leaving in October, and this almost brings on another panic attack.

"You need to talk to her. Be honest with her. She obviously trusts you."

I can tell he is deep in thought, so I wait, knowing from experience that he will talk when he is ready. *Be patient*. On the beach, holidaymakers are oblivious to my turmoil and my ever-active mind rolls back over the months I have been sitting on this wall, knowing I have come to rely on this old man for his dependability and understanding. Just like my grandfather. My heart takes a tumble – I miss Popa.

"You know," he continues after a time, "maybe she simply wants you to change the café, improve her business and then she's happy for you to go home? Who knows?"

Later that day in my apartment, Martha and I have a final discussion about the renovation work, to agree the costings, the colours, the timetable. We will close the café and start work at the weekend. Martha is relaxed and I enjoy our quiet times together cementing our friendship with the obligatory glass or two of wine. She has become a constant companion: we share similar interests and I love to hear her talk about her life, here and in New York.

Suddenly she puts down the paperwork and changes the subject. "They're having a picnic in the park next week. They have it every year around this time," she tells me. "They have a band on. I'm not sure if Daniel is singing this year—"

"Daniel?" I interrupt her.

"Yeah, he's got a great voice. Haven't you heard him sing? You need to hear him sing. He performs live occasionally and last year he did a gig at the bar on Main."

"Wow!"

"And you should go to the picnic; it's a lot of fun."

"I might watch from up here. Not much fun going alone."

"You've been on your own how long now? Two years?" she asks.

"Yes." I turn away from her intense gaze, deciding to take Stan's advice and open up to her. It's time. "You know… my family, my mum and dad, my grandparents, they all found that 'one' person. I thought when I married Jon that I had found my 'one' person too. They'd all married, stayed married, had kids, raised families and, you know, not one of them has died. I still have all my grandparents, all four of them." I pause to contemplate this. It is a blessing. I miss them all and miss being in the middle of the family. Happy memories of summer holidays spent with my maternal grandparents who had a house by the sea, happy times. "And then Jon went and died…" saying those words still causes pain in my heart and I wonder when I will be able to talk about losing him without feeling as though my guts are being pulled out through my throat. "And to be honest, after the funeral my life settled down and I went through the routine of living, you know, going to work, cleaning the house. I went running. I tried painting, stuff, even going out with friends. But nothing made sense anymore." I want her to understand. "And then this idea popped into my head to get away, somewhere far away, and the idea kind of grew and took over. One day I made the decision that it had to become a reality, but I had no idea where to go. I've always had such a tight control on my life, like it's my safety blanket, like everything was safe that way and nothing bad would happen to me again if I was in control, complete control. So, making the choice as to where to go seemed a little daunting. Then one day I simply put a pin in a map, and it landed here." I smile at the memory. "My poor dad, he was confused 'cause he thought I was doing OK. My mum was angry with me, which shocked me, and my sister was too wrapped up in her own family to be honest. The only person who whole-heartedly supported me and understood what I was doing was my best friend, Katie. Once I'd made the decision it seemed simple. I bought a ticket, rented out my house for six months and then suddenly I lost what little confidence I had left and got really, really scared. And I've been scared ever since. Scared of having nowhere to live, scared of not being able to paint, scared of that machine downstairs!"

Martha smiles and says, "And now?"

"And now I am scared…" I pause as I recognise this emotion that's been part of my life since Jon's diagnosis and has never really left me. "Scared that Katie doesn't understand, and I might be losing her, and that I don't know where life is heading. Again! And I'm scared of this second chance you are offering me because I don't know what it means – for you, for me, for the future."

It's Martha's turn to contemplate what she wants to say. I wait for her to gather her thoughts and pour us another glass of wine to lubricate the process.

"How about we take this one step at a time?" she starts, leaning forward slightly, watching me closely. "I want you to take charge of the renovations in the café. You have the most amazing ideas. I trust you.

Everything I have ever asked of you – well, you've pulled through." She points to the plans. "I like them, and I am happy for you to get on with this. Do it how you want. With my blessing. I am happy not to be involved. I have some further ideas going forward but let's do this one step at a time."

This clarification brings a measure of relief. I know where I'm at now – one step at a time. I can show her that her trust is well-placed. I can do a good job of transforming the café and help her business to move forward – at least into the twenty-first century. I can do this.

23

We all meet up at the café on Friday at eight in the morning – me, and my willing volunteers, Daniel, Sally, and Ricky – and I begin to explain how the day will work out.

"First thing is to get all the chairs and tables out into the alleyway. Sally, you're in charge of painting them the various colours, like we discussed yesterday?"

Sally gives an enthusiastic thumbs up. Our conversation had included which chairs and tables to keep, and which ones were to be thrown away and replaced.

"We need to empty everything else out of here. Some stuff can go into the kitchen and some outside into the shed or in the alleyway, in the rubbish bin—"

"Trash—"

"Rubbish bin, Sally. It's a rubbish bin! We need to empty this place. Then Daniel and Ricky, you have the job of dealing with the counter. Daniel, you have all the sizes and plans, right?"

He nods then asks, "And you?"

He grins and turns his baseball cap around so that the brim is at the nape of his neck. It looks so cute. Too cute!

"Me? Well, I am in charge—"

"Obviously!" Sally quips before I can finish.

Ricky snorts with laughter.

"I have a job too!" I state indignantly. "I am going to start drawing out the mural on the wall."

"That's OK then!" Daniel nudges Sally and winks at me.

I know they are teasing but hey… I blush profusely. This man!

"And we can get together at lunchtime and see how everything is going."

I hastily bundle everyone out of the way and on to their various assignments. It seems the whole place is in motion. Engrossed in our various tasks, the time passes peacefully as we are accompanied by the music from the radio.

Martha swans through the building around eleven, telling us all that we are "doing a fine job" and promises to be back later, then swans out again. Stan arrives a couple of minutes later offering to help and Sally commandeers him to assist with the task of painting tables and chairs. Seeing the two of them sitting together, quietly chatting and painting, it warms my hearts. Now we are complete.

Absorbed in the initial drawing out of the mural – the paper plan laid out on the floor and a grid drawn on the walls to ensure the drawing is to scale – I stand back to check the perspective, check that the sketch is working out as planned and looks right from all angles. I am scrutinising the area of wall by the front door when I sense Daniel standing behind me, inspecting it too. His proximity is still a little unsettling, though thankfully does not provoke a full-scale panic attack, although the fluttering continues. I just wish he wouldn't stand so close!

"You happy?" he asks.

"I think so. What do you think?"

"It's good. Is that supposed to be on the slant like that?" he points.

I check the sketch and the grid. "Yep. Does it look wrong?"

He takes another look. "I'll reserve judgement 'til it's all drawn out. Call me when you're done," he says as he walks away.

"Reserve judgement?" I laugh at his retreating back.

"Yep," he calls over his shoulder.

By lunchtime, satisfied with our progress, Martha returns as promised, bringing lunch which we all eat together, a happy band of workers, sitting in the alleyway where the sun was exceptionally bright. Martha is dressed in her usual linen outfit – today an emerald green. My landlady and boss, but also and more importantly, she is my friend. Second chances, eh? She catches my eye when she notices that I am watching everyone and she tips her head to one side – curious, enquiring. We smile at each other knowingly.

I rest my head against the brick wall and let me eyes flit over these people, my 'little team', who I now spend part of almost every day. Stan, a full head of white hair cropped in a military cut, dressed in old blue jeans and a flannel check shirt. I have come to admire this quiet, honourable man who is content to be around us all. He smiles readily, seems to be enjoying himself. Sitting next to him is Sally, with her ponytail bobbing as she chats. She is dressed in dungarees and is looking gorgeous – a confident young girl. Her boyfriend, Ricky, who (it turns out) is hardworking with a skill in carpentry. A useful, quiet, unassuming young man who seems to hero-worship Daniel and is happy to be included. And finally, there's Daniel with his Patriots baseball cap on backwards, white T-shirt, scruffy old jeans, and trainers (or as he would say – sneakers), scanning his mobile (or as he would say – cellphone). He has worked hard on this project, right from the beginning, with his initial advice and the architectural drawings he produced which enhanced but did not alter my original design. He has proven himself to be trustworthy and dependable during this whole renovation project and, to my astonishment, I find I am relying on him. The fact that he is slowly exerting his influence in a gentle way is acceptable; he is project managing my design. I am surprised that I feel comfortable with accepting this because he appears to be doing it instinctively and not with any purpose or ulterior motive. I guess it's how he is.

I stretch and stand up. "Let's get back to work."

Stan excuses himself with a promise to return tomorrow morning. We hug him and thank him and are rewarded with a grin and blown kisses.

"Do we all have something productive to get on with this afternoon?" Daniel asks.

Everyone thinks they do so we get back to our individual tasks. For me it is the mural and more drawing. Daniel checks on my progress regularly during the afternoon, always standing close by, making me feel light-headed. Sometimes leaning in, sending my pulse rate soaring.

At the end of the day, we have all accomplished more than we had hoped when we started this morning. The counter has been removed (amid much banging, noise and dust), the mural is nearly drawn in, and nearly all of the furniture has been painted. So, we go our separate ways with the agreement to start again tomorrow at seven – despite Ricky protesting that "it's Friday night, man!"

I decide to go for a run, listening to music, but no tears this time – just the sheer exhilaration of running in a beautiful environment after a hard day's work. I am invigorated.

On Saturday, the early start does not turn out as planned because Martha arrives with huge breakfast rolls. She seems to consider her role in all this is to feed us and we don't actually get down to doing any work until after eight. But as everyone is relaxed, I do my best to suppress the worry that we might not get all the work done on time.

I move back to my mural, having had the OK from Daniel, who tells me, "It's pretty good – could do with a bit more work though!"

My eyebrows raise slightly, and Sally laughs at us.

"He's teasing," she states. "Stop taking everything so seriously!"

I hear the familiar chuckle and Daniel pats my shoulder reassuringly before returning to his task. Standing in front of the wall – everything has been drawn in – I sigh deeply. Satisfied with how it looks, ready to paint, I prise open the lids of the paint pots, choose my brush and start by the front door, moving from right to left up the wall towards the counter.

Ricky, having cleaned up all the dust created by removing the counter, is standing with Daniel discussing their plan of action for the morning. They decide that before a rebuild it might be a good idea to whitewash all the walls that won't be covered by the mural and the ceiling. This mammoth task begins at the other end of the room so as not to disturb me.

As they get closer, I worry about splashes of paint on my mural.

"It's OK," Daniel assures me. "We'll be careful."

As I cannot protect the mural, I put a barrier of chairs in front of what's been painted and decide to leave the room just in case. I am too nervous to watch them. Emerging into the alleyway, the heat of the day is intense and hits me as I open the door. Sally has retreated into the shade thrown across by the building next door.

"Hi, how's it going?" I ask, leaning back on the wall. I can see that all the furniture we decided to keep has been transformed from 1980s honey pine to pastel shades of blue, grey, green, and antique white.

"I think I'm nearly done painting"—Sally surveys the alleyway— "now they all need varnishing and we're done. How about you – how's it going in there?"

I give her an update and add, "Daniel said it all needs two coats so I'm not sure how long that will take or how much more I'll be able to do to the mural to be honest." The nerves start to surface again. "Then when they've given the whole place two coats..."

I sit down on the step and wipe the sweat from my forehead. Worry hits me again, unexpected issues. Will it be done on time? Can I carry this off?

"It'll be fine – it'll all work out fine." Sally senses my mood and pats my hand. "We'll get it sorted."

"I hope they can get the painting done quickly so I can get back to work. I need them to get the countertops and cupboards in today as the sparky is coming tomorrow to do the electrics and put the sockets in their new places and put the coffee machine in. The plumber is due in the afternoon." I am thinking aloud.

"Why don't you get your schedule of works out and check it?"

She can see my confidence is slipping with every word and is trying to reassure me. She has a mature head on her shoulders for a young girl.

"You're right."

I groan as I stand up and head upstairs to my apartment to consult the plans. I take time to settle and find comfort in the peace and quiet of the apartment. I check and recheck. We are on schedule. I feel myself becoming calmer. A little. For a short time.

"Jane!" Daniel yells.

I flinch then rush outside and down the steps, my heart thumping furiously.

"We have a problem."

24

"You know when we took out the end of the counter yesterday, well it appears that the floor behind the counter was slightly higher than in front, so that'll have to be levelled out somehow before the new floor can be laid on Monday."

Daniel shows me as we both stand in the middle of the room. There is a distinct change in the height of the floor and the tiles behind are thicker, cracked, the wood in front old and splintered. It looks a mess.

"You're kidding me!" I state. "Surely you would have known that before, known the floor was on different levels?" I look up at him.

A muscle in his cheek clenches. "Not really," he tells me. "It's appeared because the counter is going to be shorter now—"

"So, you measured it wrong!" I accuse.

"No!" He takes a step back and gathers himself. "I measured it right, and you agreed the measurement was correct."

We take a moment to look at each other. I hold my breath. I don't need an argument with this man, and I shouldn't be taking it out on him. He takes a further step back and quietly deflects my attention by telling me the room only needed one coat of paint. I hadn't noticed and I should have. He's done a fine job. I wrench my eyes away from the floor and glance around. The room looks bigger somehow, the walls and ceiling all the same colour. Any pride he had in this job well done has evaporated.

"So, what are we going to do about the floor?" I ask him, not yet ready to apologise and still stressed that we have this extra issue to deal with.

He explains what he has in mind, and I tell him to go ahead and get it done. The tension between us still exists and the air tingles with it as I walk away, back through the alleyway and up the stairs, ignoring Sally as I go.

To be the first inside the café on Sunday morning will give me the chance to view the almost completed mural in peace, to check for any imperfections and slanting walls. Also, I want to make sure everything is ready before the arrival of the electrician and plumber. The floor issue has been dealt with, and I ate humble pie, allowing Daniel and I to part on good terms last night. Thankfully.

But when I get there, Daniel is already at work, bending down by the counter, checking, and inspecting the work he completed yesterday.

"Hello." I am surprised to see him and berate myself for staring a moment longer than necessary at his bum in the scruffy jeans. Nice!

"Morning!" he replies cheerily without raising his head from what he is doing.

I'm glad he cannot see the pink flush on my face. "You're early."

"Yep" — his voice is muffled as he moves further under the counter — "just checking stuff."

I study him closely, my eyes roaming over every aspect of him and wait for him to finish. Eventually, he slides out from under the counter and stands up. Stands close. He grins at me, knowing full well the effect it has on me, like he knows what I've been doing.

"Yep, it's OK."

"Good." I step away. I take a deep breath and repeat the words I've been saying over and over most of the night. "I'm sorry for the way I behaved yesterday," I tell him. Just to make sure.

All afternoon the atmosphere had been strained. We had worked hard and accomplished much, including the leveling off of the floor, but I had been begrudging in my praise and gratitude and slept badly as a result.

"I shouldn't have acted the way I did, and I should

have shown more appreciation." I glance at him.

He continues to smile at me.

"I'm sorry."

"Apology accepted."

He moves to pass me, and I instinctively take his hand to stop him. "I mean it."

"I know you do."

Suddenly he leans in and kisses my cheek, taking me totally by surprise.

When I have recovered (at least partially), drunk my first cup of hot coffee, and learned how to breathe normally, I ask him if he thinks we will get all the necessary jobs done today.

"I hope so, barring any more uneven floor issues."

I blush slightly.

"I gotta be back in the city in the morning and Ricky has to go to work. But yes, I think we will get most of it done. When is the guy coming to lay the floor?"

"Tomorrow. It's likely to take him all day."

"And when is the guy coming to sort out the lights?"

"He's supposed to be coming Tuesday morning and the bits of furniture I ordered are coming Tuesday afternoon. Martha wants us to re-open on Wednesday." I want to ask him if he will be around but hesitate. It's none of my business what he does and where he is.

Everyone else arriving stops our conversation and we all get back to work with the radio turned up loud. I catch sight of Ricky and Sally dancing together. They are a strange couple, in the sense that she is confident, open, and sometimes impetuous, and he seems introvert, closed and thoughtful in all he does and says – which to me, is still as little as possible. But it's an intimate moment and they look a couple who are deeply in love and happy. He kisses her cheek and she wrinkles her nose then throws back her head to laugh. Stan cuts in and demands she dance with him. She is kind and caring to the old man. I like her. She's a lovely girl. I can hear Daniel singing along to the tunes in the kitchen (Martha is right – he can sing) and I smile to myself. These are heart-warming memories to cherish (to take home with me?) and the unexpected feeling of contentment returns, the earlier tension has gone. Surveying my mural, my smile widens. It is good.

Suddenly Daniel is next to me. Standing close. He smells of sandalwood and sawdust.

"Coffee?" He offers me a mug.

"Thanks." I inhale the rich aroma and blow on the liquid; I need the caffeine.

"I like it," he states. "I like the way you carried it over the counter and across the top of the wall there." He points then looks at me.

He smiles slowly and I see the skin around his eyes crease. He smiles a lot, I can tell. He chuckles softly – a warm, familiar sound. And in that moment, something sparks between us. There is the sudden realisation – *Oh boy! I may be in trouble* – and it scares the living daylights out of me.

Martha's phone pings.

"Daniel wants to know if I have your phone number."

We are standing in the café later that evening after all the day's work is completed and everyone has gone home. Everything that should have been done – according to the schedule – has been done. Martha has been telling me how proud she is of all that has been achieved. How pleased she is with the work we have accomplished. I am reassured.

"Why?" I ask.

"I guess he wants to call you!"

I stare at her and try and figure out what it all means as she holds my gaze.

"Can I give it to him?"

"Why not – go ahead."

My phone pings within minutes. It is Daniel: 'Would you like to go to the Picnic in the Park with me?'

I show Martha the text. "Do you want to come too?" I ask her.

She laughs loudly. "Jane, it's a date! You go – he hasn't invited me. If he wanted me to go, he would have asked me first and then asked if you wanted to tag along. It's a date, dear girl!"

I stare at the phone – A DATE?

"Answer him then!"

As I do so my phone buzzes and it's a text from Katie, asking me how things are going. I reply to her first as I'm grateful we are again on speaking (texting) terms. Besides, I'm not ready to reply to his invitation. Daniel can wait!

I take some photographs and send them over to help her understand my words.

We open again on Wednesday. And how are you doing? You OK? 19.10

I'm glad everything went according to plan for Mrs. Organized but then I expect nothing less! You can always get things sorted. You sound really happy, my friend. I'm glad. I miss you x 19.20

Miss you too. Wish you were here to see this x 19.22

Me too. But you never know....... 19.23

25

Tuesday morning, I venture downstairs to check out the floor which the guy took all day yesterday to lay. It is incredible: the oak boards have been laid from front to back and give the illusion of length to the whole café. The electrician returns to fix the beautiful light shades that I found online. The metal shades have an industrial look, dark grey on the outside and white enamel inside with an exposed light bulb. They are different in size, some larger ones over the counter and smaller ones dotted around the room, interspersed with inset ceiling lights. I am so thrilled with how they transform the space.

When the books are delivered from the Blue Brolly Bookshop, I arrange them on the shelves in groups by the colour of their spines, from white through grey into charcoal and black. From red through orange into ochre and yellow then lemon. From purple into lilac and pale blue into indigo. Tweak, tweak. Love it! I then arrange some book ends and a few of the 'antiques' I picked up in the local store. In England an antique must be at least a hundred years old to be thus labelled and, given the history which stretches back way beyond Roman times, there are a lot of antiques around. In the US, however, anything which dates back to the Second World War seems to be classed as an antique, and frankly, it includes a lot of dross and forgettable items. When I went shopping for objects to display in the café, I wanted something special, something unique, and it was decidedly hard to find. Saying that, I am pleased with my purchases – though I doubt they are actually antiques! There are a couple of beautiful picture frames, some glass vases and bottles, candlesticks, lamp stands and ornaments, and I spend a happy hour arranging them with the books on the shelves at the back of the room.

I am about to finish and pack away all the boxes that the ornaments and books came in when the leather sofa, chairs and coffee table arrive. They are the finishing touch. The plans and the mood board were good, but the reality is perfect. I wanted to create a certain atmosphere: welcoming and homely, yet relaxing; rustic but modern, with wood and pale colours. I want people to sit and chat (and drink coffee!) and be comfortable. I think I've done that.

The electrician joins me in admiring what has been achieved.

"Looks real nice, ma'am," he comments.

"Thank you! I think so too."

"So, when do you open again?"

"Tomorrow morning." I turn and ask, "Would you like to come in and have a complimentary afternoon tea?"

"Yep! I'll take you up on that."

We shake hands.

"I love the lights."

He is not so sure. "They do make a difference. Unusual choice but I like them."

But even his lack of enthusiasm cannot dampen my spirits. Maybe I am starting to find my confidence, starting to find me.

Once he has packed up his tools and left, I am alone in the café. I wander around, gently running my fingers over the furniture, stroking the cushions – the colours of which match the tables and chairs – and generally absorbing the new atmosphere. It is very different. And, I think, rather lovely. I am proud of what I have helped to create. Pictures are WhatsApp'd to Katie as promised and also sent to Mum and Dad, along with a promise to Skype them tomorrow as planned. I enjoy our weekly catch up and the reassurance they give me now and have done in the past whenever my confidence slipped. They will be pleased to see the old me finally re-emerging step by step from the struggles of my past – like a butterfly from a chrysalis.

During the afternoon the humidity starts to rise, and it is hot. My apartment is an unpleasant place to be, because even with all the windows open there is no breeze, and with all the windows shut it is stifling and oppressive. So, I pack a small bag with a bottle of water, a book and towel, and head for the beach, where I hope it will be a little cooler.

It is crammed full of folks, all with the same idea and only by walking right to the far end of the beach do I manage to find some space to myself. I sit and breathe in the familiar sea air and feel my shoulders relax. We did it! We took the drawings and made it real. I am proud of myself and thankful to the others for helping. All I need now is for Martha to love it too.

That evening, I am back downstairs in the café because I want to be there when Martha arrives. I am nervous. What if she doesn't like it? At exactly the time she said she would be there, Martha sweeps in through the kitchen door, wearing the most amazing red linen outfit with a red band tied around her head, her dark curls fighting to escape. She certainly knows how to make an entrance and my admiration grows for this woman who is transforming my life.

"Are you ready for me to see the final result?" she

asks.

No preamble. No small talk – straight down to business, her business in my hands. My insides pulsate with anxiety. I nod without speaking and she sweeps past me. I follow in her wake.

She stops just inside and surveys the room then wanders around. Over to the sofa, where she runs her hand along the soft brown leather. Then to the shelves, where she picks up a glass bottle and carefully replaces it where she found it. Drifting through the café slowly, looking. Silent. At the front door she turns. Arms folded. Face determined.

"It is awesome!" She grins then comes towards me and takes both my hands in hers. "Dear girl, it is truly wonderful! I love it."

I don't know whether to laugh or cry.

"And yes, you may hug me!"

Despite the humidity, I am able to sleep well and indulge myself with a short lie-in, deciding to give running a miss for today. Stretching my weary body, I think about Jon for what appears to be the first time in – oh, I cannot remember the last time I thought about him. I smile, knowing that I do not need to think about him every day, not now, and reflecting about the past does not bring a pain above my eyes, not now. Yes, I miss him, but in the sense that I would like to be able to share these experiences with him and I would like to know how he feels about what is going on and what is happening to me. I would like him to meet my new friends and see my new life as it unfolds. I no longer ache for him. Not now.

We start the working day with a staff meeting (with no agenda) and a pep talk. All of us are excited to get to work. We have made the cakes, set up the cake stands ready for the lunch menu, and we are ready.

The door opens at ten and the electrician arrives for his complimentary afternoon tea. I try to explain the fact that it is called afternoon tea for a reason, but he simply stares at me and shrugs. Maybe this will not work with Americans after all?

He is proud to be our first customer and takes lots of selfies with us (except for Martha, who refuses point-blank) and before leaving tells us he will give us a five-star rating on TripAdvisor. Then it all goes quiet, and I start to get anxious. Not straight away, but panic creeps over me as the clock moves towards noon.

"Do you think anyone will come?" I ask Sally, rearranging the already arranged pastries on the counter. "We did send out all the invites, didn't we?"

"I delivered them yesterday. No problem."

"To everyone on Main Street?"

"Hey, don't worry. Wednesdays are always quiet like this."

"Do you think we were closed too long? Maybe we should have opened again on Monday?"

A minute later I ask, "Do you think our customers have gone to the other café down the road? Go and see."

"No way, man!" Sally exclaims. "Look! Stop frettin', will you?"

"I think it's because its afternoon tea, people think they have to come in the afternoon only. Yes, that's it."

"Jane! Be quiet!" She shakes her head in despair.

Then eventually, the people come. They order their normal sandwiches and lunches, but many of them order afternoon tea and are amazed at the food we serve them. They make nice comments. They take lots of pictures. The place starts to buzz with the sound of conversation, the clinking of cups on saucers, the hissing of the coffee machine. Sounds, sights, and smells of a busy café. Panic recedes and calm sets in. We are going to be OK.

Later in the day when it is showing four on the clock above the counter, I am pleased to see that we are still full of happy customers: families, a couple with their heads close together, a guy working on his laptop amid the bustle and noise. The ethos of the vision is taking shape, things are finally in place and a sense of excitement bubbles inside. Martha states that we should stay open until five and see what happens, so we soldier on serving cake and sandwiches until we almost run out of food.

Slowly the café empties and by five o'clock everyone has gone. There is just the three of us left. Martha turns the sign over, locks the front door and we all breathe a sigh of relief.

"Well, considering you were worried at eleven this morning, Jane, it's been a wonderful day!" Sally says as she throws herself onto the sofa and puts her feet up on the coffee table.

Martha joins her and I bring over some welcome cups of tea and the last remnants of cake crumbs as a reward for our hard work.

"We took more today than any day this summer." Martha catches sight of my stunned face. "Yes, more than July fourth! I am amazed. I think this day has been a resounding success. Good job, girls!"

She raises her cup to salute us as her phone pings. She smiles as she looks at the screen and turns the phone to show me a picture of Stan holding a huge fish. "Seems like he had a good day too!" She sends a message. There is an immediate response. She smiles again. "OK girls, let's get cleared up."

Sally groans but starts to clean away the trays and cake stands as I head to the kitchen to load the newly installed industrial dishwasher. Martha catches my hand as I go past.

"I invited Stan to bring the fish over. I thought we

might have dinner together here as a celebration. I have some champagne on ice for such an occasion. You up for that?"

"As long as I don't have to gut the thing, sure!"

"No worries, Daniel will do that."

Daniel! She did not say anything about Daniel. She said Stan had caught the fish. She invited Stan over.

"What time will they be here?" I ask.

"Around six thirty. They'll go fetch Shirley first." She smiles at me and anticipates my inner conversation. "And yes, that does give you time to get changed and showered!" She laughs.

"He sees me as I am!" I retort. I am not making a special effort for him. Black jeans and black T-shirt and apron are what he gets!

I do make a certain amount of effort, I cannot help myself as I gather enough plates, napkins, wine glasses, tea lights and pretty glass holders from upstairs to make the table presentable for dinner. Setting the table to make an impression is incredibly important. But a good impression for who? That is the question. I also bring down the obligatory fairy lights and string them around the shelves at the back of the room, all the time telling myself I am doing it to impress Stan and Shirley. Right!

Just after six thirty, Daniel comes in through the

door with the large fish in a bag which he dumps in the sink before he disappears back outside. When Stan and Shirley enter, I hug them warmly and show them to their seats, leaving them to chat with Martha.

"The table looks lovely, my dear." Shirley pats my hand and smiles. "I love what you've done to the place, Jane, it is beautiful."

I kiss her soft velvety cheek and thank her for noticing and appreciating the effort.

Stan nods his agreement and puts his arm around my shoulder. He squeezes me gently.

"Well done," he whispers.

Back in the kitchen, I find Daniel sitting on the back doorstep filleting the fish. I pop my head around at the precise moment he is gutting it.

"That's disgusting!"

He laughs. "You get used to it."

"I don't think so! Nor the smell!" I retreat inside and get on with preparing the rest of the meal of potatoes, carrots, kale, and sweetcorn.

"How do you want to cook it?" I ask him when he brings in the perfectly filleted pieces of fish.

"Why don't we seal the skin in a griddle pan and then put them into the oven to cook. You got some lemons? Almonds?"

While he is cooking, I take a look in the café. Martha has opened the champagne, and everyone is chatting away happily, so I retreat back to the kitchen so as not to disturb them and ask Daniel, "Where did you learn to fillet fish like that?"

"I grew up on a ranch in Montana and my dad always took me and my brothers fishing in the summer. He taught me how to do it." His tone is light, but I notice his shoulders hitch slightly.

"How many brothers do you have?"

"Two. Rob, he's the eldest, he runs the ranch now. Then there's me in the middle and my younger brother, Mark."

"You didn't fancy being a cowboy then?""

"Nope!" He falls silent after this sharp reply.

I sense a reluctance to talk about things so decide to change the subject and ask him about something else. "So, when did you move to Boston?"

"Right after I graduated from Harvard. I got a job with McNeil Carpenter after doing an internship with them, found a place to live and…" He pauses and bounces slowly on the balls of his feet.

I sense that again I have hit on another topic that is making him uncomfortable. He doesn't look up from sprinkling almond flakes over the fish, so I try a different approach.

"Do you want a drink? A glass of champagne?"

The change of subject brings a smile of relief and a nod.

"Why didn't you fancy being a cowboy?" I ask him as I pour us each a glass. I cannot help myself as I am intrigued. This complicated man who is so open, kind and giving, yet seems to have many family secrets that he wishes to keep hidden.

"It's not for me. Oh, don't get me wrong, I love the wide-open spaces – the land out in Montana is beautiful, and the mountains are spectacular, but that's one tough kinda life and you gotta love it. It's not for me. I'm much more a city boy"—he pauses, plates in hand— "but, you know, the older I get the more I think I'm the kinda guy who likes hanging around cafés with pretty women and goin' fishing."

He smiles and I blush as he eases past me to join the others. Serves me right for asking.

The five of us sit down for the evening meal, with Shirley, dressed in a pale pink floral summer dress, bagging her seat next to her 'toy-boy' – much to everyone's amusement. The table is pretty with the tea lights lit, and with a fresh bottle of wine poured, we chat and laugh, relaxed and happy.

I survey the table and count my blessings that I have found such good friends. I came to Oakham invisible, unknown, ready for a new adventure, and for now I have a new life, a happy, contented life. Unexpected, but so welcome. My confidence is returning – though it evaporates in a heartbeat as soon as that nagging voice in my head pipes up or someone says something mean, but on balance this positive thinking is starting to work! The residents of Oakham, and particularly these folks here, have simply absorbed me into their midst and are so nurturing and supportive.

"What are you thinking?" Daniel leans closer and whispers, his breath on my cheek.

His green eyes, bright with flashes of gold, hold mine a moment longer than is necessary and I question how much to let him in, ignoring the warm glow inside that seems to have replaced the fluttering.

"I am thinking how lucky I am to have found such good friends." I turn away and look at the others.

"They're good people," he pauses a moment then adds, "Martha's like a sister to me, a sister I never had growing up surrounded by men, cowboys. She really helped me to see how it's possible to be friends with a woman. Just friends."

I fleetingly wonder if this is telling me something. Just friends?

"At first I thought you two were a couple."

Daniel looks shocked.

"What?" Martha asks, looking over at us.

"Nothing!" we both reply together.

"No," he says, his voice low. "Only friends." He smiles.

So, he's not telling me – or is he?

Stan glances over and tilts his head on one side, contemplating us from the other end of the table.

Daniel laughs. "Jane was telling me how lucky she is to have such good friends."

I slap his arm. "Daniel!"

"She's damn right!" Stan exclaims. "We're not friends with just anyone you know!"

"And they," Daniel whispers, his breath warm on my cheek, "are like my family, more like my parents than my mom and dad ever were."

Now I'm curious. I shiver. He moves away slightly. The moment over.

Daniel and Stan are commandeered into doing the washing up while the ladies continue to chat. The night is a little cooler and there is a faint breeze which should help with sleeping if I leave the windows open for it to pass freely through the apartment.

"I'll walk you home," Daniel offers.

"I live right here!" I point out the obvious.

"I… I know where you live…"

I realise I'd missed the point, and a flutter of anxiety fills my chest. Please don't spoil a lovely day. I shrug an agreement.

We stand at the bottom of the steps. We are alone. In the dark. There is a change in the space between us. We are less relaxed. Unsure. The words 'just friends' flits through my brain. This isn't 'just friends', is it?

"You did a great job with the café," he tells me. "The little finishing touches make all the difference." I begin to play down my role, and he stops me mid-flow. "Accept the praise. Have confidence in your abilities."

I reluctantly accept and smile.

He turns to leave, hesitates, and adds, "Thank you."

"For what?"

"For coming to Oakham"—he pauses— "for being a good friend to people that mean a lot to me."

"I'll take that. Well, good night."

"Night. See you Sunday?"

"Sure." *Oh yes, the Picnic in the Park. Oh dear, is that a date? Oh no. A date!* "Sure," I repeat.

26

"Martha, you know I'm going to the Picnic in the Park with Daniel—" I pause.

Before I can continue, she interrupts. "Nice. Enjoy."

I can see she is pre-occupied, somewhere else mentally, sipping from her huge coffee mug, but I plough on regardless, getting straight to the point.

"Martha, I need to talk to you."

She looks at me.

"You're my friend."

I see her expression soften.

"Talk to me… please. Tell me about him; you're his friend too. What do I need to know? He's not married, is he?" I know I've been told his wife left him, but he might still be married.

She doesn't say a word as she regards me carefully.

Oh no! He is!

"No," she says thoughtfully.

Phew.

"He's divorced."

I wait.

"Five years ago."

I pause a moment to take this in. "I didn't know – there's so much I don't know…but then again I guess he doesn't know much about me either."

"It is only a date! Do you want a full résumé?"

"It's not a date," I state firmly.

"Whatever." She sighs then puts her cup into the sink and bustles out of the kitchen. "Come with me!"

I follow her billowing purple linen outfit into the café, where she flops down onto the leather sofa. I sit in the armchair opposite. And wait.

"Daniel did ask me if you are married. He kinda figured you couldn't be, what with leaving the UK for six months, but he wanted reassurance, like you – so I told him that no, you're not married. I didn't offer any further information and you'll have to fill in all the gaps when the time is right."

I look down at my clenched hands, my knuckles white.

"I know I am overthinking this, the same way as I overthink everything else, but I am struggling…" My voice fades.

"Why? It's only a date."

"I know." I have to start admitting to myself that yes, it's a date. "But it's, well, it's Daniel – oh, I don't know. I am not a confident, hold-it-all-together kind of woman like you are. I have only just got used to having him in the same room without jumping at his every move. He stands so close to me sometimes and it's totally unsettling, though I kind of like it too! We were becoming friends and then he goes and asks me out and changes the whole ball game. And he is far too attractive for his own good!"

Martha laughs and rolls her eyes. "Oh boy!" She leans forward, peels my taut fingers apart and gently takes my hand. "Listen," her voice soft, "all you need to know is that he is a good man and in the last five years he hasn't so much as looked at another woman." Abruptly, she sits up straight and normal service is resumed. "He's my friend so don't you go messing with his heart or with his head!" she threatens and wags a finger, smiling at the same time. "Why not let things unfold naturally." She pauses and examines my face. "I can't believe that I am giving you life lessons.

"I know. But I haven't been on a first date for decades."

"And neither has he; he'll be uptight about this too, but he must want to spend time with you, or I'd be going to the picnic!"

As much as I understand what Martha is saying, I'm not quite ready to stop finding out more.

"And why is he uncomfortable about talking about his family in Montana?"

"Ah, now that's a whole different story. Again, you will have to ask him."

"I've tried."

I can see Martha contemplating what to say next. "It's all about trust. His home life back on the ranch, his family, his ex-wife. It's all about trust and the two major women in his past – his mom and his ex, they both had an agenda. But when he trusts you, he'll tell you. OK?" She puts her hands up. "And I am saying nothing else on this or any other matter concerning Daniel. OK?"

I open the wardrobe doors wide – what to wear? Martha says it's a date – and I suppose it is — but I'm so mixed up. I thought Daniel and I were just friends, he said 'just friends', right – but what to wear?

Stepping back, I consider the contents – there are more clothes here than I brought with me from England and I briefly worry about getting them all back in my suitcase when it's time to return. What would Katie wear? She is always dressed appropriately for any occasion. But this is a first date? No. It. Is. Not! But yes, it is – oh indecisiveness!

Anxiety takes hold, so I close the wardrobe doors, leave the room, and slam the bedroom door for good measure – though no-one is there to appreciate it but me. It gives a satisfying resounding crack. Over by the window, I look out over the park – the scene of the first date. IT IS NOT A DATE! I could have declined the invite. I could have said no, but part of me wants to go – despite or in spite of this inner turmoil.

After a shower to clear my mind, I settle on a pair of white cut-off jeans, sandals and a three-quarter sleeve linen tunic. I am ready far too early and glance again in the mirror. My hair, longer than it has been for a long time, has lighter streaks amongst the waves. My make-up – I examine my eyes – is ample. I wish my eyelashes were longer, but hey!

I sit at my window overlooking the park as people gather for the evening, picnic baskets and coolers in hand, placing blankets on the ground. Daniel hadn't mentioned either and I can only assume he will bring them. This is happening, there is no denying it. My heart beats a little faster and there is a slight buzz of excitement like the buzz I felt on my first date with Jon – a link with the past, a memory that takes me down a path I'm not sure I want to go down today, but I am pleasantly relieved not to feel any anxiety at the memory, only a distance and nostalgia.

University in Liverpool, he took me on the ferry across the Mersey and sang the song by Gerry and the Pacemakers (badly) the whole way across to Birkenhead. Somehow it endeared him to me. He was making an effort; he held my hand and I felt safe. Here. Today. It is different.

Never patient at the best of times, waiting is tortuous. Why did I get dressed so early? Watching, waiting, wishing I could be cool and calm about the whole thing. I am thirty-six years old, for goodness' sake, and it's not like I've never been on a first date before. *Am I overdressed or underdressed? Is there time to change?*

I hear a vehicle draw to a stop in the alleyway between the café and the dress shop and I rush to the kitchen window to see Daniel emerging from the pick-up truck. My heart skips a beat – no going back now. I take a final glimpse in the mirror, pick up my bag, lock the door. On my way down the steps, he catches sight of me and his face breaks into a huge smile. I am taken aback by the fact that he is so pleased to see me. Maybe he thought I might back out and it is a look of relief.

"Hi." He reaches into the back of the pick-up and hands me a blanket.

"Hello."

He reaches in again and comes out with a large blue and white cooler. "Shall we find some place to sit?"

There is a spot of vacant grass under the shade of a huge oak tree. The bandstand is situated in a natural dip and there are people, chairs and blankets arrayed in a huge semi-circle, all with a great view. He puts down the cooler and I hand back the blanket, which he lays on the ground. It doesn't look very big, and I momentarily panic at the thought of having to sit so close to him. I guess he senses my hesitation, because he moves the cooler and sits down on the edge of the blanket, looking up at me expectantly.

"You can sit down. I won't bite!"

He grins at me and again I wish I could be cool, calm and collected, or at least a little more sophisticated. Carefully, I sit down, close but not too close. All this is outside my comfort zone, it's like being a teenager again. I much preferred it when we were friends and not on a date, but I can see he is trying to help me relax and yet at the same time he appears unsure as to how to react towards me. It's all rather exhausting and I contemplate getting up and leaving. Before I can follow through on that thought he offers me a drink.

"Great idea!" Relief. Alcohol. That might help.

"Beer? Wine?"

"Beer please."

Now he has something to do. He takes two bottles of Bud out of the cooler, opens them and hands me one. I thank him and watch him unload the china plates, napkins, cutlery, bowls of salad, rice, some cheese, and a bowl of big red strawberries. I am impressed; he has put some thought and effort into this.

"This is lovely, thank you," I tell him, helping myself to a few things to settle the butterflies in my stomach and the bubbles from the beer.

Thankfully it works as I slowly begin to sense a small measure of relaxation as I enjoy the food, the beer and his company. The park is lined with trees and at the edges of the paths there are a few flower beds, but mostly it's acres of grass. There's lots of children and families and the air is filled with the aroma of meat on a barbeque. This could be fun.

"How was Boston?" I ask.

"Hot. Too hot. And busy." He finishes his beer and opens a fresh bottle. "You want another?"

I shake my head as I am only halfway through mine.

"Yeah, busy. I am closing a big contract right now and meeting the client every day. I guess that's fine 'cause we can meet in my office, which is air-conditioned, but getting out onto site is a nightmare with this humidity. I'm getting through two or three shirts a day. I much prefer to be dressed like this"—he indicates towards his shorts and T-shirt— "than be all dressed up in a suit. It's a nightmare! But it's all nearly finished, just a few loose ends to tie up on Monday and I am done for the summer."

"What then? Are you moving out here?"

"Yep. Can't wait. Fishing and relaxing and maybe I'll come do some painting with you?"

"To tell the truth, I'm not getting much painting done right now. The café is so busy. The new menu is very popular, and we have folks in all day every day. I definitely need to re-negotiate my contract with Martha. Not that I have a contract per se, because she doesn't actually pay me much."

He looks amazed so I quickly elaborate.

"But then I do get to live upstairs at way below the market rate, thank goodness. I'd never be able to afford it otherwise." I contemplate telling him about camping on the café floor and the fear but no, not now. "It works for both of us, but initially I only agreed to work two days a week and one day at the weekend if the place was busy, and now it's like I'm there almost every day. Last week I only got one day off, and I slept most of that day – oh, I tell a lie, I got Tuesday afternoon off and went to the beach."

"Sounds like you need to put your foot down."

"With Martha? Are you sure?" I laugh.

"True."

We eat. We talk. I feel more settled, not quite relaxed but I'm getting there and looking around at everyone enjoying themselves, I tell myself to lighten up. Enjoy!

I recall the conversation with Martha but want to hear it from him. "Can I ask you a personal question?"

"Sure, go ahead."

"You're not married, are you?"

He holds my gaze, green eyes on blue eyes, for a really long moment. More than a moment. "No. Divorced. Five years. You?"

I continue to watch him for a reaction as I reply, "Not now. No."

Relief. I see relief. We drag our gaze elsewhere and digest the information: we are both free agents yet tied to our past.

The band comes out onto the bandstand at about nine and although they are slow to engage with the crowd, the music is good, and once people have finished eating, they start to become more involved, clapping and singing along. Some of them get up and dance — alone, together. Some gently sway to the music. I am back into the should I/shouldn't I discussion in my head when a new song starts which begs for you to dance along, but before I can dither, Daniel takes the decision out of my hands by leaping up, grabbing my hand, and pulling me up.

"Come dance; I love this song!"

Wow! This man can sing and dance! Everyone around us joins in. There are old couples amongst youngsters prancing around in time with the music, and it is a delightful atmosphere as the sun begins to set behind the buildings on Main Street. I can see my home; the clapboard is turning orange-peach with the last rays of light. It looks so pretty, and my heart is full of the joy of the moment. When the song finishes, I find I am still holding his hand. His eyes are sparkling with flecks of gold and green; he looks happy. Kissing the back of my hand, he finally lets go and I surprise myself by being a bit disappointed.

When the evening is drawing to a close, the music stops and the show ends, so we pack up the basket of food, I fold the blanket and we stroll back to the pickup to deposit everything in the back.

"Thank you for a great evening. I was really nervous about tonight," I admit, "but it turned out OK. I had a lot of fun."

"If it helps, I was nervous too. I haven't been on a first date since way back in college and that feels like a lifetime ago. But I think we did good."

"I think we did."

Neither of us quite know what to say or do next so I tell him 'Good night' and walk away. I sense he is still watching me, so when I open my gate onto the balcony I look back and wave. He smiles, waves, then gets into his pickup and drives away. Part of me is relieved and part of me wants to spend more time with him. There is so much I want to ask him, to find out about him.

I pour myself an extremely large G&T and sit in my rocking chair in the darkness, head back resting on a pillow, eyes closed – breathing in and out slowly, I go into my relaxation routine and become:

Mindful of what I can hear – The last few people are leaving the park: talking, singing, laughing. Happy chattering. The quieter hum of cars slowly making their way up and down Main Street. Peaceful sounds.

Mindful of what I can smell – The jasmine by my side gives off the most delicious aroma. The lingering smell of food and faint hint of sandalwood. I smile.

Mindful of my body – In the rocking chair, left foot resting on the ground, pushing gently then letting go, push and let go, rocking back and forth. My body is now relaxed and comfortable after the anxiety of earlier.

These emotions of peace and contentment are welcome, and I count the weeks since arriving in Oakham: fifteen weeks/three months plus – I am almost halfway through my trip. I do feel renewed, and I do feel happy, and yet it's a strange mix of emotions. I sip my gin, think about Daniel, and smile.

27

The next morning, I resolve to talk with Martha about the staffing situation and the fact that I am working five to six or even seven days a week.

"I wondered when you would ask me. I am amazed that you made it this far as cheap labour."

"I am not looking to get paid more," I inform her, "but I do need some extra hands to help. Please."

"Sure. No problem. Get on with it – hire a couple of folks. Just make sure they know that you are in charge."

My mouth opens yet no sound emits.

"Close your mouth, dear. Not an attractive look."

I close it.

"Put an advertisement in the window for part-time assistants and choose the ones you think will fit in here the best." She watches me. "Say something then."

"OK! Thank you!"

She smiles and shows her perfect even white teeth. "You do make me laugh!"

Within hours I have the details of seven youngsters,

mostly college students, who are interested in working with us. Me and my trusty wingman, Sally, interview all seven. One speaks only when spoken to and does not make eye contact, so I discount him. One speaks ALL THE TIME and never shuts up, so she is discounted too. Sally takes an instant dislike to one of the young girls, so she is not in the running. One older guy gives me the creeps by flirting with me constantly. I am looking for an employee not a boyfriend! That leaves three – two girls (Sophia and Amy) and a guy named Brody. We decide to give them an opportunity to prove themselves in the café the following afternoon.

First impressions are excellent as they arrive on time, dressed according to instructions with tied back hair (Sophia) and clean hands.

Brody is a well-built, broad-shouldered teenage boy, tanned, blond and handsome, and totally unaware of his good looks and the affect they appear to have on women young and old. He is clumsy in an energetic sort of way, like a faithful puppy, but his charm, his ability to bake and his cheeky grin get him the job.

"My mom will be so pleased," he admits with a slightly blush. "Get me out of the house and from under her feet. And it gets me away from my sisters. Thank you."

It turns out he has three sisters of varying ages, all of whom adore him but drive him crazy.

Sophia, her mousy-coloured hair scraped back from her fairly ordinary looking face, is quiet and shy, almost timid, especially when faced with the hissing machine, but then I completely understand that reaction having experienced it myself. However, there is something about her that I warm to straight away. As the afternoon progresses, she slowly opens up and I can see that there is potential there. She too can bake and is thrilled when Sally asks her to come and work with us. Her smile transforms her face.

Finally, tall Amy – six feet tall Amy – our Amazonian waitress, who strides around the room, efficient and capable, carrying plates and trays with ease and confidence. She's not much of a baker, informing us in no uncertain terms that she refuses to take part in any cake-making exercise. She has black cropped hair, eyes that penetrate your soul and the figure of a model. Sally is slightly in awe of her, but I like her sharp wit and intelligence and I believe she will complement the team. When she gets the job, she bounces up and down with glee, taking us all by surprise.

They all pass the test, so with three of them hired to work a day and a half each, I am thus freeing up my time to manage the place and go painting (the walls are empty again as sales are good). We inform Martha of what we have decided and are jointly proud of her response. "Good job!"

I interrupt my evening run to watch the sun setting over the ocean. The dazzling colours make my heart soar — pinks, crimsons, and oranges — they look like the sunsets my dad taught me to paint when I was a young child, like the sunsets Jon and I would gaze at the end of the day when on holiday in Barbados. I sigh. It's a contented sigh filled with happy memories.

As the colours fade and the moment passes, the breeze off the water picks up and brushes lightly on my arms and legs. A change in environment brings a change of mood — Katie. She's been on radio silence again. I worry. My dearest friend, married to the darling Michael for five years, a highly qualified oncologist who was unable to save her brother and now feels she has to take care of me as recompense for this 'error' which, after all, was not her fault. A close companion who fully endorsed my trip here and yet doesn't seem to be fully embracing the consequences and me moving on with my life. I sigh. A less contented sigh.

I need to talk to her; I need to see her face as I talk to her. Maybe I should invite her to come visit?

28

"You have to come to the party." Martha strikes an imposing pose which tells me I have no choice.

"Why?" I know Daniel is going to be there and it will be nice to see him again, but it has a been a long, tiring day. I was up at six this morning baking cakes, and we've been busy since opening time serving customers, making more cakes, dealing with over-excited children, dogs and (in some cases) adults, and now it is past six o'clock. A full twelve-hour day. I know Brody and tall Amy have been helping me, but I am tired. I stand my ground and frankly I admit to her, "I am exhausted, Martha. I'm hot and sweaty and my feet and my back aches!"

The expression on her face tells me I am not winning this verbal joust, so I attempt to look pathetic and wretched and put on my best stroppy-teenager face that I have not used for nearly two decades. It did not work with my parents back then and it doesn't appear to be working with my boss and landlady today.

"Go!" she sticks out her arm and points a long pink fingernail that matches her outfit perfectly at the kitchen door. "Go, shower, put on a pretty summer dress and be outside in thirty minutes. Joe is coming to give us a ride to the party."

I turn on the spot and stomp out of the room, slamming the kitchen door behind me for good measure. As I wearily climb the steps up to my balcony, I move out of the shadow thrown by the building opposite and the sun strikes my face. The jasmine fragrance hits me and I long to take a seat in my rocking chair, yet at the same time knowing that I cannot disobey Martha – she'd only come and find me, and I am not about to go to a party looking like I've put in a full day's shift and smelling like a Victoria Sponge!

I am showered, dressed and presentable as a human being by the time Joe arrives in his beat-up old Chevy truck. I take a last look in the mirror in my bedroom – a linen shift dress with pale candy stripes (a cast off from Martha that I had altered to fit), white sandals and a white crochet bag I purchased at the craft store. I notice my skin is now honey brown and my hair has grown even longer and has blonde streaks in it – the sunshine has altered my appearance as well as my mood. I smile, satisfied. Wow! Look at me! I inhale slowly and deliberately. I feel good. How did that happen?

"You ready?!" Martha yells, less 5th Avenue more Bronx on this rare occasion.

"Coming!"

We all squeeze onto the front bench seat, the old leather creased and hot to the touch. *Oh no! My dress will all be crumpled!* Then I laugh softly to myself. Since when did I become concerned about the way I looked? Joe drives us out of town, away from the crowds of tourists. Window down, arm resting on the sill, wind in my hair, going to a party with the locals. I am a local now. Things have come a long way since that chilly cool day in April. I could live this life.

Fifteen minutes later, he pulls off the road onto a dirt gravel driveway and 'parks' (better described as abandons) his Chevy alongside the other scattered vehicles on a large patch of land. To the left, occupying the huge corner plot by the crossroads, is the house: white clapboard, square, sturdy, a geometric two-storey home with a large front porch and the obligatory swing – typical American country scene. There are no fences, no gates, just wide-open spaces between the house and the road, so different to the fenced-off small gardens of England.

By the back door there is a porch with a food station that is being set up by a group of women, and behind them I can see a large garden and a pool with kids jumping in, splashing, squealing and having fun. The heat of the day is abating slightly as the sun slowly sets in the west. There is a red painted barn over to the right with its main door wide open. The sound of music floats towards me on a light breeze as I climb out of the truck and straighten my crumpled dress – sounds like a band setting up. I love live music. I smile and am glad I made the effort. This might be fun.

Following Martha over to where some folks are gathered, I notice one or two familiar faces from town: the lady from the craft store where I bought my bag, the man who runs the bookshop, and then I spot Stan playing cards with his friend, giving a good impression of being happy enough. I glance around, scanning the faces for Shirley. I can't see her. I hope she is OK. Did he come to the party by himself? I remember all the events I went to by myself the first year after Jon died and sense that old familiar pain, duller than before but sudden, and for the first time unwanted. The thought that Jon would have loved this place, these people, flies through my head. *How long before that ever leaves me? Will it ever leave me?*

Stan smiles and waves me over. "Hi, how you doin'?"

"OK, I guess. I'm tired. It's been a long day." I sit down next to him with a sigh.

"You been busy all day?"

I nod.

"Business must be good then. What a great idea you guys had of transforming the place! I tried to call in this afternoon, but it was full, no room."

"Oh, I am sorry, we're booked solid for days. I'm sorry I missed you."

"Successful, eh?"

"It is, but I want to go and paint and have time and the town to myself again – all these tourists!"

Stan laughs out loud and nudges his friend. "Sounds like one of us!"

His friend and fellow card-player pipes up, "We do need them, but we're soooo glad when they go home!"

Stan retorts, "True. Hey, how's the commission going? You done yet?"

"Almost. I am really pleased with it."

"Did you decide on a street scene? Or the beach?"

"The lady who owns the shop preferred the sketches of the beach, so we went with that, but I avoided too much of the ocean and shifted the view a little to the left to include more houses. She is pleased with what I've done so far. I haven't had much time with being so busy in the café, but I should get it finished by the weekend. You'll have to take a look."

"I can't go into a lady's dress shop!" He is horrified.

"Then bring Shirley with you! Buy her something new to wear."

The man sitting with him snorts with laughter.

"Where is Shirley?" I ask gently.

"She stayed home. She's not one for parties and she knew I'd be here with the guys, drinking beer and playing cards."

"Give her my love," I say as I leave them to their game

"You'll save a dance for me later, right?" Stan says. I tell my old friend I would be honoured and his buddies' guffaw loudly.

Martha is sitting on the porch drinking iced tea with her friends, including Jessica, who is looking imperious, surrounded by the ladies of town. She smiles at me in a superior fashion, and I quickly turn away, unwilling to get involved. I do not want to talk with anyone, particularly her, and especially after our encounter earlier in the day when she came to the café. Well actually, she came in through the kitchen, which thoroughly annoyed me – and Martha! Her attitude screamed jealousy. Her words had an appearance of pleasantness, but they had sounded barbed and mean-spirited and even Martha was stunned, ushering her back into the kitchen and eventually out of the back door. I make a mental note to talk with Martha about it as the whole episode really unsettled me. But not today. I resolve to make a determined effort to put the incident out of my mind and enjoy the moment. I want to absorb everything that is going on, to imprint it on my memory for future reference, so I slowly wander up to the barn.

My eyes become accustomed to the gloom as I lean against the door post. Daniel is setting up on the stage to the left. Well, it's not actually a stage, more an elevated part of the barn floor. I watch him with his need for everything to be exactly the right place – Where does that come from? – just like that time in the café. The bottle of drinking water, label facing toward him, his microphone exactly a certain space away from where he will stand. It makes me smile so I take a sip of beer to hide it. It is good to see him again

When he is content that everything is in exactly the right place – I can almost hear him relax – he looks up and sees me. His face lights up with a huge smile that warms my heart, prompting an involuntarily skipping of a beat.

Walking towards me, still smiling, he takes my hand, his fingers cool and soft.

"Will you wait while I finish then we can go get something to eat together?"

I nod, unable and unwilling to speak. He walks back up the barn, then turns.

"By the way, that's a real pretty dress you have on!"

The band members laugh. I dip my head and blush violently. This man makes me feel totally disconcerted and he knows it!

When we have collected our food, we find a bench to sit on and he asks me how my day has been, so I tell him: my early rising, my baking and the cakes I made. I tell him about the youngsters we hired and how tall Amy strides around the place.

"She is awesome when you see her in action and yet she is so sweet-natured."

About how Sophia is slowly emerging from her shell and is actually talking to customers in a voice that is above a whisper. I tell him about the stupid tourist with the silly little dog.

"Poor Brody! He can be ungainly at times, it's like he isn't entirely in control of his limbs." I snigger at the memory. "Well, this little dog – Brody called it a rat on a string – was in the café with its owner. Brody caught the lead with his foot as he was passing and yanked the silly little dog right off the ground and into the air. It yelped, Brody dropped the tray, and the owner went crazy! Then Martha got involved – and you know how Martha feels about dogs! She might be the patron saint of lost causes – i.e. me! – but that does not include kids or dogs! I thought she was gonna blow a fuse and point that long finger towards the door, but Sally managed to defuse the situation and calmed everyone – including the dog. We hid Martha in the kitchen 'til she had cooled down!"

He tells me all about his day and so it flows back

and forth, easy talk, no pressure, comfortable– better than last time, less nervous. But then this isn't a date. Is it?

Someone collects our plates.

"Thank you," he says and turns to me. Those green eyes. "I'd best get started in the barn – we're the warm-up act." As he gets up, he adds, "Don't leave it too long before you come in, we're only doing four songs!"

Smiling, I sit back, my head against the wall behind me, eyes closed. Full of delicious BBQ food and contentment. The light is fading fast on this beautiful day as the last rays of sun warm my face. The music starts and immediately Martha comes past on her way to the barn, waking me from my thoughts and insisting I join her.

I have always loved live music. My dad plays piano in a band, and nothing gives me greater pleasure than to sit and watch him. Live music has an immediacy to it and in the barn the sound reverberates around the walls. Daniel's voice is gentle yet powerful, filling the space. Their music is a cross between rock and country, and they are a tight-knit group of accomplished musicians. It is happy music that makes you tap your feet and clap your hands. But all too soon they have finished and bow to our applause before being replaced by another group of musicians.

Daniel comes over to join us and I accept his

invitation to dance. Most people are dancing, laughing, having fun, so why not? We find a small space on the floor and gently sway in time with the rhythm. A couple of songs later and the guy leading the band tells us, "This song is for all you love-birds out there." I let go of Daniel's hand and turn to walk away.

"Wait!" He grabs my arm, sees my reaction, and lets go. He looks me in the eye. "Please," he says softly, "wait." He moves closer. "Dance with me some more," he whispers as he moves closer, not too close but close enough.

His fingers creep across my back, touching, not touching and I step in, willing my body to relax and fighting the desire to escape. Slowly we sway in time with the music, and with each step he gets imperceptibly nearer. I close my eyes, smell the sandalwood, and breathe deeply. I can do this. He holds my hand and whispers the words of the song.

The song ends and instinctively I put space between us. I cannot help but smile because he is so happy. The creases around those green eyes are deep – he smiles a lot.

"Thank you." I start to walk away. I have no choice: I must put distance between us, between me and the intense emotions.

"Daniel!" shouts Jessica, attracting his attention.

He rolls his eyes before turning to chat with her,

giving me time and space. I head outside, lean on the door frame, and breathe deeply. It is dark now. The children no longer frolic about in the pool. Wrapped in towels, they are back with their parents and growing ever tired.

It is peaceful and I am grateful for a moment alone. An all too brief moment as Daniel appears at my shoulder.

"Nearly time for the fireworks," he tells me, his voice close to my ear sending shivers down my spine. "Don't you just love fireworks!"

We stand in silence and wait. I can sense him move closer. People start to gather; they press in, and I move sideways out of the doorway, making space, but then Daniel is right behind me. I can feel the heat of his body against my back. My heart races: *Do I want this or not? Am I ready for this?*

When the firework display bursts into the sky, I look up, and the back of my head touches his chest. *Do I leave it there?* The noise, the flashing splashes of colour, the deep boom of the explosions, all happening at the same time as his arms encircle me and he pulls me towards him. Overwhelming sensations, sounds, arms and emotions envelope me, and then all of a sudden, it's over. Silence. There is a long pause before cheers breaks into the night. I expect Daniel to let go, to open his arms, but he doesn't, and there is a long pause.

Time stands still before he turns me around to face him. I know what he is going to do. I let him. His lips soft and gentle, almost touching, just in case, just to see how I will react. He takes his time and waits for a response. Now faced with a choice, I know I will kiss him. He groans very softly and pulls me close. Stretching my arms around his back, I hold on tight.

"Nice!" he whispers.

"Very," I reply, knowing it will happen again.

I can see the crescent moon in the clear sky through my open window as I lay in bed later that night.

"I am so sorry, Jon!" I whisper out loud.

Tonight, in the cool night air, I feel like I have been unfaithful to my husband, as though I'm embarking on an affair – and yet my husband knows about it and is saying it's OK. The pain over my right eye returns for the first time in a long time. What was once familiar is now unfamiliar. I don't want to cry, it has been such a beautiful evening, but the tears flow.

"I'm sorry!" I repeat. "I think I like him, Jon. He's kind and thoughtful and handsome, but he's not you. I miss you!" In the blink of an eye, I confront the anger. "Why did you leave me? I'm too old for all this stupid teenager stuff, Jon. It is not fair!" What a mess! "This is not what I came here for." The tears begin to seep.

"I'm sorry, Jon," I repeat in a whisper.

29

After a poor night's sleep filled with disturbing dreams, I wake at stupid o'clock. The red light on the alarm tells me it is five thirty. Outside it is light. Drained and heavy with tiredness, I am definitely not ready to face another long day at work. But knowing it is my turn to open up, I take responsibility, drag myself out of bed and into the shower. I let the water pour down as memories of the previous day flood over me. I should be happy, full of the joy of a potential new romance. One part of me is ready for this new adventure, yet an overwhelming part of me is sad at leaving Jon behind, and another part of me is downright scared.

Dressed in my black cutoff jeans and T-shirt, I head downstairs. Unlocking the kitchen door, I step inside, turn off the alarm, switch on the ovens and reach for my apron. The habitual routine of baking soothes my troubled soul. I turn on the radio, begin to dance around the room, drink my coffee as the cares of my heart slowly dissipate. Suddenly, there is a knock on the back door. I stop singing and glance at the clock – 7 a.m. Martha would not knock, neither would Sally. Who is it at this time in the morning? I open the door and there stands Daniel. He grins at me.

"Hi. I made you something." He hands me a cake on a plate.

"Oh! Thank you!"

"Nice singing by the way." I shake my head as he tells me, "Yeah, I can hear it out in the alleyway." There is a momentary pause. "So… can I come in?" He hunches his shoulders, and his eyebrows raise as he tilts his head – far too appealingly for this time in the morning.

I need this time to myself and having him here makes me slightly disgruntled that I have to share my peace, my space, but I suppose if I have to share it with anyone, he is the one. I open the door wide.

"It's a cherry and coconut cake," he informs me. "The only type of cake I can bake," he apologises while looking so proud of his achievement.

What's he like, eh? He must have gotten up early this morning solely to make it for me. I should be grateful. He sees my smile as a sign and moves towards me.

"How are you this morning?" he asks, moving closer still.

"Tired…"

He touches my cheek with his finger. "You want me

to help?" he whispers, reducing the space between us even further.

I can tell from his expression that his words have meanings beyond baking cakes. I lean towards him, a smile playing on my lips.

"You can wash up," I whisper back.

"Oh! OK!"

The spell is broken. The oven timer bleeps and fills the silence in the room.

We work together, bake, chat, sing along to the radio, wash up, wipe down tables, get the café ready. Occasionally he assesses my reaction to his proximity, stepping closer, waiting then retreating.

When there is a break in proceedings, he hands me a mug of coffee and again he moves towards me, and this time I let him stand close. He rests his head next to mine. It feels such an intimate action and I let him kiss me. Gentle and soft, unsure.

"I have to go about half nine – I'm taking Stan fishing today."

"That'll be nice, the weather's calm."

He takes my untouched cup and places it on the counter. He puts his arm around my waist, pulling me in, kissing me, and just like last night, I make the choice and surrender. Suddenly the door opens and in marches Martha, dressed in linen layers of yellow and cream.

"Hey!" She is surprised by the sight in front of her as we spring apart like two startled teenagers.

Daniel says, "Morning!" blushing furiously.

"You guys having fun?" she asks, a broad smile on her face.

Daniel puts his arm across my shoulder. "I've rediscovered the art of kissing!" he proudly announces.

I cannot look at Martha.

"Well not on my time, you don't. I take it you are here to help and not to distract my chief baker and maker of coffee?!" She moves towards him, hugs him then goes into the café, laughing aloud.

He turns to me and smiles. "Oooops!" He kisses me lightly before going back to the task in hand.

We seem to have taken a step forward in our friendship, one I am not convinced I am ready to take. Don't get me wrong, I like the kissing, but now that Martha knows, now everything is out in the open, it has all become so real and I'm not sure I'm prepared for this. There is still that twinge of guilt. I sigh deeply as I batter the hell out of the contents of my bowl and tell myself to STOP OVERTHINKING!

30

Katie's imminent arrival brings a flurry of invitations from my new friends who all want to meet her and spend time with her. There are so many "Why don't we…?" to the point where I need to make a schedule of activities to ensure nothing is double booked. Part of me hates to schedule the whole time she will be in town, as I know she loves spontaneity, but it becomes a 'need' not a 'want':

Monday:	Arrive Boston Logan airport 16.20 - home, eat, relax
Tueday:	Recovery day and dinner with Martha
Wednesday:	Train to Boston and sightseeing day
Thursday:	Afternoon/Evening at Patriot Place watching NFL football with Daniel, Sally & Ricky
Friday:	Beach day and dinner with Stan and Shirley

Saturday:	Shopping and sightseeing, dinner at The Squire with Daniel
Sunday:	Relax day
Monday:	(I must work)
Tuesday:	Day at home - fly out of Logan airport 17.40

I suspect waiting (never my favourite activity) for Katie to emerge is driving Daniel crazy. Nervous anxiety causes me to get up, sit down, up, down every time someone appears at the arrivals gate. He takes my hand and raises it to his lips.

"Will you please sit?"

"Sorry," I mutter.

"You're driving me crazy!"

See, I told you so.

"Sorry! But I am excited to see her again."

"I can see that."

"And I want you to like her."

"Of course I'll like her, she's your best friend. Stop worrying, will you!"

I was concerned about asking Daniel to take me to the airport for one big reason – I haven't told Katie about him; about the fact that he's more than a friend, that he kisses me whenever he can, and I like it, and that as I start to move forward in my life, it may just include Daniel. Nothing. I've told her nothing. And I feel bad about it. On so many levels. My phone pings 'I have arrived' and I am out of my seat in an instant.

We hug so tightly we can hardly breathe and both of us are crying with joy.

"I missed you so much," she tells me. "Don't ever do this again!"

We laugh and wipe each other's tears away.

"Muppet!" she teases me.

"Sorry! I did promise myself I wouldn't cry. I'm so pleased to see you." I can sense Daniel close by. "Katie, this is Daniel. Daniel, my best friend, Katie."

I consider the two most important people in my life right now as they appraise each other momentarily before he greets her with a hug and his trademark smile. I so want them to like each other, despite the fact that neither knows how significant the other is, because I haven't told them. I feel guilty and swallow down words of explanation, knowing this is neither the time nor the place.

"Welcome. I am so glad that you're here. Maybe now Jane will stop jumping up and down like a five-year-old kid!"

"I've been such a pain!" I admit.

"Nothing changes then, eh?" Katie comments.

Daniel takes her suitcase, "Nope! Come on, let's get you home."

We make our way back to the car, arms linked, and endless chatter which continues all the way home. When Daniel drops us off at my place, I thank him profusely for his time and his patience.

"I really do appreciate it," I say. I want to kiss him but hold back.

"Go! Have fun and I'll see you guys soon."

As we head up the stairs, Katie whispers in my ear, "He's nice."

Nice?

Then as she steps inside my apartment, she exclaims, "Wow, it's even better than the photographs! I love it. Where's my room?"

I point towards her bedroom. She takes her bag and suitcase, dumps them and is back in the kitchen within minutes, getting glasses out of the cupboard and gin out of the fridge.

"Shall I?"

"Why not!"

"Oh! I bought you some things from home." She disappears with the bottle in her hand, reappears and puts it on the side, then is off again, muttering her apologies, her energy filling the room. "Here!"

She presents me with a perfectly wrapped gift that only my mum could produce, and my heart skips a beat. Suddenly, with Katie in front of me, I realise how far from home I am and tears well in my eyes.

"Open it!" she urges, trying to distract me.

It's a beautiful leather-bound journal carefully selected by my mother, and a small hand-written note that tells me she misses me and hopes I'm well. 'Write it all down', it says. I hug it to my chest, my heart thumping.

"Don't cry, Jane." Katie puts her arm around my shoulders and gives me a squeeze.

"Sorry," I say. "It's such a wrench to know she's so far away."

"Your dad sent a gift too, but it's wrapped in a bag, not as pretty as this. You want it now or will that make you cry too?"

"Tomorrow, eh?"

I ask her if she wants to contact Michael to let him know she has arrived safely – giving her the Wi-Fi code – and am surprised and rather puzzled when she looks edgy and mutters something about sending a message. This seems a bit odd but decide not to delve any deeper.

We spend all evening oblivious to time, snacking, drinking, and chatting. Eventually I hug her good night.

"It's so good to get away and to be with you," she tells me.

"I am glad you are here!" I tell her. "We are going to have the best week!"

Katie is taller than I am and has the most wonderful

head of thick white hair (genetically inherited at an early age and fully embraced) which she wears in a dramatic asymmetric bob. With bright coloured glasses, she is always striking in appearance. The bond between us, which started at university, has been cemented over the years by clothes exchange (Katie may be taller than me, but we wear the same size), secrets shared, and the ups and downs of lives well-lived. It has never been stronger than it is this morning when I cannot stop grinning at the mere sight of her, all doubts about the strength of our friendship have melted away.

After our early morning cup of tea, sitting in my big bed, she opens my wardrobe to look inside and starts trying on outfits. Much giggling follows. She then brings a couple of things from her room.

"I saw these and thought of you."

I try them on and swap them for a skirt and a dress (which she will have to wear as a tunic given the length of her legs.) Her gifts are perfect – she knows me so well. She brings me Dad's present, a new lens for my camera. Expensive, but thoughtful and not tear-provoking, thankfully. No tears today, only laughter.

Exchanges made, we prepare breakfast together and sit at the table with the view of the park.

"So, what do you want to do today? We're having dinner with Martha later but the day, what's left of it, is free. What do you fancy doing?"

"Show me around town."

Dinner that evening with Martha takes place at the Oakham Inn's bar, next to the ocean. We all agree it is a great choice as we settle at our table and order large G&Ts. Katie is my link with home and again I sense how important it is that Martha likes my best friend. I need not worry as the two of them start to chat in such an easy manner as they get to know each other. I quietly sip my drink and watch.

"I can't tell you how happy I am with the changes Jane's made to the café," Martha enthuses. "She has given the whole place a new lease of live. She and Daniel worked so hard. Have you met Daniel?"

She winks at me. My heart leaps. NO! She doesn't know. Don't bring him into the evening.

"Yes I did, yesterday."

"What do you think?"

"Martha!" I state.

"I want to know – first impressions."

Katie laughs loudly. "I think he's nice." She turns to me and frowns.

Nice?

"Katie! Can we please go back to talking about the café and how wonderful I am?" I ask, safer ground.

"You are wonderful, my dear," Martha tells me, patting my hand, "and yes, the café is so much better now, and I am very pleased. As I keep telling you. Why does she need constant reassurance?" She turns to Katie to ask the question.

"Always has done, Martha," Katie informs her. "Been like that from the day we met!"

"Where did you meet?"

The number fourteen bus up Brownlow Hill from Liverpool city centre towards my hall of residence was full that October afternoon, so I had to sit on the top deck. Thankfully I had a spare seat all to myself and I heaved my bag of textbooks and stationery onto the seat next to me, both to relieve the weight off my shoulder and to protect myself from fellow passengers. The window was covered in condensation. I wiped it to help me keep my bearings, still unsure of which stop to take, my mind a whirl of frantic thoughts as to whether I would miss the stop or be able to get off in time. I located the 'stop' button to help alleviate the growing sense of panic. While doing so, I somehow failed to notice the striking looking girl standing next to me. Dressed in bright shades of green, hair short, spiky and vibrant red, she has a sense of style which I lacked.

"Would you mind?" she said, staring at the offending bag that was occupying the seat.

I glanced around the bus. No choice. I heaved the bag onto my knees, groaning at the weight. Was I really supposed to read all these books on Renaissance art and art history before the end of term?

"Thank you."

I stared out of the window, reluctant to engage in conversation.

"You've been to the same bookshop, eh?"

I noticed she too was weighed down with books.

"Art history. You?"

"Chemistry."

I acknowledged her intelligence with a raise of the eyebrows and a "Hhhmmmm" sound which she took as a sign of friendship – both of us freshmen, away from home for the first time and somewhat lonely. By the time we both got off at the same stop, we had discovered that we both lived in the same hall of residence, and we knew we would be friends for life.

"So, you've known each other years?" Martha says.

"Years and years," Katie adds winking at me, "and I wouldn't be without her."

Dinner arrives and interrupts the flow of conversation for a moment. The food looks and smells delicious, and we quickly tuck into the freshly cooked seafood.

"So is business better now?" Katie asks, returning to

our original topic of conversation.

"So much better. We can be busy from when we open in the morning to when we close the door. We also have five stars on TripAdvisor. People have been posting reviews; so many of them are excellent reviews too. And now Jane is taking over some of the ordering and invoicing, that sort of thing. Well, it gives me the freedom to pursue what I want to do."

Interesting – I want to know what Martha intends to do next!

So does Katie. "What are you going to pursue now, Martha?"

Martha lays down her knife and fork. "I seem to be coming up to phase three of my life." She indicates with her fingers, counting them off. "Number one was my life in New York. Number two has been my life in the café and here on the Cape, and now number three – the new phase – writing. I am going to be an author."

"Wow! What are you going to write – fiction or non-fiction?"

"Oh, definitely non-fiction. I've started to write my autobiography."

Katie and I sit, eyes wide, mouths open.

"But I am saying nothing else! I want to let it all unfold on the pages. And then you can buy the book and read it for yourself!"

Her confidence is infectious, but she becomes

annoyingly tight-lipped, so we change the subject.

We finally leave the restaurant after a third round of G&Ts followed by strong coffee then a stroll back down Main Street into the warm night, content and replete.

Martha walks in front with Katie, and I listen as she tells her, "I've come to realise that Jane's trustworthy. Your friend is very dependable. I'm not normally one to let folks into my life as they so often disappoint me – dependability is vital and that's what Jane has."

But I'm leaving in October – what then?

Katie turns to me and a look passes between us – same thought.

31

On Wednesday morning, Katie and I are up far too early and take a cab ride to Hyannis Port with the aim of catching the eight o'clock bus to South Station Bus Terminal in Boston. The hour-and-a-half bus ride to get there gives us more opportunity to chat. It's like we have three months talking to catch up on in a week and only occasionally do we sit gazing out of the window at the world as it passes by.

When we eventually get out of the impressive South Street Station we turn right and go down to the harbour. The old warehouses – now apartments, coffee shops and restaurants – stand alongside the glass and steel offices surrounded by wide open spaces and the Charles River. We meander along the officially marked Harbour Walk to Long Wharf. It's a beautiful sunny day, the sky is so blue and crystal clear, and by the water it's not too humid, ideal for strolling, sightseeing and taking lots of photographs using my new lens. Thanks Dad! It is also my first time in Boston, so like a pair of tourists (Maybe – well I suppose we are. Katie definitely is a tourist, but what am I?), we take in every sight, sound and smell. Passing Quincy Market, we reach Christopher Columbus Waterfront Park, where we sit under a tree for shade and sip ice-cold lemonade, resting a while, grateful for comfortable, sensible shoes. We people watch (and pass comment) until we are sufficiently refreshed.

"This is fun!" I exclaim. "You having fun yet?"

"I am," she admits. "It's not what I expected, nothing so far is what I expected. Take Martha for instance, you could have warned me about the handshake; my fingers have only recently recovered!"

"It is fierce, isn't it!"

"Just a tad! But I do like her. I can see how much she likes you too, she respects you."

"You think?"

"Yeah, I can tell by the way she talks about you and all you've achieved since you arrived. She seems very happy having you around."

I take this information in for a moment. My old friend likes my new friend. Good.

"Come on!" I haul Katie up to standing. "Let's go – places to see!"

From the park, we go up to the New England Holocaust Memorial on Union Street, opposite Hennessy's bar. The memorial is immensely moving, and we spend a considerable length of time reading the words inscribed on the rocks and looking at the seemingly infinite list of numbers etched on the glass. So many lives. The steam from the subway rises through the grids under our feet and creates an ethereal quality to the memorial. For the first time we are lost for words, silently moving up and down the short glass walkway. When we are done, we simply sit on a bench in the park by the crossroads and internalise what we have experienced, before gathering ourselves together and strolling back to Faneuil Hall Marketplace for some shopping and a coffee.

Moving on, we walk (and talk) until we are in downtown Boston. It is an intriguing mixture of new sparkly steel and glass buildings adjacent to old original buildings from the 1600s when settlers first arrived. Old State House is particularly fascinating, and we spend time reading about the Boston massacre before strolling towards the Common and the Massachusetts State House with its golden dome. There are no skyscraper canyons like New York. The traffic is full on but does not have the same sound to it – it's almost politer and more refined, difficult to describe but definitely different. It is a beautiful city, and my camera is constantly in use.

Around one o'clock we stop for a light lunch in a lovely little café, and I get a surprise call from Daniel that sets my heart thumping. He tells me he is in town for a last-minute meeting and will be finished about half past four.

"You wanna meet up?" he asks.

Katie overhears and nods her agreement but her face seems stony.

"We could have something to eat together and then I can drive us all home. Save you guys having to ride the bus back?"

"That would be lovely."

"Great!" His voice relays his pleasure. "Where are you now?"

"Having lunch. We're opposite"– I peer out the window – "opposite the Granary Burying Ground? I think that's what it says. And we are planning to go to the Common after we've eaten and walk down Beacon Hill," I add as I consult our tourist map laid out on the table.

"OK," he says, "there is a great wine bar on Washington, it's called Sip Wine Bar and Kitchen. It's near the Opera House, you can't miss it."

I check the map. "Where is Washington Street?"

"It runs parallel to Tremont – that's the street you're on."

My finger follows the map. "Got it."

"Great. See you there about half four. Is that good for you?"

"Yes, it is. See you later. Thank you."

"No worries – gotta go." And he hangs up.

"Looks like we got ourselves a ride home!"

Katie rolls her eyes.

"What?" I retort.

"What is it with him?" Her voice seems sharp, disapproving. "He can't keep away, can he?"

"He's just being kind—"

"Yeah, right!"

She looks away. I feel guilty.

The wine bar is quiet as most people are still at work, which gives us the opportunity to choose great seats at a table by the window, preferring to be inside in the air-conditioned room than outside on the street where it is still hot and humid. The walls are painted indigo blue and the contrasting orange high-back leather chairs and granite tabletops give the bar a chic atmosphere, even without the throng of diners.

It is not long before Daniel joins us. Early on in our conversation I can see that Daniel is on a fact-finding mission.

"So, where did you guys meet?" is his opening question and I hear the story of the No. 14 bus again.

Katie continues, happy to divulge the information. Her heckles are down, which I'm relieved about, having worried the whole time that she might make a scene. "And then in our second year we managed to get rooms together in this old Georgian house about a fifteen-minute walk away from uni. Our rooms were next to each other, which was useful as it meant we technically had double the space. So, we moved both beds into Jane's room and used my room as a sitting and eating space. Even though we had to share a kitchen, we had our own fridge and bathroom, which was a godsend!" Katie rolls her eyes. "I hate communal bathrooms! And that's where we stayed 'til we graduated."

"What happened then?" he asks looking from one to the other and back to Katie.

"We went our separate ways. I went to do a Masters in oncology in London and Jane got a job teaching in Manchester and married Jon. It was obvious they were made for each other from the beginning." Katie is lost in her memories and blunders on unaware of what is happening around her. Suddenly she stops, noticing my reaction, gazes at us both and covers her mouth with both hands.

Oh no. This is not how it was supposed to happen. Daniel looks at me as my eyes well with tears. I'm desperately trying to hide the impact of hearing Jon's name.

"He died of cancer—" I manage to say by way of explanation. There is so much he needs to know. This is all going wrong.

Katie interrupts, "and Jane was completely

devastated by his death."

I can't look at her as she's making things worse.

Daniel looks like he's been slapped. "I just assumed… I thought… I didn't realise he'd died." He stops. "That must have been tough." He seems to be struggling to find the right words.

I reach out and touch his hand. Katie is forgotten. I need to reassure him. I know I've been reluctant to open up to him and now I've hurt him. "It was… I am… Well, maybe not devastated now, that was two years ago and I'm learning to live again." I pause. "With your help."

Multiple emotions cloud his eyes, sadness at my loss, uncertainty, and a dawning realisation.

"You'll always love him," he whispers.

I want to tell him more – everything – but this is not the kind of conversation you have in a wine bar, not now, but here we are. The silence is awkward, and Katie apologises. It's only then that I remember she is with us. Guilt overwhelms me as I realise that I've hurt her feelings as well.

"It's OK," I tell her. "It's just… We haven't had these kinds of conversations yet."

"I'm sorry," she repeats herself, her tone flat.

She is beginning to realise there is more to what is happening in front of her than meets the eye. I cannot look at her. I'm only just coming to terms with her brother's death and now all these complex emotions are swirling around us. I want this all to end. Now.

The apartment door closes and within seconds Katie rounds on me with the words, "What is happening?"

I stare at my feet.

"Tell me!" she yells, banging her hand down on the table, her eyes full of tears. I understand she is upset, talking about Jon, but her fury seems so unlike her.

"Why are you so angry?"

"You lied to me!"

"I didn't!"

"Clearly you did! This fella, this Daniel," she almost spits his name out, "is more than a taxi driver or the guy that helped you transform the café. My God, Jane, when he found out about Jon his face crumbled!"

"It's not what I intended."

"What isn't? Your romance with him or my finding out?!" Her voice is raised, her face animated and red.

"My romance… which isn't a romance. Not really."

"Clearly it is!" she states.

"It's not what I intended," I repeat.

"But it's happening."

"It is," I admit.

"What about Jon?" She sits down abruptly as her energy levels deplete. "He was the love of your life, remember?"

"Jon was everything to me, Katie, but he's dead and

I need to move on. He's been dead for more than two years and I've mourned him the whole time but I'm ready to move on—"

"Quickly it seems!"

"Quickly? You have no idea how much it has been eating me up inside. How I still miss him every day. How I would give anything to have him back. But he's not coming back. He's never coming back".

Silence.

I decide to cancel our trip to Foxborough the following day, citing the need to spend time with Katie. I hate doing it, but I need to mend my friendship first. Daniel is not impressed and ten minutes after I hang up the phone he is climbing my steps and asking to talk to me.

"You didn't tell her about us, did you?" is his opening remark and I now have confirmation that I've upset both of them, and I'm torn – which relationship to mend first.

I move him away from the door. I don't want Katie to hear.

Down the steps, I ask, "Us?"

"Yes! US!" He turns and places his hands on the bonnet of his pick-up truck. I hear him sigh. "We've been talking and touching. And kissing! Where did you think this was leading? There is....was going to be an 'us'!'"

To be honest, I hadn't considered where this was leading but I suddenly like the sound of 'us'. Now it could be too late. I apologise again and try to explain why I need to spend time with Katie.

"She's Jon's sister," I tell him.

His shocked face bites into my soul. "What?" he whispers.

I nod.

"What else haven't you told me, Jane?"

"Nothing!" I move towards him, run my hand over his arm, resting it finally on his hand. "Nothing," I utter, leaning in, seeking comfort.

He doesn't believe me.

"I'll leave you to it then." He straightens up, his face calm, his eyes dull and I hate myself.

"Will I see you on Saturday?"

He nods, gets into the vehicle, reversing out of the alleyway without a backward glance.

32

We sit facing each other at the table. Thankfully the view of the park means we don't actually have to make eye contact and I am hopeful that this will allow us to be honest with each other. This visit is not turning out as I had expected, and I know it is because I have not been entirely honest with my friend, and I need to apologise.

I start with, "I was happy with Jon."

Begrudgingly she acknowledges this to be true, and admits, "I miss him."

I do. I did, but not so much now. How do I tell her? I know that anger is an expression of deeply felt, long-held sadness and I can see that in her eyes. But there seems to be more than grief for Jon. Something else is troubling her; I know her too well for her to hide it from me. I tentatively reach out for her hand. She grips mine fiercely, and I'm unsure if it is out of anger or the need for support.

"I couldn't save him…" Her voice fades as she starts

to cry.

I wait. I have known her for over twenty-five years; she doesn't want a hug right now. So, I wait. We have always been so close and yet since Jon's death there has been a distance between us as we have grieved differently. I wanted to talk about Jon constantly, and Katie not so much, as talking about him brought the guilt she felt to the surface. That guilt she buried within, that became a barrier between us. Close but not so close as before.

"Then you upped and left me too." Finally, she glances at me, her eyes so like Jon's that my heart leaps as memories flood my mind. "Left me on my own…to deal with everything."

"I thought you were happy for me, for this trip?"

"I was. I am…" She pauses and wipes her face. "But" – eyes closed– "but I resented it too."

I gulp. What?

"You were free to just get up and leave and I was stuck at home with my job, and Michael and work and your parents; you just walked away."

"I needed—"

"I know you did. It's just that things haven't been great."

When I raise a questioning eyebrow for her to tell me what she means, she shakes her head, pleading with me not to ask. So I don't. But my mind goes into overdrive as we absorb these facts in silence.

"So, tell me?" Katie pleads, her head in her hands, her voice muffled.

She knows I'm hiding things and I realise that there is so much I haven't told her: the fear of failure, finding friends, feeling lost and then the real prospect of being homeless. Painfully, I relate the events.

Slowly she turns and looks at me.

"I felt we all fell over the waterfall of grief, all of us together, but then you all sailed off down the river of life to do your own thing and I was still in the whirlpool, I was floundering, and I needed to break free." I exhale noisily, trying to find the right words. "I had to prove to myself that I could cope and make a new life for myself without Jon, like you all had. And I couldn't do that at home."

Katie is obviously digesting everything I have said. As she is deep in thought, I rise and make us both a strong cup of tea and open a packet of McVities chocolate digestives that Katie brought with her. I need chocolate. Ripping open the packet and scattering crumbs, I dunk a biscuit in my tea and relish the melting deliciousness.

"The worst night ever was that night in the café, when I never felt so alone—"

"You could have come home."

"True, but then I'd be back in the same place with you taking care of me."

"I want to, it's my job, since..." Her voice fades.

I push forward the biscuits towards her.

"No Katie, it's not. I'm thirty-six years old. I need to do it by myself. That's why I couldn't share the bad bits with you. You just want to care for me. You want me at home. But I'm ready to move on. I am."

My conviction surprises me. But voicing all that's happened, telling her, has shown me how far I have come and how much I have overcome to be where I am today.

"But are you?" I reach out a hand and she does the same.

She cries. I apologise and cry. She apologises.

"And this new life... Does it include Daniel?"

"I'm not sure yet," I admit.

As I round the corner at the top of Main Street and march towards the low wall by the lighthouse, I can sense the easing of the tension in my shoulders. Katie and I have talked for hours, cried, been honest and poured out our hearts. Now we need time apart to digest what the day has given us. She promised to make dinner and I needed to escape, to breathe.

I sit down, facing the ocean, the tide is in and there are few people on the beach at this time of the day. Inhaling the familiar fragrance, I battle with myself over what has happened, trying to make sense of it all, of everything that has been said, and grateful that Katie and I have healed the breach and reached an understanding. Now I'm grateful for this place, for my thinking step and the space between us.

Slowly breathing in and out. Slowly the waves move in and out. Slowly my mind stops whirling.

"I was hoping you'd come." Daniel sits down beside me.

Instinctively I lean closer, and he drapes his arm across my shoulder as I bury my head. How did he know that I'd be here? Does he know me that well? He has obviously waited and waited – just in case. Hoping. We sit in silence for a long time and then Daniel asks me about Jon.

After the incident in the wine bar, I knew this was coming. It's only right I tell him. It does seem rather strange to be talking about the love of my life with Daniel, but he needs to know where Jon and I met and what drew me to him. He needs to know what happened and why I came to Oakham. It's a huge moment for me and I realise it's a massive relief to finally be open with him. I figure he needs reassurance as much as I do. I have to explain to him what the impact of losing Jon has had on me and my life, but no matter how I open I am, I still can't tell him everything. I can't let him know that I am afraid of letting go and feel guilty about being happy. Nor how much he is affecting me and my thoughts, my fluttering heart.

Quietly, he listens and doesn't interrupt. When I finish telling him the story, something is different. He is content, I can tell, and the mood changes.

"Thank you for being honest with me."

"I should have been from the start but it's hard… You have to give me time. Frankly I'm a mess and I'm not sure you need to get involved with me," I admit.

"I'll be the judge of that."

33

After a glorious day on the beach on Friday, soaking up the sunshine and relaxing, talking and stitching together the torn threads of friendship to weave a new, better pattern, Katie and I have dinner at Stan and Shirley's house. It is a cosy affair with Shirley making such a fuss of us and asking Katie question after question about me (again I hear about the No. 14 bus) and about England.

"It's a place we always wanted to visit but never found the time, did we, dear?"

"I went one time," Stan informs us.

"You did, dear?" Shirley's head turns sharply towards her husband. She sounds surprised. "You never mentioned it, Stanley." His full name seems to signify this missing information might be important in her life.

"Didn't I? I'm sure I did. We sailed into Portsmouth harbour one time on our way back from 'Nam, the long way round and back to Norfolk Navy Base. We were only there for twenty-four hours I guess, so I may have been to England but didn't get to see too much of the place except perhaps a bar or two!"

He winks at Katie and before a domestic ensues we ask him to elaborate. He regales us with stories of young US sailors let loose in southern England. Laughter fills the room, and any issues Shirley may have had are quickly forgotten.

The small dining table is set with pretty crockery. Shirley takes great delight in telling us all about how it came into her possession as a generous inheritance when they got married. The food she serves is delicious: meat loaf, creamed potato and corn on the cob followed by Key Lime pie. We thank her profusely for feeding us so well. I swear it will take more than one run to work it off but do not share this thought with her as she has been kind and generous. I slacken the belt on my jeans instead.

"So, you guys had a good day?" Stan asks, settling down in his recliner after dinner, hands folded over his full stomach, content and happy. He smiles at us both. "I can see you've caught the sun, Katie!"

"I know! We were on the beach today and the breeze was deceptive. You should see my shoulders!"

Shirley brings her some cream to soothe the heat and the redness. "Works wonders," she comments. "And tomorrow?"

"We're going over to a place called Cuffy's?" Katie

isn't sure so looks at me and I nod. "To buy sweatshirts and T-shirts. I am going to need an extra suitcase on the way home!" she exclaims. "I have bought so much stuff since I got here."

"Or you could leave stuff here for when you visit next time?" Stan winks at me.

On Saturday night, Daniel is taking us both out to dinner at The Squire on Main Street. Katie and I giggle and chat as we get ready and yet I am nervous. This is the first time that the two of them have been in the same room at the same time since everything exploded and everything changed, and I'm not sure what the reaction will be. I know I've repaired things with Katie, and we are back into best friend mode. I know that Daniel understands and clearly cares. But how will they respond to each other?

I need not have worried because when Daniel comes to collect us and escort us to the bar, he greets her with a big smile and a hug.

"I think we may have gotten off on the wrong foot," he tells her, holding her close, making me wish it was me in his arms. "I know that Jane here is very important to you, and I would like us to be friends too."

"Because Jane is important to you too?" she asks, smiling.

Daniel chuckles and my heart melts. "Yes, she is."

Let her go, I think.

On entering the bar, the Rob Lowe look-a-like flirt beams when he sees me. I introduce him to Katie at the same time as linking my arm through Daniel's just so he knows the score.

"Two English ladies! Hey, it's gonna be a great night!" The barman gives the impression of being thrilled as he shows us to a booth and takes our order.

The bar is filling with diners, the ceiling fans barely disturbing the air. The room is dark with wood panelling on the walls and a deep red and brown patterned carpet, but it's cosy and welcoming. Daniel is on good form and entertains Katie with stories about growing up on the ranch – all light-hearted and funny, which surprises me given that he was reluctant to talk about it before – but I do wonder if there's more to his previous life than meets the eye.

After dinner, Daniel loads up the jukebox and we move onto the dancefloor. I am surprised and unsettled when the barman asks me to dance, given the fact that it is obvious that I am with Daniel. I can tell from the expression on Daniel's face that he is not impressed. Give the barman 'A' for effort, he keeps on asking and eventually I submit. This time I am slightly more relaxed, but as soon as the tune is over, Daniel butts in and takes his place, pulling me closer. I smirk at the barman, knowing he was trying it on, and Katie thinks it's hilarious watching the two guys and feeling the testosterone flow.

As the night progresses and we have a few (too many) beers, we all laugh our way around the dancefloor – so enjoyable and yet there is a new niggling thought in the back of my mind about Katie as I watch her accepting the admiration of the young barman, watch her dance a little bit too close to him. Watch him brush her fringe back a little and whisper in her ear, and again I worry. This behaviour is out of character. I resolve to ask questions in the morning. Somethings is wrong at home.

When it's time to leave, I realise that Daniel and I are out on the street alone and it's a good minute or two (or maybe more) before Katie joins us, pink-cheeked and grinning – and not only from the amount of beer she has been drinking.

"Where've you been?" I ask rather too sharply.

"Saying goodnight." Her blush deepens and she adds, "To everyone… To everyone!"

"Oh yes?"

"Yes! Come on, let's go home." She links her arm in mine before I can reply.

34

After the excitement of the night before and the over-indulgence of alcohol, we are at home, lazing on the sofa nursing our hangovers and doing what we do best – chatting (albeit quietly).

Katie scrutinises me and I frown.

"What?"

"You know, I've not seen you looking this good for years. I'm not talking about this morning as you look as rough as a bear's arse. Neither am I talking about the last few years, obviously, but I'm talking probably ten years… You seem more alive – like you genuinely fit in your own skin again."

This surprises me, that she's recognised the change, given her reluctance and resentment of my trip. But I accept the olive branch in the manner in which it is presented.

"I was happy with Jon," I remind her.

"I know you were, but back then life was different. You guys were straight out of university, newly married, finding a home, getting jobs, and there was the daily grind of working, home, dinner, TV, bed, work. Life."

"But life here is much the same, I guess. I'm not doing anything new, I still have a home, go to work."

She stares at me, her head dipped to one side, her hair ruffled with sleep. "You look..." she struggles to find the right words. "You look... content! Yes, that's it, you look content. Happier – yes, but it's deeper than that. An inner happiness if that makes sense?"

Again, I'm surprised. "And is that OK with you?"

I think about our conversation while I contemplate this statement. Yes, I guess I am content. I'm definitely more at ease with my mind and body. The loss of Jon has waned; I miss him but do not ache for him and I rarely cry about being without him. And yet, the twinges of guilt about being with Daniel are still there – just.

"I've been thinking about what I said, what you said" —she pauses— "I shouldn't have told you I resented your leaving. It was wrong." She holds up her hand to stop me interrupting. "I know I've said it before, but I want to say it again. I am pleased for you. I am proud of you, and I want you to feel free to move on and be happy. You do have a right to be happy, I realise that now."

I smile gratefully. "Thank you. And yeah, you're right. I do have a nice place to live, an easy job. I paint, I run. I have new friends, yes. I suppose I am content.

Happy. I still miss of all of you, though."

I reach out to hold her hand and she nods in understanding, telling me, " I told you it was alright to be happy again."

"Talking of happy." I scrutinise her and frown. "Last night—"

Katie has the decency to look shamefaced. "I was drunk," she admits.

"So, you were with the barman?"

"It was one kiss—"

"Katie!"

"I was drunk, and it was one, well maybe two." I stare at her. "Don't look at me like that! It was no more than a kiss. And I promise I won't go near the bar again."

"But why? Are you not happy with Michael?"

"I guess…"

But I am not convinced, and Katie tries to bring the topic of conversation back to neutral ground while we eat our breakfast.

"Martha's brilliant, don't you think?" Katie exclaims, hoping, I can tell, that I will let the matter drop. For now. "What a woman! When she came into the café yesterday morning, we were sitting and chatting, and she was telling me some more about her life in New York and some of the people she has met over the years – like really famous people. Did you know she was a friend of Jackie Kennedy?"

"No way!"

"She was! Apparently, Martha used to supply her with clothes, shoes, and bags – like as a personal shopper? Martha would get stuff together each season and take them over to Jackie's apartment and let her choose her outfits. This was after JFK died, but wow, I was impressed. And she told me she used to go to Studio 54 on West 54th Street and hang out with everyone there. You know that book Martha told us she wants to write about her life back then? Well, I think she's writing it right now."

"Is she?"

I experience a pang of jealousy that Katie has been told all this information and not me, but it passes. I am simply pleased that the two of them have enjoyed each other's company and that they seem to like each other.

"So that's why she's been missing in the café so much recently. I wondered what she was up to and now it all makes sense. I thought she was only at the stage of planning this book and not actually doing it already."

A sense of panic rises in my chest. *But I haven't made any commitment to her to stay and work in the café!* I push it down. I'll think about that later.

"Yes, from what she said, it seems she's started writing. Wouldn't you love to read that book?"

"I would. I wonder if there'll be any juicy bits in it!"

"Jane!" She laughs. "You know, I bet there are! You couldn't be mixed up with that kind of crowd and not know some secrets. I wonder if it'll be a kiss and tell story?"

"I don't think so, do you? Martha is too classy for that."

"True, but she is rather intimidating too – so sophisticated and elegant."

"I remember when I first met her, she shook my hand. She almost broke every bone!"

"Tell me about it – my hand is better now but only just!"

That first encounter, that first handshake seems so long ago now.

"But you know, underneath that hard exterior there's a lovely lady. She's been so kind to me, she cares and that's what makes her so special."

Katie contemplates this information and asks, "So, while she's not been in the café, has she been handing things over to you? I noticed the ordering books and invoices on your dining table the other day?"

"She has been, yes. She got me to hire the new staff last month – you met Brody yesterday?"

Katie nods.

"I love that boy! Recently she's had me opening up in the morning too and then cashing up at the end of the day."

"So, you're like the manager now? Do you think she's considering handing the café over to you? She did mention at dinner that she was entering the third phase of her life, didn't she?"

"It has crossed my mind." I tell her about the discussion I had with Stan. "But really, I have no idea. Maybe she's simply making the most of me while I am here. After all, she knows I'm only here 'til October."

I get up from the sofa in an effort to quell the rising panic.

"You sure?" Katie asks, curious.

"Sure." *Am I?*

Katie then asks, "Has it been fun working and living here? Is it what you expected?"

Is it?

"To be honest, I didn't have any expectations. I decided it was important to come here with an open mind, ready to accept whatever came along. But you know, it's been an amazing experience so far—"

"So far?"

"Yeah, so far. But you know, thinking about it, living here has been a surprisingly unsettling business in many ways." Yet again, I'm struggling to find the right words. Struggling with everything this conversation is stirring up inside, about being honest.

"Why unsettling?"

Katie keeps asking questions, she keeps making me

think about where I am and how I feel, and I am lost in thought for a moment or two while washing up the breakfast dishes. She can see the mental struggle and waits patiently. I dry my hands of the tea-towel and sit down next to her.

"I've found it all fairly familiar. I know it's a foreign county but at least it's one we're familiar with from films and TV, you know, and I have felt comfortable being here. After all, we do speak the same language."

"Almost!"

I snort with laughter. "Yeah, almost! I've had that conversation with Daniel. But you know, being here, well, it's starting to feel permanent and yet I know it is only temporary. And I guess that's why it's unsettling."

Katie is making me assess what has happened and the implications. I find it refreshing and yet disturbing at the same time (if that is possible!)

"How much longer are you staying? Until October you said?"

"Yeah, I fly back to England on the fifteenth."

"Home! You didn't say fly back home!"

We stare at each other. Silence.

Then Katie fills the space with, "Well you have a couple of months left yet."

"I guess."

The silence returns as we digest these details.

"Are you coming home?" she asks.

I cannot find the right words. I don't know, but tell her, "I guess I will have to leave as my visa expires on the fifteenth and if I don't, then that would mean I was here illegally, and I could end up in jail."

"Not a good idea."

"Nope. But, you know," I pause before commenting, "my life is here now." As soon as the words come out I realise it is the truth. What is there back in England? My house, true, but no job, no husband. Friends – yes, family – yes, but I would have to build my whole life back up from scratch and start again. Is that what I want?

"I can see that," Katie almost whispers.

"But I have you in England. Mum and Dad, grandparents, my sister and her baby girl, my house…" My voice fades unconvincingly.

"Your Mum and Dad, they'll be fine. They are both fit and healthy and they could come visit you here and you could go visit them. Back home?"

"Home – where is it?" I ask her. "This is home and yet that is home too."

"Confused.com."

We laugh uneasily and Katie changes the subject.

"I like this room. It's warm and cosy. You have a nice place here."

That's too close to the other conversation so she tries again. "I love Stan."

We are back on safe ground. Relief all round.

"I do too – isn't he just the nicest man? So kind and thoughtful. And Shirley too."

"How long have they been married?"

"About sixty years I think."

"Wow! That is a long time. You can tell though, by the way they interact with each other, they even finish each other's sentences."

We reminisce about our dinner with Stan and Shirley, and I tell her about our time painting together and some of the stories he has told me.

"I feel safe when he's there beside me. He has this calm, unhurried manner about him that soothes my soul. He has offered me some wise words while I have been here." I nod. "Yes, I love him and Shirley very much."

"Talking of love," Katie takes my hand and pats it gently. "Let's talk about the elephant in the room, shall we?" She turns to face me. I recognise her body language and her tone; I have heard it and seen it before.

"Am I in trouble?" I ask.

"That depends on—"

"On what?"

"On what you are going to tell me." She stares at me.

"About what?" I deliberately avoid the issue, the elephant in the room.

"Daniel!" she states. "Daniel! That man who obviously has the hots for you. I saw the way he held you last night when you were dancing. He watches your every move and would walk on hot coals for you, and who you – apparently – are oblivious to!"

"Ah yes! Daniel."

"Yes, Daniel."

"I'm sure he'll be thrilled when I tell him you called him an elephant!"

"Stop avoiding the issue, Jane!"

"Moi?!"

"Is he a good kisser?" She giggles like a teenager.

"Katie!"

"Well?"

I smile. A slow smile of pleasure.

"I'll take that as a yes then."

I nod.

"You had sex yet?"

"Katie!"

"Well?"

"No. We. Have. Not!"

"He'd have you tomorrow—"

I start to get up, but she grabs my arm.

"Sit down! I'm sorry, sweetie."

"You want me to tell you about him then I'll tell you, but not that… Not yet."

"Why? A summer fling might do you some good.

When was the last time you had a good seeing to? I bet it's years!" She laughs and rocks back and forth.

"I do not need a good seeing to, thank you very much! And I am not the sort to have a summer fling, or any other sort of fling – you of all people should know that?"

Besides, given Daniel's reaction to hearing Jon's name and Katie's words, I'm not sure he wants just a summer fling. Deep down, I get the feeling he might want more.

"Remember Mick?" I ask.

This brings Katie up short as her mind fires back to the first year at uni and the guy in our art history class with the meltingly brown eyes and the husky voice.

"Mick!" Katie laughs loudly. "Oh yes. I remember him. You were way too serious even back then and you always took the moral high ground."

"He was really up for an end of term thing but not me." I shake my head. "Besides – way too serious. And if I remember correctly, you were making your way through the front row of the rugby team, having enough flings for the pair of us!

She has the temerity to blush. "Oh OK! You win. So, talk to me."

I tell her how Daniel and I met and how I felt when he first starting hanging around the café, how my feelings used to thrill and frighten me in equal measure.

"Overthinking."

"Maybe." I pause. "OK. True. But I didn't figure that coming here I would find another man; it was the last thing I expected, and when Daniel started taking an interest, well it was the last thing I wanted. I felt I was cheating on Jon." I hold up my hand to stop her. "Yes, I know he's dead and yes, I know I'm not cheating on him, but that is how it made me feel!"

"So, what changed?" she enquires.

"I'm not sure anything has truly changed; I still clam up when he gets too close, he still makes my heart flutter and I'm not sure what I want from him," I admit.

"He's seemed pretty chewed up about what I blurted out at the bar the other day."

"He did, didn't he."

"It was as if he realised that you have never fallen out of love with Jon."

"Well, I haven't. But now I kind of allow myself to go with the flow and then something happens, and I withdraw. I don't want to hurt him, and yet clearly I have, but I can't seem to stay away."

There is a moment of silence, and my head is filled with Daniel's smile, his smell and his kisses.

"Have you noticed he has a soft chuckle when he's happy?"

"Can't say I have."

"And his eyes are green, and they sparkle when he

smiles."

"You always did have a thing for eyes."

"And he slowly broke down the barriers. He's never rushed me, and I think I'm beginning to be more and more comfortable around him."

I tell her about going to his house for the first time.

"Old-fashioned courting eh? A knight in shining armour. A gentleman."

"And," I add, "he can sing and dance."

"Dancing is a bonus – our Jon had two left feet and no sense of rhythm."

We laugh at the memory and then fall once more into a companionable silence.

"So, if you won't have a summer fling with him, what's going to happen? Where's this going to end?"

She looks kindly at me, like she knows it might not end well. It has never before occurred to me that my heart might be broken by this man, this trip.

"I don't know. But I think if he has figured things out so far that he will figure things out going forward."

"And you are happy to let this just evolve?" she asks.

I stop for a moment, mull over the question. "I have learned while I have been here that things have a way of sorting themselves out if you simply leave them alone. Look at where I live – and I have a job. OK, so I don't get paid a whole lot, but you know, I have lived here for four months and have more money now than I had when I arrived. I have good friends who care about me, a couple who give me wise words and seem to guide me…" I pause.

"And a handsome man who clearly adores you."

"And a handsome man who clearly adores me. What's not to like?"

35

After the most relaxing day on Sunday when all we did was sit around, drink and eat and chat some more, I have to work Monday morning, so Katie spends some time upstairs packing what she can and deciding whether to take Stan's advice and leave some clothes behind (for next time!) or to buy another suitcase. When she is done – or rather, when she has done all she can do under the circumstances – she comes downstairs to the café and lends a hand, washing up, serving customers. Her phone is constantly 'pinging' as she texts backwards and forwards. She tells me it's her Michael. I ask if everything is OK between them. She nods and continues to clear the tables.

"You want a job?" I ask her.

"You coming home ever?" she retorts.

Later that afternoon, while I am in the kitchen, Jessica comes into the café. That woman has the skin of a rhino and the temerity to waltz in here as though nothing has happened. Ostensibly she is looking for

Martha, but I know she's come to meet Katie, to find out who she is and to see if there is anything she needs to know, any dirt she can dig up on me to then gossip about to put Daniel off.

I did not actually see the encounter, but as we are closing the door at five, Katie informs me, "I met Jessica today."

I am immediately on guard as I reply, "Oh yes?"

"I was surprised, after what you'd said about her. She seems a nice lady."

My raised eyebrows invite her to tell me more.

"She spoke well of you—"

"Did she now?"

"Yes, she did. She said how much you had done to help Martha's business. And how you seem to have made friends. Though she did start asking lots of questions and she asked me when you were going home."

"What did you tell her?"

"I didn't tell her anything. I remembered the emails you'd sent me about her, and I have to admit I was wary. I said she'd have to ask you as I wasn't sure when you were leaving."

"Thank you."

"Why are you so worried about her?"

Katie sits down on the sofa and puts her feet up on the coffee table, inviting me to join her. I bring over coffee and cake.

"Because being in her company for longer than five minutes brings me out in a rash and every time I see her she makes a sarcastic remark or a biting comment like 'You working here now?' or 'Are you a qualified interior designer?' And last week she came into the café through the back door and straight into the kitchen – which Martha didn't like – and she was so mean to me, even Martha was stunned. I don't trust Jessica as far as I could throw her, to be honest, and if she ever sees me with Daniel… Whoa… If looks could kill."

"She sounds jealous to me."

"Too right, though why she thinks Daniel would ever consider her…." My voice fades. I can feel the tension rise in my chest. I eat cake. It helps.

"Jealousy, that's it. You have to feel sorry for her—"

"No, you don't. You just have to avoid her!" I state.

"You can't do that all the time, not if she's in the habit of coming in here unannounced. She obviously feels that your presence in town is a threat to her friendship with Martha. Now interestingly, Martha doesn't see it the same way, so focus on that. Have you tried being nice to Jessica?"

I admit I haven't.

"Well maybe you should."

"What? Kill her with kindness?"

"Not killing, literally, but it might make a difference.

If not, then don't take it personally."

I eat more cake and ponder on this.

We sit in bed on our final morning together, mug of tea in hand, and do what we have done every morning – chat.

"I have so enjoyed having you here."

I frown at her comment as arguing and shouting, and the anger has really upset me and left a mark on my heart. I know things are mended but…

"Yes, even with all that!" She knows what I am thinking. She kisses my cheek. "Nothing like a good argument to clear the air and any misunderstanding."

I admit she's right and thank her for caring and forgiving.

"It's been a blast," she says in a passable American accent.

I smile at my best friend. "Are you going to be alright going home?"

She pauses before answering, knowing she's been avoiding this topic of conversation the whole time she's been with me. Her eyes meet mine.

"Come on," I encourage her. "You can tell me. Will you be OK when you get back home?"

"I think so, yes. This week, the space between us, between Michael and I, it's helped me to get some perspective. Things have been a bit rough but a lot of that is my fault, working too hard, not paying enough attention, but I have realised that I do love him. We've been texting back and forth and the lines of communication are open again – we're going to be OK. And I've had a great time with you. I miss you, but you know, you've moved on. I can see that now."

"We will always be friends."

She hugs me tightly. "Always. But I can see that you have a new life here and I am happy for you, I really am, but my life is at home with Michael. I'm going to go back, and I'm going to make every effort to put things right between us."

"I'm glad. I was worried for a time there, especially after the barman incident."

Katie has the decency to be a little shamefaced. "I blame the beer!"

"Yeah, right! I'm glad you're going to sort things out. I love your Michael very much, he's a good

man."

"We lost sight of each other, that's all. Both of us working hard and not having time to be together. I can see that now and, although I've had the best time, I have missed him. It'll be OK, Jane, promise."

"That's good."

We are both reassured. We know it's safe to say goodbye and go our separate ways.

"You do know I'm going to cry later, don't you?" I

say.

She nods. "Me too."

We sit quietly for a moment.

"What should I do, Katie?"

She puts her hand on my arm to comfort me and sighs deeply. "It's a toughie, my friend. Like I said, you are happy here—"

"I know, but at the same time this is not what I came here for. I came to find myself."

"Have you considered the fact that this might be the new you – your new life? Here in America?"

"If that's the case," That would be nice! "what do I do to make it happen?"

"Do some research? Talk to these people, find out what's possible."

More quiet moments.

"And Daniel?"

"What about him?"

"Do I want a new life with him?"

"I think you do."

"Does he want me?"

She snorts. "Pleeeaaasssse!"

I look at her and tears seep from my eyes. "You think?"

"I know."

36

Katie has gone home. The emotion of saying goodbye to her at the airport has left its mark on me and I am bereft. As Daniel drives the two of us back to Oakham, I run through what has just happened. Katie and I had clung together at the security gate, both of us unwilling to be the first to let go. Both of us weeping. She knows me so intimately, knows my thoughts and ends my sentences for me, knowing exactly how I feel. She's able to help me see through all the rubbish, right to the heart of any matter, and now she has left me and gone back to England to sort her own life out. She has helped me clarify my thoughts about being in America, the people I have met and, in particular, how I am feeling about Daniel. She has confirmed that it is OK for me to be with him, to kiss him and hold him. To be happy.

But saying goodbye had been so hard.

"I shall miss you," she had said as she hugged me again and brushed the tears from my face.

Daniel had put his arm around my shoulder and

moved me slightly away from Katie.

"She has to go; she has a flight to catch. You have to go!"

"I know," we'd said in unison, followed by a laugh.

She'd walked away, handing over her bag for scanning, going through the metal detector and out to the other side where, when I stood on my tiptoes, I could still see the top of her head.

"Bye!" I'd yelled, not caring who heard, who saw or what they thought. "I love you!"

"Bye!" came back the response and then she was gone.

I had turned to Daniel, and he wiped away the final tears gently with his thumbs. He'd kissed me softly and said, "Let's go home."

Home. My home in Oakham, Massachusetts, US of A.

When, a couple of hours later he finally parks up outside the apartment, it is early evening, and the sun is low in the sky. My sadness lingers and I do not want to be by myself, but on the other hand I do not want to invite Daniel up for coffee in case he gets the wrong idea and thinks it's more than coffee. Besides, my apartment is my space and I am not ready to share that space with him. I wonder if he can sense this inner dilemma and my reluctance to leave, reluctance to ask.

"You wanna go down to the beach a while?" he asks

quietly. "It might be a great sunset?"

I must look relieved – he just has the ability to know what to say. *Yes, that's a great idea!*

"Yes, please."

"Great! So why don't you grab a sweater and I'll get some beer from the store and meet you back here in, say, fifteen minutes?"

I grab my camera too, use the bathroom to freshen up and replace the mascara I lost at the airport, get some fruit from the fridge, and put it all in my trusty backpack.

Down at the beach we find a place to sit, and Daniel builds a fire from driftwood in a hole in the sand – carefully standing the logs up to form a pyramid. I take photographs of him, finding wood, building the fire. It is the first time I have had the opportunity. I realise of all the things I have photographed since I have arrived, he is not one of them and suddenly I need to take as many as I can: his face in the light, in the shade and in the flicker of the flames, from the left, the right, face on and from behind. I want to capture everything about him on film. I even manage to get a shot mid-chuckle and notice how he closes his eyes and dips his chin in that moment. That moment, that movement, that sound which warms my heart.

Satisfied that I have every nuance to view at home later, I turn to the scenery: the beach, the sea and the sunset, the beautiful sky.

"You done yet?" he asks, patiently emptying the bag and producing beer and food. "Here" — he hands me a bottle — "come, sit. Turn that thing off."

I snuggle closer, resting my head on his shoulder. I smile to myself at the beauty that surrounds me, the peace of the evening, the sound of the sea. The beach has a special cool fragrance at this time of night.

"It's beautiful here."

"This is one of my favourite places to come and sit. I like to be able to think and get a handle on life," he tells me.

I listen to the quiet sound of the waves lapping on the shore. All the people have gone home except for a few, like us, who are here for the sunset. We silently, almost reverently, watch the sky turn from the pale blue of the early evening to pink, through vibrant orange, to red and finally into a deep indigo. Sitting in companionable silence, leaning in towards each other, I am at peace. Daniel adds a log to the fire and it momentarily spits and crackles before it too settles down. I exhale again with a deep contentment now all the earlier sadness has evaporated.

"I am glad you like it here. You are the first person I've brought here since…"

He takes a sip of beer. I sense a moment and can hardly breathe. Normally he stops talking at this point.

Will he tell me more today? Will he trust me with the truth about his past?

"My ex, she hated the beach. Oh, she liked the views pretty much, but mostly from behind glass. She didn't like sand between her toes, and she didn't like sand in her food. She was ultra-clean and kinda fussy and was always complaining so I stopped bringing her here. She kinda spoiled it. I came by myself." He takes a moment to look out at the horizon. "And now you're here with me." He turns and looks at me, his face in shadow, then he leans down and kisses me gently.

"Where did you two meet?" I ask, taking advantage of the opening, testing it slightly.

"She was a year ahead of me in college. She was super-efficient and focused, organising all kinds of groups and faculties, and I guess, that's what first attracted me to her. It was a slow burn for me, keeping an eye on her from afar, admiring her and yet she kinda scared me too – so organised and on track. I wanted to be in that particular college because it was a long way from Montana. I took architecture because I'm interested in buildings and maybe I was drifting, but not her. Initially I liked the fact that she took charge and knew without doubt what it was she wanted. Unfortunately, that trait was also the dominant one in our marriage and what finally pulled us apart. She had to be in control of everything, including me. I mean,

I like to have everything in precisely the right place, don't get me wrong, you've seen me with plates and bowls" — he takes another sip of beer — "but she was" — he hesitates again — "she was uber-controlling and I couldn't handle it in the end. It was too much. The older I get, the less control I need or want and the less drive I have. I love chilling out on the beach, playing my guitar, and seeing where the day takes me, and that would have driven her crazy." Again, he sips his beer. "You hungry?" he asks.

The moment passes but the insight is important to me on two levels: I know something about her (though not her name, interestingly) and what drives him crazy, but more important than that, I realise he trusts me.

We talk about Katie and the last week.

"So, you like my best friend?"

"She's awesome! And she's funny, always saying words in a strange way. Her accent is more pronounced than yours."

"Is it? Have I lost some of my English accent?"

He nods. "Yeah, some of it. But that's OK! You have what I would call a mid-Atlantic accent now."

"Neither here nor there."

He murmurs his agreement.

"That's a bit how I feel right now, neither here nor there, like I belong in both places, both places are home, but neither is at the same time, if that makes sense?" I know it doesn't, and his lack of response confirms my suspicions.

Conversation fades into an easy and friendly silence, each with our own thoughts as the fire slowly dies down. The night has a slight chill to it now, an onshore breeze, and it's time to leave. Daniel extinguishes all flames with the sand, leaving it safe.

We walk slowly arm in arm back to the apartment. I recall the first time I walked from the beach back to town and retell the day to Daniel; all the things I can remember, the spring flowers, the sidewalks, the houses. It seems so long ago now.

"The houses are so different here; they're all made with wood and covered in clapboard. In England, we build our houses with brick mainly, or stone, like in the Cotswolds. The local stone there is an ochre, yellow colour and all the cottages are built using it – it is picturesque. You would love it."

"I bet I would."

"You must come visit me sometime."

"I'd like that," he says quietly as we both take in the fact that I will have to leave, the same as Katie left this morning.

I will have to go back to my other home, the other place that was home, is home, but doesn't feel like home anymore. I stop and take his hands in mine. I take a deep breath before I ask – I need to know things, and here in the darkness, I have to ask.

"When we were at the airport today, saying goodbye to Katie, I got to thinking that in two months' time, that'll be me... leaving. I want you to be honest with me, Daniel." I pause. "Our friendship..."

I look at him and, even in the shadows, my eyes plead, 'Help me out here, please.' His eyes tell me, 'No – you say it out loud. You tell me what you want from me.'

"Our friendship..." I don't want to call it by any other name. Not yet. "Will it last beyond October, given the distance?" I hold my breath. I've put it out there. All I need now is some reassurance from him. Constant reassurance.

"I would like it to last, yes." He speaks slowly, carefully.

That's a good start. "It's not what I expected when I came here – This. You. Me."

"Me neither. But I'm happy with it."

Reassurance. Katie told me it was alright to be happy.

"I am too," I say.

"Do you have to leave?"

"Yes. My visa runs out."

"Have you checked out what you can do about staying in the US?"

"Not yet."

Suddenly I don't want to be reminded of it anymore. This evening has been beautiful and special. So, I fill the ensuing silence. "I can't believe how much has happened since we first met." I want to tell him 'I like having you as a friend,' but I hesitate.

"I know! You didn't like me at first, did you?" He pulls me towards him and wraps his arms round me, holding me tight before we start to walk again. Home.

I laugh, embarrassed. "I wouldn't go that far!"

"Oh, I would." That soft chuckle. "I remember the first time I saw you… when you looked at me in the bookshop, your eyes were so wide. I thought, 'My goodness, they're blue!'"

He noticed my eyes. The first thing I noticed about him were his green eyes! How strange.

"Then I almost knocked you over outside the café and then later when I saw you behind the counter at Martha's place – well, you were like a cat on a hot tin roof! You didn't trust me as far as you could throw me!"

He remembers everything!

"Well, if I remember correctly, you did fire question after question at me!"

"I know. I did come on a bit strong. Sorry."

"I forgive you!"

We say goodnight at the bottom of my steps.

"Thank you."

I wrap my arms around his neck, and he pulls me

closer to him.

"What for?"

"Everything."

"Be specific." He kisses my nose.

"For being nice and kind towards Katie."

He kisses my left cheek.

"For being my friend."

He kisses my right cheek.

"For taking me to the beach."

He kisses my forehead. I close my eyes and he kisses feather-like each eyelid. My insides are melting.

"For letting me take pictures of you."

He kisses me long and deep.

"My pleasure," he says, and then he lets go. He walks away with a wave and a smile. "See you Friday!"

37

I slowly become aware of the sunlight and awaken from sleep. My bedroom is filled with light, deliciously bright light, and my first thought is Daniel. I smile to myself and stretch. August, the longest month of the year – it started with heat and humidity, which means there are few places to go to find relief, so I am grateful that my air-con unit is working full-time and the faint hum accompanies my thoughts. My smile broadens as I relive our time on the beach, the way we were talking and reassuring each other, watching the fire, sitting arm in arm, quiet and peaceful and content. Happy.

Katie said it's OK to be happy and she's right, but what truly makes me happy is that Daniel talked about his ex-wife, about being in Oakham and how that made him feel and how different his life is here to his life in the city. He felt safe and secure enough to trust me with information about his life, his past. And he knows about Jon.

I stretch again and decide to go for a run before

breakfast. I take my usual and now familiar route out of town and then along past the lighthouse and my thinking wall and back into town. Despite the humidity, my body flows, my breathing is even and steady, not laboured. I am flying along, exhilarated and empowered by the hit of endorphins.

Thirty minutes later the shower is pouring warm water over me, wiping away sweat and muscle ache, refreshing me for the day ahead, a day of work in the café.

Downstairs the café is quiet. Empty. I turn on the radio, find some up-beat music, tie my apron around my waist and move around the room, swaying, dancing, humming softly to myself and getting everywhere ready for the customers.

Sophia arrives around eight o'clock. She has taken over from Brody as my trusty cake-maker. It turns out she is a genius in the kitchen and every day makes the most delicious cakes and biscuits, cookies and brownies. What is more, she loves to bake, and the customers love to eat what she produces. And Brody is more than grateful that she has taken over the responsibility. He prefers to serve the customers, chat with the ladies, and annoy us – all with a cheeky smile on his face. I am thrilled that Sophia is enjoying her summer job and fret slightly as to how we will manage once she returns to Boston. By the end of this longest month people will start thinking about school starting, apple-cider and the leaves turning from green to orange and brown. Maybe before she leaves I will get her to fill a freezer with food or bribe her to return every weekend to keep it fully stocked. I'm still wondering how much bribing that might take as she greets me cheerfully and briefly joins in the singing and dancing. I am glad she seems to enjoy being here as much as I do. It has been wonderful to watch her evolve and grow over the last weeks, like watching a flower unfold, petal by petal. Each cake that she bakes – some of which are Mum's recipes – that sells out or is complimented by a customer has given her a shot of confidence. Each smile is slightly wider. Her haircut last week gives her a more grown-up appearance and the sun has given her skin a summer glow. Each day her timidity decreases, and she becomes braver to the point where she can now actually look Brody in the eye and speak face to face with him and give instructions to tall Amy. I am amazed and thrilled in equal measure.

"What delights do we have in store today?" I ask her.

She shows me some recipes she found online that she wants to try.

"They could be delicious! Go for it," I say, keen to encourage and support her endeavours.

Sally and Brody arrive together about half nine and

we have a team meeting and a coffee together.

Sally enquires, "Are we taste-testing something this morning?"

She grins at Sophia, who fetches a sample for each of us. I love the smoothness of the mousse cake and the sweet lemony tang of the icing on the lemon drizzle cake. They are truly divine.

"Epic!" is Brody's response.

He loves being our solitary male and basks in our adoration. Our 'younger brother', we guide and educate him and he in turn watches out and protects us. We love him and are irritated by him in equal measure. Having the teenagers around has changed the atmosphere in the café for the better. They're young and vibrant, yet respectful and hard-working.

"I agree! Can I lick the plate?" Sally laughs.

"Let's get down to business." I take charge as this can so easily – and regularly does – get completely out of hand. "It's likely to be a busy day with all the normal customers, especially at lunch time, but I think we have" —I consult the diary— "how many bookings for afternoon tea later?"

Sophia has already checked. "There are four: one at two o'clock – a couple are booked in then; two parties at three o'clock – both have four people in each party… no wait, one has five people; and then the final family of… let me see, there are six of them coming at four o'clock."

"Excellent – so seventeen servings in total." I make a note. "And do we have sufficient bread, fillings and scones, etc?"

"We will have." Sophia has proved to be an expert not only at baking cakes but organising the afternoon tea presentations and I am confident to delegate this role into her more than capable hands.

"OK, I'll leave that with you. So, the rest of us, when these bookings come in, please can we all find time to help with serving tea? Without neglecting the counter and the other customers, of course?"

They all nod in agreement and discuss other matters pertaining to the day in front of us. When all are happy with what's in store, we get to work. I can hear their lively chatter as they go about their assigned tasks. We turn down the volume on the radio and open the front door.

Martha swans in around eleven, beautifully dressed in lilac linen. She moves in a perfumed cloud around the room. The two of us take time to sit and catch up over a morning coffee and a piece of cake.

"How are things?" she asks.

Every morning we have the same discussion: takings, bookings, staff issues and any other matter she needs to be concerned about. I might be managing the café but she's the boss.

"Sounds like you have it all under control." She seems pleased and nods her approval.

"I think we do. They're a great bunch. They've all settled in, and we get along just fine and work together as a team. What do you think of the mousse cake Sophia made this morning?" I notice the plate in front of Martha on the coffee table is clean, every morsel and crumb has been eaten.

"Absolutely delicious!"

"She's a gift to baking."

"What are we going to do when she goes back to college?"

"I was thinking the same thing this morning!" I tell her. "I wonder if bribery might work? A bonus to come and work weekends? What do you think?"

"Whatever works. Just keep tight hold of her – she is a great kid."

"They all are. I am going to miss them when they leave, and things get quiet around here in a week or so's time."

People leaving is not a good thing in my mind – I miss having Katie around. But besides that, I like things exactly the way they are right now. Can I capture this moment in time, this day, this week, this month and hold on to it and never let it go?

"And what am I going to do when you leave?" Martha asks.

I let my gaze wander around the room from where I am sitting on the sofa at the back of the café. I cannot bring myself to think about that time. I am enjoying life in a way I had not expected.

"I don't want to leave," I whisper.

"And how about Daniel?" she adds quietly.

"Daniel." I blush slightly and smile. "I don't know… I'm trying not to think about it yet. I know I will have to, sooner or later, but not today. Today's a lovely day. Tomorrow."

She shakes her head and frowns.

Thursday is my day off, so I indulge in a lie-in. I sit in bed and read my book and then put my head back, close my eyes, and breathe!

The day stretches in front of me, and I briefly wonder what Daniel is doing today. Shall I text him? I decide against it. He said 'see you Friday' so I will see him then. Thinking of him reminds me of the photographs I took, and I leap out of bed, grab my camera, and download all the shots onto my laptop. I examine each one in detail: the shape of his nose, the way the light catches the slight grey flecks of hair on his head and in his goatee. The frown lines between his eyes, the way his right ear lobe kicks out a little but the left one does not. I notice his kissable lips are kind of thin with the bottom one a fraction bigger, and he has a line along his left cheek from the end of his lip down, and when he's not smiling, it makes him look almost sad. But when he smiles, his eyes crease up. I delete those that are out of focus or unflattering and after a contented hour or two looking at this man who has found his way into my heart, I finally get out of bed and head to the bathroom for a shower.

Later, I decide to draw and paint some of the buildings further up Main Street on the way out of town, and also to call in on the lady in the clothes shop. She is thrilled with the mural she commissioned and is excited to tell me that many of her customers have posted comments on Facebook and Instagram. She tells me she has folks all over the place who want a mural too. I briefly contemplate setting up my own Facebook page to promote my artwork but quickly dismiss the venture as I know I only have a couple of weeks left of my stay. Still, I give her permission to hand out my phone number and we'll see what happens. She complains about the weather and the fact that the humidity is so high, telling me she is shutting early today so that she can get the shutters up.

"There's a storm blowing in Saturday night into Sunday morning."

The next morning, I decide to have an early (5.30 a.m. early) run before the heat of the day makes any sort of movement incredibly sticky due to the blanket of humidity that hangs over everywhere, everyone and everything. Even the air seems charged and there is a palpable tension in the atmosphere that I have not experienced before. The heat gets into my bones, into my head, causing a muzzy ache.

After a shower and something to eat, I walk (slowly) up town towards Stan and Shirley's house to visit them and take some flowers. They greet me warmly and welcome me into their home. I'm content when I am with them; they seem to have the ability to make me feel calm, soothed and comforted, and I realise something important needs to be said.

"I do love you," I tell Shirley as she hugs me tightly.

"Why thank you, my dear. I love you too. I am so glad you came to live here in our town."

We smile at each other, and I hug Stan and tell him I love him too. He grins at me and pats my hand.

"Come. Sit. We'd go out on the porch but it's way too hot for me, so come tell me what you have been up to lately, brighten my day!"

We sit in their lounge, a well-used and well-loved room filled with the memorabilia of their lives. A tall, glass-fronted cupboard contains all the plates and dishes which are so treasured from their wedding day. It is a homely, informal space, slightly faded and worn but not so as you'd notice much. I sit on the sofa next to Stan and tell him the ordinary everyday stuff I am dealing with. I tell him about going to the beach with Daniel after dropping Katie off at the airport and how Daniel felt he could talk about his past with me.

"See! I told you to be patient and wait and he would learn to trust you!"

We sit, chat and drink coffee, and a pleasant hour or two passes before I must leave to go back to work.

"Thank you for having me."

"Our pleasure. Come again, any time."

"I will do," I promise.

I amble back to the café and am about to reach for the handle on the front door when it suddenly opens. I step back. There he is.

He chuckles softly and says, "We must stop meeting like this," before hugging me close. "You still OK to go out and eat later? Say eight o'clock?"

I nod.

"I'll drop by and pick you up then."

And just like that, he is gone. A huge grin spreads over my face as I watch him walk away. Cute bum.

The café is exceptionally quiet this afternoon, with noticeably fewer people around town, as though they are all hiding away. It makes me uneasy. With Martha's advice about making the place secure for tomorrow ringing in our ears, we decide to close early. Ricky arrives about four o'clock to check that the boards are in a good condition – the ones that will cover the front of the café and my huge windows upstairs in readiness for the storm that the local weather station threatens will arrive overnight Saturday. I am curious as to why we need to go to such lengths.

"Surely it's just a storm?" I ask.

Turns out it is a stupid question. Everyone shakes their heads.

"You've never experienced a storm in these parts, have you?"

I admit that I have not.

"Better to be safe than sorry," Ricky informs me. "Make sure your cell phone is charged and you have flashlights in case the power goes down. You got drinking water and a go bag?"

"A go bag?"

"Sure – a bag with all your essentials in it in case we have to evacuate."

"Evacuate? Ricky, you're scaring me now."

"It may not get so bad, but better to be safe than sorry. You'll be fine. I'll call back tomorrow to put up the boards."

While I am grateful for his obvious concern, I find Sally to discover what might (or might not) be in store on Saturday night.

She tells me, "We get a big storm at least once every summer. It might be the tail end of a hurricane, but to be honest they usually make landfall around the Carolinas, so it's probably a tropical storm. Can you feel the tension?"

I nod.

"Yep, there's a storm on the way."

"This is where I stayed when I first arrived," I tell Daniel as we walk through the front lobby of Oakham Inn later that evening and out into the garden restaurant. *Was that only four months ago?*

Jessica is on reception and waves a greeting to Daniel but shouts that she cannot stop and chat as she is dealing with a guest. Thank goodness. I wasn't sure about eating here, just in case, and didn't want to worry Daniel, but walking through reception made me a little nervous. I held his hand tight and he smiled at me knowingly. I've not crossed paths with Jessica for some time now and I'm hoping that over that period her feelings towards me might have softened, but I am reluctant to find out just in case. Who knows if being seen with Daniel might add to her jealousy. It seems ridiculous but as I'm so unsure about her and her motives, I deem it wise to stay well clear of her. And yet Daniel wanted to come here and eat, and I felt stupid bringing up the issues as they might sound petty when spoken aloud.

The garden is perfect; the late-summer flowers

beds are full of fragrant colourful blooms. There are candles in glass jars in amongst the flowerbeds and on the tables too. It is magical. The trees have fairy lights wound around the branches and the tables are set for dinner, not too close together, so that conversations can be private. I am glad that I made an effort and dressed up.

We order and Daniel chooses a bottle of champagne.

"What are we celebrating?" I ask.

"Life!" he announces. "And friendship." He winks at me.

I smile, happy and much more relaxed now, comfortable going out on a date with him. I can do this! And yet, despite this, there is an unmistakable tension in the atmosphere which somehow influences our evening. When Jessica comes over to the table, my heart beats a little faster.

"Well, hello." She smiles sweetly at Daniel and through gritted teeth says, "Are you guys having a great evening?" She doesn't look at me.

"Yes, thank you."

"That's good," she says and departs, still not looking at me or acknowledging my presence, thankfully.

I command my heart to slow down and my mind to stop overthinking. *Everything is fine. Be calm. It's OK.* The food is tasty and filling, and the champagne manages to brings a heady mix to a romantic evening.

And yet it feels like there's been a slight shift in our dynamics that is elusive, but I can sense it, unsure but aware.

After dinner, we slowly walk home arm in arm. When we get to my steps, Daniel pulls me to him and kisses me deep and long. A groan of delight emits from him, and I can tell from the heat in his body that this is something more. For a brief second I panic and try to stop myself from becoming stiff in his arms. I so enjoy his kisses and even the slight prickle of the hair on his chin, but this has expectations attached to it. I move almost imperceptibly away.

"Sorry," I whisper.

Sensing the change in my mood, he lifts my chin, and our eyes meet. Even in the darkness I can see how emotional he is.

"When you're ready."

"Not yet."

His thumb strokes my cheek in a movement I find so reassuring. I close my eyes briefly as the feelings he evokes sweep over me and threaten to drown me. Again, I move away ever so slightly. To protect myself.

"I'll wait," he whispers and smiles.

"Thank you."

He lightly kisses my lips and walks away. A tear escapes and silently rolls down my cheek.

"Sorry," I whisper again, but he is too far away to hear me apologise for I know not what.

38

We know it is coming and some people prepare, and some carry on as normal. During the day, we heed the warnings and close the café early. Ricky comes over as promised and boards up the front windows and all my windows upstairs, which makes the place dark and oppressively gloomy. Everyone is checking that folks are OK. I am still unsettled by what might happen, having never experienced a tropical storm before. Sally tries to reassure me again with the fact that this happens at least once every summer and it is nothing to worry about, but still, it niggles at me. The rain and the wind are due to strike during the early hours of the morning, and we are going to be at the heart of the storm. People tell wild tales which unfortunately makes my anxiety worse. Martha tells me to "Stop fretting!"

"Are we still going out to the bar later? Is it safe?" I ask.

"Sure. It's a storm, an ex-hurricane."

"Sally mentioned that."

"But remember it's an ex-hurricane. It'll be fine. And we're still going out tonight, so I'll collect you around seven thirty. Be ready!"

Despite all the pre-storm activity, it is reassuring to see that all the locals are taking things in their stride and life is carrying on as normal: shopping, driving, baking. Even the night out at the bar isn't cancelled and I wonder if things are going to be as bad as they make out. I take a cool shower and get a sense of the tension diminishing with the flow of the water. I calmly dress and breathe evenly. I can do this.

So, when Martha and I take our seats at the bar of The Squire, beer bottles in hand, I am almost relaxed and looking forward to a pleasant evening. We chat, the barman continues to flirt with me and yes, this is going to be a fine time.

Around nine, Daniel appears on the little stage in the corner of the room and my heart swells with pride. I want to cheer but the applause is polite and muted, so I refrain – let's not embarrass the poor man! Martha and I smile at each other as he adjusts the microphone.

He introduces himself and the band, eyes down – no eye contact. He strums his guitar and checks it is in tune. I can tell he has already done it a hundred times before. He whispers to the other guys in the band, "and one, two…" and he begins to play. I am entranced. The music is clear and sharp, the notes he sings warm and true, and it is beautiful. The prickle on my skin makes the hairs on my arms stand up and salute him. I smile again, watching him visibly unwind, and when the applause rings out after the last note he looks directly into the room and makes eye contact with the audience. For the first time he smiles. I know it is going to be alright.

Three songs into the set and we are up on our feet with him and the band. We are dancing and clapping and into the mood he has subtly created in The Squire.

Two songs later he slows it down by sitting back on his stool, taking a sip of beer, and allowing the audience to take a breath and rest a while. I scan the room; people are enjoying the evening as much as I am. There are lots of happy faces.

"I met someone a coupl'a month's back," he tells the crowd. "Amazing blue eyes." He chuckles softly. "Drives me crazy, she does."

I become wary. The audience capture the change in mood. They watch his every move, hang onto every word, and they laugh quietly too. He fiddles with the tuners at the end of the neck of the guitar and strums.

"Know what I mean, guys?"

Some nod. I'm curious. *Why is he telling people these things?*

"And to add to everything else" — he chuckles

again — "she's from England and talks real strange. I know you guys think you speak English, but boy – not like this!"

They all laugh. I half expect folks to turn around and stare, realising he's talking about me. I cannot take my eyes off him but am mortified. *Why, Daniel?* I can feel the heat on my face. *Why?* He strums and sings

"You say tomato, she says tomarto! You say potato, she says potarto!"

More laughing. More embarrassment on my part. He is avoiding eye contact with me deliberately. I try to get off my bar stool but Martha, sensing what is happening, pats my leg and makes me stay put. He strums again.

"So… anyways. I heard this song a week or so back, on the radio, and it really captures how I'm feeling right now, so me and the guys learned how to play it. First time tonight, so be patient please, and it goes something like this…"

There are lyrics about breath and life and love and heartbeats and emotions. It's beautiful. It is as though he is looking right into my heart and soul. My emotions swirl, my eyes water. It's breathtaking. All I can see is him. It is powerful stuff.

The applause breaks the spell and he's quickly into a fast tune, the mood changes once more with clapping, cheering, and dancing.

"Last song."

The crowd responds with a low groan.

"Gotta go!" He tells them and plays one last song, and the appreciation is evident.

Later, when The Squire closes, we stand in the street a while, saying goodnight, our voices echoing up and down the pavement. Everywhere is closed and boarded up. Daniel walks me home and checks that I have my mobile phone on and fully charged, with a go bag ready, just in case. I assure him that all is well and not to worry. Neither of us mention what just happened, the embarrassment, the emotions, nor the implications. All the tension from earlier in the day has thankfully dispersed, (in the weather and between us) and although there is an eerie calm, I feel they may have made a fuss about nothing. It's just a storm.

My apartment is dark and in a weird way it's cosy and safe. It isn't long before I am tucked up in bed. It's quiet and peaceful and soon I am asleep.

Sometime later – How many hours? Not sure – I wake with a jolt to the sound of my phone ringing. The room is inky pitch black and yet it's so noisy now; the wind howls around the building, buffeting and rattling the boards that cover the windows. I can hear the rain; it is heavy and relentless.

Disorientated, I fumble in the dark for the bedside

lamp, knocking over my glass of water in the process. Water on my arm, my bed, my face. I whisper a curse, switch on the light, and answer the call.

"Hello?"

"Jane! Jane!" Martha sounds frantic. "Get up. Dress quickly! Daniel is on his way over to get you. You gotta get over to Stan's house. Now! It's awful, Jane. Come quick!" And she is gone.

Why is Daniel coming? What is so awful? I shake my head. Think clearly!

I throw on some jeans and a sweat top over my sleeping T-shirt. I find socks and trainers and I am making my way out of the bathroom, having hastily cleaned my teeth and washed my face, when Daniel knocks on the door.

He is pale under his tan. The lines on his face are more clearly etched.

"I'll grab my bag."

He nods.

We leave.

Outside, the storm is fierce and even getting down the steps to the pick-up truck is an effort, but once inside the comfort of the cab, drenched in rainwater, we smile tightly at each other.

"What's happening?"

Daniel explains that Martha called him. "She's with Stan and apparently a tree has fallen on his house."

I gasp. "Oh no! Is anyone hurt?"

Daniel isn't sure but given Martha's urgent calls, then yes, maybe someone is hurt.

The wipers are on full speed, trying desperately to clear away the lashing water. I hope that no-one else is on this road out of town as it is barely visible through the torrential rain. The wind buffets us, shunting the vehicle around. The noise is deafening, and for the first time there is a real sense of fear. I move slightly towards Daniel. Seeking comfort.

"This isn't good. I don't like this," I admit.

He does not respond. He needs all his powers of concentration merely to steer us in a straight line. We pull into the once familiar street where Stan and Shirley live. The blue emergency lights flash across the sky, illuminating the rain which is now falling in sheets. The houses seem smaller, the street feels narrower, and I can see the tree, a huge old oak tree, across the road, lit up by headlights, blocking our path.

"Wow!" Daniel utters. He turns to me and momentarily I see fear in his eyes too.

The wind drives the rain horizontally into our faces. Coming from England, I associate wind and rain with cold, but this wind and rain is surprisingly warm. I draw closer to Daniel, take his hand as we walk the length of the tree, the gnarled bark shiny and wet. We pick our way around the roots, which stretch twenty feet into the air, ripped out of the ground, gouging a hole in the earth. Once past the tree, a scene of devastation opens in front of us. There are people everywhere, some busy, some standing, looking on in disbelief. We momentarily pause to take it all in: flashing lights, rain and wind, the noise, Martha and Stan, and the tree which has landed on the corner of Stan's house, completely flattening part of it. The rest of the house leans precariously towards the tree like a house of cards ready to collapse at any moment. And all the time, blue light, red light, darkness.

On the grass by the road, Martha and Stan are standing huddled together, their arms wrapped around each other, heads bent close, totally drenched, and oblivious to what is going on around them: the fire service guys going in and out, the additional sound of the chainsaw over and above the noise of wind and rain. All senses are overwhelmed, and I want to close my eyes to the scene and my ears to the deafening sounds. I let go of Daniel's hand and run towards my friends.

Martha sees me over Stan's shoulder. I can see she has been crying.

"Stay with him a while," she shouts over the noise.

She moves towards Daniel, and I go and hug my dear friend Stan, holding him upright. His face is crumpled, his eyes red and swollen.

"She's gone!"

I can barely hear him.

"Gone?" I ask.

He turns and points at the tree. He can't tell me what has happened.

"Ma'am?"

I peer through the rain at the fireman standing in front of me, dripping wet.

"Ma'am," he repeats. "It ain't safe to stand here no more, can you guys move further away from the house, please?"

"Stan, come on. Stan." I try to get him to move away.

"I can't leave Shirley," he responds, suddenly stronger. He stands up straighter.

"We will take care of her, sir." The fireman helps me to get Stan moving. "Come on, sir, let's get you to the ambulance, let's take care of you first." He is gentle and kind.

"My Shirley! My Shirley!" Stan wails, the pain etched on his face.

I still cannot piece together what has happened as we slowly walk Stan over to the ambulance where Martha and Daniel are waiting. Perhaps he's confused by it all and they're trying to rescue Shirley. If he's OK, then surely she must be OK too. Right? We hand him over to a paramedic who sits him down inside the ambulance out of the rain, wrapping him in a blanket and talking to him soothingly.

I turn to Daniel. "What's happened?"

The lights continue to flash, and his face is in shadow, then blue, then red, then shadow, wet with rain and etched in grief. He puts his arms around me and draws me into him, holds me tight. He shudders and I realise he is now sobbing. Minutes later, it seems like forever, he puts his mouth to my ear, unable to speak out loud.

"The tree fell on the house. Landed right on top of Shirley as she was sleeping."

I gasp, shaking my head. He cradles my face and kisses my cheeks over and over again.

"She never knew what happened." His voice cracks with emotion.

"Where was Stan?"

"In the kitchen fixing a drink."

"No!"

The full horror of what has happened hits me and my knees buckle. Daniel catches me, holds me up and we cling together in the pouring rain, drenched and shivering.

39

Much later, all of us — well, there are only the four of us now — go back to the safety of Daniel's house as the storm starts to abate. We find Stan some dry clothes while Daniel lights a fire and I fix food as Martha watches Stan like a hawk. No-one speaks. What is there to say?

Martha refuses dry clothes. I take a pair of jeans and a cotton shirt from Daniel. We all sit. Silent. Lost in our own thoughts and our own sorrow.

Suddenly Stan starts to talk, and the story of the night unravels. He sounds calm and kind of numb, as though telling us about something that has happened to someone else.

"I got up to make a cup of cocoa as we couldn't sleep, the storm, it was so noisy. I went into the kitchen and bang!" He almost shouts the last word, then his face crumbles and he starts to cry. "Why didn't I stay another five minutes with her? Why?"

My instinct is to go and hold him, but Martha gets

there first.

"Why didn't I ask her to go make a drink? I would have died, and she would be here now. I should have stayed with her. She died alone. I should have stayed and been there for her. I let her down when she needed me the most," he sobs.

Martha tries to soothe him. Useless, empty words. She holds him and tries to make him strong. An impossible task for now. I put my head in my hands and weep, shocked at seeing Stan in such distress, seeing his calm exterior crumble.

The wind outside is quieter now and all I can hear is crying. I want to block my ears to this sound too. The sound of crying, the sound of death. The night Jon died sounded like this night and all the emotions return, raw and powerful.

Death – the act of dying. I never understood why people say, 'they died peacefully in their sleep.' Death is brutal.

The afternoon before Jon died, the two of us had been able to have a conversation about inane, normal everyday things: "How's the cat?" "Have to you paid the milkman?" Between periods of sleep, he had seemed restless and agitated, so the nurse, who explained that this was 'normal', had administered a sedative to help him to cope and I had sat and watched him sleep. At least I can say that was peaceful. The room in the hospice was filled with spring sunshine and I stared out into the garden at life passing by, normal everyday life, listening to him breathe.

As there was nothing else I could do and I needed a change of clothes and something to eat, and his parents were arriving to sit with him, I had kissed his cheek, said goodbye and left, telephoning them on the drive home to tell them how the afternoon had progressed and what they would find when they arrived.

An hour or so later I had received the call I had been expecting and dreading at the same time: "Come back, Jane." I knew what those words meant. I drove back to the hospice, my mind racing. I'm not ready for this. I'm not ready to say goodbye. Not yet.

The nurse had let me in the side door with a sympathetic smile and guided me back to Jon's room, her arm around my waist. He was asleep but his breathing was now erratic, uneven, loud. His mother wrapped her arms around me. Katie sobbed quietly in the corner. His best friend was slumped in a chair and smiled briefly as he nodded a greeting. Jon's father joined us, and we held each other, imparting what meagre strength we had left so that we could face what was about to happen. The inevitable.

I went over to the bed and took Jon's hand in mine.

"Hello, my love," I'd whispered. I had turned to his mum.

"His hands are cold."

She had nodded. I pulled the blanket over them to warm them. It made no difference.

"Why are they cold?" I asked, stroking them gently so as not to hurt him.

The nurse next to the bed, having entered unnoticed. "His body is shutting down."

I had stared at her. This is it then? *She had checked his vitals and left us alone. We stood and stared at him before each of us took a seat and waited. The hours passed quicker than I thought possible, each one brought a small change, a change closer to the end. His breathing became unusual, and I enquired why – turns out the breathing pattern has a name; someone had taken the time to name the imminent death breathing pattern. Jon became agitated, fighting the inevitable, and we became agitated too, desperate for him to breathe and desperate for the trauma and the agony to end, for his sake and for ours. The nurse arrived and administered more drugs. He calmed. He breathed his last. He died. I don't have much experience of death, but that was truly brutal.*

Martha decides sometime later, I'm not sure when, to go home and change. Stan is persuaded to go to bed and try to rest. Daniel sits in a chair in the bedroom, keeping him under observation, protecting him. I curl up on the sofa under a blanket, not sure if I will be able to sleep, but desperate to escape the day, the night.

Within hours the sun rises, and the first rays fall across my face and gently bring me back into the day. I stretch to relieve the tension in my neck and shoulders. Glancing around the elegant space, I stand and am drawn towards the glass wall and the view beyond. I totally get why Daniel lives here. The house is quiet, peaceful and, despite the tragedy of the storm the night before, it feels tranquil and calm.

I make coffee, three cups, strong and steaming, and finding a tray, carry them to the bedroom where I find Daniel still in the same chair, next to Stan, dozing. He wakes instantly, glances at Stan and ushers me out of the room.

"Let him sleep," he whispers.

We take our mugs and go back to the kitchen, where I am drawn once more to that view. I lean my head on Daniel's shoulder. He shifts his mug to the other hand and puts his arm around me and I welcome the comfort this brings. He will deal with this; he will take care of things. I sigh involuntarily as he kisses the top of my head. Silent reassurance that together we can face today. Today we have to deal with the fallout from the storm. The world may be quiet and calm, and for a moment it's like it didn't really happen. But an old man, our dear friend, is asleep in the bedroom and when he wakes up it will all become dreadfully real. The sun rises in the sky exactly like any other ordinary day.

"My husband died on a morning like this, just after the sun rise."

He kisses the top of my head again and pulls me closer.

Martha returns dressed from head to toe in yellow, informing us it is the ancient royal Tudor colour of mourning which Anne Boleyn wore when she heard that Henry VIII's first wife Catherine had died.

"Besides," she adds, "I look like a crow in motion when I wear black!"

She goes to see Stan and we can hear them talking quietly. Daniel and I sit in companionable silence. Words will come later.

A knock at the door reveals a couple of grim-faced police officers. Martha brings Stan back and we assemble in the lounge where, remarkably professional and detached, we discuss details and facts:

- Your house will need to be knocked down and re-built, sir. (Police Officer)
- He can stay with me. (Martha)
- Can I see her? (Stan)
- Not advisable. (Police Officer)
- We can deal with the paperwork and arrange a

funeral then? (Martha)

- Yes ma'am. (Police Office)
- We can go get his things. (Daniel)
- Yes sir. (Police Officer)

The tears are dried for the time being. Practicality takes over. Organisation overrides emotions and plans are put into place. Stan is cared for and protected.

Later that same day, Daniel and I go back to Stan's house to find that the tree has been sliced up and split into logs and there is a huge pile stacked up neatly on the front lawn. There is no sign of the killer except this stack of wood, and I want to burn the lot. The right side of the house is completely flat, demolished, and all trace of Shirley is gone. I am angry at her death, but I know from experience that anger is a useless reaction and will only damage me. It is so sad, tragic even, but anger won't reverse the events of last night nor bring her back. There is no-one around, the place is deserted, but I know that the neighbours must have seen us drive up to the house. We wander around and pick up what is left, fragments of their lives lived. Remnants of their life together. We have to preserve what we can, I tell myself. It all feels too helpless. I can see tears in Daniel's eyes again and I want to ease his anguish. I place my hand on his cheek and softly brush his lips with my fingertip. His pain is raw, and I sense he has been thinking of times past like me.

"My dad was paralysed in a storm like the one we had last night." He pauses and looks around but sees something else, someplace else. "He got caught out on the ranch in a big storm that blew in from the mountains. He was on his way home and the horse got spooked by the noise and reared. Dad is an experienced horseman and this horse had reared up before so Dad thought he would come back down again but the horse lost his footing. Dad fell to the ground and the horse rolled on top of him, crushing the lower vertebrae in his spine. It was hours before we found him." Daniel's mouth is a tight line. "We had the horse destroyed because he broke a leg and Dad never rode again." He stares past me. He is back in Montana. Another life-changing storm.

"We will get through this," I say, not sure I believe it but at the same time I hope it's true. We have both been through tough times like this before and survived.

He pulls me to him. We cling together amidst the wreckage of Stan's home and see different scenes, lost in our individual memories.

He moans, shakes his head almost imperceptibly then stands tall once more. "We are gonna need a van to take everything out of here that Stan wants."

"A lifetime of possessions."

"And find some place to store it."

"Where to start?"

"We'll ask Stan what he wants to do."

Stan informs us later that he wants to see the house.

"What?" we all say in unison.

"I want to say goodbye and collect all my things."

"Are you sure?" Martha asks gently.

"Man, it's a mess!" Daniel tells him.

"I am sure!" he states resolutely.

We all go together.

40

There isn't a sound in the car on the way over, each of us lost in our own thoughts, friends united and yet divided by grief. As Daniel drives into the street, we all seem to sit up a little straighter, prepared to face the next arduous challenge.

The house is deserted except now there is a policeman standing guard, who informs us that the 'building' will have to be demolished tomorrow afternoon and we are to take what we want, or to organise the removal of furniture and contents by the morning. *It isn't a 'building'! It's a house, his home, a home full of memories.* I want to shout at him and rail against the absurdity of it all.

The bright red front door is open to the world and the elements. Slowly, with a measure of trepidation, we enter one at a time. As Stan wanders through the ruins of his life he tells us we can demolish the lot, he doesn't want anything, he has changed his mind. He turns to leave, but Martha gently stops him.

"But this is your life."

"It was my life. They are just things. They mean nothing without Shirley," he tells her, but as he moves around the rooms that remain safe to enter, he starts to quietly reminisce about when they met, when they bought this and that.

Martha, Daniel, and I watch each other and make mental notes so that these specific items can be gathered and stored for a time when he is ready to receive them back into his life. I pick up a china cup and saucer which have fallen from the cupboard in the sitting room and slip it into my bag to give to him later. Maybe I will keep it in the café – just for him. So many of the other pieces have been broken but a few are still intact and can be collected later. Next to the shattered pieces of a shattered life is a frame containing a photograph from their wedding day. I hand it to Martha who momentarily looks as though she will cry. A deep frown builds a furrow on her brow. She blinks, takes the frame, and mouths a 'thank you'.

This room always reminded me of Grandma Doris's living room; the style of furniture, the colours and my heart takes a tumble at the thought of losing her, walking around her house picking up the pieces of her life after she's gone. A lump in my throat threatens to choke me. I swallow it down.

Finally, on leaving, Stan tries to close his front door

only to discover that it no longer fits. He sighs and puts his hand on the painted frame. He bows his head and instantly I am transported back four months to when I left my house for an uncertain future. I move forward to stand close to him and hear him whisper, "Goodbye old friend, thank you for many happy memories." As his voice cracks, he sniffs and attempts to collect himself. He straightens up, and with tears in his eyes tells me, "Time to leave."

All I can do is nod and take his hand – united. He no longer has a home; I no longer know where my real home is. We slowly walk back to the car to return to Daniel's house.

When I am convinced that Stan is safe and resting and there is nothing more to see or say, Martha drives the two of us back to the café, which the kids are running today. Entering through the back door we find the place is subdued. Don't get me wrong, there are a lot of people sitting at tables eating and drinking, but hardly anyone raises their voice above a whisper. Many of the locals have gathered, familiar faces, and when I walk in they turn and watch me. I can feel the tears well. Before they can fall, Brody comes towards me and holds me tight, murmuring how sorry he is. Sophia is openly sobbing, and I notice that many of the customers are too. We are all grieving for Shirley but also for Stan. Our collective bereavement is a reaction to the loss we are feeling as a community.

The whole town is in shock. Yes, the boards are removed from the windows, the powerlines reconnected, and the sand put back on the beach. Yes, folks return to their everyday lives, but the storm has left its mark – one injured tourist, two damaged cars, several upturned boats and Shirley's death – all of us have been affected by several hours of wind and rain. I simply feel numb.

And in the following days the heartbreak keeps me from sleeping. I'm not entirely sure I eat anything resembling a proper meal. It is grief, I know; the helplessness etched into every waking moment. Yet it somewhat surprises me, as I've only known Stan and Shirley for a few short months. I suppose I am closer to Stan, but that's probably because I have spent more time with him; hours and hours side by side painting together, and that brings a closeness which leads to imparting secrets and keeping confidences. I told Shirley I loved her and it's true, and yet there's a sense of the grief being mixed with regret. Regret that I didn't take the time to get to know her better, lost opportunities to spend time with her. And maybe it's the fact that my dear friend is totally destroyed by the death of his wife.

Even the weather seems to be grieving; there is a faint dew on the ground in the morning. The odd leaf is losing its grip on the summer green and is turning a pale yellow with the promise of stunning autumn colours to come.

While running I wonder if the change to the beautiful array of fall colours will arrive before I depart. Repeating: October fifteenth, five beats. Oct.O.Ber.Fift.teenth. Five steps. Over and over in rhythm with my breathing – five in – five out, October fifteenth. I cannot stop thinking about it. What to do? Where to live? Go home? Stay? October fifteenth. Running may do my body some good, but my mind is in disarray and a sense of agitation and discontentment adds to the swirl of emotions. Today we must plan a funeral and I am not looking forward to being there. I know I will cry. I know it will be upsetting. Grief is exhausting – it ebbs and flows like the tide, in and out, sometimes close, sometimes distant, but it's there all the time. Beyond control, beyond belief. It never leaves.

We meet at Daniel's house and sit quietly, talking in hushed tones. Why does no-one shout and scream about the futility of it all? I breathe and try to stay calm and am grateful that Martha is in total control. She has withdrawn all her emotions and hidden behind the barrier of logic and efficiency. She puts forward ideas and waits for Stan's response, Daniel's view, my opinion. We decide collectively and move to the next point. Flowers, cremation or burial, service, food, guests. All dispatched swiftly and calmly.

Daniel is withdrawn too, and I am unable to approach him, to hold his hand, to hold him, as he holds himself rigidly, remotely, and my heart aches with the need to comfort him.

Stan is quiet and he too shows little reaction: he is stoic, quietly answering Martha's questions as though it's someone else's funeral we are organising, not that of his beloved wife. When we finish, he sighs and as he does so, deflates. We all hold it together, in a way supportive but at the same time isolated. Together but apart, all of us grieving differently and I need to remember to respect that. Slowly, tears roll down my cheeks at the despair I feel.

And then I realise that I must tell Katie. A text is too informal. If I call her, I will cry. I decide to send an email, taking the time to choose the words carefully. I'll do it later.

From: Jane [mailto: janenjon28@web.com]

Sent: 1 September 22.00

To: Katie@Katiesplace.web.com

Subject: Evening

Hi Best Friend,

I'm sorry I have not been in touch recently. We've had the most dreadful time, Katie.

There was a big storm. We had to board up all the windows downstairs and in my apartment. The whole town seemed to go into lockdown. It was rather frightening, I have to say.

In the night, a tree fell on the corner of Stan's house, and it killed Shirley. I'm sorry to have to let you know with an email but every time I talk about it, I cry and, to be honest, today I am fed up with the tears.

It's been the worst few days since, well since Jon died, and all the memories keep flooding back. I also got to thinking about my grandparents - I still have all four of them; aren't I the lucky one? But if I come and live here… if I stay - then I might never see them again. All these thoughts are going round and round in my head. I can't sleep.

We're all dealing with it differently: Martha is Mrs Efficiency, Stan is stoic, and Daniel has withdrawn into himself, and I am struggling with that too, and you seem so far away, and I need a hug.

I miss you.

Love you loads.

Jane

From: Katie [mailto: Katie@Katiesplace.web.com]

Sent: 1 September 22.23

To: janenjon28@web.com

Subject: Love you

I'm so sorry. Oh Jane, so very sorry. Sorry, so sorry to hear about Shirley – it must be distressing for you all. I cannot imagine.

My heart aches for Stan too, what a lovely man. He is so kind and gentle. Please send him my love and give him a big hug from me.

Don't worry about Martha and Daniel, they'll work it out themselves, but I can see why you are struggling. Just hold yourself together, my dear. You can do this.

I miss you too, my friend and I wish I could come and give you a big hug, but Michael and I are off on holiday in the morning, a second honeymoon. As soon as we get back, I'll be in touch again. Promise.

Love you. Hold it together.

Katie

Reading the email again, I get the sense that Katie and Michael have repaired the damage to their marriage and a second honeymoon is just what they need. It makes me smile – a bright light in the dark skies of my grief.

Martha's role as Mrs Efficiency extends to dealing with Stan's belongings from the house. She organises a van and takes Daniel over to collect the items they consider worth retaining and preserving, including the china, leaving me to sit with Stan. No-one wants to leave him alone. The house is emptied of all the remnants of his life accumulated over the decades and moved to a storage unit outside town.

None of us is present to witness the demolition of Stan's home, but the day after I decide to go for a run in that direction. As I enter the street I am shocked by the sight that greets me. The huge hole in the ground where the tree once stood has been filled in and grassed over – they laid lawn on it, like it was never there. The wood pile has vanished like the death-dealing tree never existed and the plot of land where once stood their home is bare and raw, the wound open and sore.

I stand and stare, sobbing silently. Sobbing for the fragility of life; Shirley's life snuffed out in a moment. My grandparents coming to the end of their lives without me. Potentially. For my life – I caught a glimpse of how it might be, living here with my new friends, being part of their lives. But with Daniel withdrawn and remote, unreachable, I feel the fragility of our relationship and the person I was becoming, confident, capable. It all seems to have disappeared in a flash of a stormy night.

41

It is early morning, a week after the storm and two days before the funeral. I am alone in the café, now fully established in town as the English Tearoom, in a place I love, a place I helped to create. My usual contentment is mixed with the sadness that continues to follow me like a grey cloud, close then distant, back and forth, unpredictable. From the radio I hear the words of a song that stirs this sadness. I turn it off. I cannot listen. Tears seep and I accept them, letting them flow and not suppressing them. Yet this feeling of being stuck in no man's land, this thought lingers; I'm neither here nor there, with nowhere fixed and the restlessness that fills my days affects my nights and my sleep. I yawn and long to go back to bed.

My reverie is interrupted by the sound of the back door opening. I shake myself and cannot help but smile at the sight of Brody. He advances towards me, this handsome young man, arms open wide and hugs me so tightly it's hard to breathe. For a teenage boy, he shows an amazing amount of intuition and concern.

"You OK?" he asks, looking me in the eye.

"I will be," I admit.

He nods, satisfied, then he lets go, walks away and turns the radio back on as he passes. I briefly consider turning it off again. *No. Breathe. I can do this.*

Not long after, Martha arrives and we sit with our morning coffee discussing the day ahead, which includes what we will require for the funeral food-wise, and how we will accommodate everyone.

"I think it's important we have this place for friends to gather… after…"

I agree with a nod while staring down at my notes. It is a moment before I realise that Martha has stopped talking. I look up. She is crying. Why I find this astonishing, I don't know, but I do. Her hard exterior has crumpled and it's a distressing sight. *Do I leave her? Ignore her and let her be? Do I hug her? What?*

I decide on a compromise and sit next to her on the sofa. As I take hold of her hand she starts to sob uncontrollably. No words can help at this point, so I sit quietly and stroke the back of her hand until she recovers.

"I'm so sorry about that." She finds a tissue and wipes her face, her eyes, and blows her nose.

"No need."

She sighs deeply. "Wow, that came from deep within.

Sorry, my dear. I hope I didn't…" Her voice fades.

I can see she is trying to rebuild that exterior protective wall. I wait patiently. She will tell me. I have seen this before.

"I'm not good at accepting comfort," she explains. "I've always relied on myself. I even grieved for my father by myself, and I've always seen self-sufficiency as a virtue." She takes a sip of her (now cold) coffee.

I decide to make us both a fresh cup and bring them back to the table.

"Thank you." I can see she has used my absence to recover completely and the Martha I know and love is back. "Shirley has always been like a mother to me. I never had a relationship with my biological mother, she was aloof and cold. I had a nanny from the day I was born, and she was the one who took care of me, Nanny Rogers. I saw my mother for an hour each evening after my bath and before bedtime. It was a strained time for us both. When I moved here, Shirley kind of adopted me and took care of me in a way I had never experienced before, and to lose her…" She sniffs then sits upright, shoulders back. She will not break down again. "She helped me put my life back together again after Daddy died, she was there when I needed her the most and now she's gone…" She takes a deep breath and a moment or two passes, then, "Right! Let's get on with things, shall we?"

Normal service is resumed.

The morning of the funeral dawns clear and bright. I am physically present in the day and my emotions are currently under control, but my mind flashes back years – Jon. That morning, I woke up in our big bed by myself. This morning, I wake up in my big bed by myself. The parallels are continuous and will be all day – I know it, the links are undeniable. If I had a stronger faith in God, a faith beyond simple inherited belief, now would be a good time to ask for help and the strength to cope with another funeral on another continent. Instead, I take a shower and try to prepare myself for the day that lies ahead.

On the drive over to church I stare out of the window like I did two years ago, quietly contemplating how the world carries on as normal. It's an ordinary morning: the tourists enjoy their vacation totally unaware, the kids eating ice cream, the shops selling souvenirs. But the world isn't normal nor ordinary anymore, is it? I wonder what Stan finally picked out to wear today. Helping him to choose was hard, and all the time I was wishing Martha had taken on the responsibility. Would it be the same suit he wore when they got married (after getting over the surprise that he still had the suit and that it still fitted) or the Navy uniform he keeps in the old chest?

Martha and I arrive at the church early and there is a chill inside despite the growing summer heat of the day; she inspects every flower arrangement, and every detail has been organised to perfection. The ladies who are always in charge of flowers in church have done a fine job, and the entrance and the nave are filled with fragrance and colour. We too are dressed brightly, precisely as Stan requested. I bought a new yellow and white dress for the occasion and Martha has a linen outfit of peach, cream and orange with a matching bandana on her head to keep her black curls in place. She looks amazing and I follow her lead by trying to be efficient, cool, calm and collected.

As we stand in the entrance, I notice the pale blue sky has white fluffy benign clouds. The weather is kind of soothing and so different from ten days ago when it assaulted the senses. Breathing deeply, a smile fixed on my face, I help Martha to receive the guests and well-wishers: friends from town, all three kids from the café and their respective families, along with Sally and Ricky (who is dressed in a suit and is sombre), the lady from the dress shop, Jessica (who smiles a genuine smile at me for the first time) and so many more. Folks whisper self-consciously, wondering what the etiquette for a funeral is – who to talk to, where to look, should I smile? The place fills up rapidly leaving the front pew empty for the four of us.

Daniel and Stan arrive eventually. Stan knew he would not be able to face everyone before the funeral service so asked if it would be alright to arrive last. I notice there is a smile on his face as he acknowledges members of the congregation. He has chosen to wear his wedding suit. Daniel, on the other hand, looks drawn and ashen, and though a smile fleetingly passes over his face, it doesn't touch his beautiful green eyes as the two of them move swiftly down the aisle towards the vicar and the front pew. There is no coffin – again at Stan's request. He wants to celebrate her life. She will be buried on another day, privately. Stan does not want to be present. He cannot watch her being placed in the ground just like I couldn't watch them bury Jon. Links, so many links.

We take our seats with Stan on the end, his head held erect, the strain in his neck from the effort is obvious. A nerve twitches. He gazes into space, both hands limp on his knees, the sparkle gone from his eyes. The initial acute grief was so powerful and yet turns out to be transient. Now even this short time after, we are moving into a different phase. Numb has become unfeeling. I glance again towards Stan and see myself two years ago. I close my eyes. I. Can. Do. This.

The ceremony is poignant and sweet, and we laugh, and we sigh. We even shed a tear or two. The vicar knew Shirley well and describes her in such a beautiful way that we are all pleased and smile at her memory, except for Daniel who is barely holding it together. His distress is tangible as he grips my hand throughout the whole ceremony until my fingers turn white and I lose all sense of feeling. During the final prayer, he lets out an audible sob that breaks my heart.

Finally, when the funeral service is over, Stan is gracious in receiving the condolences of his friends. With Martha by his side, he makes his way out of the church and into the sunshine of the graveyard, where people have gathered to chat. I take Daniel to the car and leave him alone to recover.

There is an open invitation back to the café, where Sally is now in charge with Brody, tall Amy and Sophia to help her; they are doing a great job of welcoming the guests and making sure everyone has something to eat and something to drink. I thank each one of them, knowing it must be tough to work on a day such as this. I take time to make sure that Sally is coping as I know she is taking Shirley's death as badly as we are.

"How you doing?"

"Holding up," she says with a small smile as she wrinkles her nose. "You?"

"About the same. Thank you for helping out today, I couldn't face it."

"No worries."

"You're doing a great job."

"Wouldn't be any place else."

We smile and I hug her briefly to let her know I care

without making either of us too emotional. Not now. Not yet. Later. Maybe.

I smile at folks, not quite believing how many are here, and wander, trying to be efficient and friendly, while Martha ensures that Daniel and Stan are alright. Coping. OK. Just.

About four o'clock it suddenly all becomes too much for me, seeing Daniel in such pain, Stan being so stoic, all the people around me. The noise and the pressure is overpowering, and I need to escape. I slip out into the kitchen and close the door for a measure of privacy. I rest my head against the cool glass in the back door and quietly let the tears flow. Slowly my sense of being overwhelmed eases. Amy finds me.

"You OK?" she asks.

Why do we always ask such a stupid question when it's obvious that we're not and yet we all do it?! I sniff, nod and wipe away the tears. She hands me a tissue.

"I'm fine," I tell her. We both know I am lying.

Eventually folks drift off home. I pay the kids double time and thank them again for all their hard work and finally, finally there are four of us. Sitting quietly. Lost in our own thoughts.

Stan clears his throat and says, "Shirley would have loved today. Thank you for making it such a special day. I really appreciate all your help."

"I like the fact that everyone took a flower home.

Where did you get that idea from, Jane?" Martha asks.

"From Jon's funeral. We filled the church with spring flowers just like he asked. But they die so quickly, and he knew I hated to see flowers die so he told me to make sure that the people who came took the flowers home with them. I made up bunches of daffodils and tulips. Everybody loved it."

"Nice touch."

We all look at the vase of flowers, taken from the church, on the coffee table in front of us.

"My Shirley loved flowers. The first house we lived in after we got married, she wasn't too bothered about the inside, but she couldn't wait to get out into that tiny garden and plant some flowers. I was just home from the Navy. It was a cosy house. We had our whole future in front of us."

I hear Daniel sniff; I cannot look at him, sitting in the chair, slightly away from us, isolated. He hasn't spoken for what seems like hours.

"We, sorry she… planted all sorts of flowers, like these. I don't know what they're called but she would smile at me and say, 'never mind, Stanley'." He smiles. "She was so patient and kind. She was a good wife, and she would have made a great mother… I wish we'd been able to have kids," he says wistfully.

I can hear Daniel again; he is so emotional, but now all of us are choosing to ignore him. The pull to go and comfort him is so strong, unbearably strong.

"But never to be," Stan concludes.

Silence returns. All of us lost in our own thoughts and our own histories. Martha is about to speak when Daniel whispers, "We couldn't have kids either."

I turn to look at him.

"My fault," he adds.

The silence that haunts the room is tangible. My heart is thumping. I glance towards Stan and then back at Martha. *Do you know what he's talking about?* The spark of anxiety grows with every silent second.

"It was not your fault, Daniel," Martha tells him calmly. "It's just one of those things."

He shakes his head. "Nope. My fault and that's why she left me." *WHAT?* He looks right at me, his eyes bright with tears. "Left me because I couldn't give her what she wanted, couldn't give her a child she so desperately wanted, wanted more than me." He is so sad, but also angry, bitter. I have not seen this before. It's new. "She left me and married some guy within months of our divorce, and she's got two kids now."

Struggling to control my reaction, desperate that he doesn't see my shock, I don't know what to say or even if he needs to hear anything.

"Daniel, son, it really isn't your fault," Stan tells him. The effort of consoling him is depleting the last dregs of Stan's energy and he seems to shrink into the chair under the strain.

"Shirley always used to tell me that," he sniffs again.

"And she's right," Martha chips in. "It's all in the past now. History."

"We should look to the future now," Stan adds.

How did this all become about Daniel? Surely today should be about Stan?

"And how are we supposed to do that?" Daniel suddenly snaps. Abruptly, he gets up and leaves.

"Let him go," Martha tells me as she sees me start to move.

"But he's hurting."

"I know he is but let him be. This anger, this frustration, he needs to work it out himself."

"I've never seen him like this."

"It's very rare," she tells me. "Very."

"Jane, he loved Shirley so much; they were close," Stan says. "He feels her loss deeply. She nourished him and helped him to heal, she was almost like a mother to him."

There's a theme going here.

"When his wife left him, he was in a bad place and Shirley was there for him, more than we were, I think." He glances at Martha for confirmation then turns to me. "He's over her, he's over it all." He is trying to reassure me. "But I guess this has brought it all back to him. He's lost the one person who helped him. He feels lost."

"It's brought a lot of the past back for all of us," Martha comments almost to herself.

"It has," I add. "But the past… it never leaves you. Today reminded me so much of Jon's funeral." I sigh. "It's tough."

We all silently agree; we are all grappling with our own issues, our own past experiences. Suddenly I can bear it no longer and, ignoring Martha's advice, I stand up.

"I should go to him."

Daniel is sitting on my steps.

"Hi."

"Hi."

"You OK?" I ask that stupid question warily.

He looks up, eyes bloodshot, and nods. "I guess. Tough day. I'm sorry for what I said back there. It shouldn't be about me; we should be supporting Stan really."

I long to touch him, to hold him, but decide instead to sit down next to him. Not too close. He puts his head in his hands once more.

"I miss her so much."

Who? Shirley or your wife?

"She helped put me back together again."

Phew, Shirley! Immediately I feel guilty about being concerned about such things on a day like today.

"She loved me unconditionally. Accepted me and

she always knew what to say at the right time. She was so special."

"I can see that."

"I'm sorry for storming out like that."

"It's OK."

We sit quietly for a moment.

"I wish I'd known her more," I confess.

He looks up and smiles weakly. At least it's a smile. "She was a wonderful woman. She was like my second mom."

There's that theme.

"She called me her toy boy, but I hope she thought of me as a son. She couldn't have children, couldn't hold onto one for nine months."

"They made it through though. As a couple."

"Yeah, well lucky them." He sounds bitter again. "My ex hardly bothered to work it out or get through it. She moved on."

"Then she missed out on something special. She missed out on being with you."

His eyes are red from crying. He puts his head back in his hands as though it's too heavy to hold. There are no more words. He is hunched over. I put my hand on his back and stroke him gently. He makes no move, he has withdrawn. I cannot reach him.

42

The day after the funeral and the world feels subdued. The weather is calm; people who venture into the café are holding muted, hushed conversations. Sally and I go about our business without the usual banter. We're both tired but thankfully, work helps to keep my mind occupied. Martha arrives around noon and even she is withdrawn. All of us are dealing with the grief and the sadness of losing Shirley, as well as the emotions of the funeral. There is a lot of silence, and the occasional tear is swiftly wiped away.

Jessica calls in and spends a few minutes with Martha. Both Sally and I are immediately wary and grateful that we don't have to deal with her. It's the last thing we need right now. And yet seeing her slumped in her chair, obviously distressed, I feel a sense of pity and sympathy.

My face must reveal this as Sally whispers, "Don't you start feeling sorry for her."

"Why? Don't you think those tears are genuine?"

"Genuine? Ha! I doubt she's got a genuine bone in her body."

I scrutinise Jessica. Her tears appear real enough, and Martha's body language seems to support that. I venture over and ask if they need anything.

Jessica looks up, tear stained. "No thank you."

I move to leave them.

"Jane," she calls me back. "Jane… I want to apologise for the way I've treated you."

I don't know who's more surprised, me or Martha.

"I have behaved badly," she admits.

Martha turns to me and her eyes ask, 'what?'

I am lost for words.

The café is silent. I want to say, 'That's OK', but it's not. I want to believe she means it, but history tells me to be on my guard. So, I smile and say, "You must have had your reasons." Sounds so stupid, but there it is. I know she has this hard exterior, and I know her past has moulded her. We will never be friends, but I could at least show I understand and acknowledge her apology, whether it's genuine or not.

"I can see that you're a good person and I'm sorry I doubted you. The way you handled yesterday" — she sniffs — "and helped Stanley. It was very kind of you. Shirley was a good friend and I shall miss her."

"We all will," Martha adds.

We all agree on something. I am lost for words. This

is weird. I have to walk away.

The beginning of September means that the kids – Brody, Sophia and tall Amy – will be going back to college. It feels like everyone is leaving and I am losing people I love all the time. It definitely feels like I am losing Daniel as he continues to be withdrawn. I tell Martha how worried I am by his behaviour.

"I'm worried too," she agrees, as a frown crosses her face.

"I have never seen him like this before, have you? I know he's missing Shirley, we all are, but this seems more somehow?"

"I have seen it a couple of times, whenever he talks about his dad and his mom, it's like they bring out the worst in him, but then I kind of get that." She pauses to consider her next words. "But then if his ex-wife becomes a topic of conversation, that can get him riled up. The way she behaved towards him was atrocious and I think at the time he struggled with the rejection. I guess this is his way of dealing with the stress of losing someone he loved. He loved his parents, he loved his wife — sorry, ex-wife — and he was abandoned by them."

"I wish I could reach him."

"I know, sweetie. He is still there, honestly. Clearly, it'll take time."

I flop down on the sofa opposite her. It is the end of another busy day and I want to tell her that time is something I don't have much of. The last week has been hell and suddenly it is all too much and the pain above my right eye strikes and tears flow. At first they are silent and go un-noticed, and then a sob is emitted, then another one, and before I know it I'm rocking back and forth, unable to control what is happening, swamped by the well of emotions as they overflow.

Sometime later, now empty and hollow, the tears dry and I start to breathe normally. Calmly, I sit up and find Martha close by, anxious and concerned.

"Sorry."

"Please don't be sorry, my dear girl. Would you like coffee or something stronger?"

"Something stronger, I think. Please."

Martha finds a bottle of red wine and two glasses, pours us both a large measure. She sits and asks, "So what brought that on?" and waits for my response.

Heaving a huge sigh, I open up to her about how I have been feeling: reliving Jon's funeral, watching all of us grieve, losing Daniel and having to go home, all of it, and the helplessness that accompanies these events.

And then I ask, "And how about you?"

"Me?"

"Yes, are you coping? You said it brought a lot of the past back for you too."

"Ah, yes. So, I did." She takes a huge swig of wine then tops up her glass. "Where to start?"

I wonder if she is going to tell me more about her parents and what happened when her father died. I can see her deciding on how to tell the truth and where to begin, but I am not prepared for what follows.

"While I was in college, I went to Yale to study law, in my second year I went to London to do a semester at the Inns of Court. You heard of them?"

I nod.

"There I met a most wonderful man." Her eyes soften at the memory. "James. His name was James, and we were in love and everything was simply wonderful. A glorious summer. We went everywhere together: dining at the Ritz, weekends in the country at some amazing country estates. I have never been happier… Then I fell pregnant."

I can see she is struggling to keep the long-hidden emotions under control. Martha is a survivor and proud of the fact. She holds herself upright. I almost hold my breath. Not what I expected. At. All. There is a long silence as Martha swirls the remaining wine in her glass, lost in memories. I wait patiently for her to continue. I don't think I say anything even if I wanted to, I am so stunned by the revelation.

"Unfortunately, James wasn't as happy as I was about this turn of events. You see, he had a great future ahead of him, all planned out. He was going to become a great barrister and then a judge and finally he would be appointed to the Supreme Court." She catches the surprised expression on my face. "Oh yes, I've followed his career with interest. But you see, back then an American wife and a child was not part of his plan, nor the plan his family had for him. He came from a noble family. So, I was cast off, like a used rag. Abandoned."

That had got to hurt.

"I came back to the US, and mother – well, she exploded with indignation. You should have seen her – white with rage. She told me I had let the family down. I was unmarriable now. I was a disgrace. You get the picture?"

I nod again.

Another sigh. More wine. "She ordered me out of the country before my figure started to change shape, to avoid any scandal, and back to England to have my baby. Back to England, I ask you. How cruel! She knew I wouldn't be able to see James. She did it on purpose, I'm convinced of it. I stayed with a distant aunt who lived in Buckinghamshire. When my daughter was born, I held her in my arms for three whole days before giving her up for adoption and returning to the US."

My heart breaks when I look at her. She is doing a supreme job of containing whatever is happening inside. The strain is visible in the lines on her face, which I've never noticed before.

"In my mind, she has always been Jemima," she adds wistfully. "I love that name and it suited her perfectly. She will be about thirty-six years old now..."

The words hang in the air.

43

Wondering what to do with my day, I'm passing my spare room when I spot the paints and paper, lying there abandoned since before the storm. Instantly, I decide to go out and capture the change in the weather, the changing of the season, and take my wise friend, Stan, with me.

I call Martha to ask if he is up for a few hours by the lake and am pleasantly surprised and delighted when she tells me "Yes" and that she would drive him over in about an hour. She too will join us, "Though I am NOT going to paint!" she states before hanging up abruptly. I am used to her sudden disappearance; she hates using the telephone and considers it an instrument of torture. She has a smart phone but rarely uses it, much to everyone's frustration – except Martha's.

We've not spoken much since our conversation and I'm not sure how she will react to my knowing her secret, to being so vulnerable. And I'm still not sure how I feel about what she's told me. All this continues to pile emotion on top of emotion. I know I am going to have to deal with it all before it swamps me and I cannot cope. Finding myself is proving to be tricky. Or maybe I should accept that this is me – the overthinker, the worrier, the emotional wreck!

Down by the lake, I set up my easel and put on the large canvas. I want to stand and paint today. I want to use a big brush. I want to make huge slashing marks on the canvas. Angry, frustrated large dark paint marks.

I painted like this when Jon died, when I hated the world for leaving me bereft. Immersed in my angst, it takes time for me to become aware that Martha and Stan have arrived and are making their way down to where I am standing, splashed with paint. Martha looks at the canvas and out at the view in front of her and back at the canvas.

"That's not what I see!" she comments. "But hey, what do I know? Is it impressionistic or something?" She frowns as she tries to understand what I have created.

"It's representative but not real." I sound pompous without meaning to and sigh deeply as I put down my brush. "Actually, it's just an angry painting."

"Angry?" She squints at me. "Oh OK." She takes a step back. "I'll leave you guys to it, I guess. I'll be in the car if you need me. Stan, she is angry today. Don't take no stick from her. OK?"

So, the old Martha we all love is back behind her barrier. I am almost relieved. Stan shakes his head wisely and sets up his own easel and canvas without saying a word. His mere presence brings that welcome sense of calm. It is soothing and the negative emotions subside oh so slightly. He raises his pencil and starts to draw. I sit down on the soft grass and watch him, hoping to somehow absorb his inner peace. Eventually he speaks.

"You wanna talk about it?"

I cannot help myself; I need to empty out all the past. Again.

"It's always been my most hated part of the year – March. For a time, I also hated Fridays, and if Friday ever coincided with twenty-ninth of any month – well… dreadful. Thankfully, Friday, March twenty-ninth only occurs every six years, so I guess I have that to look forward to."

The irony is not lost on Stan, and he smiles at me.

"The weeks and months passed, people offered me sympathy which I accepted, then they moved on and I stayed put. I lost that special status of the recently bereaved. Life moved on. Slowly. I thought I'd get over it and that grief would go away, and life would get back to 'normal'. Then I realised that it was always going to be there. I was changed forever. I would have to adjust and adapt and find a new normal." I stop for a moment to think about the impact my words are having on Stan. Again, not very supportive; I appear to be more concerned about me, me, me. I try and change my tone to sound more positive. "Just like you're going to have to find a new normal."

Stan smiles as though he can hear what's going on in my head and tells me he has dealt with death before, when he was in the Navy. More than death, with trauma and the life-changing injuries of his fellow sailors.

"Grief is strange, don't ya think?" Stan says as his eyes scan the horizon.

I nod. He pauses for a moment, lost in thought.

"Funny, but I grieved when I left the Navy despite all the horrors of war. I missed the camaraderie of being in the forces, the brotherhood. That took time to get over and adjust when I got home. But you know, you just get on with life, I guess. I have no words that would be of any use to you," he continues, "no words that can do you any good."

He watches me intently, and we both have tears in our eyes. He is blurred but I am comforted by his presence. I tell him more about why I came to the US, hoping that my tone is more positive. I tell him how I feel about him, Martha and Shirley, and eventually about Daniel. All my insecurities emerge despite my best efforts, but I share, and we discuss, and I pack them away as if I'd told someone a big secret, as though it was no longer my burden to carry. Stan knows all about my pain and sorrow at losing Jon. He knows now how I feel about Daniel. He understands and shares the moment, precious as it is.

"I'm sorry I offloaded all that. You don't need to hear this right now, do you?"

"No need to be sorry."

"But you have enough to deal with yourself without listening to all my woes." I put my hand on his arm and lean my head onto his shoulder. Contact is comforting.

"That's true," he admits. "But that doesn't mean I can't listen to you, my dearest girl."

"Thank you. I do appreciate it." I pause. "How're you doing?"

"OK, I guess. Some days I make it through in one piece and others I barely hold myself together. I miss her. She was my lifetime companion, and now life, well it carries on, I guess, like you said. The sun comes up each morning. I eat. I sleep. I do stuff, but it has so little meaning now. I sometimes wish I could go to sleep and not wake up, join her wherever she is. I'm not sure what my future looks like now."

"I wish I had known her for longer."

"Me too."

"But you do have a future, you know. You have me."

"I know."

"And Daniel and Martha too, we all love you and you do have so much to live for."

He doesn't reply. He's not convinced.

"You OK at Martha's house?"

He nods. "I love that woman. She's the best!" He pats my hand. "You've been so wonderful too, my dear. I don't know what I'd have done without you all."

"That's what friends are for."

"True."

"And you could always come and work at the café with me. I always need a spare pair of hands."

He laughs. "You're kiddin', right?"

"No, I'm not! Martha is handing me more and more responsibility and taking less interest in the day to day running of the place now she's in the middle of writing this book. I can hire who I like. And I'd like to hire you now that the kids are leaving and going back to college!"

He laughs again. "We'll see!"

We go back to our painting. And this time I can paint what is in front of me and not what is in my heart.

Oakham's Labour day activities that took place at the weekend seem to have passed us all by while we were working flat out. So, to celebrate the end of summer, and for the kids, we decide to have a going-away party in the park – a picnic to say goodbye. All their families and friends are invited. We eat and drink and laugh and chat, and strangely enough, it's a refreshing change for all of us after the events of the previous weeks. We play rounders (sorry – baseball) and flake out on the grass after all the running, throwing and cheering. It's good to see Daniel joining in – he looks better, though in quiet moments the sadness is etched on his face. He's not been around much, and I miss his soft chuckle, his smile and his kisses. Stan is invited and sits next to Martha, quiet but calm. He smiles a lot, which lifts my heart.

The kids are excited by the new term, the prospect of going back to university and what the future holds for them. But for me it is painful to say goodbye and let them go. I don't tell them this – they have their lives in front of them and no-one and nothing should hold them back, especially me. But I want to hang on to them and the summer and the wonderful times we've spent together. I don't want things to change. I want everything to stay as it is right now, and yet knowing that's impossible, I smile and hug them and wish them well.

Tall Amy is going away for the first time and is a little anxious but also excited about leaving home and being independent, having new experiences. She weeps when she says goodbye and tells me it's been the best summer ever. I figure it's because she has found love for the first time with an equally tall young man called Josh whom she introduced me to earlier, but she says it's because of me. I am not so sure. She promises to keep in touch and visit me in England. I cannot speak to her about it. I don't know where I will be – in England or back here?

Sophia is up for some bribery and promises to fill the freezer with cakes and cookies, and also to return as often as she can to bake some more. She too has had a brilliant summer and is not sure she wants to go back to college or take a catering course and find work in a kitchen. I tell her she can work for me anytime and we cry when we hug and say goodbye.

Brody, my handsome Brody, hugs me so tightly I can hardly breathe, and tells me I'm the best and how much he enjoyed his summer, and asks can he come again next year. He has no idea of my inner turmoil and I do not burden him with it – I simply nod. I ask him not to be a stranger and he tells me he'll be my friend for life.

Three great kids. We have become a great tight-knit team. I shall miss them all so much. It has been a lovely day and as everyone is packing up and making plans to depart, I find myself next to Daniel. I take his hand and raise it to my lips.

"Hi."

"Hi."

"You OK?" I ask him. There's that stupid question again!

He sighs. "I guess."

I move closer to him, contemplating my next move, before standing on the tips of my toes to reach him, then kiss him gently.

"I miss you," I whisper.

"I'm sorry."

His eyes brighten with tears. Then he wraps his arms around me and kisses me deep and with such longing that my heart swells with all the emotions I have been feeling and trying to suppress. He's still there. He still feels the same. Relief mixes with joy, and for a moment all the sadness is forgotten. "I've missed you too."

"You want to go for a walk on the beach?"

I am both relieved and pleased when he nods his agreement.

Holding hands, we stroll up Main Street and down to the beach but decide to sit on the grass by the lighthouse instead of venturing down onto the sand.

"How do you think Stan's doing?" I ask him. "You've seen him more than me."

"We went fishing yesterday – yeah, he seems OK. He's a different generation to us, not one to show his emotions."

"Stoic."

He nods. "I guess so. He's trying to be positive and

to think of the good times they spent together. He says he's fine and he appears to be happy at Martha's."

We discuss the plans he's drawing up for the garage conversion – a permanent place for Stan to live.

"It'll give him a measure of independence, but with Martha right there, that's gonna give him some security too."

"He doesn't say much."

"I know, but that's his way of dealing with it all."

I tell him about going painting (but not about what we discussed) and we agree that keeping him occupied will help heal his wounds, hopefully. I take a moment to wonder if I should ask then decide to go for it.

"And how do you think you're dealing with it all?"

He sighs deeply and lies back on the grass, staring at the sky, which has the first hint of stars sparkling in the darkening blue. "I'm kind of getting my head around it. I think the shock has worn off; the trauma of that night is easing somewhat." He pauses, closing his eyes. "You know, all the things that happen to us in the past, they never leave us, do they?"

He briefly opens his eyes and looks at me to see if I agree with him. I do. He closes them again. I wait. There has to be more to say.

"My mom, the way she treated me different than my brothers, really affected my life. I know my younger brother resented me; my older one ignored me most of the time. Mom encouraged me to excel at school and the better grades I got, the more touchdowns I scored, the more I succeeded, the worse it got and the more she made a fuss. She thought she was encouraging me, but no matter what I did, it wasn't enough. It was never enough. If only she'd treated us all the same." He sounds so wistful. "In the end I had to leave, leave home, Montana, everyone. I had to escape and make my own life."

The struggle of reliving those days is almost physical, his body is tense, his hands clenched.

"Then I met" — he still cannot say her name — "and we built a life together. We were happy… for a time. We were both successful, we had a good social life, friends, a great apartment. We even bought the house here. I thought we had it all."

I am holding my breath.

"Then her biological clock started to tick so loud, but we couldn't seem to conceive. We went to see the doctor and had some tests done." He pauses again.

This is painful for him, I can tell. But I also know he needs to tell me in order to help me to understand what's happening to him.

"Turns out I have a low sperm count and the chances of us having a baby were remote, possible but remote. We looked at getting IVF treatment, but over the weeks and months, her need to be in control and the sorrow that seems to surround us, well we drifted. Drifted apart. She worked more because it seemed to give her something to focus on. Then she got offered a promotion and we discussed it. Well, shall I say she told me about it. I don't recall ever having any input into that conversation. Then one day she came home from work and told me she'd decided to take the promotion and she was moving to Oregon! Oregon, I ask you!" He sighs again. "She just packed up what she wanted from the apartment, told me to find a lawyer as she wanted a divorce, and she left."

Wow! That is heartless. I hunch my knees up closer and hug them tightly, not knowing what to say. What can I say? The poor man has been badly treated by the women in his life.

"That was five years ago." He sits up and looks at me. "I've not looked at another woman since, until now. Until you."

It sounds like he is open to trying again. With me. My doubts surface, doubts about me, him. About us moving forward. I push them away resolutely. Unwilling to share. Not now.

44

Daniel is due back in the city. Normally it is at the beginning of September, around Labor Day weekend, that he packs up the house and moves back to Boston, but this year he does not leave as though he senses the need to stay, for all of us to be together.

As the days pass I find I am capable of building a new 'normal', a world without Shirley in it, a life where everyone is sad. I've done it before and I can do it again. I have more good days than bad days, and if I have happy moments, they do not make me feel guilty. My resolve and strength are re-emerging with each passing moment. I want to be happy. I want to look to the future, though what that future is I am still not sure.

On a particularly positive day, I venture online to find out if I can renew my B-2 visa, only to discover I cannot renew but need to reapply and to do that I have to be out of the country. Canada maybe? Negativity replaces positivity. The research makes me unsure as to what to do next, how to proceed. Should I make the effort to plan my return, or should I simply say 'thank you for a great six months' and go back to England? But then my thoughts fly to Daniel. He needs my support now more than ever. He opened his heart to me; I can't break it. Yet I don't feel strong enough to take on the pressure of being someone else's happiness. Everything I have achieved since I have been here. I have grown. I am not the person I was when I left England, but insecurities and lack of confidence swiftly return and the act of staying positive takes its toll. The emotional tiredness of the shock of Shirley's death and dealing with the emotional behaviour of my friends, and now this. Frankly, it's exhausting. They are all so wrapped up in their own grief, how can I burden them? I still feel guilty about saying anything to Stan. I could talk with Katie, but she's so far away, geographically and physically. Alone and lonely, I keep it inside.

The sun floods in through the kitchen window. The cafe is a place that is guaranteed to soothe my soul and I love the sense of satisfaction I get every time a cake is decorated and finished and set on the counter for the customers. But more than anything I love my boss. She is a smart, beautiful woman, a lively New Yorker – you can take the girl out of 5th Avenue but not 5th out of the girl – and today she is wearing a wonderful bohemian outfit of multi-coloured pink.

In a very business-like manner – which as I have come to understand belies hidden depths – she asks me, "When are you leaving us?" Her tone when emotions are involved – cool and distant.

"I have to leave mid-October."

"How long will you be gone?"

"Why?" I reply.

She looks straight at me and it's like her handshake – bone crushing. I know she cares for me, and I suddenly realise she needs to know, and the uncertainty disturbs her. She hides behind her up-tight upbringing at times like this.

"I want to know about your plans for returning."

"I haven't given it much thought yet. I mean, I have thought about it... To be honest, I can't stop thinking about it," I babble, pause, then admit, "but I haven't made any plans. Yet."

"Well, I would very much like you to think about it and to make some plans, please." Each word is precise and clipped. "I have a book deal to fulfil—"

"A book deal, that's brilliant!"

"Thank you," she pauses, and I sense her deflate slightly and that concerns me. She's been keeping up this strong exterior since Shirley died and it's taking its toll. "You have proved to me that you can run this place." She waves her hands to take in our surroundings. "You handle the responsibilities well and I'm confident in your abilities. I want to concentrate on this book, on writing, and I want to move away from running this place, but that means I need someone to run it for me and I need to know your plans, so," — she pauses again and almost wills herself to resume her defensive mode — "I'd appreciate it if you get sorting things out and let me know ASAP."

With that she leaves the kitchen.

The conversation plays on my already whirling mind: What do I want? What are my plans? When I stuck that pin in the map, closed down my life in the UK and came to Cape Cod, without any expectations – and frankly with little thought of what would happen at the end of the six months – had I expected a nice extended holiday? I had hoped to 'find myself' and now I am coming to the end of my time here, what am I going to do next? Stay or go? There is so much going on in my head, so many conflicting thoughts, so many other people to consider, a sense of panic rises in my chest – that expanding balloon of emotion. I attempt to breathe deeply and tell myself to 'just get on with working and think about it later.'

Martha bustles back into the kitchen, business-like and aloof, and asks what cakes will be made for today so that she can write out the cards. I shake myself out of reverie and concentrate. I imitate her body language. I can do this. Later, I will think about it later.

But later I am going to Daniel's house for dinner, an unexpected invitation that makes me happy and yet, with overthinking mode in full flow, it makes me slightly nervous given how he has been recently. Only after immediately saying yes, thank you, did I subsequently worry about being in the house alone with him and what expectations he might have. Maybe it's dinner with a friend. (OK, a friend who I've shared a few kisses with!) Maybe it's to chat and reconnect after the events of the past days, weeks. Or maybe something more? I concede that overthinking is such a dreadful trait!

On the walk over to Daniel's – trying to get a handle on my thoughts, wrestling with all the complex emotions, to log them away in their various compartments and find some clarity – I relish the freshness of the early evening; the humidity has left us (thankfully), the air is slightly crisp, not cool but different. I stride out and make a determined effort to put order to my brain; it's hard work and there isn't enough time. I need time. I need space.

Daniel greets me with broad smile that calms my nerves. At least he looks pleased to see me. He's wearing his favourite collarless shirt and waistcoat that I have seen many times before, with a pair of faded worn Levi's. I notice his feet are bare.

"Hi."

He kisses my cheek. No hug then. Still wary.

"Hello. How are you?" I ask uncertainly.

"There are good days and bad days and I've not been too good today, to be honest. I don't know what's wrong with me, I thought I'd be feeling better by now," he admits.

"We all take time to grieve, Daniel, and we all take different amounts of time and do it in different ways."

"I guess. It's good to have you here though." He smiles again and his eyes have a measure of their sparkle which I find encouraging.

I take hold of his hand and am reassured with a slight squeeze. I like being close to this man and I admit to myself that I've missed his touch, his smile and his kisses. So how is it going to feel when I am three thousand miles away? My heart does a somersault.

"Dinner smells good."

"It's my one speciality."

One speciality or not, the food is delicious: he has made his own pasta which he serves with a beautiful light and creamy sauce. I compliment his culinary skills. Sitting at the dining table, with soft music in the background, we eat, we chat, we relax, and it is like old times between us, and contentment returns. Dessert is a lemon soufflé which stays upright – no mean feat!

"I am seriously impressed," I tell him when he proudly places the soufflé in front of me.

"I'm thinking a drum roll might be appropriate," he quips.

"You can cook, you sing, play guitar, you paint. Is there anything you can't do?"

He is quiet for a moment as though contemplating his response. "Well yeah, to be honest, there are two things I can't do…"

"And they are?" I prompt him as his voice fades away.

"I can't whistle!" he announces.

Unfortunately, I laugh out loud and immediately apologise.

"It's true!" he insists and shows me.

It is true. He cannot whistle!

"But that's hardly life hindering, is it? Unless you want to be a cowboy or a shepherd? So, what's the one other thing you can't do?"

Again, he is quiet and the words Stan said to me – what seems like a long time ago now – go through my head: 'It's a trust thing. When he trusts you, then he will open up to you.'

He takes my plate and stacks it on his while he contemplates what he will say next. "I can't swim."

"Oh, OK."

No laughter this time. Just quiet acceptance and patience, waiting on the rest of the story. His green eyes momentarily lose their spark as memories flood his mind. I want to reach out and offer reassurance but dare not move. Are we back in a dark place again?

"When I was a kid, I think I told you, we lived on a ranch and Dad used to take us boys fishing. I never liked the big river out back of our place; it made such a noise and when you're eight or nine years old, it's a big old thing. Dad would wait 'til it wasn't in full flow, but still, it was intimidating for a young kid. My big brother, he could fish OK, and he would tease me, pick on me and call me all sorts of names about my not wanting to get into the water. Anyways, this one day I decided I'd show him I could do this. Dad fitted me out with waders, and we stood in the river up to thigh deep and he showed me how to cast. I was doing OK. I hadn't caught anything, but I was doing OK." He pauses for a moment and sips his glass of wine, licks his lips. "Anyhow, this one time I was casting, I stepped back to flick the rod and slipped. I went down and under the water, and my waders – which were kinda like dungarees – they filled with water, and I got swept down river." He stops. Another sip. "Dad had to haul me out. I nearly drowned."

I can hear the fridge humming in the kitchen above the expanse of silence.

"Dad was not best pleased, and we never spoke about it then nor any time since and he never took me fishing again. He focused on my elder brother and I got sidelined." He looks at me and I am surprised that there isn't any signs of anger or resentment. He's dealt with this. "And I can't swim."

The words hang in the air before I whisper, "Wow."

He nods and sighs.

"And yet you go fishing with Stan out on the ocean."

"I do, you're right, but the ocean isn't half as scary somehow. I don't know. Maybe being with Stan keeps me calm. And I do love fishing." He smiles. "Just not in rivers wearing waders." His eyes twinkle.

I am relieved to see him return, at least partly, to his old self. The intimacy between us that I felt at the beach returns too. My heart swells with… what? Love? Or too early to tell?

"You want some coffee?" He takes the plates and stands up to go to the kitchen.

"Yes, please."

And the moment passes.

After we have finished eating, washing up and cleared everything away, neat and tidy and precise (his cupboards put mine to shame and I make a mental note not to let him see the chaotic mess), he asks me, "You remember the first time you came here?"

"I do, yes."

"You said how you thought the stars might look great from the deck given that there is no light pollution out here?"

"Oh yes!"

"Well, let's go look at them. You wanna go look at them?" he says, turning out the lights.

It takes a moment or two for my eyes to adjust. Being plunged into darkness puts me on edge and somehow. He senses my trepidation, so he takes my hand and slowly guides me outside onto the deck. I lie down on the wooden lounger and he lies on the one right next to me. Thankfully, the awesome array of stars is stunning and distracts me from where I find myself. Momentarily we are dumbstruck by their beauty. He is right, there is no light pollution, and I don't recall having ever seen so many stars. The moon is full and, in imitation of Tom Hanks in the scene from the film Apollo 13, I put my thumb up and blot it out.

"I remember that scene," he comments. "Would you like to go?"

"Where? To the moon? No. No thanks – would you?"

"No. I don't think so." We gaze up at the sky for several minutes before he asks, "Where would you like to go?"

"Anywhere?"

"Sure – your dream place to go see?"

"I would love to go to the Caribbean!" I do not need to even think about it. "Warm and sunny, white beaches, blue skies, turquoise ocean. I imagine it to be like paradise. What about you?"

"I'll go with that, though I do love to ski too. I love the mountains in the winter. Can you ski?"

"I tried it a couple of times while I was at uni, and again the first year Jon and I were married, but it scares me. Skiing itself doesn't, but the lifts do."

There is a slight pause.

"How long were you and Jon married?"

But before I can answer, a shooting star flies across the sky.

Daniel points. "Quick! Make a wish!"

Instantly I think, I wish I could live here. And then immediately I start to overthink things. Why that? Why did I wish that?

Both of us are lost in our thoughts, our wishes. Neither of us tell. Our hands touch and there is an electric pulse that passes between us, an excitement yet fear in my heart, butterflies in my stomach. He leans over to kiss me and I accept his advances, welcome the contact. Seeing this as an invitation, Daniel moves across to my lounger and snuggles closer. Things get more involved.

I try to accept what is happening, to relax and enjoy it, I really do. After all, we are grown adults, I've done this before and maybe it was inevitable that this was going to happen. *I like this man. He is kind and gentle and he obviously cares for me, but is this what I want?*

His passion intensifies. I feel all my senses hit hyper-alert. My fingers tingle from the adrenaline. My lungs constrict. And I panic.

"No!" I almost shout. "Please. No!" I push him away. "I'm not ready for this… I'm sorry." I gulp for air. "I'm afraid."

"Of what?" His voice is thick with emotion.

"Of you, me, this, everything. Oh, I don't know. I can't explain." I sit up and put my head in my hands, trying to breathe as the tears start to flow. *Why am I crying?* I want to escape. *Why can't I simply accept this and love this man?*

Daniel slowly repositions himself and sits next to me, close but not too close.

"I'm sorry," I mutter. It seems like all I do is end up apologising to this man who simply wants to love me.

"Why are you sorry?"

"I just can't."

"Why not?"

"Because..." I take a deep breath. "Because I don't know what that means for me, you, us? We're friends, you said you wanted to be friends after I leave in October, but this… this is more… you want more, don't you?" He nods. "But I'm leaving in a couple of weeks and—"

"Have you done any research into the visa thing?"

"Not really," Which is true, half true.

"Surely you can renew it? I did ask you to check into it ages ago."

"I know you did. I haven't had the time." I avoid looking at him. How can I possibly explain to him how worried I am about the whole thing? About everything.

"Well maybe you should." I turn to him as his tone takes on a sharper edge. "What is it you want, Jane?"

"Why are you cross with me?"

"I'm not cross with you, I'm" — I can see him searching for the right words — "I'm frustrated that you don't seem to want to sort things out. You could have found the time. Don't you want to stay?"

"I can't stay. I have to leave when my visa expires. I don't know what I want."

The words tumble out and now he knows I've been holding back.

"And then what? Are you willing to leave it all hanging?"

I can't look at him. I can't explain. He shakes his head.

"I told you how I feel, but you… you seem to be holding back. Why can't you trust me? I thought we were making headway together but you kinda brushed me off."

"Is that why you invited me here? For this?"

"Sure! Why not?" There is a slight hint of sarcasm in his voice. "Isn't it kind of natural for two people who are attracted to each other to want to have sex? You are attracted to me, right?"

"Of course."

"So why won't you just let go?"

"I'm afraid."

"So you keep saying!" His voice sounds louder. He shakes his head as though he knows he's gone too far.

I am trying to stay calm. I am trying not to cry again. I am trying to find a way to explain myself. "I've never… I'm not…" This is all wrong. "The only man I have ever slept with is Jon. I haven't had sex for over three years, and it doesn't feel right to sleep with you at the drop of the hat."

"Drop of a hat!"

He stands up indignantly. Obviously, I have failed to explain myself.

"We've known each other for months! I have been so patient."

"I know."

"I waited like you asked."

"I know."

How did we get to this place? A place where the distance between us is so vast. Where we obviously want different things.

"I'm sorry. I know you are disappointed in me and it's not what you wanted. I'm sorry. Take me home, please."

The drive home is silent. He's upset but I cannot help him or comfort him, and to be honest, I'm not sure I want to as I am struggling to deal with my own emotions.

"I've let you down. Forgive me," I whisper when he stops on Main Street.

He does not park in the alley way as he would do normally, and I take this as a further sign of his reaction to our outburst. He doesn't even glance at me.

I get out and stand on the sidewalk, watching him drive away.

In bed, the maelstrom of thoughts and emotions is almost too much to bear. I have this niggling sense of guilt towards Jon, but also towards Daniel for not accepting his advances. Add to this a measure of indignation that he can't understand how difficult this is for me. For the first time, there is loneliness. *I knew it was all too good to be true. Maybe I just do not deserve this. Maybe it is time to go home as we're not seeing this relationship in the same way. I will think about it again in the morning.* And then I promptly burst into tears.

45

The seagulls are silent in awe of the colours of the sky. The seaweed, dried, crispy, crunches under my feet as I walk along the water's edge. Calm water, lapping cool and clear over my bare feet, reflecting the colours of the sunset.

The day is ending, and I fear so is my trip. I have been churning everything over in my mind all day and this stroll along my favourite piece of sand has helped me to clarify everything. I don't want to wait until the fifteenth of next month. I want to go home now. Some may think I'm running away, others that I have failed, but no, I'm ready to go home. All I need to do now is muster up the courage to tell Martha and stick to my guns.

Is it relief that I have finally made the decision, or the sense of calm I always feel down here by the ocean? Whatever, my mind made up, I stroll home, past the clapboard houses and pretty gardens. The seasons have unfolded on these evening walks and now the leaves crowd the pavements, scrunched up and brown, heaped in piles driven by the breeze into corners.

Main Street is quiet, only a few folks are around. As I enter the alleyway, my breath is taken from me. There sitting on the steps — Daniel. My heart leaps and threatens to burst out of my chest, taking all my resolve with it. Doubts return.

He stands, nervous, his hands shoved in the pockets of his jeans. He nods.

"Hi," I whisper, not getting too close.

He nods again and extracts his wallet. Opening it, he gives me a fragile piece of grass, woven into the shape of a heart. It's beautiful.

"Made you this this afternoon," he tells me.

"Thank you."

"I've been thinking—"

"So have I."

"You go first."

"No. you." I want to know what he's thinking.

"Last night…" He pauses. "I probably overstepped the mark. But…" I watch him swallow. "I want you."

My heart does its fluttery thing.

"I want you in my life."

"Are you sure?" I ask, and out of the corner of my eye I see a photograph lying by his feet.

As I pick it up, I hear him gasp. It's him. And her!

"Are you sure?" I ask, my tone different. The

question is now different. "I think this fell out of your wallet!"

He snatches it. "It doesn't mean anything."

"Then why is it still in your wallet?" I demand.

He starts to tear it in two. I am shocked. How could a beautiful moment turn so quickly. He isn't ready to move on any more than I am ready to let go and accept how I feel about him. Any doubts evaporate. I made the right decision and I tell him so!

His face reflects his feelings: shock, distress and pain, but I cannot stop the words.

"Go then!" he states when I finish.

46

The following morning, Daniel's final words ringing in my head, I am wrecked. I probably slept for a few hours, if that, and as a result I am irritable and short-tempered. Sally dodges me as best she can; we avoid eye-contact, unsure what to say or do.

Martha arrives for our early morning briefing and can sense that something is wrong. She makes me stay in the kitchen, out of sight. Pointing with her long finger, she says, "You will only frighten the customers looking like that." She follows me, closing the door behind her. "You wanna tell me what's wrong?" The anguish is clear on her face; she is distressed to see me this way and obviously has no understanding of what has happened.

I shake my head. "No."

Martha sighs dramatically. "Is this because Daniel has left town? He called me late last night; told me he'd changed his mind and was going back to the city."

I'm not surprised given what happened, but I cannot

hide the fact that it hurts and maybe I was wrong.

Then out of frustration, Martha barks, "You're no use to me here – go paint, go run, go do something. Go!"

Two people who mean the world to me have uttered the same word in a matter of hours — go! I leave without another word. I cannot tell her what happened last night nor what is happening inside.

I go running and all the time I am crying. As I reach the shore, I sit on the low wall – my thinking step – and try to analyse what is happening. I breathe deeply and take in the now familiar view in front of me. Six months I have been sitting on this wall. I came here on a cold April day, afraid of the future and what it might hold, never thinking it would include such wonderful people, happy memories, and a summer to remember. And now it's autumn and summer is over. I slump forward, my head in my hands. This adventure is coming to an end. Do I really want it to end? Or do I want it to carry on through autumn until the snows of winter fall and then on into spring and another summer and another summer.

Breathing deeply, I sit up straight, deep down knowing the answer. I love this view. I love this place and I love these people. I know I do, so what's the issue? I've done everything I can, transformed the café, helped and supported Stan, and now I've ruined everything. It's definitely over with Daniel, so it is time to leave. But is it really what I want? I cannot believe that I am swinging so strongly one way and then the other and back again.

As these thoughts race round and round, a familiar face comes into view. Dressed in his habitual dungarees, but with a hoodie and a scarf today to fend off the cool sea breeze, he is more stooped since Shirley died, but my old friend Stan is a sight for my poor sore eyes, and I find myself smiling and crying at the same time. I am so glad he is here; maybe he can help me. Talk some sense into me. Help bury my insecurities.

He sits down beside me. I link my arm through his and bury my head in his shoulder and silently seep tears.

"You OK?" he whispers.

There's that stupid question again.

"Not really but I'm very glad that you're here."

"You wouldn't think so by the number of tears you're crying." He hands me a tissue. "You wanna tell me what's going on?"

I relate my conversation with Martha and her demands to know what I plan to do moving forward. He doesn't question me; he patiently waits for me to carry on, somehow knowing there's more. I convey the events of that fateful dinner with Daniel.

"Did you know he can't swim?" I ask.

Stan smiles.

"Of course, you did," I sigh and tell him what happened next (well, most of it!)

"It's all been building up to this, my dearest girl," he says quietly. "You've had the best summer, right?"

I nod.

"Deep down, you don't wanna go back to England, do you?"

I shake my head.

"You know, you deserve to be happy, my dear." He pats my hand, his fingers cool, the skin thin. "Jon is dead, and you must remember life is learned backwards but lived forwards – so live life. Make the most of the time you have. Believe me, it will go too quickly. Tell Daniel how you feel. Trust me when I tell you he feels the same way."

"How can I know that?" I think of the heart of grass then the words we spoke flood in. "Yesterday, we said harsh things and now he's left town. I might never see him again." The tears start again, evidence of my true feelings. I want to see him again.

"Maybe you should leave then?"

I am shocked by Stan's words, his tone of voice.

"But I think you're just running away."

"Do you?" I ask. "Do you really?"

He nods. "I don't want this to end badly. I don't want him hurt."

We sit for a moment. Stan has never been so forthright with me. He means this.

"Besides," he adds, his voice calmer now, quieter. "I think you guys are made perfect for each other."

"You do?"

"Yes. Take a chance on him. It'll all work out fine. I know you don't think so right now, 'cause you're worried about so many things, aren't you?"

I nod again.

"Stop overthinking."

This last comment makes me smile briefly and I sit upright, brush away my tears.

"There's no need to be afraid of the future, you know."

I briefly wonder if he's had this same type of conversation with Daniel or is it solely me who needs his wise words, his reassurance.

I look at him. It's like he knows what's going on in my head.

"I was afraid when I first came here," I admit.

"And see how things turned out."

"True."

"So don't be afraid. Where's the strength and resilience you showed coming all this way to our little town? Dig deep. Find it again."

"But I've made such a mess of things," I tell him.

"Then mend them."

With a renewed sense of purpose, he instils in me, I instinctively text Daniel: "Sorry." Then my stomach churns with worry and doubts.

Almost immediately, as though he is waiting for me, watching out for something from me, I get a reply: "Me too."

"What do I say to him now?" I ask Stan.

"I don't know. But you'll figure it out."

47

After another night of disturbed sleep, I haul my aching heart and body into work. Around noon, Martha arrives, and we take time to discuss the plans for the rest of the day. The café is much quieter now, with mainly locals about town. The harbour master has been in for his morning cup of full-fat three-shot coffee, no chit-chat. There are one or two out-of-season tourists, but mostly it's quiet.

Satisfied that everything is under control, Martha enquires, "I need to get the rest of this one chapter written and it's driving me to distraction, can you cope without me for a couple of hours?"

She watches me carefully with her piercing eyes. I nod, unconvincingly.

"OK!" She stands and makes a move to leave. "Well, I think that's everything."

She busies herself behind the counter and I can sense she is still watching me, then suddenly she confronts me and demands some sort of explanation for my behaviour and my silence, which I haltingly provide, in part.

"He's disappeared. I'm afraid to text him again. I have hurt him, I must have." I pile plates and cups on to the tray. "He said stuff that... and I said things... even I don't really understand half of it because I was falling apart and all I want to do is explain."

"Then explain," Daniel's voice whispers from behind me.

I spin around and drop the tray as I am confronted by those green eyes. He's here.

"Martha sent for me; told me it was an emergency."

I scramble to pick up all the broken pieces and put them back on the tray.

At the same time, Martha says, "Well it is an emergency! My café is being run by a blotchy-faced grumpy woman and I won't stand for it! Please, go into the kitchen and sort this out. Please!"

Reluctantly, nervously, we agree. The kitchen feels small, filled as it is with our emotions. I am surprised by this turn of events and have not prepared what I will say, how I will say it, nor thought about his reaction to what I may or may not say. All I seem to have done is cry. He takes my hand gently in his. He stands close but not too close.

"Hi," he whispers. "You wanna tell me what's going on?"

"I'm sorry I hurt you." Seems like a good place to start. "I'm sorry I wasn't honest with you about the visa thing. I have done some research and it turns out I can't renew my visa while I'm here. I have to go home to England and reapply. I didn't check into it anymore because it scared me, and I don't know what timespan we're dealing with here."

"Why didn't you tell me this before?"

"I don't know."

"Don't you trust me?"

"Yes, of course I do, but to be honest, I've been a little unsure about you, about us this last few weeks. You've not exactly been approachable recently."

"I've been dealing with Shirley's death—"

"I know, but why couldn't we deal with it together? I have been dealing with it too, you know." My voice starts to get louder.

"You hardly knew her!" He almost hurls the words at me, and I can see that sense of frustration rising in him as he tries to figure out how to deal with what's going on.

"That's not fair!" I add childishly. "She was my friend too!"

We stare at each other, bristling. Surprised that we are capable of causing pain, yet seemingly unable to stop.

"Hey!" Martha strides into the kitchen. "Hey!" She

points at us one at a time. "Enough! You guys take your lovers' tiff elsewhere. Not in my kitchen. Go!"

We go for a drive. Neither of us speak now that more hurtful words are out there, hanging in the air between us. I can hear them in my head amid the silence, bouncing back and forth, damaging a fragile trust.

Finally, after what seems like hours, Daniel pulls off the highway and parks up facing the ocean. The heat of the summer's day has dissipated and as the sun starts to set it shimmers on the water, jewel-points of light.

We sit. I breathe in and whisper, "Talk to me." I pause. "Please."

His eyes briefly skim over my face. "I thought you wanted to explain what happened?"

Is he angry with me? Or is he as upset as I am at the turn of events?

"I deserve that," I state.

He sighs, staring out of the window.

"Where shall I start?" *He deserves to know everything. I must somehow try and regain his trust.* "You know that my intention behind the trip was to find myself."

He nods but doesn't look at me. At least he's listening.

"But also, to find a purpose to my life and that didn't include finding another man." I can't face him. My insides are like jelly. Quietly, I continue, "Jon was the only man I ever loved, ever slept with. Yes, I've had boyfriends, but they were more friends as my heart was very seldom involved. I gave my heart to Jon. I thought it would be forever, then I kind of buried it with him when he died." I pause to gather my thoughts. "He's been gone for over two years now and I wanted… I wanted—" I pause. This is so hard. "Life was tough without him. I felt trapped by my life and couldn't see a future, any future. So, I quit my job and came here – to find myself, to find out what I want from life, what's important, because nothing felt right, nothing felt important. When Jon was diagnosed…" I stop and breathe, trying desperately to hold it all together. "I remember that day so clearly. When we were called into the doctor's room, the oncologist greeted us with a smile and a handshake and I must have seen this as a positive sign, any sign of something positive. Anything. We sat side by side at the doctor's desk and I could see he had the results on the screen, and he was asking Jon questions and then he said, 'I have some important news.' Jon and I, we looked at each other and then at the doctor. The monitor was turned towards us, and the scan of Jon's brain was there, and right in the middle of his brain was a hole – a black hole is the only way I can describe it. 'That's your tumour. And I'm afraid the news isn't good.' The doctor was still talking but I wasn't taking anything in. My world turned grey and colourless. My chest ached and I remember turning to the wall 'cause I didn't want Jon to see my reaction, but suddenly I was sobbing and apologising, and Jon was comforting me. Me!" It's still raw even after all this time. "The nurses gave me a cup of tea and the doctor started to explain the whole diagnosis again – medical details, long words, you know, long, frightening words. He explained that the tumour was inoperable, but they would try chemotherapy. I remember thinking, 'TRY? What do you mean, try?' We were all holding hands, all three of us, and he was speaking so softly and kindly, telling us what the plan was going forward. Then Jon asked, 'How long have I got?' I remember staring at him, thinking, 'What?' and I heard the doctor say, 'Six, maybe eight months at the most.' My husband appeared to be perfectly healthy. He'd played football at the weekend, and we'd run the night before. 'He can't be ill,' I thought, 'look at him. He's not dying.' Jon turned and looked at me and he'd got tears in his eyes. I remember he said to me, 'Good job I didn't buy a season ticket then, eh?' But neither of us smiled. I watched him every day, slowly die. He died by inches, and it tore me apart."

"I'm sorry."

Daniel stares at our hands. I slowly become aware that we are now holding hands; he must have taken hold of mine as I was lost in my memories. There is silence again.

"I feel that meeting you has changed my life. But I doubt everything. I'm afraid. I was afraid when Jon was sick, afraid when he died." I can hear my voice getting tighter. "I was afraid when I came here and I'm afraid now."

"I have my insecurities too, you know," he says softly.

We sit for a moment and assess this mutual admission.

"I know you do."

"And I'm sorry that I yelled at you, back there, in the kitchen."

I lean over and kiss his cheek.

"And I've been thinking about what happened when you came over to my house." He carefully chooses his words. "I over-reacted. Sorry."

"No, I'm sorry. I should have… I want you to understand what happened."

He watches me as it's my turn to choose my words carefully.

"It was a great evening, really it was. The food you cooked was delicious, and I was having fun and beginning to relax. I like being with you. I do." My mind is whirling, not sure what to say next and not wanting to blow this – it feels like I am only going to get one chance. "And Stan tells me I deserve to be happy, but I'm having a hard time accepting that. You made a move and I panicked. I don't just want to have sex with you and then leave. I can't do it, Daniel. I don't want this to be a summer fling. It feels like something more, but I don't want to hope… and besides, I'm not that kind of woman, and when you looked at me, it was so intense."

"I looked at you that way because" — he searches my face — "because I love you."

We stare at each other.

I nod, almost imperceptibly. "Oh!"

SILENCE.

Suddenly, the cab of the pickup truck doesn't feel big enough to contain all the emotions that are flying around. I must get out and find space. To breathe. Daniel follows, takes hold of my hand and we walk along the sand by the sea. We sit and watch the sun go down. Then it's dark and again we are lying side by side looking up at the stars, holding hands.

"Tell me more about your dad. And your mum."

"When Dad broke his back in the storm, life at the ranch got real tough – for all of us. My big brother took over the running of the place. He was always gonna do that anyways. I had no interest in being a cowboy and Dad didn't approve of me – used to call me 'pretty boy'."

He pauses. I wish I could see his face.

"Mom turned after that. She was never too keen about being stuck way out in the mountains of Montana, but I guess she must have loved Dad. But he turned angry and she turned bitter. So, I left and came out East. She always wanted me to make something of myself, something away from home. Something she could be proud of."

"I am sure she's proud of you – you have achieved so much."

"She has no idea what I have achieved. I haven't spoken to either of them for years now."

"And you've never been back?"

"Nope. Oh, I called home a couple of times once I was settled. I even wrote a letter but got nothing back. Ever. I was Mom's favourite son and that rankled with my brothers and my dad too. She kinda wanted me to be more than them somehow, and yet when I did what she wanted, I got nothing back. Nothing. But Dad… I spent most of my life trying to get his approval for the things that I did — passing a test, being quarterback of the football team, getting into college with straight A's — but nothing seemed to please him. So, when I left, I figured nothing I ever did in life would impress him, so why tell him anything."

I thought about my dad, my encouraging, supportive and loving father, and felt a sadness in my heart for Daniel.

"I did invite Mom to graduation, but she didn't turn up. I guess she wasn't too impressed either."

"I'm sorry."

"I live with it. You? You get on well with your mom and dad?"

"Yes, I do. They're great parents. I had a wonderful childhood." I realise how blessed I am. "They've always been kind and supportive of every decision I made, even the one to come here, though they didn't fully understand my reasons. I miss them."

I tell him about what life was like for us as a close-knit family of four, plus dog. My mind brings back thoughts about leaving them permanently. How will we all cope being so far apart every day? Me here, them there? What about my grandparents – I might never see them again. My heart somersaults at the thought.

"And they were there with me every step of the way with Jon."

All these pieces of information, like pieces of a jigsaw, forming a picture of who we are and what we are by what has happened to us in the past. Daniel squeezes me hand as if to say, 'I get this.'

"Where did you guys meet?"

"We met at university in Liverpool. In the first term. I was in the library reading something and he sat next to me. I remember he kept interrupting me and asking questions. He really annoyed me. Then a week later it happened again, and the week after that 'til he finally plucked up the courage to invite me out. Seems Katie told him all about me and he spent more and more time with us in our student digs. We were inseparable after that." I pause. It all seems such a long time ago. "What about you and your wife?"

"Ex-wife." He confirms her status. "I met her in college, I think I told you?"

I nod, realise he cannot see me, and quietly agree with him.

"We were married twelve years. Very driven woman. Ambitious, career-minded, and for a time we were both that way. Then she changed."

He rolls over and even in the darkness, I can make out his features. I want to touch him, but I dare not move. He reaches out and touches my cheek. Seeking comfort.

"She's married to some guy in Chicago now."

I reach up and touch his fingers. They are cool. I shiver and he pulls me close, closer. The physical closeness is reassuring, we need it. We hold each other for some time, assimilating what has passed between us.

"So, you see, the women in my life – well, things have not always gone to plan. After she left me, I vowed I would never trust a woman again, and then you came along and stole my heart."

My voice is muffled in his chest. "But I'm scared."

"Of what?"

"That I will love you and you will die." There it is – I said it. You will die and I will not cope.

Suddenly the intimacy appears to be too much for him. He stands and I can hear him take a deep breath. I stand too and take his hand in mine.

"You have to give me time. I want you. I do. Believe me, I really do, but I need time, Daniel." I sigh deeply. "You tell me you love me—"

"I do love you—"

"And I don't want to lose you or go back to England without you. But I know I'm going to have to leave you here. All of this – it scares me. I'm afraid of being here and my loved ones in England, my grandparents might die, and I never see them again. But there's this underlying deep fear – that you will die." I stare at him, searching his face, his green eyes.

I can see he is choosing his words carefully. No platitudes, no promises.

"As far as I know, right now I am a healthy human being. I will do my upmost not to die…" His voice fades away.

We stand in silence for a moment or two.

"You cannot live the rest of your life without letting people love you, because you are the most wonderful woman it has been my privilege to know. And whatever you say, I will still love you. So how about you let me love you, and we'll see what happens, eh?"

He pulls me close. The air is now chilled and I shiver slightly.

"Come on, let's go," he says.

Back to the car and with a blanket wrapped around us, we talk some more, hours and hours more – pouring out our thoughts and our desires, our pasts and our potential futures. Trust, a new emotion, a fragile one, helps us to be honest. His gentleness gives me confidence and is calmly reassuring. He makes me smile and we laugh. We make promises.

"Wow! It's half four. The sun will be coming up soon. You hungry?" he asks.

I realise that I am.

"Let's go get something to eat. I know a great place in Rhode Island."

"Rhode Island? How far away is that?"

"Not too far."

He pulls out of the parking lot and back onto the road and then onto the highway heading north. I must have dozed off. The emotional strain of the last few hours, the day before and the day before that have taken their toll and I feel drained. Drained but now happy. Happy that we have resolved our difficulties, laid bare our feelings, and established common ground to move forward.

Turns out 'not too far' takes almost two hours and we end up having early morning breakfast at The Beehive café in downtown Bristol, Rhode Island, overlooking Independence Park and Bristol Harbour. Daniel gets a text from Martha – 'Are you guys still alive?' – and he sends her pictures of the wonderful food we are eating.

It is well worth the eighty-six-mile round trip. Many hours later, Daniel pulls into the alleyway next to the café and drops me off at home.

"I love you," he says with a smile. "Something big happened today."

A tear seeps from my eyes. A happy tear. I kiss him on the cheek. "Thank you for listening and caring."

"My pleasure. Do you love me?" he asks, needing to know. "Because if you love me, we can sort all the other things out together. If you love me then we can make the future different, for both of us. So do you love me?"

I gaze deep into those sparkly green eyes – the eyes I first saw in the bookshop – take a deep breath and say, "Yes. Yes, I do. I love you."

He grins. "I'm glad. And we're OK now?"

I nod. There is no fuss, no drama in his words, he clearly needs hope that 'we' are a possibility.

48

I have always been an overthinker. Katie tells me that if overthinking was an Olympic sport that I'm a gold medal winner – every time! Some call it navel-gazing, some self-absorption or pre-occupation, but whatever you label it, I am good at it and cling to it like a security blanket. I try and compartmentalise the problems, thus reducing the amount of stress each problem causes me, putting them in my mental filing cabinet and getting them out one at a time, trying to deal with them and remove them completely or put them back for another time.

The worst thing that can possibly happen is that the mental filing cabinet gets knocked over and all the issues/files fall out onto the floor and get mixed up. That happened when Jon died, when my foundations in life seismically shifted and nothing felt quite the same again. Suddenly, I was a widow – a title that brings all sorts of connotations and expectations I was not ready to accept. Yes, I had a house and a job and a family who loved and cared for me, but Jon was gone, my other half had vanished, and I was alone and heartbroken. Unprotected.

Hence the move to Cape Cod. For the first time ever, I did something without thinking about it, without analysing the actions or the consequences. I just did it. Yes, it scared the living daylights out of me and yes, on the flight over there was a minor panic and a 'What the hell am I doing?' moment. Then another wobble while driving south from Boston airport to Oakham, but I got through it thanks to a lengthy coffee stop and some severe words with myself. I did it and that made me proud.

Fast-forward six months and here I am lying on the sofa, over-analysing my life and, instead of grasping it with both hands, I am overthinking and reverting to type.

The autumnal sunshine fills the room, and it is still warm enough to have the door open; the light breeze is refreshing. It is decision time. My filing cabinet has all the drawers open, the contents of each file is scattered, and there is a desperate need to put everything back where it should go. Concentrating for a minute or two on my breathing to help me to be mindful of what I am doing, mentally I examine each 'file': the home I have created, the summer I have experienced, the friends I have made. All of them indicate one thing – I love being here! I even love the humidity, the way I paint, the way I look. What was I thinking?!

I am about to get up and check the visa application system again when my phone pings. Daniel. I smile. My Daniel.

"Do you love me?" his message reads. "Tell me again."

As I am texting back, I hear footsteps on the stairs and the balcony gate opens, closes and Martha pokes her head around the door.

"Hi!" She is breezy and bright, dressed head to toe in autumnal colours that match the trees I can see through my beautiful windows. I briefly consider the view and the fact that I will miss seeing it during the winter. My heart skips a beat.

"What you doin'?" she asks.

This is an obvious question – I'm lying on the sofa – but don't say so.

"Not a lot, just thinking… well, probably overthinking."

"Oh, OK. I was wondering if you fancied some lunch."

"That would be lovely."

The phone pings again.

"Daniel," I tell her.

"How are things with you guys?"

A huge grin appears on my face, one I cannot

suppress.

"That good, huh?"

I start to bounce up and down with excitement. "He loves me!"

Martha laughs. "I could've told you that weeks ago, merely by the way the guy looks at you. Don't tell me you didn't see that?"

I shake my head. "I guess I've been reluctant to admit that he's won me over. All this time, he's shown that he cares for me, in the way he deals with me, always taking my feelings into consideration. He has patiently accepted every apology and then yesterday he told me he loves me." Saying it out loud and sharing this precious information makes it even more real. "He makes me feel safe and secure. I know he'll always protect me and take care of me." I take a deep breath. "And that's very important."

"You're one lucky lady."

I agree with her.

There is a moment of peace in the room, then Martha asks, "So what you doing about getting your visa sorted?"

"I was just about to recheck that, but I will have to leave on fifteenth. I have to be out of the country when I reapply."

"So, you'll go back to England?"

"Afraid so, even for a short time." What happens

then? "But you know what?"

"What?"

"Daniel has gotten me this far—"

"No, you have gotten yourself this far!"

"Agreed, but we have survived this, Daniel and I, and I am sure that between us we can figure it out." I refuse to let anything, any doubt or insecurity, to dampen this day. I am happy. I am in love.

"Let's do lunch!"

"And drink champagne!"

"Exactly!"

49

That evening in the bar, having a beer, Daniel asks if I am working the next day.

"I have something I wanna show you and then I thought we might go to lunch someplace nice?"

"That sounds interesting. I'm sure Sally will cover for me. What time will you pick me up?"

He picks me up about ten o'clock, once I have arranged for Sally – my ever-loyal friend and support – to cover for me. We drive out of town inland for about twenty to thirty minutes.

"Where we going?"

"It's a surprise."

A frown crosses his face when he sees my reaction.

"It's a nice surprise," he confirms.

"Can I reserve judgement?" I ask.

"Sure."

I get the feeling he's a little on edge and I wonder where we are going and why.

"I thought you were going back to the city this

week?"

"I was, but I have been meeting with some people about plans for the future." He tells me no more.

When I can stand the silence no longer and Daniel is not forthcoming, I ask, "Plans?"

He chuckles softly. He knows what he is doing – piquing my interest and telling me nothing at the same time.

"Come on, Daniel! Tell me!"

He laughs again. "I am thinking of moving out to the Cape." He waits for a response and when he doesn't get one, he continues. "It's always been my plan to move here full time, but life has pushed it forwards a few years and now it's part of a five-year plan, not a retirement plan. I have been meeting potential clients regarding some home/interior design work with a view to starting my own architectural firm out here."

"And giving up your partnership in Boston?"

"Mmnnnn, thinking about it," he confirms.

He looks relaxed about this plan, his hand loosely holding the steering wheel, his arm resting on the open window as we drive along.

I take in this information and wonder about the timing. I want to ask him why but I'm reluctant. So, I get him talking about his new clients, his ideas for their properties.

"I don't want to be in the city, with all the hustle and

bustle. I've been with the same company since leaving college. I wanna change, to stride out and do something new, something that excites me. Or maybe I am getting old! And this summer's made me reflect on all sorts of things, re-evaluate, you know… and then Shirley dying." He pauses, glances over. "You being here."

"Me?"

"Yeah. You." He briefly glances over again before driving off the main highway, down a side road and finally onto a dirt track, coming to a stop next to a vacant lot, a field that is overgrown with wildflowers and grass. Over to the left I can see a clump of oak trees in full autumnal splendour, and beyond that some water.

"This is it?" I ask.

He nods, and that soft chuckle melts my heart. "Come on."

He takes my hand as we walk over to the trees and down to the lake.

"This is Middle Pond in Marston Mills."

He leads me over the uneven ground towards the pretty lake, the shores dotted with houses and jetties and an abundance of trees. The water is clear and blue, but it's not a pond, it's a lake — in England it's called a lake.

"Why is it all overgrown?" I ask him.

"This lot has been vacant for years due to a family

feud, but it's all been settled in court now and I heard on the grapevine, through an associate of mine, that it's coming on the market at the end of the month. I wanted to come and bring you here to see what you think."

He keeps his eyes on me as though he is searching for something in my reaction. But I am unsure what he is saying (or meaning) by those words so only manage to look confused, which makes him smile.

When we get down to the water's edge, he stops and turns around to glance back at the lot and then full circle back to the water.

"It's bigger than I thought."

I have no reply as it's all new to me.

"I was thinking of buying it and building a house here."

"But you have a house. A great house overlooking the ocean."

"True. But I bought that house a long time ago."

"But the view —"

"Isn't everything. That house has too many memories now. It's time for a new view, new memories and maybe a bigger house?"

"If you build here, what will you do with that house?"

"I could sell it to fund the building of this one or maybe rent it out?"

I look back at the lot. "You could build a reasonably

big house here."

This seems to trigger some sort of reaction in Daniel, and he starts to explain, "How about the living quarters, you know, the sitting room with an open fireplace, and the dining space and the kitchen over here?" He strides out and opens his arms wide, to the left and to the right. "To take in that view of the lake. I'm not thinking open-plan, one big room like I have now, but designing something that was semi-open-plan with views through to each area, leading you on to explore. What d'ya think?"

Before I can answer, he marches over to the next spot, and I follow.

"And here in another block, I thought we might have a workspace, an office for me and a place to design and stuff, and maybe an art studio…" His voice fades.

We? Studio? He said 'we!' Was it a slip of the tongue or does he mean 'we', as in him and me – together? Is this his way of 'sorting things out together?'

He moves over to the trees, pulling me along with him.

"And here," he announces, "the master suite with that as a view. And then two maybe three other bedrooms for guests, and another bathroom here?"

He points and smiles broadly. I can tell he is enjoying himself.

"This isn't a passing fancy, is it?" I ask him. "You've

given this some thought? You already have a design in your head, an image of what you want to build here."

He grins at me. "I do. Yes," he admits. "I've known about this land for a number of years and always had my eye on it. But it was never available, and I never had a good enough reason to move to a new house and build something bespoke."

A reason to build a new house?

"And now?" I almost whisper.

"And now I have you…"

We look intently at each other and once more it's too raw, too emotional. We have both declared our love and yet we are both still insecure, unsure. He visibly pulls himself together and gives a little shrug, bouncing a little on the balls of his feet, the way he always does when he is uncomfortable or nervous. We look back at the lake.

"Nice view," I say. "I like it."

He sees this as a positive and starts to wax lyrical about the sights and sounds that are in his head concerning the house. It is fun to witness his enthusiasm and his joy. It makes me laugh as we stroll down to the water's edge and walk along the wooden deck out over the water. He sits down, legs dangling over the edge, inviting me to sit next to him.

"You like the view?" he asks.

I do.

"Shall we get a boat?"

"We could do."

"And a dog?"

"A dog?"

He nods. "Gotta have a dog."

"When I get back," I remind him of realities.

"I've been thinking about that," he tells me. "And I think I have a solution."

Our eyes meet. I want to know what this means.

"I love you with every fibre of my being," Daniel starts then coughs quietly to clear his throat, "and I have done since the moment I first laid eyes on you in the bookstore. I know that's a lot to take in, but it's true." He gazes off into the distance for a moment then takes my hand in his. "I can't imagine spending another day without you. I'm not sure how we're gonna sort this whole thing out, but I tell you now, I want to sort it out. I want to live the rest of my life with you by my side, holdin' my hand, makin' my dreams, our dreams, come true. I hope you feel the same."

He pauses, sinking to one knee. My heart thumps.

"And that you'll do me the honour of being my wife."

He is watching me, his beautiful green eyes glistening with tears of joy.

"Marry me, Jane?"

Every sense in my body is acutely aware of this

moment. This is the perfect solution.

I nod again and again, realising that I love this man too much not to take a leap into the unknown.

"Yes."

He grins.

"Yes, please."

The End.

ABOUT THE AUTHOR

The idea of writing a blog came to me on a road trip in the summer of 2017 during a 1000 miles road trip from Boston, Massachusetts, to Savannah, Georgia and back with my husband (Mr B) and my best friend (BFF).

Once I'd started writing, I couldn't stop – the words just flowed and the website www.mytop5ofeverything.com was born with the help of the multi-talented Beki Hawley.

Before long the kernel of an idea for a novel was planted after a trip to Cape Cod. I watered the idea and it grew – into a first draft of 80,000+ words. Many drafts later and I am embarking on a new career path as I'm hitting semi-retirement – as an author, with my first novel, A New England Escape.

I'm a wife, a friend, a mum and a grandma to 4 beautiful children.

ACKNOWLEDGEMENTS

This book would not be possible without a long list of folks, so here goes:

To my dear friends Ruthi and Lisa from across the pond for introducing me to Cape Cod, taking me on a road trip and to Farmer's Daughter for Sunday lunch. You encourage and inspire me.

To the talented Beki Hawley who created my website www.mytop5ofeverything.com, and helped me to showcase my writing and photography in a beautiful format – the blog.

To Karen Kelly, who I met in Waterstones, a self-published author who encouraged me to keep going with my writing and introduced me to Siân-Elin Flint-Freel.

To Siân – my long-suffering editor and friend. Who corrected my grammar, fed me cake, dried my tears, and help me produce this book.

To the wonderful Michelle Catanach, who transformed the manuscript into a book and did it in a calm, professional and stunning way.

To Jo Giles, Emily Cowen, Barbara Skews, and all those who read draft after draft and helped me to perfect my writing.

To all of you and to Mr. B – my rock – thank you. Your time, energy, support, and expertise are much appreciated.

And to you – for buying my book. If you have enjoyed reading it, do please help me spread the word – by posting a review on Amazon, by posting something on social media or simply by telling your friends and family.

I am an independent publisher, and your support is priceless.

Thank you.

QUESTIONS FOR READING GROUPS

1. What was your favourite part of the book?
2. Who was your favourite character and which character did you relate to the most?
3. Is there a scene that has stuck with you since you finished reading the book?
4. How did the book have an impact on you?
5. What surprised you most about the book?
6. How did your opinion of the characters change as you read it?
7. If you could ask the author anything, what would it be?
8. Why do you think Jane needed to escape to Oakham?
9. What did Jane gain from being in Oakham?
10. Grief is mentioned a number of times in the book – how did that impact differently on the characters?

Printed in Great Britain
by Amazon

43928346R00274